POPULAR TALES,

BY THE AUTHOR OF THIS VOLUME.

———o———

I.—MARIAN GREY.

II.—'LENA RIVERS.

III.—MEADOW BROOK.

IV.—HOMESTEAD on the HILLSIDE.

V.—DORA DEANE.

VI.—COUSIN MAUDE.

——o——

PRICE $1 25 EACH.

MARIAN GREY;

OR, THE

HEIRESS OF REDSTONE HALL.

BY

MRS. MARY J. HOLMES,

AUTHOR OF "LENA RIVERS," "TEMPEST AND SUNSHINE," ETC., ETC.

NEW YORK:

Carleton, Publisher, 413 Broadway.

M DCCC LXIII.

TO

N. C. MILLER,

OF NEW YORK,

MY MUCH ESTEEMED FRIEND,

AND

FORMER PUBLISHER,

THIS STORY OF MARIAN GREY

IS RESPECTFULLY

DEDICATED,

BY

THE AUTHOR.

MARIAN GREY.

CHAPTER I.

GUARDIAN AND WARD.

The night was dark and the clouds black and heavy which hung over Redstone Hall, whose massive walls loomed up through the darkness like some huge sentinel keeping guard over the spacious grounds by which it was surrounded. Within the house all was still, and without there was no sound to break the midnight silence save the sighing of the autumnal wind through the cedar trees, or the roar of the river, which, swollen by the recent heavy rains, went rushing on to meet its twin sister at a point well known in Kentucky, where our story opens, as "The Forks of the Elkhorn." From one of the lower windows a single light was shining, and its dim rays fell upon the face of a white-haired man, who moaned uneasily in his sleep, as if pursued by some tormenting fear. At last, as the old-fashioned clock struck off the hour of twelve, he awoke, and glancing nervously toward the corner, whence the sound proceeded, he whispered, "Have you come again, Ralph Lindsey, to tell me of my sin?"

"What is it, Mr. Raymond?" and a young girl

glided to the bedside of the old man, who, taking her hand in his, the better to assure himself of her presence, said, "Marian, is there nothing in that corner yonder—nothing with silvery hair?"

"Nothing," answered Marian, "nothing but the lamplight shining on the face of the old clock. Did you think there was some one here?"

"Yes—no. Marian, do you believe the dead can come back to us again—when we have done them a wrong—the dead who are buried in the sea, I mean?"

Marian shuddered involuntarily, and cast a timid look toward the shadowy corner, then, conquering her weakness, she answered, "No, the dead cannot come back. But why do you talk so strangely to-night?"

The old man hesitated a moment ere he replied.—"The time has come for me to speak, so that your father can rest in peace. He has been with me more than once in this very room, and to-night I fancied he was here again, asking why I had dealt so falsely with his child."

"Falsely!" cried Marian, kissing tenderly the hand of the only parent she had ever known. "Not falsely, I am sure, for you have been most kind to me."

"And yet, Marian," he said, "I have done you a wrong—a wrong which has eaten into my very soul, and worn my life away. I did not intend to speak of it to-night, but something prompts me to do so, and you must listen. On that night when your father died, and when all in the ship, save ourselves and the watch, were asleep, I laid my hand on his forehead, and swore to be faithful to my trust. Do you hear, Marian—faithful to my trust. You don't know what that meant, but *I* know, and I've broken my oath to the dying—and from that grave in the ocean he comes to me sometimes, and with the same look upon his face which it wore that Summer afternoon when we laid him in the sea, he asks why justice has not been done to you. Wait, Marian, until I have finished," he continued, as he saw her about to speak; "I know

I have not long to live, and I would make amends; but, Marian, I would rather—oh, so much rather, you should not know the truth until I'm dead. You will forgive me then more readily, won't you, Marian? Promise me you will forgive the poor old man who has loved you so much—loved you, if possible, better than he loved his only son."

He paused for her reply, and half bewildered, Marian answered, "I don't know what you mean—but if, as you say, a wrong has been done, no matter how great that wrong may be, it is freely forgiven for the sake of what you've been to me."

The sick man wound his arm lovingly around her, and bringing her nearer to him, he said, "Bless you, Marian—bless you for that. It makes my deathbed easier. I will leave it in writing—my confession. I cannot tell it now, for I could not bear to see upon your face that you despised me. You wrote to Frederic, and told him to come quickly?"

"Yes," returned Marian, "I said you were very sick and wished to see him at once."

For a moment there was silence in the room; then, removing his arm from the neck of the young girl, the old man raised himself upon his elbow and looking her steadily in the face, said, "Marian, could you love my son Frederic?"

The question was a strange one, but Marian Lindsey was accustomed to strange modes of speech in her guardian, and with a slightly heightened color she answered quietly, "I do love him as a brother—"

"Yes, but I would have you love him as something nearer," returned her guardian. "Ever since I took you for my child it has been the cherished object of my life that you should be his wife."

There was a nervous start and an increase of color in Marian's face, for the idea, though not altogether disagreeable, was a new one to her, but she made no reply, and her guardian continued, "I am selfish in this wish, though not wholly so. I know you could be happy with him, and in no other way can my good name be saved from disgrace. Promise me, Marian, that you will be his wife very soon after I am dead, and before all Kentucky is talking of my sin. You are not too young. You will be sixteen in a few months, and many marry as early as that."

"Does *he* wish it?" asked Marian, timidly; and her guardian replied, "He has known you but little of late, but when he sees you here at home, and learns how gentle and good you are, he cannot help loving you as you deserve."

"Yes he can," answered Marian with childish simplicity. "No man as handsome as Frederic ever loved a girl with an ugly face, and I heard him tell Will Gordon, when he spent a vacation here, that I was a nice little girl, but altogether too freckled, too red-headed, and scrawney, ever to make a handsome woman," and Marian's voice trembled slightly as she recalled a speech which had wrung from her many tears.

To this remark Col. Raymond made no reply — for he too, had cause to doubt Frederic's willingness to marry a girl who boasted so few personal charms as did Marian Lindsey then. Rumors, too, he had heard, of a peerlessly beautiful creature, with raven hair and eyes of deepest black, who at the north kept his son a captive to her will. But this could not be; Frederick must marry Marian, for in no other way could the name of Raymond be saved from a disgrace, or the vast possessions he called his be kept in the family, and he was about to speak again when a heavy tread in the hall announced the approach of some one, and a moment after, Aunt Dinah, the housekeeper, appeared. "She had come to sit up with her marster," she said, "and let Miss Marian go to bed, where children like her ought to be."

At first Marian objected, for though scarcely conscious of it herself, she was well enough pleased to sit where she was and hear her guardian talk of Fred eric and of what she had no hope would ever be; but when Aunt Dinah suggested to her that sitting up so much would make her look yellow and old, she yielded, for Frederic was a passionate admirer of beauty, and she well knew that she had none to lose. Kissing her guardian good night, she hurried to her chamber, but not to sleep, for the tumult of thought which her recent conversation had awakened kept her restless and wakeful. Under ordinary circumstances she would have wondered what the wrong could be at which Col. Raymond had hinted, but now she scarcely remembered it, or if it occurred to her at all, she instantly dismissed it from her mind as some trivial thing which the weak state of her guardian's mind magnified into a serious matter.

Thirteen years before our story opens, Marian had embarked with her father on board a ship which sailed from Liverpool to New York. Of that father she remembered little save that he was very poor, and that he talked of his poverty as if it were something of which he was proud. Pleasant memories, though, she had of an American gentleman who used often to take her on his lap, and tell her of the land to which she was going; and when one day her father laid him down in his berth, with the fever as they said, she remembered how the kind man had cared for him, holding his aching head and watching by him till he died;—then, when it was all over, he had taken her upon his knee and told her she was to be his little girl now, and he bade her call him father—telling her how her own dead parent had asked him to care for her, who in all the wide world had no near relative. Something, too, she remembered about an old coarse bag, which had troubled her new father very much, and which he had finally put in the bottom of his trunk, throwing overboard a few articles of clothing to make room for it. The voyage was long and stormy, but they reached New York at last, and he took her to his home—not Redstone Hall, but an humble farm-house on the Hudson, where he had always lived. Frederic was a boy then—a dark haired handsome boy of eleven, and even now she shuddered as she remembered how he used to tease and worry her. Still he liked her, she was sure—and the first real grief which she remembered was on that rainy day when, with an extra pull at her long curls, he bade her good-by and went off to a distant boarding school.

Col. Raymond, her guardian, was growing rich, and people said he must have entered into some fortunate speculation while abroad, for, since his return, prosperity had attended every movement; and when, six months after Frederic's departure, he went to Kentucky and purchased Redstone Hall, then rather a dilapidated building, Mrs. Burt, his housekeeper, had wondered where all his money came from, when he used to be so poor. They had moved to Kentucky when Marian was five and a half years old—and now, after ten years' improvement, there was not in the whole county so beautiful a spot as Redstone Hall, with its terraced grounds, its graveled walks, its plats of grass, its grand old trees, its creeping vines, its flowering shrubs and handsome park in the rear. And this was Marian's home;—here she had lived a rather secluded life, for only when Frederic was with them did they see much company, and all the knowledge she had of the world was what she gleaned from books or learned from the negress Dinah, who, "having lived with the very first families," frequently entertained her young mistress with stories of "the quality," and the dinner parties at which her presence was once so indispensable. And Marian, listening to these glowing descriptions of satin dresses, diamonds and feathers, sometimes wished that she were rich, and could have a taste of fashion. To be sure, her guardian bought her always more than she needed—but it was not hers, and without any particular reason why she should do so, she felt that she was a dependent and something of an inferior, especially when Frederic came home with his aristocratic manners, his graceful mustache, and the soft scent of perfumery he usually carried with him. He was always polite and kind to Marian, but she felt that there was a gulf between them. He was handsome; she was plain—he was rich; she was poor—he was educated, and she—alas, for Marian's education—she read a great deal, but never yet had she given herself up to a systematic course of study. Governesses she had in plenty, but she usually coaxed them off into the woods, or down by the river, where she left them to do what they pleased, while she learned many a lesson from the great book of nature spread out so beautifully before her. All this had tended to make and keep her a very child, and it was not until her fourteenth year that any thing occurred to develop the genuine womanly qualities which she possessed.

By the death of a distant relative, a little unfortunate blind girl was left to Colonel Raymond's care, and was immediately taken to Redstone Hall, where she became the pet of Marian, who loved nothing in the whole world as dearly as the poor blind Alice. And well was that love repaid; for to Alice Marian Lindsey was the embodiment of everything beautiful, pure and good. Frederic, on the contrary, was a kind of terror to the little Alice. "He was so precise and stuck up," she said; "and when he was at home Marian was not a bit like herself." To Marian, however, his occasional visits to Redstone Hall were sources of great pleasure. To look at his handsome figure, to listen to his voice, to anticipate his slightest wish and minister to his wants so quietly that he scarcely knew from whom the attention came, was happiness for her, and when he smiled upon her, as he often did, calling her "a good little girl," she felt repaid for all she had done. Occasionally, since her guardian's illness, she had thought of the future when some fine lady might come to Redstone Hall as its mistress, but the subject was an unpleasant one, and she always dismissed it from her mind. In her estimation, there were few worthy to be the wife of Frederic—certainly not herself—and when the idea was suggested to her by his father, she regarded it as an utter impossibility. Still it kept her wakeful, and once she said softly to herself, "I could love him so much if he would let me, and I should be so proud of him, too." Then, as she remembered the remark she had heard him make to his college friend, she covered her face with her hands and whispered, sadly, "Oh, I wish I wasn't ugly." Anon, however, there came stealing over her the thought that in the estimation of others she was not as plain as in that of Frederic Raymond. Every body seemed to like her, and if she were hideous looking they could not. Alice, whose darkened eyes had never looked upon the light of day, and who judged by the touch alone, declared that she was beautiful, while old Dinah said that age would improve her as it did wine, and that in time she would be the handsomest woman in all Kentucky.

Never before had Marian thought so much of her personal appearance—and now, feeling anxious to know exactly what her defects were, she arose, and lighting the lamp, placed it upon her dressing bureau —then throwing a shawl around her shoulders, she sat down and minutely inspected the face which Frederic Raymond called so homely. The features were regular enough, but the face was very thin—"scrawney," Frederic had said, and the cheek bones were plainly perceptible. This might be the result of eating slate-stones; Dinah, who knew everything, said it was, and mentally resolving thereafter to abjure everything of the kind, Marian continued her investigations. It did not occur to her that her complexion was surpassingly fair, nor yet that her eyes were of a most beautiful blue, so intent was she upon the freckles which dotted her nose and a portion of her face. Slate-stones surely had nothing to do with these, and she knew of no way of remedying this evil—unless, indeed, *poulticing* should do it.—She would consult Dinah on the subject, and feeling a good deal of confidence in the negress' judgment, she passed on to what she considered her crowning point of ugliness—her *hair!* It was soft, luxuriant and curly, but alas, it bore the color which, though accounted beautiful in Mary Stuart's time, has long since been proscribed by fashion as horrid and unbecoming. Turn which way she would, or h[illegible]e lamp in any position she chose, it was still re[illegible]k, decided red—and the tears came to Mari[illegible]s she recalled the many times when, as a bo[illegible]ric taunted her with being a "red-head" or a "[illegible]ck-top," just as the humor suited him. Suddenly she remembered that among her treasures was a lock of her mother's hair, and opening a rosewood box she took from it a shining tress which she laid upon the marble top of her bureau, and then bent down to admire its color, a beautiful auburn, such as is rarely seen—and which, when seen, is sure to be admired.

"And this was my mother's," she whispered, smoothing caressingly the silken hair. "I must resemble her more than my father, who my guardian says was dark. I wish I was like her in everything, for I believe she was beautiful," and into the mind of the orphan girl there crept an image of a bright-haired, sweet-faced woman, whose eyes of lustrous blue looked lovingly into her own—and this was her mother. She had seen her thus in fancy many a time, but never so vividly as to-night, and unconsciously she breathed the petition, "Let me look like her some day, and I shall be content."

The gray morning light was by this time stealing through the window, and overcome with weariness and watching, Marian fell asleep, and when, two hours later, old Dinah came in to wake her, she found her sitting before the glass, with the lamp still burning at her side, and her head resting on her arms, which lay upon the low bureau.

"For the dear Lord's sake, what are you doing?" was Dinah's exclamation, which at once roused Marian, who unhesitatingly answered,

"I got up to look in the glass, and see if I was so very homely."

"Humbly! Nonsense, child," returned old Dinah. "You look like a picter lyin' thar with the sun a shinin' on yer har, and makin' it look like a piece of crimson satin."

The compliment [illegible]ubtful one, but Marian knew it was well m[illegible]d, without a word in reply, commenced her [illegible]ng toilet. That day, somewhat to her disappointment, her guardian did not resume the conversation of the previous night. He was convinced that Marian could be easily won, but he did not think it wise to encourage her until he had talked with his son, whose return he looked for anxiously. But day after day went by, and it was in vain that Alice listened, and Marian watched, for the daily stage. It never stopped at the gate; and each time that the old man heard them say it had gone by, he groaned afresh, fearing Frederic would not come until it was too late.

"I can at least tell him the truth on paper," he said to himself at last, "and it may be he will pay more heed to words, which a dead father wrote, than to words which a living father spoke."

Marian was accordingly bidden to bring him his little writing desk, and then to leave the room, for he would be alone when he wrote that letter of confession. It cost him many a fierce struggle—the telling to his son a secret which none save himself and God had ever known—aye, which none had ever need to know if he would have it so—but he would not. The secret had worn his life away, and he must make reparation now. So, with the perspiration dropping from every pore, he wrote; and, as he wrote, in his disordered imagination, there stood beside his pillow the white-haired Englishman, watching carefully to see that justice was [illegible] at last to Marian. Recently several letters had passed between the father and his son concerning the marriage of the latter with Marian —a marriage every way distasteful to the young man, who, in his answer, had said far harsher things of Marian than he really meant, hoping thus to put an end to his father's plan. She was "rough, uncouth, uneducated and ugly," he said, "and if his father did not give up that foolish fancy, he should positively hate the red-headed fright."

All this the old man touched upon—quoting very words his son had used, and whispering to himself, "Poor—poor Marian, it would break her heart to know that he said that, but she never will—she never will;" and then, with the energy of despair, he wrote the reason why she must be the wife of his son, pleading with him as only a dying man can plead, that he would not disregard the wishes of his father, and begging him to forget the dark-haired Isabel, who, though perhaps more beautiful, was not—could not—be as pure, as gentle and as good as Marian.

The letter was finished, and 'mid burning tears of remorse and shame the old man read it through.

"Yes, that will do," he said. "Frederic will heed what's written here. He'll marry her or else make restitution;" and laying it away, he commenced the last and hardest part of all—the confessing to Marian how he had sinned against her.

Although there was no tie of blood between them, the gentle young orphan had crept down into his inmost heart, where once he treasured a little golden-haired girl, who, before Frederic was born, died on his lap, and went to the heaven made for such as she. In the first moments of his bereavement, he had thought his loss could never be repaired, but when, with her soft arms around his neck, Marian Lindsey had murmured in his ear how much she loved the only father she had ever known, he felt that the angel he had lost was restored to him tenfold in the little English girl. He knew that she believed that there was in him no evil, and his heart throbbed with agony as he nerved himself to tell her how for years he had acted a villain's part, but it was done at last, and with a passionate appeal for her forgiveness, and a request that she would not forget him wholly, but come some time to visit his lonely grave, he finished the letter, and folding it up, wrote upon its back, "*For Marian;*" then, taking the one intended for Frederic, he attempted to write, "*For my Son,*" but the ink was [illegible]e from his pen, there was a blur before his eyes, and though he traced the words he left no impress, and the letter bore no superscription to tell to whom it belonged. Stepping upon the floor, he dragged his feeble limbs to the adjoining room, his library, and placing both letters in his private drawer, retired to his bed, where, utterly exhausted, he fell asleep.

When at last he awoke, Marian was sitting by his side, and to her he communicated what he had done, telling her where the letters were, and that if he died ere Frederic's return, she must give the one bearing the words "For my Son" to him.

"You will not read it, of course," he said, "or ever seek to know what its contents are."

Had Marian Lindsey been like many girls, the caution would have insured the reading of the letter at once, but she fortunately shrank from anything dishonorable, and was blessed with but a limited share of woman's curiosity; consequently, the letter was safe in her care, even though no one ever came to claim it. All that afternoon she sat by her guardian, and when as usual the stage thundered down the turnpike, leaving no Frederic at the door, she soothed him with the hope that he would be there to-morrow. But the morrow came and went as did other to-morrows, until Col. Raymond grew so ill that a telegram was despatched to the truant boy, bidding him hasten if he would see his father again alive.

"That will bring him," the old man said, while the big tears rolled down his wrinkled face. "He'll be here in a few days," and he asked that his bed might be moved near the window, where, propped upon pillows, he watched with childish impatience for the coming of his boy.

CHAPTER II.

FATHER AND SON.

A TELEGRAM from Frederic, who was coming home at last! He would be there that very day, and the inmates of Redstone Hall were thrown into a state of unusual excitement. Old Dinah in jaunty turban and clean white apron, bustled from the kitchen to the dining room, and from the dining room back to the kitchen, jingling her huge bunch of keys with an air of great importance, and kicking from under her feet any luckless black baby which chanced to be in her way, making always an exception in favor of "Victoria Eugenia," who bore a striking resemblance to herself, and would one day call her "gran'mam." Dinah was in her element, for nothing pleased her better than the getting up a "tip top dinner," and fully believing that Frederic had been half starved in a land where they didn't have hoe-cake and bacon three times a day, she determined to give him one full meal, such as would make his stomach ache for three full hours at least!

Mr. Raymond, too, was better than usual to-day, and at his post by the window watched eagerly the distant turn in the road where the stage would first appear. In her chamber, Marian was busy with her toilet, trying the effect of dress after dress, and at Alice's suggestion deciding at last upon a pale blue, which harmonized well with her fair complexion.

"Frederic likes blue, I know," she thought, as

she remembered having heard him admire a dress of that color worn by a young lady who had once visited at Redstone Hall.

Dinah, when consulted as to the best method of making red hair dark, had strongly recommended "possum ile and sulphur, scented with some kind of essence;" but to this dye Marian did not take kindly. She preferred that her hair should retain its natural color, and falling as it did in soft curls around her face and neck, it was certainly not unbecoming. Her toilet was completed at last—Alice's little hands had decided that it was perfect—the image reflected by the mirror was far from being ordinary-looking, and secretly wondering if Frederic would not think her tolerably pretty, Marian sat down to await his coming. She had not been seated long when Alice's quick ear caught the sound of the distant stage, and in a few moments Marian from behind the half-closed shutter, was watching the young man as he came slowly up the avenue, which led from the highway to the house. His step was usually bounding and rapid, but now he lingered as if unwilling to reach the door.

"'Tis because of his father," thought Marian. "He fears he may be dead."

But not of his father alone was Frederic thinking. It was not pleasant coming home; for aside from the fear that his father might really die, was a dread of what that father might ask him to do. For Marian as a sister, he had no dislike, for he knew she possessed many gentle, womanly virtues, but from the thoughts of making her his wife he instinctively shrank. Only one had the shadow of a claim to bear that relation to him, and of her he was thinking that September afternoon as he came up the walk. She was poor, he knew, and the daughter of his landlady, who claimed a distant relationship with his father; but she was beautiful, and a queen might covet her stately bearing, and polished, graceful manner. Into her heart he had never looked, for satisfied with the fair exterior, he failed to see the treachery lurking in her large black eyes, or yet to detect the fierce, stormy passions, which had a home within her breast.

Isabella Huntington, or "Cousin Bell," as he called her, was beautiful, accomplished, and artful, and during the year that Frederic Raymond had been an inmate of her mother's family, she had succeeded in so completely infatuating the young man that now there was to him but one face in the world, and that in fancy shone upon him even when it was far away. He had never said to her that he loved her, for though often tempted so to do, something had always interposed between them, bidding him wait until he knew her better. Consequently he was not bound to her by words, but he thought it very probable that she would one day be his wife, and as he drew near to Redstone Hall, he could not forbear feeling a glow of pride, fancying how she would grace that elegant mansion as its rightful mistress. Of Marian, too, he thought—harsh, bitter thoughts, mingled with softer emotions as he reflected that she possibly knew nothing of his father's plan. He pitied her, he said, for if his father died, she would be alone in the world. After what had passed, it would hardly be pleasant for him to have her there where he could see her every day;—she might not be agreeable to Isabel either, and he should probably provide for her handsomely and have her live somewhere else—at a fashionable boarding school, perhaps!

Magnanimous Frederic! He was growing very generous, and by the time he reached the long piazza, Marian Lindsey was comfortably disposed of in the third story of some seminary far away from Redstone Hall!

The meeting between the father and son was an affecting one—the former sobbing like a child, and asking of the latter why he had tarried so long. The answer to this question was that Frederic had been absent from New Haven for three weeks, and that Isabel, who took charge of his letters, neglected to forward the one written by Marian. At the mention of Isabel, the old man's cheek flushed, and he said, impatiently, "the neglect was an unpardonable one, for it bore on its face 'In haste.' Perhaps, though, she did it purposely, hoping thus to keep you from me."

Instantly Frederic warmed up in Isabel's defence, saying she was incapable of a mean act. He doubted whether she had observed the words "In haste" at all, and if she did she only withheld it for the sake of saving him from anxiety as long as possible.

At this moment there was the sound of little uncertain feet near the door, and Alice groped her way into the room. She was a fair, sweet-faced little child, and taking her upon his knee, Frederic kissed her affectionately, and asked her many questions as to what she had done since he was home six months before. Seldom before had he paid her so much attention, and feeling anxious that Marian should be similarly treated, the little girl, after answering his questions, said to him, coaxingly,

"Won't you kiss Marian, too, when she comes down? She's been ever so long dressing herself and trying to look pretty."

Instantly the eyes of the father and son met—those of the former expressive of entreaty, while those of the latter flashed with defiance.

"Go for Marian, child, and tell her to come here," said Mr. Raymond.

Alice obeyed, and as she left the room, Frederic said bitterly, "I see she is leagued with you. I had thought better of her than that."

"No, she isn't," cried the father, fearing that his favorite project was in danger. "I merely suggested it to her once—only once."

Frederic was about to reply, when the rustling of female garments announced the approach of Marian. To Colonel Raymond she was handsome then, as with a hightened bloom upon her cheek and a bashful light in her deep blue eyes, she entered timidly and offered her hand to Frederic. But to the jealous young man she was merely a plain, ordinary country girl, bearing no comparison to the peerless Isabel. Still he greeted her kindly, addressed to her a few trivial reremarks, and then resumed his conversation with little Alice, who, feeling that matters were going wrong, rolled her eyes often and anxiously toward the spot where she knew Marian was sitting—and when at last the latter left the room, she said to Frederic, "Isn't Marian pretty in her blue dress, with all those curls? There are twenty of them, for I heard her count them. Say she *is* pretty, so I can tell her and make her feel good."

Frederic would not then have admitted that Marian was pretty, even had he thought so, and biting his lip with vexation, he replied, "I do not particularly admire blue, and I detest cork-screw curls."

Marian was still in the lower hall, and heard both the question and the answer. Darting up the stairs, she flew to her chamber, and throwing herself upon the bed, burst into a passionate flood of tears. All in vain had she dressed herself for Frederic Raymond's eye—curling her hair in twenty curls, even as Alice had said. He hated blue—he hated curls—cork-screw curls particularly. What could he mean? She never heard the term thus applied before. It must have some reference to their color, and clutching at her luxuriant tresses she would have torn them from her head, had not a little childish hand been laid upon hers, and Alice's soothing voice murmured in her ear, "Don't cry, Marian; I wouldn't care for him. He's just as mean as he can be, and if I owned Redstone Hall, I wouldn't let him live here, would you?"

"Yes—no—I don't know," sobbed Marian. "I don't own Redstone Hall. I don't own anything, and I most wish I was dead."

Alice was unaccustomed to such a burst of passion,

and was trying to frame some reply, when the dinner bell rang, and lifting up her head, Marian said, "Go down, Alice, and tell Dinah I can't come, and if she insists, tell her I *won't!*"

Alice knew she was in earnest, and going below she delivered the message to Dinah in the presence of Frederic, who silently took his seat at the table.

"For the dear Lord's sake, what's happened her now?" said Dinah, casting a rueful glance at Marian's empty chair.

"She's crying," returned Alice, "and she dislikes somebody in this room awfully; 'taint you, Dinah, nor 'taint me," and the blind eyes flashed indignantly at Frederic, who smiled quietly as he replied, "Thank you, Miss Alice."

Alice made no reply, and the dinner proceeded in silence. After it was over, Frederic returned to his father, who had been nerving himself for the task he had to perform, and which he determined should be done at once.

"Lock the door, Frederic," he said, "and then sit by me while I say to you what I have so long wished to say."

With a lowering brow Frederic complied, and seating himself near to his father, he folded his arms and said, "Go on, I am ready now to hear—but if it is of Marian you would speak, I will spare you that trouble, father," and Frederic's voice was milder in its tone. "I have always liked Marian very much as a sister, and if it so chances that you are taken from us, I will be the best of brothers to her. I will care for her and see that she does not want. Let this satisfy you, father, for I cannot marry her. I do not love her, for I love another; one compared to whom Marian is as the night to the day. Let me tell you of Isabel, father," and Frederic's voice was still softer in its tone.

The old man shook his head and answered mournfully, "No, Frederic, were she as fair as the morning

I could not wish her to be your wife. I have never told you before, but I once received an anonymous letter concerning this same Isabel, saying she was treacherous and deceitful, and would lead you on to ruin."

"The villain! It was Rudolph's doings," muttered Frederic; then in a louder tone he said, "I can explain that, I think. When Isabel was quite young, she was engaged conditionally to Rudolph McVicar, a worthless fellow whom she has since discarded. He is a jealous, malignant creature, and has sworn to be revenged. He wrote that letter, I am sure. It is like him."

"It may be," returned the father, "but I distrust this Isabel. Her mother, as you are aware, is a distant relative of mine. I know her well, and though I never saw the daughter, I am sure she is selfish, ambitious, deceitful and proud, while Marian is so good."

"Marian is a mere child," interrupted Frederic.

"Almost sixteen," rejoined the father, "and before you marry her she will be older still."

"Yes, yes, much older," thought Frederic, continuing aloud, "Listen to reason, father. I certainly do not love Marian, neither do I suppose that she loves me. Now if you have our mutual good at heart, you cannot desire a marriage which would surely result in wretchedness to both."

"I have thought of all that," returned the father. "A few kind words from you would win Marian's love at once, and when once won she would be to you a faithful, loving wife, whom you would ere long learn to prize. You cannot treat any woman badly, Frederic, much less Marian. I know you would be happy with her, and should desire the marriage even though it could not save me from dishonor in the eyes of the world."

"Father," said Frederic, turning slightly pale,

"what do you mean? You have in your letters hinted of a wrong done to somebody. Was it to Marian? If so, do not seek to sacrifice my happiness, but make amends in some other way. Will money repair the wrong? If so, give it to her, even to half your fortune, and leave me alone."

He had touched a tender point, and raising himself in bed, the old man gasped, "Yes, yes, boy—but you have no money to give her. Redstone Hall is not mine, not yours, but hers. Those houses in Louisville are hers—not mine, not yours. Everything you see around you is hers—all hers; and if you refuse her, Frederic—hear me—if you refuse Marian Lindsey, strict restitution must be made, and you will be a beggar as it were. Marry her, and as her husband you will keep it all and save me from disgrace.—Choose, Frederic, choose."

Mr. Raymond was terribly excited, and the great drops of perspiration stood thickly upon his forehead, and trickled from beneath his hoary hair.

"Is he going mad!" thought Frederic, his own heart throbbing with a nervous fear of coming evil, but ere he could speak his father continued, "Hear my story, and you will know how I came by these ill-gotten gains," and he glanced around the richly furnished room. "You know I was sent to England, or I could not have gone, for I had no means with which to meet the necessary expenses. In the streets of Liverpool I first saw Marian's father, and I mistook him for a beggar. Again I met him on board ship, and making his acquaintance, found him to be a man of no ordinary intellect. There was something about him which pleased me, and when he became ill, I cared for him as for a friend. The night he died we were alone, and he confided to me his history. He was an only child, and, orphaned at an early age, became an inmate of one of those dens of cruelty—those schools on the Dotheboys plan. From this bondage he escaped at last, and then for more than thirty years employed his time in making and saving money. He was a miser in every sense of the word, and though counting his money by thousands—yes, by tens of thousands, he starved himself almost to death. No one suspected his wealth—not even his young wife, Mary Grey, whom he married three years before I met him, and who died when Marian was born. She, too, had been an only child and an orphan; and as in England there was none to care for him or his, he conceived the idea of emigrating to America, and there lavishing his stores of gold on Marian. She should be a lady, he said, and live in a palace fit for a queen. But death overtook him, and to me he entrusted his child with all his money—some in gold, and some in bank notes. And when he was dying, Frederic, and the perspiration was cold on his brow, he made me lay my hand there and swear to be faithful to my trust as guardian of his child. For her, and for her alone, the money must be used. But, Frederic, I broke that oath. The Raymonds are noted for their love of gain, and when the Englishman was buried in the sea, the tempter whispered that the avenue to wealth, which I so long had coveted, was open now—that no one knew or would ever know of the miser's fortune; and I yielded. I guarded the bag where the treasure was hidden with more than a miser's vigilance, and I chuckled with delight when I found it far more than he had said."

"Oh, my father, my father!" groaned Frederic, covering his white face with his hands, for he knew now that he was penniless.

"Don't curse me, boy," hoarsely whispered the old man; "Marian will not. She'll forgive me—for Marian is an angel; but I must hasten. You remember how I grew gradually rich, and people talked of my good luck. Very cautiously I used the money at first so as not to excite suspicion, but when I came to Kentucky, where I was not known, I was less fearful, and launched into speculations, until now they say I am the wealthiest man in Franklin county. But it's hers —it's Marian's—every cent of it is hers. Your education was paid for with her money; all you have and are you owe to Marian Lindsey, who, by every law of the land, is the heiress of Redstone Hall."

He paused a moment, and trembling with emotion, Frederic said, "Is there nothing ours, father? Our old home on the Hudson? That, surely, is not hers?"

"You are right," returned the father; "the old shell was mine, but when I brought Marian home, it was not worth a thousand dollars, and it was all I had in the world. Her money has made it what it is. I always intended to tell her when she was old enough to understand, but as time went by I shrank from it, particularly when I saw how much you prized the luxuries which money alone can buy, and how that money kept you in the proud position you occupy.— But it has killed me, Frederic, before my time—and now at the last do you wonder that I wish restitution to be made? I would save you from poverty, and my name from disgrace, by marrying you to Marian. She must know the truth, of course, for in no other way can my conscience be satisfied—but the world would still be kept in ignorance."

"And if I do not marry her, oh, father, must it come—poverty, disgrace, everything?"

The young man's voice was almost heart-broken in its tone, but the old man wavered not as he answered —"Yes, Frederic, it must come. If you refuse, I must deed it all to her. The lawyer, of course, must know the cause of so strange a proceeding, and I have no faith that he would keep the secret, even if Marian should. I left it in writing in case you did not come, and I gave you my dying curse if you failed of restoring to Marian her fortune. But you are here—you have heard my story, and it remains for you to choose. You have never taken care of yourself—have never been taught to think it necessary—and how can you struggle with poverty. Would that Isabel join her destiny with one who had not where to lay his head?"

"Stop, father! in mercy stop, ere you drive me mad!" and starting to his feet Frederic paced the floor wildly, distractedly.

A dark cloud had fallen upon him, and turn which way he would it enveloped him in its dark folds. He knew his father would keep his word, and he desired that he should do so. It was right, and he shrank from any further injustice to the orphan, Marian, with whom he had suddenly changed places. He was the dependent now, and hers the hand that fed him.—Frederic Raymond was proud, and the remembrance of his father's words, "Her money paid for your education; all you have and are, you owe to Marian Lindsey," stung him to his inmost soul. Still he could not make her his wife. It would be a greater wrong than ever his father had done to her. And yet if he had never seen Isabel, never mingled in the society of beautiful and accomplished women, he might, perhaps, have learned to love the gentle little girl, whose presence, he knew, made the life and light of Redstone Hall. But he could not do it now, and going up to his father, he said hesitatingly, as if it cost a bitter, agonized struggle to give up all his wealth, "I cannot do it, father; neither would Marian wish it if she knew. Send for her now," he continued, as a new idea flashed upon him, "tell her all, here in my presence, and let her choose for me; but stay," he added, quickly, coloring crimson at the unmanly selfishness which had prompted the sending for Marian, a selfishness which whispered that the generous girl would share her fortune with him; "stay, we will not send for her. I can decide the matter alone."

"Not now," returned the father. "Wait until to-morrow at nine o'clock. If you do not come to me then, I shall send for Lawyer Gibson, and the writings will be drawn. I give you until that time to decide; and now leave me, for I would rest."

He motioned toward the door, and glad to escape from an atmosphere which seemed laden with grief, Frederic went out into the open air, and Col. Raymond was again alone. His first thought was of the letter—the one intended for his son. He could destroy that now—for he would not that Marian should ever know what it contained. She might not be Frederic's wife, but he would save her from unnecessary pain; and exerting all his strength, he tottered to his private drawer, and took the letter in his hand. It was growing very dark within the room, and holding it up to the fading light, the dim-eyed old man read, or thought he read, "For my Son."

"Yes, this is the one," he whispered—"the other reads 'For Marian,'" and hastening back to his bedroom he threw upon the fire burning in the grate, the letter, but, alas, the wrong one—for in the drawer still lay the fatal missive which would one day break poor Marian's heart, and drive her forth a wanderer from the home she loved so well.

That night Frederic did not come down to supper. He was weary with his rapid journey, he said, and would rather rest. So Marian, who had dried her tears and half forgotten their cause, sat down to her solitary tea, little dreaming of the stormy scene which the walls of Frederic's chamber looked upon that night. All through the dreary hours he walked the floor, and when the morning light came struggling through the windows, it found him pale, haggard, and older by many years than he had been the day before. Still he was undecided. "Love in a cottage" with Isabel, looked fair enough in the distance, but where could he get the "cottage?" To be sure, he was going through the form of studying law, but he had never looked upon the profession as a means of procuring his livelihood, neither did he see any way by which he could pursue his studies, unless, indeed, he worked to defray the expense. He might, perhaps, saw wood. Ben Gardiner did in college—Ben with the threadbare coat, cowhide boots, smiling face and best lessons in the class. Ben liked it well enough, and so, perhaps, would he! He held his hands up to the light; they were soft and white as a girl's. They would blister with the first cut. He couldn't saw wood—he couldn't do anything. And would Isabel love him still when she knew how poor he was. It seemed unjust to doubt her, but he did, and he remembered sundry rumors he had heard touching her ambitious, selfish nature. Anon, too, there crept into his heart pleasant memories of a little, quiet girl, who had always sought to do him good, and ministered to his comfort in a thousand unobtrusive ways. And this was Marian, the one his father would have him marry; and why didn't he? when the marrying her would insure him all the elegances of life to which he had been accustomed, and which he prized so highly. She was a child yet; he could mold her to his will and make her what he pleased. She might be handsome some time. There was certainly room for improvement. But no, she would never be aught save the plain, unpolished Marian, wholly unlike the beautiful picture he had formed of Redstone Hall's proud mistress. He could not marry her, he would not marry her, and then he went back to the question, "What shall I do, if I don't?"

As his father had said, the Raymonds were lovers of wealth, and this weakness Frederic possessed to a great degree. Indeed, it was the foundation of all his other faults, making him selfish and sometimes overbearing. As yet he was not worthy to be the husband of one as gentle and good as Marian, but he was passing through the fire, and the flames which burned so fiercely, would purify and make him better. He heard the clock strike eight, and a moment after breakfast was announced.

"I am not ready yet; tell Marian not to wait," was

the message he gave the servant; and so another hour passed by, and heard the clock strike nine.

His hour was up, but he could not yet decide. He walked to the window and looked down on his home, which never seemed so beautiful before as on that September morning. He could stay there if he chose, for he felt sure he could win Marian's love if he tried. And then he wondered if his life would not be made happier with the knowledge that he had obeyed his father's request, and saved his name from dishonor. There was the sound of horses' feet upon the graveled road. It was the negro Jake, and he was going for Lawyer Gibson.

Rapidly another hour went by, and then he heard the sound of horses' hoofs again, but this time there were two who rode, Jake and the lawyer. In a moment the latter was at the door, and the sound of his feet, as he strode through the lower hall, went to the heart of the listening young man like bolts of ice. He heard a servant call Marian and say that his father wanted her; some new idea had entered the sick man's head. He had probably decided to tell her all before he died, but it was not too late to prevent it, the young man thought; he could not be a beggar, and with a face as white as ashes, and limbs which trembled in every joint, he hurried down the stairs, meeting in the hall both Marian and the lawyer.

"Go back," he whispered to the former, laying his hand upon her shoulder; "I would see my father first alone."

Wonderingly Marian looked into his pale, worn face and bloodshot eyes; then motioning the lawyer into another room, she, too, followed him thither, while Frederic sought his father's bedside, and bending low whispered in the ear of the bewildered and half-crazed man that he would marry the Heiress of Redstone Hall!

CHAPTER III.

DEATH AT REDSTONE HALL.

For two days after the morning of which we have written, Colonel Raymond lay in a kind of stupor from which he would rouse at intervals, and pressing the hand of his son who watched beside him, he would whisper faintly, " God bless you for making your old father so happy. God bless you, my darling boy."

And Frederic, as often as he heard these words, would lay his aching head upon the pillow and try to force back the thoughts which continually whispered to him that a bad promise was better broken than kept, and that at the last he would tell Marian all, and throw himself upon her generosity. Since the morning when he made the fatal promise he had said but little to her, though she had been often in the room, ministering to his father's comfort—and once in the evening when he looked more than usually pale and weary, she had insisted upon taking his place, or sharing at least in his vigils. But he had declined her offer, and two hours later a slender little figure had glided noiselessly into the room and placed upon the table behind him a waiter, filled with delicacies which her own hand had prepared, and which she knew from experience would be needed ere the long night was over. He did not turn his head when she came in, but he knew whose step it was; and in his heart he thanked her for her thoughtfulness, and compelled himself to eat what she had brought because he knew how disappointed she would be if in the morning she found it all untouched.

And still he was as far from loving her now as he had ever been; and on the second night, as he sat by his sleeping father, he resolved, come what might, he would retract the promise made under such excitement. "When father wakes, I'll tell him I cannot," he said, and anxiously he watched the clock, which pointed at last to midnight. The twelve long strokes rang through the silent room, and with a short, quick gasp his father woke.

"Frederic," he said, and in his voice there was a tone never heard there before. "Frederic, has the light gone out, or why is it so dark? Where are you, my son? I cannot see."

"Here, father—here I am," and Frederic took in his the shriveled hand which was cold with approaching death.

"Frederic, it has come at last, and I am going from you; but before I go, lay your hand upon my brow, where the death sweat is standing, and say again what you said two days ago. Say you will make Marian your wife, and that until she is your wife she shall not know what I have done, for that might influence her decision. The letter I have left for her is in my private drawer, but you can keep the key.—Promise, Frederic—promise both, for I am going very fast."

Twice Frederic essayed to speak, but the words "I cannot" died on his lips, and again the faint voice—fainter than when it spoke before, said, "Promise, my boy, and save the name of Raymond from dishonor!"

It was in vain he struggled to resist his destiny.—The pleading tones of his dying father prevailed. Isabel Huntington—Marian Lindsey—Redstone Hall—everything seemed as nought compared with that father's wishes, and falling on his knees the young man said, "Heaven helping me, father, I will do both."

"And as you have made me happy, so may you be happy and prospered all the days of your life," returned the father, laying his clammy hand upon the brown hair of his son. "Tell Marian that dying I blessed her with more than a father's blessing, for she is very dear to me. And the little helpless Alice—she has money of her own, but she must still live with you and Marian. Be kind to the servants, Frederic. Don't part with a single one—and—and—can you hear me, boy? Keep your promise as you hope for heaven hereafter."

They were the last words the old man ever spoke—and when at last Frederic raised his head he knew by the white face lying motionless upon the pillow, that he was with the dead. The household was aroused, and crowding round the door the negroes came, their noisy outcries grating harshly on the ear of the young man, who felt unequal to the task of stopping them. But when Marian came, a few low spoken words from her quieted the tumult, and those whose services were not needed dispersed to the kitchen, where, forgetful of their recent demonstrations of grief, they speculated upon the probable result of their "old marster's death," and wondered if with the new one they should lead as easy a life as they had done heretofore.

The next morning the news spread rapidly, not only that Colonel Raymond was dead, but also that he had died without a will—this last piece of information being given by Lawyer Gibson, who, a little disappointed in the result of his late visit to Redstone Hall, had several times in public expressed his opinion that it was all the work of Frederic, who wanted everything himself, and feared his father would leave something to Marian Lindsey. This seemed very probable; and in the same breath with which they deplored the loss of Colonel Raymond, the neighbors denounced his son as selfish and avaricious. Still he was now the richest man in the county, and it would not be politic to treat him with disrespect—so they came about him with words of sympathy and offers of assistance, all of which he listened to abstractedly, and when they asked for some directions as to the arrangements for the burial, he answered, "I do not know—I am not myself to-day—but go to Marian. I will abide by her decision."

So to Marian they went; and hushing her own great grief—for she mourned for the departed as for a well loved father—Marian told them what she thought her guardian would wish that they should do. It is not customary in Kentucky to keep the dead as long as at the North, and ere the sun of the first day was low in the west a grave was made within an enclosure near the river side, where the cedar and the fir were growing, and when the sun was setting, a long procession wound slowly down the terraced walk, bearing with them one who when they returned came not with them, but was resting quietly where the light from the windows of his former home could fall upon his peaceful grave.

CHAPTER IV.

KEEPING THE PROMISE.

Four weeks had passed away since Colonel Raymond was laid to rest. The negroes, having finished their mourning at the grave and at church on the Sabbath succeeding the funeral, had gone back to their old light-hearted way of living, and outwardly there were no particular signs of grief at Redstone Hall. But two there were who suffered keenly, and suffered all the more that neither could speak to the other a word of sympathy. With Alice Marian wept bitterly, feeling that she was indeed homeless and friendless in the wide world. From Dinah she had heard the story of the Will, and remembering the events of that morning when Lawyer Gibson, as she supposed, had come to draw it, she thought it very probable. Still this did not trouble her one half so much as the studied reserve which Frederic manifested toward her. At the funeral he had offered her his arm, walking with her to the grave and back; but since that night he had kept aloof, seeing her only at the table, or when he wished to ask some question which she alone could answer.

In the first days of her sorrow she had forgotten the letter which her guardian had left for her, and when she did remember it and go to the private drawer where he said it was, she found the drawer locked.—Frederic had the key, of course, and thinking that if a wrong had indeed been done to her, he knew it, too, she waited in hopes that he would speak of it, and perhaps bring her the letter. But Frederic Raymond had sworn to keep that letter from her yet awhile, and he dared not break his vow. On the night after the burial he, too, had gone to the private drawer, and, taking the undirected missive in his hand, had felt strongly tempted to break its seal and read. But he had no right to do that, he said; all that was required of him was to keep it from Marian until such time as he was at liberty to let her read it. So, with a benumbed sensation at his heart, he locked the drawer and left the room, feeling that his own destiny was fixed, and that it was worse than useless to struggle against it. He could not write to Isabel yet, but he wrote to her mother, telling her of his father's death, and saying he did not know how long it would be ere they saw him again at New Haven. This done, he sat down in a kind of torpor, and waited for circumstances to shape themselves.—Marian would seek for her letter, he thought, and missing the key, would come to him, and then—oh, how he hoped it would be weeks and months before she came, for when she did he knew he must tell her why it was withheld.

Meantime, Marian waited day after day vainly wishing that he would speak to her upon the subject; but he did not, and at last, four weeks after her guardian's death, she sought the library again, but found the drawer locked as usual.

"It is unjust to treat me so," she said. "The letter is mine, and I have a right to read it."

Then, as she recalled the conversation which had passed between herself and Colonel Raymond on that night when he first hinted of a wrong, she wondered if he had said aught to Frederic of her. Most earnestly she hoped not—and yet she was almost certain that he had, and this was why Frederic treated her so strangely. "He hates me," she said bitterly, "because he thinks I want him—but he needn't, for I wouldn't have him now, even if he knelt at my feet, and begged of me to be his wife; I'll tell him so, too, the first chance I get," and sinking into the large arm chair Marian laid her head upon the writing desk and wept.

The day had been rainy and dark, and as she sat there in the gathering night and listened to the low moan of the October wind, she thought with gloomy forebodings of the future, and what it would bring to her.

"Oh, it is dreadful to be so homeless—so friendless, so poor," she cried, and in that cry there was a note of desolation which touched a chord of pity in the heart of him who stood on the threshold of the door, silently watching the young girl as she battled with her stormy grief.

He did not know why he had come to that room, and he surely would not have come had he expected to find her there. But it could not now be helped; he was there with her; he had witnessed her sorrow, and involuntarily advancing toward her he laid his hand lightly upon her shoulder and said, "Poor child, don't cry so hard."

She seemed to him a little girl, and as such he had addressed her; but to the startled Marian it mattered not what he said—there was kindness in his voice, and lifting up her face, which even in the darkness looked white and worn, she sobbed, "Oh, Frederic, you don't hate me, then?"

"Hate you, Marian," he answered, "of course not. What put that idea into your head?"

"Because—because you act so cold and strange, and don't come near me when my heart is aching so hard for him—your father."

Frederic made no reply, and resolving to make a clean breast of it, Marian continned, "There's nobody to care for me now, and I wish you to be my brother, just as you used to be, and if your father said any thing else of me to you he didn't mean it, I am sure; I don't at any rate, and I want you to forget it and not hate me for it. I'll go away from Redstone Hall if you say so, but you mustn't hate me for what I could not help. Will you, Frederic?" and Marian's voice was again choked with tears.

She had stumbled upon the very subject uppermost in Frederic's mind, and drawing a chair near to her, he said, "I will not profess to be ignorant of what you mean, Marian. My father had some strange fancies at the last, but for these you are not to blame. Did he say nothing to you of a letter?"

"Yes, yes," answered Marian quickly, "and I've been for it so many times. Will you give it to me now, Frederic? It's mine, you know," and Marian looked at him wistfully.

Frederic hesitated a moment, and misapprehending the motive of his hesitancy, Marian continued,

"Do not fear what I may think. He said a wrong had been done to me, but if it has not affected me heretofore, it surely will not now—and I loved him well enough to forgive anything. Let me have the letter, won't you?"

"Marian," and Frederic trembled with strong emotion, "the night my father died, I laid my hand upon his head and promised that you should not see that letter until you were a bride."

"A bride!" Marian exclaimed passionately, "I shall never be a bride—never—certainly not yours!" and the little hands worked nervously together, while she continued. "I asked you to forget that whim of your father's. He did not mean it—he would not have it so, and neither would I," and Frederic Raymond could almost see the angry flash of the blue eyes turned so defiantly toward him.

Man-like he began to feel some interest now that there was opposition, and to her exclamation "neither would I," he replied softly, "Not if I wish it, Marian?"

The tone rather than the words affected the young

girl, thrilling her with a new-born delight; and laying her hand again upon the desk, she sobbed afresh, not impetuously, this time, but steadily, as if the crying did her good. Greatly she longed for him to speak again, but he did not. He was waiting for her, and drying her tears, she lifted up her face, and in a voice which seemed to demand the truth, she said: "Frederic, do you wish it? Here, almost in the room where your father died, can you say to me truly that you wish me to be your wife?"

It was a perplexing question, and Frederic Raymond felt that he was dealing falsely with her, but he made to her the only answer he could—"Men seldom ask a woman to marry them unless they wish it."

"I know," returned Marian, "but—do—would you have thought of it if your father had not first suggested it?"

"Marian," said Frederic, "I am much older than yourself, and I might never have thought of marrying you. He, however, gave me good reasons why I should wish to have it so—in all sincerity I ask you to be my wife. Will you, Marian? It seems soon to talk of these things, but he so desired it."

In her bewilderment Marian fancied he had said, "I do wish to have it so," but she would know another thing, and not daring to put the question to him direct, she said, "Do men ever wish to marry one whom they do not love?"

Frederic understood her at once, and for a moment felt strongly tempted to tell her the truth, for in that case he was sure she would refuse to listen to his suit and he would then be free, but his father's presence seemed over and around him, while Redstone Hall was too fair to be exchanged for poverty; and so he answered, "I have always loved you as a sister, and in time I will love you as you deserve. I will be kind to you, Marian, and I think I can make you happy"

He spoke with earnestness, for he knew he was deceiving the young girl, and in his inmost soul he determined to repair the wrong by learning to love her, as she said:

"And suppose I refuse you, what then?"

Marian spoke decidedly, and something in her manner startled Frederic, who now that he had gone thus far, did not care to be thwarted.

"You will not refuse me, I am sure," he said.—"We cannot live together here just as we have done, for people would talk."

"I can go away," said Marian, mournfully, while Frederic replied,

"No, Marian, if you will not be my wife, *I* must go away; Redstone Hall cannot be the home of us both, and if you refuse I shall go—soon, very soon."

"Won't you ever come back?" asked Marian, with childish simplicity; but ere Frederic could answer, the door suddenly opened and old Dinah appeared, exclaiming as her eye fell upon them, "For the dear Lord's sake, if you two ain't settin' together in the dark, when I've done hunted everywhar for you," and Dinah's face wore a very knowing look, as setting down the candle she departed, muttering something about "when me and Philip was young."

The spell was broken for Marian, and starting up, she said, "I cannot talk any more to-night. I'll answer you some other time," and she hurried into the hall, where she stumbled upon Dinah, who greeted her with "Ain't you two kinder hankerin' arter each other, 'case if you be, it's the sensiblest thing you ever done. Marster Frederic is the likeliest, trimmest chap in Kentuck, and you've got an uncommon heap of sense."

Marian made no reply but darted up the stairs to her room, where she could be alone to think. It seemed to her a dream, and yet she knew it was a reality. Frederic had asked her to be his wife, and though she had said to herself that she would not marry him even if he knelt at her feet, she felt vastly like revoking that decision! If she were only sure he loved her, or would love her; and then she recalled every word he had said, wishing she could have looked into his face and seen what its expression was. She did not think of the letter in her excitement.—She only thought of Frederic's question, and she longed for some one in whom she could confide. Alice, who always retired early, was already asleep, and as her soft breathing fell on Marian's ear, she said, "Alice is much wiser than children usually are at six and a half. I mean to tell her," and, stealing to the bedside, she whispered, "Alice, Alice, wake up a moment, will you?"

Alice turned on her pillow, and when sure she was awake, Marian said impetuously, "If you were me, would you marry Frederic Raymond?"

The blind eyes opened wide, as if they doubted the sanity of the speaker; then quietly replying, "No, indeed, I wouldn't," Alice turned a second time upon her pillow and slept again, while Marian, a good deal piqued at the answer, tormented herself with wondering what the child could mean, and why she disliked Frederic so much. The next morning it was Alice who awoke Marian and said, "Was it a dream, or did you say something to me last night about marrying Frederic?"

For a moment Marian forgot that the sightless eyes turned so inquiringly toward her could not see, and she covered her face with her hands to hide the blushes she knew were burning there.

"Say," persisted Alice, "what was it?" and half willingly, half reluctantly, Marian told of the strange request which Frederic had made, saying nothing, however, of the letter, for if Colonel Raymond had done her a wrong, she felt it a duty she owed his memory to keep it to herself.

The darkened world in which Alice lived, had matured her other faculties far beyond her age, and though not yet seven years old, she was in many things scarcely less a child than Marian, whose story puzzled her, for she could hardly understand how one who had seemed so much her companion could think of being a married woman. Marian soon convinced her, however, that there was a vast difference between almost seven and almost sixteen, and still she was not reconciled.

"Frederic is well enough," she said, "and I once heard Agnes Gibson say he was the best match in the county, but somehow he don't seem to like you. Ain't he stuck up, and don't he know a heap more than you?"

"Yes, but I can learn," answered Marian, sadly, thinking with regret of the many hours she had played in the woods when she might have been practising upon the piano, or reading the books which Frederic liked best. "I can in time make a lady perhaps—and then you know if I don't have him, one of us must go away, for he said so."

"Oh," exclaimed Alice, catching her breath and drawing nearer to Marian, "wouldn't it be nice for you and me to live here all alone with Dinah, and do just as we're a mind to. Tell him you won't, and let him go back where he came from."

"No," returned Marian, "if either goes away, it will be me, for I've no right here, and Frederic has."

"You go away," repeated Alice. "What could you do without Dinah?"

"I don't know," returned Marian mournfully, a dim foreboding as it were of her dark future rising up before her. "I can't sew—I don't know enough to teach, and I couldn't do anything but die!"

This settled the point with Alice. She would rather Marian should marry Frederic than go away and die, and so she said, "I'd have him, I reckon," adding quickly, "You'll carry the keys, then, won't you, and give me all the preserves and cake I want?"

Thus was the affair amicably adjusted between the two, and when at the breakfast table she met with

Frederic, she was ready to answer his question; but she chose to let him broach the subject, and this he did do that evening when he found her alone in his father's room. He had decided that it was useless to struggle with his fate, and he resolved to make the best of it. How far Redstone Hall, bank notes, stock and real estate influenced this decision we cannot say, but he was sincere in his intention of treating Marian well, and when he found her by accident in his father's room, he said to her kindly, "Can you answer me now?"

Marian was not yet enough accustomed to the world to conceal whatever she felt, and with the light of a new happiness shining on her childish face, she went up to him, and laying her hand confidingly upon his, she said, "I will marry you, Frederic, if you wish me to."

A strange enigma is human nature. When the previous night she had hesitated to answer, Frederic was conscious of a vague fear that she might say no—and now that she had said yes, he felt less pleasure than pain, for the die he knew was cast. A more observing eye than Marian's would have seen the dark shadow which flitted over his face, and the sudden paling of his lips, but she did not; she only saw how he shook off her hand without even so much as touching it, and all the novels she had ever read would surely have sanctioned so modest a proceeding as that! But novels, she reflected, were not true, and as she was an actor in real life, she must accept whatever that life might bring. Still she was not quite satisfied, and when Frederic, fancying he should feel better if the matter were well over, said to her, "There is no reason why we should delay—my father would wish the marriage to take place immediately, and I will speak to Dinah at once," she felt that with him it was a mere form, and bursting into tears she said passionately, "You are not obliged to marry me. I certainly did not ask you to."

For a moment Frederic stood irresolute, and then he replied, "Don't be foolish, Marian, but take a common sense view of the matter. I am not accustomed to love-making, and the character would not suit me now when my heart is so full of sorrow for my father. Many a one would gladly take your place, but"—here he paused, uncertain how to proceed and still keep truth upon his side—then, as a bright thought struck him, he added, "but I prefer you to all the girls in Kentucky. Be satisfied with this, and wait patiently for the time when I can show you that I love you."

His manner both frightened and fascinated Marian, and she answered through her tears, "I will be satisfied, and wait."

Frederic knew well that Marian was too much of a child to manage the affair, and after his interview with her, he sought out Dinah, to whom he announced his intentions.

"There is no need of delay," he said, "and two weeks from to-day is the time appointed. There will be no show—no parade—simply a quiet wedding in the presence of a few friends, who will dine with us, of course. The dinner, you must see to, and I will attend to the rest."

Amid ejaculations of surprise and delight, old Dinah heard what he had to say—and then, boiling over with the news, hastened to the kitchen, where she was soon surrounded by an astonished and listening audience, the various members of which were affected differently, just according to their different ideas of what "marster Frederic's" wife ought to be. Among the negroes at Redstone Hall were two distinct parties, one of which having belonged to Mr. Higgins, the former owner of the place, looked rather contemptuously upon the other clique, who had been purchased of Mr. Smithers, a neighboring planter, and were not supposed to have as high blood in their veins as was claimed by their darker rivals. Hence between the democratic Smitherses and the aristocratic

Higginses was waged many a fierce battle, which was usually decided by old Dinah, who, having belonged to another family still, "thanked the Lord that she was neither a Higginses nor a Smitherses, but was a peg or so above such low-lived truck as them."

On this occasion the announcement of Master Frederic's expected marriage was received by the Smitherses with loud shouts of joy and hurrahs for Miss Marian. The Higginses, on the contrary, though friendly to Marian, declared she was not high bred enough to keep up the glory of the house, and Aunt Hetty, who led the clan and was a kind of rival to old Dinah, launched forth into a wonderful stream of eloquence.

"Miss Marian would do in her place," she said, "but 'twas a burnin' shame to set such an onery thing over them as had been oncet used to the quality. 'Twas different with the Smitherses, whose old Miss was bed rid with a spine in her back, and hadn't but one store carpet in the house. But the Higginses, she'd let 'em know, had been 'customed to sunthin' better. Oh," said she, "you or'to seen Miss Beatrice the fust day Marster brought her home. She looked jest like a queen, with that great long switchin' tail to her dress, a wipin' up the walk so clean that I, who was a gal then, didn't have to sweep it for mor'n a week—and them *ars* she put on when she curchied inter the room and walkin' backards sot down on the rim of the cheer—so"—and holding out her short linsey-woolsey to its widest extent, the old negress proceeded to illustrate.

But alas for Aunt Hetty—her intention was anticipated by stuttering Josh, the most mischievous spirit of all the Smithers clan. Quick as thought the active boy removed the chair where she expected to land, pushing into its place an overflowing slop-pail, and into this the discomfited old lady plunged amid the execrations of her partisans and the jeers of her opponents.

"You Josh—you villain—the Lord spar me long enough to break yer sassy neck!" she screamed, as with difficulty she extricated herself from her position and wrung her dripping garments.

"Sarved you right," said Dinah, shaking her fat sides with delight. "Sarved you right, and the fust one that raises thar voice agin Miss Marian 'll catch sunthin' a heap wus than dirty dishwater."

But Dinah's threat was unnecessary, for with Hetty's downfall the star of the Higginses set, leaving that of the Smitherses still in the ascendant!

Meantime Marian was confiding to Alice the story of her engagement, and wondering if Frederic intended taking a bridal tour. She hoped he did, for she so much wished to see a little of the world, particularly New York, of which she had heard such glowing accounts. But nothing could be less in accordance with Frederic's feelings than a bridal tour—and when once Marian ventured to broach the subject, he said that under the circumstances it would hardly be right to go off and enjoy themselves, so they had better stay quietly at home. And this settled the point, for Marian never thought of questioning his decision. If they made no journey, she would not need any additions to her wardrobe, and she was thus saved from the trouble which usually falls to the lot of brides.—Still it was not at all in accordance with her ideas—this marrying without a single article of finery, and once she resolved to indulge in a new dress at least. She had ample means of her own, for her guardian had been lavish of his money, always giving her far more than she could use, and during the last year she had been saving a fund for the purpose of surprising Alice and the blacks with handsome Christmas presents.—The former was to have a little gold watch, which she had long desired, because she liked to hear it tick—but the watch and the dress could not both be bought, and when she considered this, Marian generously gave up the latter for the sake of pleasing the blind girl.

Among her dresses was a neat, white muslin, given her by Colonel Raymond only the Summer. previous, and this she decided should be the wedding robe, for black was gloomy, she said, and would almost seem ominous of evil.

And so the childish bride elect made her simple arrangements, unassisted by any one save Dinah and the little Alice, the latter of whom was really of the most service, for old Dinah spent the greater portion of her time in grumbling because "Marster Frederic didn't act more lover-like to his wife that was to be."

Marian, too, felt this keenly, but she would not admit it, and she said to Dinah, "You can't expect him to be like himself when he's mourning for his father."

"Mournin' for his father," returned Dinah,—"and what if he is? Can't a fellow kiss a gal and mourn a plenty too? Taint no way to do to mope from mornin' till night like you was gwine to the gallus. Me and Phil didn't act that way when he was settin' to me—but I 'spect they've done got some new fangled way of courtin' jest as they hev for everything else—but I'm satisfied with the old fashion, and I wish them fetch-ed Yankees would mind their own business and let well 'nough alone."

Dinah felt considerably relieved after this long speech, particularly as she had that very morning made it in substance to Frederic--and when that evening she saw the young couple seated upon the same sofa, and tolerably near to each other, she was sure she had done some good by "ginnen 'em a piece of her mind."

Among the neighbors there was a great deal of talk, and occasionally a few of them called at Redstone Hall, but these only came to go away again, and comment on Frederic's strange taste in marrying one so young, and so wholly unlike himself. It could not be, they said, that he had really cared about the Will, else why had he so soon taken Marian to share his fortune with him? But Frederic kept his own counsel, and once when questioned on the subject of his marriage and asked if it were not a sudden thing, he answered haughtily, "Of course not—it was decided years ago, when Marian first came to live with us."

And so amid the speculations of friends, the gossip of Dinah, the joyous anticipations of Marian, and the harrowing doubts of Frederic, the two weeks passed away, bringing at last the eventful day when Redstone Hall was to have once more a mistress.

CHAPTER V.

THE BRIDAL DAY.

"It was the veriest farce in all the world, the marriage of Frederic Raymond with a child of fifteen;" at least so said Agnes Gibson of twenty-five, and so said sundry other guests who at the appointed hour assembled in the parlor of Redstone Hall, to witness the sacrifice—not of Frederic as they vainly imagined, but of the unsuspecting Marian.

He knew what he did, and why he did it, while she, blindfolded as it were, was about to leap into the uncertain future. No such gloomy thoughts as these, however, intruded themselves upon her mind as she stood before her mirror and with trembling fingers made her simple bridal toilet. When first the idea of marrying Frederic was suggested to her nearly as much pride as love had mingled in her thoughts, for Marian was not without her ambition, and the honor of being the mistress of Redstone Hall had influenced her decision. But during the two weeks since her engagement, her heart had gone out toward him with a deep absorbing love, and had he now been the poorest man in all the world and she a royal princess, she would have spurned the wealth that kept her from him, or gladly have laid it at his feet for the sake of staying with him and knowing that he wished it. And this was the girl whom Frederic Raymond was about to wrong by making her his wife when he knew he did not love her. But she should never know it, he said—should never suspect that nothing but his hand and name went with the words he was so soon to utter, and he determined to be true to her and faithful to his marriage vow.

Some doubt he had as to the effect his father's letter might have upon her, and once he resolved that she should never see it; but this was an idle thought, not to be harbored for a moment. He had told her when she asked him for it the last time that she should have it on her bridal day; for so his father willed it, and he would keep his word. He had written to Isabel at the very last, for though he was not bound to her by a promise he knew an explanation of his conduct was due to her, and he forced himself to write it. Not a word did he say against Marian, but he gave her to understand that but for his father the match would never have been made—that circumstances over which he had no control compelled him to do what he was doing. He should never forget the pleasant hours spent in her society, he said, and he closed by asking her to visit the future Mrs. Raymond at Redstone Hall. It cost him a bitter struggle to write thus indifferently to one he loved so well, but it was right, he said, and when the letter was finished he felt that the last tie which bound him to Isabel was sundered, and there was nothing for him now but to make the best of Marian. So when on their bridal morning she came to him and asked his wishes concerning her dress, he answered her very kindly, "As you are in mourning you had better make no change, besides I think black very becoming to your fair complexion."

This was the first compliment he had ever paid her, and her heart thrilled with delight, but when, as she was leaving the room he called her back and said, still gently, kindly, "Would you as soon wear your hair plain? I do not quite fancy ringlets," her eyes filled with tears, for she remembered the corkscrew curls, and glancing in the mirror at her wavy hair, she wished it were possible to remedy the defect.

"I will do the best I can," she said, and returning to her room, she commenced her operations, but it was a long, tedious process, the combing out of those curls, for her hair was tenacious of its rights, and even when she thought it subdued and let go of the end, it rolled up about her forehead in tight round rings, as if spurning alike both water and brush.

"I'd like to see the man what could make me yank out my wool like that," muttered Dinah, who was watching the straightening process with a lowering brow, inasmuch as it reflected dishonor upon her own crisped locks. "If the Lord made yer har to curl, war it so, and not mind every freak of his'n. Fust you know, he'll be a-wantin' you to war yer face on t'other side of yer head, but 'taint no way to do. You must begin as you can hold out. In a few hours you'll have as much right here as he has, and I'd show it, too, by pitchin' inter us niggers and jawin' to kill. I shall know you don't mean nothin' and shan't keer. Come to think on't, though, I reckon you'd better let me and the Smitherses be and begin with them Higginses. I'd give it to old Hetty good—she 'sarves to be took down a button hole lower, if ever a nigger did, for she said a heap o' stuff about you."

Marian smiled a kind of quiet happy smile and went on with her task, which was finished at last, and her luxuriant hair was bound at the back of her head in a large flat knot. The effect was not becoming and she knew it, but if Frederic liked it she was satisfied, even if Dinah did demur, telling her she looked like "a cat whose ears had been boxed." Frederic did not like it, but after the pains she had taken he would not tell her so, and when she said to him, "I am ready," he offered her his arm and went silently down the stairs to the parlor, where guests and clergymen were waiting.

The day was bright and beautiful, for the light of

the glorious Indian Summer sun was resting on the Kentucky hills, and through the open window the murmuring ripple of the Elkhorn came, while the balmy breath of the south wind swept over the white face of the bride, and lifted from her neck the few stray locks which, escaping from their confinement, curled naturally in their accustomed place. But to the assembled guests there seemed in all a note of sadness, a warning voice which said the time for this bridal was not yet; and years after, when the beautiful mistress of Redstone Hall rode by in her handsome carriage, Agnes Gibson told to her little sister how on that November day the cheeks of both bride and bridegroom paled as if with mortal fear when the words were spoken which made them one.

Whether it were the newness of her position, or a presentiment of coming evil Marian could not tell, but into her heart there crept a chill as she glanced timidly at the man who stood so silently beside her, and thought, "He is my husband." It was, indeed, a sombre wedding—"more like a funeral," the guests declared, as immediately after dinner they took their leave and commented upon the affair as people always will. Oh, how Frederic longed yet dreaded to have them go. He could not endure their congratulations, which to him were meaningless, and he had no wish to be alone. He was recovering from his apathy, and could yesterday have been his again, he believed he would have broken his promise. But yesterday had gone and to-morrow had come—it was to-day, now, with him, and Marian was his wife. Turn which way he would, the reality was the same, and with an intense loathing of himself and a deep pity for her, he feigned some trivial excuse and went away to his room, where, with the gathering darkness and his own wretched thoughts, he would be alone.

With strange unrest Marian wandered from room to room, wondering if Frederic had so soon grown weary of her presence, and sometimes half wishing that she were Marian Lindsey again, and that the new name by which they called her belonged to some one else. At last, when it was really dark—when the lamps were lighted in the parlor and Alice had wept a bitter, passionate good night in her arms and gone to sleep, she bethought her of the letter. She could read it now. She had complied with all the stipulations, and there was no longer a reason why it should be withheld. She went to Frederic's door; but he was not there, and a servant passing in the hall said he had returned to the parlor while she was busy with Alice. So to the parlor Marian went, finding him sitting unemployed and wrapped in gloomy thought. He heard her step upon the carpet, but standing in the shadow as she did, she could not see the look of pain which flitted over his face at her approach.

"Frederic," she said, "I may read the letter now—will you give me the key?"

Mechanically he did as she desired, and then with a slightly uneasy feeling as to the effect the letter might have upon her, he went back to his reflections, while she started to leave the room. When she reached the door she paused a moment and looked back. In giving her the key he had changed his position, and she could see the suffering expression of his white face. Quickly returning to his side, she said anxiously, "Are you sick?"

"Nothing but a headache. You know I am accustomed to that," he replied.

Marian hesitated a moment—then parting the damp brown hair from off his forehead she kissed him timidly and left the room. Involuntarily Frederic raised his hand to wipe the spot away, but something stayed the act and whispered to him that a wife's first kiss was a holy thing and could never be repeated!

Through the hall the nimble feet of Marian sped until she stood within her late guardian's room, and there she stopped, for the atmosphere seemed oppressive and laden with terror.

"'Tis because it's so dark," she said, and going out into the hall, she took a lamp from the table and then returned.

But the olden feeling was with her still—a feeling as if she were treading some fearful gulf, and she was half tempted to turn back even now, and ask Frederic to come with her while she read the letter.

"I will not be so foolish, though," she said, and opening the library door she walked boldly in; but the same Marian who entered there never came out again!

CHAPTER VI.

READING THE LETTER.

Oh, how still it was in that room, and the click of the key as it turned the slender bolt echoed through the silent apartment, causing Marian to start as if a living presence had been near. The drawer was opened, and she held the letter in her hand, while unseen voices seemed whispering to her, "Oh, Marian, Marian—leave the letter still untouched. Do not seek to know the secret it contains, but go back to the man who is your husband, and by those gentle acts which seldom fail in their effect, win his love. It will be far more precious to you than all the wealth of which you are the unsuspecting heiress."

But Marian did not understand—nor know why it was she trembled so. She only knew she had the letter in her hand—her letter—the one left by her guardian. It bore no superscription, but it was for her, of course, and fixing herself in a comfortable position, she broke the seal and read:

"*My Dear Child:*"

There was nothing in those three words suggestive of a mistake—and Marian read on till, with a quick, nervous start, she glanced forward, then backward—and then read on and on, until at last not even the fear of death itself could have stopped her from that reading. That letter was never intended for her eye—she knew that now, but had the cold hand of her guardian been interposed to wrest it from her, she would have held it fast until she learned the whole. Like coals of living fire, the words burned into her soul, scorching, blistering as they burned—and when the letter was finished she fell upon her face with a cry so full of agony and horror that Frederic in the parlor heard the wail of human anguish, and started to his feet, wondering whence it came.

With the setting of the sun the November wind had risen, and as the young man listened it swept moaning past the window, seeming not unlike the sound he had first heard. "It was the wind," he said, and he resumed his seat, while, in that little room, not very far away, poor Marian came back to consciousness, and crouching on the floor, prayed that she might die. She understood it now—how she had been deceived, betrayed, and cruelly wronged. She knew, too, that she was the heiress of untold wealth, and for a single moment her heart beat with a gratified pride, but the surprise was too great to be realized at once, and the feeling was soon absorbed in the reason why Frederic Raymond had made her his wife. It was not herself he had married, but her fortune—her money—Redstone Hall. She was merely a necessary incumbrance, which he would rather should have been omitted in the bargain. The thought was maddening, and, stretching out her arms, she asked again that she might die.

"Oh, why didn't he come to me?" she cried, "and tell me? I would gladly have given him half my fortune—yes, all—all—rather than be the wretched thing I am, and he would have been free to love and marry this—"

She could not at first speak the name of her rival—but she said it at last, and the sound of it wrung her heart with a new and torturing pain. She had never heard of Isabel Huntington before, and as she thought how beautiful and grand she was, she whispered to herself, "Why didn't he go back to her, and leave me, the red-headed fright, alone? Yes, that was what he wrote to his father. Let me look at it again," and the tone of her voice was bitter and the expression of her face hard and stony, as taking up the letter she read for the second time that "she was uncouth, uneducated and ugly," and if his father did not give up that foolish fancy, Frederic would positively "hate the red headed fright." Her guardian had not given up the foolish fancy, consequently there was but one inference to be drawn.

In her excitement she did not consider that Frederic had probably written of her harsher things than he really meant. She only thought, "He loathes me—he despises me—he wishes I was dead—and I dared to kiss him too," she added. "How he hated me for that, but 'twas the first, and it shall be the last, for I will go away forever and leave him Redstone Hall, the bride he married a few hours ago," and laying her face upon the chair Marian thought long and earnestly of the future. She had come into that room a happy, simple-hearted, confiding child, but she had lived years since, and she sat there now a crushed but self-reliant woman, ready to go out and contend with the world alone. Gradually her thoughts and purposes took a definite form. She was ignorant of the knotty points of law, and she did not know but Frederic could get her a divorce, but from this publicity she shrank. She could not be pointed at as a discarded wife. She would rather go away where Frederic would never see nor hear of her again, and she fancied that by so doing he would after a time at least be free to marry Isabel. She had not wept before, for her tears seemed scorched with pain, but at the thought of another coming there to take the place she had hoped to fill, they rained in torrents over her white face, and clasping her little hands convulsively together, she cried—"How can I give him up when I love him so much—so much?"

Gradually there stole over her the noble, unselfish thought, that because she loved him so much, she would willingly sacrifice herself and all she had for the sake of making him happy—and then she grew calm again and began to decide where she would go. Instinctively her mind turned toward New York city as the great hiding place from the world. Mrs. Burt, the woman who had lived with them in Yonkers, and who had always been so kind to her, was in New York she knew, for she had written to Colonel Raymond not long before his death, asking if there was anything in Kentucky for her son Ben to do. This letter her guardian had answered and then destroyed with many others, which he said were of no consequence, and only lumbered up his drawer. Consequently there was no possibility that this letter would suggest Mrs. Burt to Frederic, who had never seen her, she having come and gone while he was away at school, and thus far the project was a safe one. But her name—she might some time be recognized by that, and remembering that her mother's maiden name was *Mary Grey*, and that Frederic, even if he had ever known it, which was doubtful, had probably forgotten it, she resolved upon being henceforth MARIAN GREY, and she repeated it aloud, feeling the while that the change was well —for she was no longer the same girl she used to know as Marian Lindsey. Once she said softly to herself, "Marian Raymond," but the sound grated harshly, for she felt that she had no right to bear that name.

This settled, she turned her thoughts upon the means by which New York was to be reached, and she was glad that she had not bought the dress, for now she had ample funds with which to meet the expense, and she would go that very night, before her resolution failed her. Redstone Hall was only two miles from the station, and as the evening train passed at half-past nine, there would be time to reach it, and write a farewell letter, too, to Frederic, for she must tell him how, though it broke her heart to do it, she willingly gave him everything, and hoped he would be happy when she was gone forever. Marian was beautiful then in her desolation, and so Frederic Raymond would have said, could he have seen her with the light of her noble sacrifice of self shining in her eyes, and the new-born, womanly expression on her face. The first fearful burst was over, and calmly she sat down to her task—but the storm rose high again as she essayed to write that good-by, which would seem to him who read it a cry of despair wrung from a fainting heart.

"Frederic—*dear Frederic*," she began, "can I—may I say *my husband* once—just once—and I'll never insult you with that name again?

"I am going away forever, Frederic, and when you are reading this I shall not be at Redstone Hall, nor anywhere around it. Do not try to find me. It is better you should not. Your father's letter, which was intended for you, and by mistake has come to me, will tell you why I go. I forgive your father, Frederic—fully, freely forgive him—but *you*—oh, Frederic, if I loved you less I should blame you for deceiving me so cruelly. If you had told me all I would gladly have shared my fortune with you. I would have given you more than half, and when you brought that beautiful Isabel home I would have loved her as a sister.

"Why didn't you, Frederic? What made you treat me so? What made you break my heart when you could have helped it? It aches so hard now as I write, and the hardest pain of all is the loss of faith in you. I thought you so noble, so good, and I may confess to you here on paper, I loved you so much—how much you will never know, for I shall never come back to tell you.

"And I kissed you, too. Forgive me for that, Frederic. I didn't know then how you hated me.—Wash the stain from your forehead, can't you?—and don't lay it up against me. If I thought I could make you love me, I would stay. I would endure torture for years if I knew the light was shining beyond, but it cannot be. The sight of me would make you hate me more. So I give everything I have to you and Isabel. You'll marry her at a suitable time, and when you see how well she becomes your home, you will be glad I went away. If you must tell her of me, and I suppose you must, speak kindly of me, won't you?—You needn't talk of me often, but sometimes, when you are all alone, and you are sure she will not know, think of poor little Marian, who gave her life away, that one she loved the best in all the world might have wealth and happiness.

"Farewell, Frederic, farewell. Death itself cannot be harder than bidding you good-by, and knowing it is for ever."

And well might Marian say this, for it seemed to her that she dipped her pen in her very heart's blood, when she wrote that last adieu. She folded up the letter and directed it to Frederic—then taking another sheet she wrote to the blind girl:

"DEAREST ALICE—Precious little Alice. If my heart was not already broken, it would break at leaving you. Don't mourn for me much, darling. Tell Dinah and Hetty, and the other blacks, not to cry—and if I've ever been cross to them, they must forget it now that I am gone. God bless you all. Good by—good by."

The letters finished, she left them upon the desk, where they could not help being seen by the first one who should enter—then stealing up the stairs to the closet at the extremity of the hall, she put on her bonnet, vail and shawl, and started for her purse, which was in the chamber where Alice slept. Careful, very careful were her footsteps now, lest she should waken the child, who, having cried herself to sleep, was resting quietly. The purse was obtained, as was also a daguerreotype of her guardian which lay in the same drawer—and then for a moment she stood gazing at the little blind girl, and longing to give her one more kiss; but she dared not, and glancing hurriedly around the room which had been hers so long, she hastened down the stairs and out upon the piazza. She could see the light from the parlor window streaming out into the darkness, and drawing near she looked through blinding tears upon the solitary man, who, sitting there alone, little dreamed of the whispered blessings breathed for him but a few yards away. It seemed to Marian in that moment of agony that her very life was going out, and she leaned against a pillar to keep herself from falling.

"Oh, can I leave him?" she thought. "Can I go away forever, and never see his face again or listen to his voice?" and looking up into the sky she prayed that if in heaven they should meet again, he might know and love her there for what she suffered here.

On the withered grass and leaves near by there was a rustling sound as if some one was coming, and Marian drew back for fear of being seen, but it was only Bruno, the large watch dog. He had just been released from his kennel, and he came tearing up the walk, and with a low savage growl sprang toward the spot where Marian was hiding.

"Bruno, good Bruno," she whispered, and in an instant the fierce mastiff crouched at her feet and licked her hand with a whining sound, as if he suspected something wrong.

One more yearning glance at Frederic—one more tearful look at her old home, and Marian walked rapidly down the avenue, followed by Bruno, who could neither be coaxed nor driven back. It was all in vain that Marian stamped her little foot, wound her arms round his shaggy neck, bidding him return; he only answered with a faint whine quite as expressive of obstinacy as words could have been. He knew Marian had no business to be abroad at that hour of the night, and, with the faithfulness of his race, was determined to follow. At length, as she was beginning to despair of getting rid of him, she remembered how pertinaciously he would guard any article which he knew belonged to the family—and on the bridge which crossed the Elkhorn, she purposely dropped her glove and handkerchief, the latter of which bore her name in full. The ruse was successful, for after vainly attempting to make her know that she had lost something, the dog turned back, and, with a loud, mournful howl, which Marian accepted as his farewell, he laid himself down by the handkerchief and glove, turning his head occasionally in the direction Marian had gone, and uttering low plaintive howls when he saw she did not return.

Meantime Marian kept on her way, striking out into the fields so as not to be observed—and at last, just as the cars sounded in the distance, she came up to a clump of trees growing a little to the left, and on the opposite side of the road from that on which the depot stood. By getting in here no one would see her at the station, and when the train stopped she came out from her concealment, and bounding lightly upon the platform of the rear car, entered unobserved. As the passengers were sitting with their backs toward her, but one or two noticed her when she came in, and these scarce gave her a thought, as she sank into the seat nearest to the door, and drawing her vail over her face trembled violently lest she should be recognized, or at least noted and remembered. But her fears were vain, for no one there had ever seen or heard of her—and in a moment more the train was moving on, and she, heart-broken and alone, was taking her bridal tour!

CHAPTER VII.

THE ALARM.

In her solitary bed little Alice slumbered on, moaning occasionally in her sleep, and at last when the clock struck nine, starting up and calling "Marian, Marian, where are you?" Then, remembering that Marian could not come to her that night, she puzzled her little brain with the great mystery, and wept herself to sleep for the second time.

In the kitchen old Dinah was busy with various household matters. With Frederic she had heard in the distance the bitter moan which Marian made when first she learned how she had been deceived, and like him she had wondered what the sound could be—then as a baby's cry came from a cabin near by, she had said to herself, "some of them Higgins brats, I'll warrant. They're allus a squallin'," and, satisfied with this conclusion, she had resumed her work. Once or twice after that she was in the house, feeling a good deal disturbed at seeing Frederic sitting alone without his bride, who, she rightly supposed, "was somewhar. But 'tain't no way," she muttered; "Phil and me didn't do like that;" then reflecting that "white folks wasn't like niggers," she returned to the kitchen just as Bruno set up his first loud howl. With Dinah the howl of a dog was a sure sign of death, and dropping her tallow candle in her fright, she exclaimed—"for the Lord's sake who's gwine to die now? I hope to goodness 'taint me, nor Phil, nor Lid, nor Victory

Eugeny," and turning to Aunt Hetty, who was troubled with vertigo, she asked if "she'd felt any signs of an afterplax fit lately?"

"The Lord," exclaimed old Hetty, "I hain't had a drap o' blood in me this six month, and if Bruno's howlin' for me, he may as well save his breath;" but in spite of this self-assurance, the old negress, when no one saw her, dipped her head in a bucket of water by way of warding off the danger.

Thus the evening wore away until at last Dinah, standing in the doorway, heard the whistle of the train as it passed the Big Spring station.

"Who s'posed 'twas half-past nine," she exclaimed. "I'll go this minit and see if Miss Marian wants me."

Just then another loud piercing howl from Bruno, who was growing impatient, fell upon her ear and arrested her movements.

"What can ail the critter," she said—"and he's down on the bridge, too, I believe."

The other negroes also heard the cry, which was succeeded by another and another, and became at last one prolonged yell, which echoed down the river and over the hills, starting Frederic from his deep reverie and bringing him to the piazza, where the blacks had assembled in a body.

"'Spects mebbe Bruno's done cotched somethin' or somebody down thar," suggested Philip, the most courageous of the group.

"Suppose you go and see," said Frederic, and lighting his old lantern Philip sallied out, followed ere long by all his comrades, who, by accusing each other of being "skeered to death," managed to keep up their own courage.

The bridge was reached, and in a tremor of delight Bruno bounded upon Phil, upsetting the old man and extinguishing the light, so that they were in total darkness. The white handkerchief, however, caught Dinah's eye, and in picking it up she also felt the glove, which was lying near it. But this did not explain the mystery—and after searching in vain for man, beast or hobgoblin, the party returned to the house, where their master awaited them.

"Thar warn't nothin' thar 'cept this yer rag and glove," said Dinah, passing the articles to him.

He took them, and going to the light saw the name upon the handkerchief, "Marian Lindsey." The glove too, he recognised as belonging to her, and with a vague fear of impending evil, he asked where they found them.

"On the bridge," answered Dinah; "somebody must have drapped 'em. That handkercher looks mighty like Miss Marian's hem-stitched one."

"It is hers," returned Frederic—"do you know where she is?"

"You is the one who orto know that, I reckon," answered Dinah, adding that she "hadn't seen her sense jest after dark, when she went up stars with Alice."

Frederic was interested now. In his abstraction he had not heeded the lapse of time, though he wondered where Marian was, and once feeling anxious to know what she would say to the letter, he was tempted to go in quest of her. But he did not—and now, with a presentiment that all was not right, he went to Alice's chamber, but found no Marian there. Neither was she in any of the chambers, nor in the hall, nor in the dining room, nor in his father's room, and he stood at last in the library door. The writing-desk was open, and on it lay three letters—one for Alice, one for him, the other undirected. With a beating heart he took the one intended for himself, and tearing it open, read it through. When Marian wrote that "she gave her life away," she had no thought of deceiving him, for her giving *him* up was giving her very life. But he did not so understand it, and sinking into a chair he gasped, "Marian is dead!" while his face grew livid and his heart sick with the horrid fear.

"Dead, Marster Frederic," shrieked old Dinah—"who dars tell me my chile is dead!" and bounding forward like a tiger, she grasped the arm of the wretched man, exclaiming, "whar is she the dead? and what is she dead for? and what's that she's writ that makes yer face as white as a piece of paper?—Read, and let us hear."

"I can't, I can't," moaned the stricken man. "Oh, has it come to this? Marian, Marian—won't somebody bring her back?"

"If marster 'll tell me whar to look, I'll find her, so help me, Lord," said uncle Phil, the tears rolling down his dusky cheeks.

"You found her handkerchief upon the bridge," returned Frederic, "and Bruno has been howling there—don't you see? She's in the river!—She's drowned! Oh, Marian—poor Marian, I've killed her—but God knows I did not mean to;" and in the very spot where not long before poor Marian had fallen on her face, the desolate man now lay on his, and suffered in part what she had suffered there.

It was a striking group assembled there. The bowed man, convulsed with strong emotion, and clutching with one hand the letter which had done the fearful work. The blacks gathered round, some weeping bitterly and all petrified with terror, while into their midst when the storm was at its hight the little Alice groped her way—her soft hair falling over her white night dress, her blind eyes rolling round the room, and her quick ear turned to catch any sound which might explain the strange proceedings. She had been roused from sleep by the confusion, and hearing the uproar in the hall and library, had felt her way to the latter spot, where in the doorway she stood asking for Marian.

"Bless you, honey, Miss Marian's dead—drownded," said Dinah, and Alice's shriek mingled with the general din.

"Where's Frederic?" asked the little girl, feeling

intuitively that he was the one who needed the most sympathy.

At the sound of his name Frederic lifted up his head, and taking the child in his arms, kissed her tenderly, as if he would thus make amends for his coldness to the lost Marian.

"'Tain't no way to stay here like rocks," said Uncle Phil at last. "If Miss Marian's in the river, we 'd better be a fishin' her out," and the practical negro proceeded to make the necessary arrangements.

Before he left the room, however, he would know if he were working for a certainty, and turning to his master, said, "Have you jest cause for thinkin' she's done drownded herself—'case if you hain't, 'tain't no use huntin' this dark night, and it's gwine to rain, too. The clouds is gettin' black as pitch."

Thus appealed to, Frederic answered, "She says in the letter that she's going away forever, that she shall not come back again, and she spoke of giving her life away. You found her handkerchief and glove upon the bridge, with Bruno watching near, and she is gone. Do you need more proof?"

Uncle Phil did not, though "he'd jest like to know, he said, "why a gal should up and dround herself on the very fust night arter she'd married the richest and han'somest chap in the county—but thar was no tellin' what gals would do. Gener'ly, though, you could calkerlate on thar doin' jest con-tra-ry to what you'd 'spect they would, and if Miss Marian preferred the river to that twenty-five pound feather-bed that Dinah spent mor'n an hour in makin' up, 'twas her nater, and 'twan't for him to say agin it. All he'd got to do was to work!"

And the old man did work, assisted by the other negroes and those of the neighbors who lived near to Redstone Hall. Frederic, too, joined, or rather led the search. Bareheaded, and utterly regardless of the rain which, as Uncle Phil had prophesied, began to fall in torrents, he gave the necessary directions, and when the morning broke, few would have recognized the elegant bridegroom of the previous day in the white-faced, weary man, who, with soiled garments and dripping hair, stood upon the narrow bridge, and in the grey November morning looked mournfully down the river as it went rushing on, telling no secret, if secret, indeed, there were to tell, of the wild despair which must have filled poor Marian's heart and maddened her brain ere she sought that watery grave.

Before coming out he had hurriedly read his father's letter, and he could well understand how its contents broke the heart of the wretched girl, and drove her to the desperate act which he believed she had committed.

"Poor Marian," he whispered to himself, "I alone am the cause of your sad death;" and most gladly would he then have become a beggar and earned his bread by the sweat of his brow, could she have come back again, full of life, of health and hope, just as she was the day before.

But this could not be, for she was dead, he said, dead beyond a doubt; and all that remained for him to do was to find her body and lay it beside his father. So during that day the search went on, and crowds of people were gathered on each side of the river, but no trace of the lost one could be found, and when a second time the night fell dark and heavy round Redstone Hall, it found a mournful group assembled there.

To Alice Frederic had read the letter left for her, and treasuring up each word the child groped her way into the kitchen, where, holding the note before her sightless eyes as if she could really see, she repeated it to the assembled blacks,

"Lor' bless the child," sobbed Dinah from behind her woolen apron, "I knowed she would remember me."

"And me," joined in Hetty. "Don't you mind how I is spoke of, too? She was a lady, every inch of her, Miss Marian was, an' if I said any badness of her, I want you to forgive me, Dinah. Here's my hand," and these two old ladies took each other's hand in token that they were joined together now in one common sorrow.

Indeed, for once, the Higginses and Smitherses forgot their ancient feud and united in extolling the virtues of the lost one. After reading the letter as many as three times—for when their grief had somewhat subsided, the blacks would ask to hear it again, so as to have fresh cause for tears—Alice returned to the parlor, where she knew Frederic was sitting. Her own heart was throbbing with anguish, but she felt that his was a sorrow different from her own, and feeling her way to where he sat she wound her little arms around his neck, and whispered tenderly: "We must love each other more now that Marian is gone."

He made no answer except to take her on his lap and lay her head upon his bosom; but Alice was satisfied with this, and after a moment she said, "Frederic, do you know why Marian killed herself?"

"Oh, Alice, Alice," he groaned. "Don't say those dreadful words. I cannot endure the thought."

"But," persisted the child, "she couldn't have known what she was doing, and God forgave her.—Don't you think He did? She asked him to, I am sure, when she was sinking in the deep water."

The child's mind had gone further after the lost one than Frederic's had, and her question inflicted a keener pang than any he had felt before. He had ruined Marian, body and soul, and Alice felt his hot tears dropping on her face as he made her no reply. Her faith was stronger than his, and putting up her waxen hand, she wiped his tears away, saying to him, "We shall meet Marian again, I know, and then if you did anything naughty which made her go away, you can tell her you are sorry, and she'll forgive you, for she loved you very much."

Alice's words were like arrows to the heart of the

young man, and still he felt in the first hours of his desolation that she was his comforting angel, and he could not live without her. More than once she asked him if he knew why Marian went away, and at last he made her answer, "Yes, Alice, I do know, but I cannot tell you now. You would not understand it."

"I think I should," persisted the child, "and I should feel so much better if I knew there was a reason."

Thus importuned, Frederic replied, "I can only tell you that she thought I did not love her."

"And did you, Frederic. Did you love her as Marian ought to be loved?"

The large brown blind eyes looked earnestly into his face, and with that gaze upon him Frederic Raymond could not tell a lie, so he was silent, and Alice, feeling that she was answered, continued, "But you would love her now if she'd come back."

He couldn't say yes to that, either, for he knew he did not love her even then, though he thought of her as a noble, generous-hearted creature, worthy of a far different fate than had befallen her—and had she come back to him, he would have striven hard to make the love which alone could atone for what she had endured. But she did not come—and day after day went by, during which the search was continued at intervals, and always with the same result—until when a week was gone and there was still no trace of her found, people began to suggest that she was not in the river at all, but had gone off in another direction.—Frederic, however, was incredulous—she had no money that he or any one else knew of, or at least but very little. She had never been away from home alone, and if she had done so now, somebody would have seen her ere this, and suspected who it was—for the papers far and near teemed with the strange event, each editor commenting upon its cause according to his own ideas, and all uniting in censuring the husband, who at last was described as a cruel, unfeeling wretch, capable of driving any woman from his house, particularly one as beautiful and accomplished as the unfortunate bride! It was in vain that Frederic winced under the annoyance—he could not help it—and the story went the rounds, improving with each repetition, until at last an Oregon weekly outdid all the rest by publishing the tale under the heading of "Supposed Horrible Murder." So much for newspaper paragraphs.

Meantime Frederic, too, inserted in the papers advertisements for the lost one, without any expectation, however, that they would bring her back. To him she was dead, even though her body could not be found. There might be deep, unfathomable sink-holes in the river, he said, and into one of these she had fallen—and so, with a crushing weight upon his spirits, and an intense loathing of himself and the wealth which was his now beyond a question, he gave her up as lost and waited for what would come to him next.

Occasionally he found himself thinking of Isabel, and wondering what she would say to his letter.—When he last saw her, she was talking of visiting her mother's half-brother, who lived at Dayton, Ohio, and he had said to her at parting, "If you come as far as that, you must surely visit Redstone Hall."

But he had little faith in her coming—and now he earnestly hoped she would not, for if he wronged the living he would be faithful to the dead; and so day after day he sat there in his desolate home, brooding over the past, trying to forget the present, and shrinking from the future, which looked so hopeless now. Thoughts of Marian haunted him continually, and in his dreams he often heard again the wailing sound, which he knew must have been her cry when she learned how she had been deceived. Gradually, too, he began to miss her presence—to listen for her girlish voice, her bounding step and merry laugh, which he had once thought rude. Her careful forethought for his comfort, too, he missed—confessing in his secret heart at least that Redstone Hall was nothing without Marian.

And now, with these influences at work to make him what he ought to be, we leave him awhile in his sorrow, and follow the fugitive bride.

CHAPTER VIII.

MARIAN.

ONWARD and onward—faster and faster flew the night Express, and the wishes of nearly all the passengers kept pace with the speed. One there was, however, a pale-faced, blue-eyed girl, who dreaded the time when the cars would reach their destination, and she be in New York! How she had come thus far safely she scarce could tell. She only knew that every body had been kind to her, and asked her where she wished to go; until now the last dreadful change was made—the blue Hudson was crossed—Albany was far behind, and she was fast nearing New York. Night and day she had traveled, always with the same dull, dreary sense of pain—the same idea that to her the world would never be pleasant, the sunshine bright, or the flowers sweet again. Nervously she shrank from observation—and once, when a lady behind her, who saw that she was weeping, touched her shoulder and said, "What is the matter, little girl?" she started with fear, but did not answer until the question was repeated—then she replied, "Oh, I'm so tired and sick, and the cars make such a noise!"

"Have you come far?" the lady asked, and Marian answered, "Yes, very, very far," adding, as she remembered with a shudder the din and confusion of the larger cities, "Is New York a heap noisier than Albany or Buffalo?"

"Why, yes," returned the lady, smiling at the strange question. "Have you never been there?"

"Once, when a child," said Marian, and the lady continued, "You seem a mere child now. Have you friends in the city?"

"Yes, all I have in the world, and that is only one," sobbed Marian, her tears falling fast at words of sympathy.

The lady was greatly interested in the child, as she thought her, and had she been going to New York would have still befriended her, but she left at Newburgh, and Marian was again alone. She had heard much of New York, but she had no conception of it—and when at last she was there, and followed a group through the depot up to Broadway, her head grew dizzy and her brain whirled with the deafening roar. Cincinnati, Louisville, Buffalo and Albany combined were nothing to this, and in her confusion she wou d have fallen upon the pavement had not the crowd forced her along. Once, as a richly dressed young lady brushed past her, she raised her eyes meekly and asked where "Mrs. Daniel Burt lived?"

The question was too preposterous to be heeded, even if it were heard, and the lady moved on, leaving Marian as ignorant as ever of Mrs. Burt's whereabouts. To two or three other ladies the same question was put, but Mrs. Daniel Burt was evidently not generally known in New York, for no one paid the slightest attention—except indeed to hold tighter their purse-strings, as if there were danger to be apprehended from the slender little figure which extended its ungloved hand so imploringly. After a time, a woman from the country, who had not yet been through the hardening process, listened to the question—and finding that Mrs. Daniel Burt was no way connected with the Burts of Yates county, nor the Blodgetts of Monroe, replied that she was a stranger in the city, and knew no such person—but pretty likely Marian would find it in the Directory—and as a regiment of soldiers just then attracted her attention, she turned aside, while Marian, discouraged and sick at heart, kept on her weary way, knowing nothing where she was going, and, if possible, caring less. When she came opposite to Trinity Church, she sank down upon the step, and drawing her vail over her face, half wished that she might die and be buried there in the enclosure where she saw the November sunshine falling on the graves. And then she wondered if the roar of the great city didn't even penetrate to the ears of the sleeping dead, and, shudderingly, she said, "Oh, I would so much rather be buried by the river at home in dear old Kentucky. It's all so still and quiet there."

Gradually, as her weariness began to abate, she grew interested in watching the passers-by, wondering what every body was going down that street for, and why they came back so quick! Then she tried to count the omnibuses, thinking to herself, "Somebody's dead up town, and this is the procession." The deceased must have been a person of distinction, she fancied, for the funeral train seemed likely never to end. And, what was stranger than all, another was moving up while this was coming down! Poor Marian! she knew but little of the great Babylon to which she had so recently come, and she thought it made up of carts, hacks, omnibuses and people—all hurrying in every direction as fast as they could go. It made her feel dizzy and cross-eyed to look at them, and leaning back against the iron railing, she fell into a kind of conscious sleep, in which she never forgot for an instant the roar which troubled her so much, or lost the gnawing pain at her heart. In this way she sat for a long time, while hundreds and hundreds of people went by, some glancing sideways at her, and thinking she did not look like an ordinary beggar, while others did not notice her at all.

At last, as the confusion increased, she roused up, staring about her with a wild, startled gaze. People were going home, and she watched them as they struggled fiercely and ineffectually to stop some loaded omnibus, and then rushed higher up to a more favorable locality.

"The funeral was over," she said. The omnibusses were most all returning, and though she had no idea of the lapse of time, she fancied that it might be coming night, and the dreadful thought stole over her—"What shall I do then? Maybe I'll go in the church, though," she added. "Nobody, I am sure, will hurt me there," and she glanced confidingly at the massive walls which were to shield her from danger and darkness.

And while she sat there thus, the night shadows began to fall—the people walked faster and faster—the omnibus drivers swore louder and longer—the crowd became greater and greater—and over Marian there stole a horrid dread of the hour when the uproar would cease—when Wall street would be empty, the folks all gone, and she be there alone with the blear-eyed old woman who had seated herself near by, and seemed to be watching her.

"I will ask once more," she thought. "Maybe some of these people know where she lives." And, throwing back her vail, she half rose to her feet, when a tall, disagreeable looking fellow bent over her and said—"What can I do for you, my pretty lass?"

For an instant Marian's heart stood still, for there was something in the rowdy's appearance exceedingly repulsive, but when he repeated his question, she answered timidly, "I want to find Mrs. Daniel Burt."

"Oh, yes, Mrs Daniel Burt. I know the old lady well—lives just round the corner. Come with me and I'll show you the way," and the great red, rough hand was about to touch the little slender white one resting on Marian's lap, when a blow from a brawny fist sent the rascal reeling upon the pavement, while a round, good-humored face looked into Marian's, and a kindly voice said, "Did the villain insult you, little girl?"

"Yes—I reckon not—I don't know," answered Marian, trembling with fright, while her companion continued, "'Tis the first time he ever spoke civil to a woman then. I know the scamp well—but what are you sittin' here alone for, when everybody else is goin' hum?"

Marian felt intuitively that *he* could be trusted, and she sobbed aloud, "I havn't any home, nor friends, nor anything."

"Great Moses!" said the young man, scanning her closely, "you ain't a beggar—that's as sure as my name is Ben Burt—and what be you sittin' here for, any way?"

Marian did not heed his question, so eagerly did she catch at the name Ben Burt.

"Oh, sir," she exclaimed, grasping his arm, "are you any way related to Mrs. Daniel Burt, who once lived with Colonel Raymond at Yonkers?"

"Wall, ra-ally now," returned the honest-hearted Yankee, "if this don't beat all. I wouldn't wonder if I was some connected to Mrs. Daniel Burt, bein' she brung me up from a little shaver, and has licked me mor'n a hundred times. She's my mother, and if it's her you're looking for we may as well be travelin', for she lives all of three miles from here."

"Three miles!" repeated Marian, "that other man said just around the corner. What made him tell such a lie?"

"Yeu tell," answered Ben, with a knowing wink, which however failed to enlighten Marian, who was too glad with having found a protector to ask many questions, and unhesitatingly taking Ben's offered arm she went with him up the street, until she found the car he wished to take.

When they were comfortably seated and she had leisure to examine him more closely, she found him to be a tall, athletic, good-natured looking young man, betraying but little refinement either in personal appearance or manner, but manifesting in all he did a kind, noble heart, which won her good opinion at once. Greatly he wondered who she was and whence she came, but he refrained asking her any questions, thinking he should know the whole if he waited. It seemed to Marian a long, long ride, and she was beginning to wonder if it would never end, when Ben touched her arm and signified that they were to alight.

"Come right down this street a rod or so and we're there," said he, and following whither he led, Marian was soon climbing a long, narrow stairway to the third story of what seemed to her a not very pleasant block of buildings.

But if it were dreary without, the sight of a cheerful blazing fire, which was disclosed to view as Ben opened a narrow door, raised her spirits at once, and taking in at a glance the rag carpet, the stuffed rocking chairs, the chintz-covered lounge, the neat-looking supper table spread for two, and the neater looking woman who was making the toast, she felt the pain at her heart give way a little, just a little, and bounding toward the woman, she cried, "You don't know me, I suppose. I am Marian Lindsey, Colonel Raymond's ward."

Mrs. Burt, for it was she, came near dropping her plate of buttered toast in her surprise, and setting it down upon the hearth, she exclaimed, "The last person upon earth I expected to see. Where did you come from, and how happened you to run afoul of Ben?"

"I ran afoul of her," answered Ben. "I found her a cryin' on the pavement in front of Old Trinity, with that rascal of a Joe Black, makin' b'lieve he was well acquainted with you, and that you lived jest round the corner."

"Mercy me," ejaculated Mrs. Burt, "but do tell a body what you're here for—not but I'm glad to see you, but it seems so queer. How is the old Colonel, and that son I never see—Ferdinand, ain't it—no Frederic, that's what they call him?"

At the mention of Frederic, Marian gave a choking sob and replied: "Colonel Raymond is dead, and Frederic—oh, Mrs. Burt, please don't ask me about him now, or I shall surely die."

"There's some bedivilment of some kind, I'll warrant," muttered Ben, who was a champion of all woman kind. "There's been the old Harry to pay, or she wouldn't be runnin' off here, the villain," and in fancy he dealt the unknown Frederic a far heavier blow than he had given the scapegrace Joe.

"Well, never mind now," said Mrs. Burt, soothingly. "Take off your things and have some supper; you must be hungry, I'm sure. How long is it since you ate?"

"Oh, I don't know," answered Marian, a deathlike paleness overspreading her face; "not since yesterday, I reckon. Where am I? Everything is so confused!" and overcome with hunger, exhaustion and her late fright, Marian fainted in her chair.

Taking her in his arms as if she had been an infant, Ben carried her to the spare room, which, in accordance with her New England habits, Mrs. Burt always kept for company, and there on the softest of all soft beds he laid her down; then, while his mother removed her bonnet and shawl, he ran for water and camphor, chafing with his own rough fingers her little clammy hands, and bathing her forehead until Marian came back to consciousness.

"There, swaller some cracker and tea, and you'll feel better directly," said Mrs. Burt; and, like a very child, Marian obeyed, feeling that there was something delicious in being thus cared for after the dreadful days she had passed. "You needn't talk to us tonight. There will be time enough to-morrow," continued Mrs. Burt, as she saw her about to speak; and fixing her comfortably in bed, she went back to Ben, to whom she told all that she knew concerning Marian and the family with whom she had lived.

"There's something that ain't just right, depend on't," said Ben, sitting down at the table. "That Frederic has served her some mean caper, and so she's run away. But she hit the nail on the head when she came here."

By the time supper was over, Marian's soft, regular breathing told that she was asleep, and taking the lamp in his hand, the curious Ben stole to see her. Her face was white as marble, and even in her sleep the tears dropped from her long eye-lashes, affecting Ben so strangely that his coat-sleeve was more than once called in requisition to perform the office of a handkerchief.

"Poor little baby! You've been misused the wust kind," he whispered, as with his great hand he brushed her tears away, and then went noiselessly out, leaving her to her slumbers.

It was a deep, dreamless sleep which came to Marian that night, for her strength was utterly exhausted, and in the atmosphere of kindness surrounding her, there was something soothing to her irritated nerves. But when the morning broke and the roar of the waking city fell again upon her ear, she started up, and gazing about the room, thought, "where am I, and what is it that makes my heart ache so?"

Full soon she remembered what it was, and burying her face in the pillows, she wept again bitterly, wondering what they were doing far away at Redstone Hall, and if anybody but Alice was sorry she had gone. A moment after Mrs. Burt's kind voice was heard asking how she was, and bidding her be still and rest. But this it was impossible for Marian to do. She could not lie there in that little room and listen to the din which began to produce upon her the same dizzy, bewildering effect it had done the previous day, when she sat on the pavement and saw the omnibuses go by. She must be up and tell the kind people her story, and then, if they said so, she would go away—go back to those graves she had seen yesterday, and lying down in some hollow, where that horrid man and blear-eyed woman could not find her she would die, and Frederic would surely never know what had become of her. She knew she could trust both Mrs. Burt and Ben, and when breakfast was over, she unhesitatingly told them everything, interrupted occasionally by Ben's characteristic exclamations of surprise and his mother's ejaculations of wonder.

Mrs. Burt's first impulse was, that if she were Marian she would claim her property, though of course she would not live with Frederic. But Ben said *No* —"he'd work his finger-nails off before she should go back. His mother wanted some one with her when he was gone, and Marian was sent to them by Providence. Any way," said he, "she shall live with us a while, and we'll see what turns up. Maybe this Fred'll begin to like her now she's gone. It's nater to do so, and some day he'll walk in here and claim her."

This picture was not a displeasing one to Marian, who through her tears smiled gratefully upon Ben, mentally resolving that should she ever be mistress of Redstone Hall she should remember him. And thus it was arranged that *Marian Grey*, as she chose to be called, should remain where she was, for a time at least, and if no husband came for her, she should stay there always as the daughter of Mrs. Burt, whose motherly heart already yearned toward the unfortunate orphan. Both Mrs. Burt and Ben were noble types of diamonds in the rough. Neither of them could boast of much education or refinement, but in all the great city there were few with warmer hearts or kindlier feelings than the widow and her son. Particularly was this true of Ben, who in his treatment of Marian only acted out the impulse of nature; if she had been aggrieved, he was the one to defend her, and if she bade him keep her secret, it was as safe with him as if it had never been breathed into his ear. Nearly all of Ben's life had been passed in factories, and though now home on a visit, he was still connected with one in Ware, Mass. Very carefully he saved his weekly earnings, and once in three months carried or sent them to his mother, who, having spent many years in New York city, preferred it to the country. Here she lived very comfortably on her own earnings and those of Ben, whose occasional visits made the variety of her rather monotonous life. The other occupants of the block were not people with whom she cared to associate, and she passed many lonely hours. But with Marian for company it would be different, and she welcomed her as warmly as Ben himself had done.

"You shall be my little girl," she said, laying her hand caressingly on the head of Marian, who began to think the world was not as cheerless as she had thought it was. Still the old dreary pain was in her heart—a desolate, home-sick feeling, which kept her thoughts ever in one place and on one single object—the place, Redstone Hall, and the object, Frederic Raymond. And as the days went by, the feeling grew into an intense, longing desire to see her old home once more—to look into Frederic's face—to listen to his voice, and know if he were sorry that she was gone. This feeling Mrs. Burt did not seek to discourage, for though she was learning fast to love the friendless girl, she knew it would be better for her to be reconciled to Mr. Raymond, and when one day, nearly four weeks after Marian's arrival, the latter said to her, "I mean to write to Frederic and ask him to take me back," she did not oppose the plan, for she saw how the great grief was wearing the young girl's life away, making her haggard and pale, and writing lines of care upon her childish face.

That night there came to Marian a paper from Ben, who, having far outstaid his time, had returned the week before to Ware. Listlessly she tore open the wrapper, and glancing at the first page, was about throwing it aside, when a marked paragraph arrested her attention, and, with burning cheeks and fast-beating heart, she read that "Frederic Raymond would gladly receive any information of a young girl who had disappeared mysteriously from Redstone Hall."

"Oh!" she exclaimed, springing to her feet, "I am going home—back to Frederic. He's sent for me—see!" and she pointed out to Mrs. Burt the advertisement. "*Can* I go to-night?" she continued. "*Is* there a train? Oh, I am so glad."

Mrs. Burt, however, was more moderate in her feelings. Mr. Raymond could scarcely do less than advertise, she thought, and to her this did not mean that he wished the fugitive to return for any love he bore her. Still, she would not dash Marian's hopes at once, though she would save her from the cold reception she felt sure she would meet, should she return to Redstone Hall, unannounced. So, when the first excitement of Marian's joy had abated, she said: "I should write to Mr. Raymond, just as I first thought of doing. Then he'll know where you are, and he will come for you, if he wants you, of course."

That "if he wants you" grated harshly on Marian's ear; but, after her past experience, she did not care to thrust herself upon him, unless sure that he wished it, and concluded to follow Mrs. Burt's advice. So she sat down and wrote to him a second letter, telling him where she was, and how she came there, and asking him in her child-like way, to let her come back again.

"Oh, I want to come home so much," she wrote; "if you'll only let me, you needn't ever call me your wife, nor make believe I am—at least, not until you love me, and I get to be a lady. I'll try so hard to learn. I'll go away to school, and maybe, after a good many years are gone, you won't be ashamed of me, though I shall never be as beautiful as Isabel. If you don't want me back, Frederic, you must tell me so. I can't feel any worse than I did that day when I sat here in the street and wished I could die. I didn't die then, maybe I shouldn't now, and if you *do* hate me, I'll stay away and never write again—never let you know whether I am alive, or not; and after seven years, Ben Burt says, you will be free to marry Isabel. She'll wait for you, I know. She won't be too old then, will she? I shall be almost twenty-three, but that is young, and the years will seem so long to me if you do not let me return. May I, Frederic? Write, and tell me Yes; but direct to Mrs. Daniel Burt, as I shall then be more sure to get it. I dare not hope you'll come for me, but if you only would, and quick, too, for my heart aches so, and my head is tired and sick with the dreadful noise. Do say I may come home. God will bless you if you do, I am sure; and if you don't, I'll ask Him to bless you just the same."

The letter closed with another assurance that she gave to him cheerfully all her fortune—that she neither blamed his father, nor himself, nor Isabel, nor anybody. All she asked was to come back!

Poor little Marian! The pain in her heart was not so intense, and the noise in the street easier to bear after sending that letter, for hope softened them both, and whispered to her, "he'll let me come," and in a thousand different ways she pictured the meeting between herself and Frederic. Occasionally the thought intruded itself upon her, "what if he bids me keep away," and then she said, "I'll do it if he does, and before seven years are gone, maybe I'll be dead. I hope I shall, for I do not want to think of Isabel's living there with him!"

She had great faith in the seven years, for *Ben* had said so, and Ben, who was very susceptible to female charms, believed it, too, and the thought of it was like a ray of sunshine in the dingy, noisome room where all day he worked, sometimes reckoning up how many *months* there were in seven years—then how many *weeks*—then how many *days*, and finally calling himself a *fool* for caring a thing about it. When the newspaper article came under his eye, the sunshine left the dirty room, and after he had sent the paper to Marian he cared but little how many months or weeks or days there were in seven years, and he felt angry at himself for having *sweat* so hard in making the computation!

And so, while Marian in the city waits and watches for the message which will, perhaps, bid her come back, and Ben, in the noisy factory, waits also for a message which shall say she has gone, and his mother is again alone, the letter travels on, and one pleasant afternoon, when the clerk at Cincinnati makes up the mail for Frankfort, he puts that important missive with the rest and sends it on its way.

CHATER IX.

ISABEL HUNTINGTON.

All day and all night it rained with a steady, unrelenting pour, and when the steamboat which plies between Cincinnati and Frankfort stopped at the latter place, two ladies from the lower deck looked drearily over the city, one frowning impatiently at the mud and the rain, while the other wished in her heart that she was safely back in her old home, and had never consented to this foolish trip. This wish, however, she dared not express to her companion, who, though calling her mother, was in reality the mistress—the one whose word was law, and to whose wishes everything else must bend.

"This *is* delightful," the younger lady exclaimed, as holding up her fashionable traveling dress, and glancing ruefully at her thin kid gaiters, she prepared to walk the plank. "This is charming. I wonder if they always have such weather in Kentucky."

"No, Miss, very seldom, 'cept on strordinary 'casions," said the polite African, who was holding an umbrella over her head, and who felt bound to defend his native State.

The lady tossed her little bonnet proudly, and turning to her mother, continued: "Have you any idea how we are to get to Redstone Hall?"

At this question an old gray-haired negro, who, with several other idlers, was standing near, came forward and said, "If it's Redstone Hall whar Miss wants to go, I's here with Marster Frederic's carriage. I come to fotch a man who's been out thar tryin' to buy a house of marster in Louisville."

At this announcement the face of both ladies brightened perceptibly, and pointing out their baggage to the negro, who was none other than our old friend Uncle Phil, they went to a public house to wait until the carriage came round for them.

"What do you suppose Frederic will think when he sees us?" the mother asked; and the daughter replied, "He won't think anything, of course. It is perfectly proper that we should visit our relations, particularly when we are as near to them as Dayton, and they are in affliction, too. He would have been displeased if we had returned without giving him a call."

From these remarks the reader will readily imagine that the ladies in question were Mrs. Huntington and her daughter Isabella. They had decided at last to visit Dayton, and had started for that city a few days after the receipt of Frederic's letter announcing his father's death: consequently they knew nothing of the marriage, and the fact that Colonel Raymond was dead only increased Isabel's desire to visit Redstone Hall, for she rightly guessed that Frederic was now so absorbed in business that it would be long ere he came to New Haven again; so she insisted upon coming, and as she found her Ohio aunt not altogether agreeable, she had shortened her visit there, and now with her mother sat waiting at the Mansion House for the appearance of Phil and the carriage. That Isabel was beautiful was conceded by every one, and that she was as treacherous as beautiful was conceded by those who knew her best. Early in life she had been engaged to Rudolph McVicar, a man of strong passions, an iron will and indomitable perseverance. But when young Raymond came, and she fancied she could win him, she unhesitatingly broke her engagement with Rudolph, who, stung to madness by her cold, unfeeling conduct, swore to be revenged. This threat, however, was little heeded by the proud beauty. If she secured Frederic Raymond, she would be above all danger, and she bent every energy to the accomplishment of her plan. She knew that the Kentuckians were proverbial for their hospitality, and feeling sure that no one would think it at all improper for her mother and herself to visit their cousin, as she called Frederic, she determined, if possible, to prolong that visit until asked to stay with him always. He had never directly talked to her of love, consequently she felt less delicacy in going to his house and claiming relationship with him; so when Phil came around with the carriage, she said to him, quite as a matter of course, "How is Cousin Frederic since his father's death?"

"Jest tolable, thankee," returned the negro, at the same time saying, "Be you marster's kin?"

"Certainly," answered Isabel, while the negro bowed low, for any one related to his master was a person of distinction to him.

Isabel had heard Frederic speak of Marian, and when they were half way home, she put her head from the window and said to Phil, "Where is the young girl who used to live with Colonel Raymond—Marian was her name, I think?"

"Bless you," returned the negro, cracking his whip nervously, "haint you hearn how she done got married to marster mighty nigh three weeks ago?"

"Married! Frederic Raymond married!" screamed Isabel; "it is *not* true. How dare you tell me such a falsehood?"

"Strue as preachin', and a heap truer than some on't, for I seen 'em joined with these very eyes," said Phil, and, glancing backward at the white face leaning from the window, he muttered, "'spects mebby she calkerlated on catchin' him herself. Ki, wouldn't she and Dinah pull har though. Thar's a heap of Ole Sam in them black eyes of hern," and, chirruping to his horses, Philip drove rapidly on, thinking he wouldn't tell her that the bride had run away—he would let Frederic do that.

Meantime, Isabel, inside, was choking—gasping—crying—wringing her hands and insisting that her mother should ask the negro again if what he had told them were so.

"Man—sir"—said Mrs. Huntington, putting her bonnet out into the rain, "is Mr. Frederic Raymond really married to that girl Marian?"

"Yes, as true as I am sittin' here. Thursday'll be three weeks since the weddin'," was the reply, and with another hysterical sob, Isabel laid her head in her mother's lap.

Nothing could exceed her rage, mortification and disappointment, except, indeed, her pride, and this was stronger than all her other emotions and that which finally roused her to action. She would not turn back now, she said. She would brave the villain and show him that she did not care. She would put herself by the side of his wife and let him see the contrast. She had surely heard from him that Marian was plain, and in fancy, she saw how she would overshadow her rival and make Frederic feel keenly the difference between them, and then she thought of the discarded Rudolph. If everything else should fail, she could win him back—he had some money, and she would rather be his wife than nobody's!

By this time they had left the highway, for Redstone Hall was more than a mile from the turnpike, and Isabel found ample opportunity for venting her ill-nature. Such a road as that she never saw before, and she'd like to know if folks in Kentucky lived out in the lots. "No wonder they were such heathen! you nigger," she exclaimed, as Phil drove through a brook; "are you going to tip us over, or what?"

"Wonder if she 'spects a body is gwine round the brook," muttered Phil, and as the carriage wheels were now safe from the water, he stopped and said to the indignant lady, "mebby Miss would rather walk the rest of the way. Thar's a heap wus places in the cornfield, whar we'll be pretty likely to get oversot."

"Go on," snapped Isabel, who knew she could not walk quite as well as the mischievous driver.

Accordingly they went on, and ere long came in sight of the house which even in that drenching rain looked beautiful to Isabel, and all the more beautiful because she felt that she had lost it. On the piazza little Alice stood, her fair hair blowing over her face, and her ear turned to catch the first sound which should tell her if what she hoped were true. Old Dinah, who saw the carriage in the distance, had said there was some one in it, and instantly Alice thought of Marian, and going out upon the piazza, she waited impatiently until Phil drove up to the door.

"There are four feet," she said, as the strangers came up the steps; "four feet, but none are Marian's," and she was turning sadly away, when she accidentally trod upon the long skirt of Isabel, who, snatching it away, said angrily, "child, what are you doing—stepping on my dress?"

"I didn't mean to; I'm blind," answered Alice, her lip quivering and her eyes filling with tears.

"Never you mind that she dragon," whispered Uncle Phil, thrusting into the child's hand a paper of candy, which had the effect of consoling her somewhat, both for her disappointment and her late reproof.

"Who is that ar?" asked Dinah, appearing upon the piazza just as Isabel passed into the hall. "Some of marster's kin!" she repeated after Uncle Phil. "For the Lord's sake, what fotched 'em here this rainy day, when we's gwine to have an ornery dinner—no briled hen, nor turkey, nor nothin'. Be they quality, think?"

"'Spects the young one wants to be, if she ain't," returned Phil, with a very expressive wink, which had the effect of enlightening Dinah with regard to his opinion.

"Some low flung truck, I'll warrant," said she, as

she followed them into the parlor, where Isabel's stately bearing and glittering black eyes awed her into a low courtesy, as she said: "You're very welcome to Redstone Hall, I'm sure. Who shall I tell marster wants to see him?"

"Two ladies, simply," was Isabel's haughty answer, and old Dinah departed, whispering to herself, "Two ladies simple! She must think I know nothin' 'bout grarmar to talk in that kind of way, but she's mistakened. I hain't lived in the fust families for nothin'," and knocking at Frederic's door, she told him that "two simple ladies was down in the parlor and wanted him."

"Who?" he asked, in some surprise, and Dinah replied:

"Any way, that's what she said—the tall one, with great black eyes jest like coals of fire. Phil picked 'em up in Frankford, whar they got off the boat. They's some o' yer kin they say."

Frederic did not wish to hear any more, for he suspected who they were. It was about this time they had talked of visiting Dayton, and motioning Dinah from the room, he pressed his hands to his forehead, and thought, "Must I suffer this, too? Oh, why did she come to look at me in my misery?" Then, forcing an unnatural calmness, he started for the parlor, where, as he had feared, he stood face to face with Isabel Huntington.

She was very pale, and in her black eyes there was a hard, dangerous expression, from which he gladly turned away, addressing first her mother, who, rising to meet him, said:

"We have accepted your invitation, you see."

"Yes, ma'am," he replied, and he was trying to stammer out a welcome, when Isabel, who all the time had been aching to pounce upon him, chimed,

"Where is Mrs. Raymond? I am dying to see my new cousin" and in the eyes of black there was a reddish gleam, as if they might ere long emit sparks of living fire.

"Mrs. Raymond!" repeated Frederic, the name dropping slowly from his lips. "Mrs. Raymond! Oh! Isabel, don't you know? Havn't you heard?"

"Certainly I have," returned the young lady, watching him as a fierce cat watches his helpless prey. "Of course I have heard of your marriage, and have come to congratulate you. Is your wife well?"

Frederic raised his hand to stop the flippant speech, and when it finished he rejoined: "But havn't you heard the rest—the saddest part of all? Marian is dead!—drowned—at least we think she must be, for she went away on our wedding night, and no trace of her can be found."

The fiery gleam was gone from the black eyes—the color came back to the cheeks—the finger nails ceased their painful pressure upŏn the tender flesh—the shadow of a smile dimpled the corner of the mouth, and Isabel was herself again.

"Dead! Drowned!" she exclaimed. "How did it happen? What was the reason? Dreadful, isn't it?" and going over to where Mr. Raymond stood, she looked him in the face, with an expression she meant should say, "I am sorry for you," but which really did say something quite the contrary.

"I cannot tell you why she went away," Frederic answered, "but there was a reason for it, and it has cast a shadow over my whole life."

"Marian was a mere child, I had always supposed," suggested Isabel, anxious to get at the reason why he had so soon forgotten herself.

"Did you get my last letter—the one written to you?" asked Frederic, and upon Isabel's replying that she did not, he briefly stated a few facts concerning his marriage, saying it was his father's dying request, and he could not well avoid doing as he had done, even if he disliked Marian. "But I didn't dislike her," he continued, and the hot blood rushed into his face.

"She was a gentle, generous hearted girl, and had she lived, I would have made her happy."

If by this speech Frederic Raymond thought to deceive Isabel Huntington, he was mistaken, for, looking into his eyes she read a portion of the truth and knew there was something back of all—a something between himself and his father which had driven him to the marriage. What it was she did not care then to know. She was satisfied that the bride was gone—and when Frederic narrated more minutely the particulars of her going, the artful girl said to herself, 'She is dead beyond a doubt, and when I leave Redstone Hall, I shall know it, and mother, too!"

It was strange how rapidly Isabel changed from a hard, defiant woman, to a soft, sparkling, beautiful creature, and when, in her plaid silk dress of crimson and brown, with her magnificent hair bound in heavy braids about her head, she came down to dinner, Aunt Dinah involuntarily dropped another courtesy, and whispered under her teeth, "The Lord, if she ain't quality after all." Old Hetty, too, who from a side door looked curiously in at their guests, received a like impression, pronouncing her more like Miss Beatrice than any body she had ever seen. To Alice, Isabel was all gentleness, for she readily saw that the child was a pet; so she called her darling and dearest, smoothing her fair hair and kissing her once when Frederic was looking on. All this, however, did not deceive the little blind girl, or erase from her mind the angry words which had been spoken to her, and that evening, when she went to Frederic to bid him good night, she climbed into his lap and said: "Is that Miss Isabel going to stay here always?"

"Why, no," he answered. "Did you think she was?"

"I did not know," returned Alice, "but I hoped not, for I don't like her at all. She's very grand and beautiful, Dinah says, but I think she must look like a snake, and I want her to go away, don't you?"

Frederic would not say yes to this question, and he remained silent. Had he been consulted, he would rather that she had never come to Redstone Hall, but now that she was there, he did not wish her away. It would be inhospitable, he said, and when next morning she came down to breakfast, bright, fresh and elegant in her tasteful wrapper, he felt a pang, as he thought, "had I done right, she might have been the mistress of Redstone Hall," but it could not be now, he said, even if Marian were dead, and all that day he struggled manfully between his duty and his inclination, while Isabel dealt out her highest card, ingrafting herself into the good graces of the Smitherses by speaking to them pleasant, familiar words, exalting herself in the estimation of the Higginses by her lofty, graceful bearing, and winning Dinah's friendship by praising Victoria Eugenia, and asking if that fine looking man who drove the carriage was her husband. Then, in the evening, when the lamps were lighted in the parlor, she opened the piano and filled the house with the rich melody of h r cultivated voice, singing a sad, plaintive strain, which reminded Alice of poor, lost Marian, and carried Frederic back to other days, when, with a feeling of pride, he had watched her snowy fingers as they gracefully swept the keys. He could not look at them now—he dared not look at her, in her ripe glowing beauty, and he left the room, going out upon the piazza, where he wiped great drops of sweat from his face, and almost cursed the fate which had made it a sin for him to love the dark-haired Isabel. She knew that he was gone, and rightly divining the cause, she dashed off into a stirring dancing tune, which brought the negroes to the door, where they stood admiring her playing and praising her queenly form.

"That's somethin' like it," whispered Hetty, beating time to the lively strain. "That sounds like Miss Beatrice did when she done played the pianner. I 'clare for't, I eenamost wish Marster Frederic had done chose her. 'Case you know t'other one done drowned herself the fust night," she added quickly, as she met Dinah's rebuking glance.

Dinah admired Isabel, but she could not forget Marian; though like her sex, whether black or brown, she speculated upon the future, when "Marster Frederic would be done mournin'," and she wondered if "old miss," meaning Mrs. Huntington, would think it necessary to stay there, too. Thus several days went by, and so pleasant was it to Frederic to have some one in the house who could divert him from his gloomy thoughts, that he began to dread the time when he would be alone again. But could he have looked into the heart of the fair lady, he would have seen no immediate cause of alarm. Isabel did not intend to leave her present quarters immediately, and to this end her plans were laid. From what she had heard she believed Marian Lindsey was dead, and if so, she would not again trust Frederic away from her influence. Redstone Hall needed a head—a housekeeper—and as her mother was an old lady, and also a relative of Frederic, she was just the one to fill that post. Their house in New Haven was only rented until March, and by writing to some friends they could easily dispose of their furniture until such time as they might want it. Alice needed a governess, for she heard Frederic say so; and though the little pest (this was what she called her, to herself) did not seem to like her, she could teach her as well as any one. It would be just as proper for her to be Alice's governess as for any one else, and a little more so, for her mother would be with her.

And this arrangement she brought about with the most consummate skill, first asking Frederic if he knew of any situation in Kentucky which she could procure as a teacher. That was one object of her visit, she said. She must do something for a living, and as she would rather teach either in a school, or in a private family, she would be greatly obliged to him if he would assist her a little. Hardly knowing what he was doing, Frederic said something about Alice's having needed a governess for a long time; and quickly catching at it, Isabel rejoined, "Oh! but you know I couldn't possibly remain here, unless mother staid with me. Now, if you'll keep her as a kind of overseer-in-general of the house, I'll gladly undertake the charge of dear little Alice's education. She does not fancy me, I think, but I'm sure I can win her love. I can that of almost any one—children I mean, of course;" and the beautiful, fascinating eyes looked out of the window quite indifferently, as if their owner were utterly oblivious of the fierce struggle in Frederic's bosom.

He wished her to stay with him—oh, so much! But was it right? and would he not get to loving her? No, he would not, he said. He would only think of her as his cousin—his sister, whose presence would cheer his solitary home. So he bade her stay, and she bade her mother stay, urging so many reasons why she should, and must, that the latter consented at last, and a letter was dispatched to New Haven, with directions for having their furniture packed away, and their house given up to its owner. This arrangement at first caused some gossip among the neighbors, who began to predict what the end would be, and, also, to assert more loudly than ever their belief that Marian was not dead. Still, there was no reason why Isabel should not be Alice's governess, particularly as her mother was with her; and when Agnes Gibson pronounced her beautiful, accomplished, and just the thing, the rest followed in the train, and the health of the "northern beauty" was drunk by more than one fast young man.

In the kitchen at Redstone Hall there was also a discussion, in which the Higginses rather had the preference, inasmuch as the lady in question was after their manner of thinking. Old Dinah wisely kept silent, saying to herself, "a new broom sweeps clean, and I'll wait to see what 'tis when it gets a little wore. One thing is sartin, though, if she goes to put on ars, and sasses us colored folks, I'll gin her a piece of my mind. I'll ask her whar she come from, and how many niggers she owned afore she come from thar."

It was several days before Alice was told of the arrangement, and then she rebelled at once. Bursting into tears, she hid her face in Dinah's lap, and sobbed, "I can't learn of her. I don't like her. What shall I do?"

"I wish to goodness I had larning'," answered Dinah, "and I'd hear you say that foolishness 'bout the world's turnin' round and makin' us stan' on our heads half the time, but I hain't, and if I's you I'd make the best on't. I'll keep my eye on her, and if she makes you do the fust thing you don't want to, I'll gin her a piece of my mind. I ain't afraid on her. Why, Gibson's niggers say how they hearn Miss Agnes say she used to make her own bed whar she came from, and wash dishes, too! Think o' that!"

Thus comforted, Alice dried her tears, and hunting up the books from which she had once recited to Marian, she declared herself ready for her lessons at any time.

"Let it be to-morrow, then," said Isabel, who knew that Frederic was going to Lexington, and that she could not see him even if she were not occupied with Alice.

So, the next morning, after Frederic was gone, Alice went to the school-room, and drawing her little chair to Isabel's side, laid her books upon the lady's lap, and waited for her to begin.

"You must read to me," she said, "until I know what 'tis, and then I'll recite it to you."

But Isabel was never intended for a teacher, and she found it very tedious reading the same thing over and over, particularly as Alice seemed inattentive and not at all inclined to remember. At last she said, impatiently, "For the pity's sake how many more times must I read it. Can't you learn anything?"

"Dont—don't speak so," sobbed Alice. "I'm thinking of Marian, and how she used to be with me. It's just six weeks to-day since she went away. Oh, I wish she'd come back. Do you believe she's dead?"

Isabel was interested in anything concerning Marian, and closing the book, she began to question the child, asking her among other things, if Marian did not leave a letter for Mr. Raymond, and if she knew what was in it."

"No one knows," returned the child; "he never told—but here's mine," and drawing from her bosom the soiled note, she passed it to Isabel, who scrutinized it closely, particularly the handwriting.

"Of course she's dead, or she would have been heard from ere this," said she, passing the note back to Alice, who, not feeling particularly comforted, made but little progress in her studies that morning, and both teacher and pupil were glad when the lessons of the day were over.

Before starting for Lexington, Frederic had sent Josh on some errand to Frankfort, and just after dinner the negro returned. Isabel was still alone upon the piazza when he came up, and as she was expecting news from New Haven, she asked if he stopped at the post-office.

"Ye-e-us 'm," began the stuttering negro, "an' I d-d-d-one got a h-h-eap on 'em, too," and Josh gave her six letters—one for herself and five for Frederic.

Hastily breaking the seal of her own letter, she read that their matters at home were satisfactorily arranged—a tenant had already been found for their house, and their furniture would be safely stowed away. Hearing her mother in the hall, she handed the letter to her and then went to the library to dispose of Frederic's. As she was laying them down she glanced at the superscriptions, carelessly, indifferently, until she came to the last, the one bearing the New York postmark;

then, with a nervous start she caught it up again and examined it more closely, while a sickening, horrid fear crept through her flesh—her heart gave one fearful throb and then lay like some heavy, pulseless weight within her bosom. Could it be that she had seen that handwriting before? Had the dead wife returned to life, and was she coming back to Redstone Hall? The thought was overwhelming, and for a moment Isabel Huntington was tempted to break that seal and read. But she dared not, for her suspicion might be false; she would see Alice's note again, and seeking out the child she asked permission to take the letter which Marian had written. Alice complied with her request, and darting away to the library Isabel compared the two. They were the same. There could be no mistake, and in the intensity of her excitement, she felt her black hair loosening at its roots.

"It is from her, but he shall never see it, never!" she exclaimed aloud, and her voice was so unnatural that she started at the sound, and turning saw Alice standing in the door with an inquiring look upon her face, as if asking the meaning of what she had heard.

Isabel quailed beneath the glance of that sightless child, and then sat perfectly still, while Alice said, "Miss Huntington, are you here? Was it you who spoke?"

Isabel made no answer, but trembling in every limb, shrank farther and farther back in her chair as the little, groping, outstretched arms came nearer and nearer to her. Presently, when she saw no escape, she forced a loud laugh, and said, "Fie, Alice. I tried to frighten you by feigning a strange voice. You want your letter, don't you? Here it is. I only wished to see if in reading it a second time I could get any clue to the mystery," and she gave the bit of paper back to Alice, who, somewhat puzzled to understand what it all meant, left the room, and Isabel was again alone. Three times she caught up the letter with the intention of breaking its seal, and as often threw it down, for, unprincipled as she was, she shrank from that act, and still, if she did not know the truth, she should go mad, she said, and pressing her hands to her forehead, she thought what the result to herself would be were Marian really alive.

"But she isn't," she exclaimed. "I won't have it so. She's dead—she's buried in the river." But who was there in New York that wrote so much like her? She wished she knew, and she might know, too, by opening the letter. If it was from a stranger, she could destroy it, and he, thinking it had been lost, would write again. She should die if she didn't know, and maybe she should die if she did.

At all events, reality was more endurable than suspense, and glancing furtively around to make sure that no blind eyes were near, she snatched the letter from the table and broke the seal! Even then she dared not read it, until she reflected that she could not give it to Frederic in this condition—she might as well see what it contained; and wiping the cold moisture from her face she opened it and read, while her flesh seemed turning to stone, and she could feel the horror creeping through her veins, freezing her blood and petrifying her very brain. *Marian Lindsey lived!* She was coming back again—back to her husband, and back to the home which was hers. There was enough in the letter for her to guess the truth, and she knew why another had been preferred to herself. For a moment even her lip curled with scorn at what she felt was an unmanly act, but this feeling was soon lost in the terrible thought that Marian might return.

"Can it be? Must it be?" she whispered, as her hard, black eyes fastened themselves again upon the page, blotted with Marian's tears. "Seven years—seven years," she continued, "I've heard of that before," and into the wild tumult of her thoughts there stole a ray of hope. If she withheld the letter from Frederic, and she must withhold it now, he would never know what she knew. Possibly, too, Marian might die, and though she would have repelled the accusation, Isabel Huntington was guilty of murder in her heart, as she sat there alone and planned what she would do. She was almost on the borders of insanity, for the disappointment to her now would be greater and more humiliating than before. She had no home to go to—her arrangements for remaining in Kentucky were all made, and Redstone Hall seemed so fair that she would willingly wait twice seven years, if, at the expiration of that time, she were sure of being its mistress. It was worth t.ying for, and though she had but little hope of success, the beautiful demon bent her queenly head and tried to devise some means of effectually silencing Marian, so that if there really weie anything in the seven years the benefit would accrue to her.

"She's a litle silly fool," she said, "and this Mrs. Daniel Burt she talked about is just as silly as herself. They'll both believe what is told to them. I may never marry Frederic, it is true, but I'll be revenged on Marian. What business had she to cross my path, the little red-headed jade!"

Isabel was growing excited, and as she dared do anything when angry, she resolved to send the letter back.

"I can imitate his handwriting," she thought; "I can do anything as I feel now," and going to her room, she found the letter he had written to her mother.

This she studied and imitated for half an hour, and at the end of that time wrote on the blank page of Marian's letter, "Isabel Huntington is now the mistress of Redstone Hall."

"That will keep her still, I reckon," she said, and taking a fresh envelope, she directed it to "Mrs. Daniel Burt," as Marian had bidden Frederic do. "'Twas a fortunate circumstance, her telling him that, for 'Marian Lindsey' would have been observed at once," she thought; and then, lest her resolution should fail her, she found Josh and bade him take the letter to the post-office at the Forks of Elkhorn not very far away.

Nothing could suit Josh better than to ride, and stuttering out something which nobody could understand, he mounted his rather sorry-looking horse and was soon galloping out of sight. In the kitchen Mrs. Huntington heard of Josh's destination, and when next she met her daughter, she asked to whom she had been writing.

"To some one, of course," answered Isabel, at the same time intimating that she hoped she could have a correspondent without her mother troubling herself.

The rudeness of this speech was forgotten by Mrs. Huntington in her alarm at Isabel's pale face, and she asked anxiously what was the matter?

"Nothing but a wretched headache—teaching don't agree with me," was Isabel's reply, and turning away, she ran up the stairs to her room, where, throwing herself upon the bed, she tried to fancy it all a dream.

But it was not a dream, and Marian's anguish was scarcely greater than her own at that moment, when she began to realize that Frederic and Redstone Hall were lost to her forever. There might be something in the seven years, but it was a long, dreary time to wait, with the ever-haunting fear that Marian might return, and she half wished she had not opened the letter. But her regrets were unavailing now, and resolving to guard her secret carefully and deny what she had done, if ever accused of it, she began to consider how she should hereafter demean herself toward Frederic. It would be terrible to have him making love to her, she thought, for she would be compelled to tell him no, and if another should become her rival, she could not stand quietly by and witness the unlawful deed.

"Oh, if I or Marian had never been born, this hour would not have come to me," she cried, burying her face in the pillows to shut out the fast increasing darkness which was so hateful to her.

Already was she reaping the fruit of the transgression, and when an hour later she heard the voice of Frederic in the hall, she stopped her ears, and, burying her face still closer in the pillows, wished again that either Marian or herself had never seen the light of day.

CHAPTER X.

FREDERIC AND ALICE.

All the day long Frederic had thought of Marian—thought of the little blue-eyed girl, who just six weeks before went away from him to die. To die. Many, many times he said that to himself, and as often as he said it, he thought, "perhaps she is not dead," until the belief grew strong in him that somewhere he should find her, that very day it might be. He wished he could, and take her back to Redstone Hall, where she would be a barrier between himself and the beautiful temptation which it was so hard for him to resist. Manfully had he struggled against it, going always from its presence when the eyes of lustrous black looked softly into his own, and when he heard, as he often did, the full rich-toned voice singing merry songs, he stopped his ears lest the sweet music should touch a chord which he said was hushed forever.

"It might have been," he thought sometimes to himself, but the time was past, and even if Marian were dead, he must not take another to share the wealth so generously given up. And Marian was dead, he had always believed until to-day, when she seemed to be so near, that on his return at night to Redstone Hall he had a half presentiment that he might find her there, or at least some tidings of her.

All about the house was dark, but on the piazza a little figure was standing, and as its dim outline was revealed to him, he said, involnntarily: "That may be Marian, and I am glad, or at least I will be glad," and he was hurrying on, when a light from the hall streamed out upon the figure, and he saw that it was Alice waiting for him. Still the impression was so strong that after kissing her, he asked if no one had been at the Hall that day.

"No one," she answered, and with a vague feeling of disappointment, he led her into the house.

Alice's heart was full that night, for accidentally she had heard old Hetty and Lyd discussing the probable result of Isabel's sojourn among them, and the very idea shocked her, as if they had trampled on Marian's grave.

"I'll tell Frederic," said she to herself, "and ask him is he going to marry her," and when after his supper he went into the library to read the letters which Mrs. Huntington told him were there, she followed him thither.

It was not Frederic's nature to pet or notice children much, but in his sorrow he had learned to love the little helpless girl dearly, and when he saw her standing beside him with a wistful look upon her face, he smoothed her soft brown hair and said: "What does my blind bird want?"

"Take me in your lap," said Alice, "so I can feel your heart beat and know if you tell me true."

He complied with her request, and laying her head against his bosom, she began, "be we much related?"

"Second cousins, that's all."

"But you love me, don't you?"

"Yes, very much."

"And I love you a heap," returned the little girl. "I didn't use to, though—till Marian went away. Frederic, Marian isn't dead!" and, lifting up her head, Alice looked at him with a truthful, earnest look, which seemed to say that she believed what she asserted.

Frederic gasped a short, quick breath, and Alice continued, "wouldn't it be very wicked for you to love anybody else. I don't mean me—because I'm a little blind girl—but to love somebody and marry them with Marian alive?"

"Certainly it would be wicked," he replied; and Alice continued, "Aunt Hetty said you were going to marry Isabel, and it almost broke my heart. I never thought before that Marian wasn't dead, but I knew it then. I felt her right there with us, and I've felt her ever since. Dinah, too, said it seemed to her just like Marian was alive, and that she hoped you wouldn't make—perhaps I ought not to tell you, but you don't care for Dinah—she hoped you wouldn't make a fool of yourself. Frederic, do you love Isabel Huntington?"

"Yes," dropped involuntarily from the young man's lips, for there was something about that old little child which wrung the truth from him.

"Did you love her before you married Marian?"

"Yes," he said again, for he could not help himself. There was silence a moment, and then Alice, who had been thinking of what he told her once before, said, interrogatively, "Marian found it out, and that was why she thought you didn't love her and went away?"

"That was one reason, but not the principal one."

"Do you think Isabel as good as Marian?"

"No, not as good—not as good," and Frederic was glad that he could pay this tribute to the lost one.

After a moment Alice spoke again:

"Frederic, do you believe Marian is dead?"

"I have always thought so," he answered, and Alice replied: "But you don't know for certain; and I want you to promise that until you do you won't make love to Isabel, nor marry her, nor anybody else, will you, Frederic?" and putting both her little hands upon his forehead, she pushed back his hair and waited for an answer.

Many times the young man had made that resolution, but the idea of thus promising to another was unpleasant, and he hesitated for a time; then he said:

"Suppose we never can know for certain—would you have me live all my life alone?"

"No," said Alice, "and you needn't, either; but I'd wait ever so long, ten years, anyway, and before that time she'll come, I'm sure. Dinah says maybe she will, and that perhaps we shan't know her, she'll be so changed—so handsome," and as if the power of prophecy were on her, Alice pictured a beautiful woman who might come to them sometime as their lost Marian, and Frederic, listening to her, felt more willing to promise than he had been before.

A glow of hope was kindled within his own bosom, and when she finished he said to her:

"I will wait, Alice—wait ten years for Marian."

Blessed Alice! When the mother, whose grave was grass-grown now and sunken, first knew her only child was blind, she murmured against the dealings of Providence, and in the bitterness of her heart asked:

"Why was my baby born? and what good can it ever do?"

She who had questioned thus was dead, while the good the little girl was to do was becoming, each day, more and more apparent. Helpless and blind though she was, she would keep the strong man from falling, and when his heart grew faint with hope deferred, her gentle, earnest words would cheer him on to wait a little longer. Marian was not dead to her, and so sure of it did she seem that when the interview was ended, and Frederic was left alone, he bowed his head reverently and said:

"If Marian be, indeed, alive, will the good Father send me some tidings of her, and so keep me from sin?"

Oh! could the writing desk before him have told how only that afternoon there had lain upon its velvet cover a message from the lost one—a sweet, childlike petition for him to take her back, even though he could not love her—he would have gone for her then, and, bringing her to the home which was not his, but hers, he would have placed her between himself and the temptation, yielding to her all honor and respect until his heart should say it loved her. But the time was not yet, and he must suffer longer—must pass through deeper waters; while Marian, too, must be molded and changed into a bride who, far better than the queenly Isabel, could do the honors of Redstone Hall.

CHAPTER XI.

THE LETTER RECEIVED.

It was baking-day at Mrs. Burt's, and the good lady bustled in and out—her cap strings pinned over her head, her sleeves tucked up above her shoulders, and her face, hands and apron covered with flour. Occasionally as she rolled out the short pie crust, or sliced the juicy apple, she glanced at the rain-drops pattering against the window, and said encouragingly, "I don't care for the rain, for I've get a big umbrella and the best kind of overshoes;" and as often as she related the cheering words, they brought a smile to the thin, white face of the young girl who sat in the large, stuffed easy-chair, and did not offer to share the labors of her aunt, as she called her.

Marian was sick. Strong excitement had worn her strength away, and since she had sent the letter to Frederic, her restless anxiety for the answer had made her so weak that she kept her bed nearly all the time, counting the days which must elapse ere she could possibly hope to hear, and then, when the full time was out, bidding Mrs. Burt wait one more day before she went to the office, so as to be sure and get it. She had made due allowance for delays, and now she was certain that it had come. She would sit up that day, she said, for she felt almost well; and if Frederic told her to come home, she should start to-morrow and get there Saturday night, and she fancied how people would stare at her, and be glad to see her, too, on Sunday, when she first went into church, for she "should go, any way." Alice, too, would be delighted, and kiss her so many times; and then she wondered if Frederic wouldn't kiss her, too — she thought he might just once, she'd been so long away, and she said to herself that "she would draw back a little, and let him know she wasn't so very anxious."

Poor Marian, how little was she prepared for the cruel blow awaiting her! The pies were made at last, as was the ginger-bread and crispy snaps; the apple dumplings, Marian's favorite dessert, were steaming on the stove; the litter was cleared away, the carpet swept, the oil-cloth washed, the chairs set back; and then exchanging her work dress for a more respectable delaine, Mrs. Burt put over the kettle to boil, "for after her wet walk, she should want a cup of tea," she said, and, leaving Marian to watch the pie baking in the oven, she started on her errand.

"I mean to have the table ready when she gets back," said Marian—"for if I don't make her think I'm well, she won't let me start so soon;" and, exerting all strength, she set the table for dinner in the neatest possible manner, even venturing upon the extravagance of bringing out the best white dishes, which Mrs. Burt only used on great occasions. "When I get some, I'll send her a new set with gilt bands," the little girl said, as she arranged the cups, and then stepped back to witness the effect. "Oh! I wish she'd come," she continued, glancing at the clock; but it was not time yet, and, resuming her rocking-chair, she tried to wait patiently.

But it seemed very long and very tiresome, sitting there alone, listening to the rain and the ticking of the clock. It is strange how the most trivial circumstance will sometimes stamp itself indelibly upon the memory. The steam from the dumplings, which Marian thought she should enjoy so much, filled the room with a sweet, sickly odor, and for many, many years she remembered now faint it made her feel. But 'twas a pleasant faintness now; everything was pleasant, for wasn't she going home, back to Redstone Hall—back to Frederic, who, if he didn't love her now, would learn to love her, for Mrs. Burt said so; Mrs. Burt, who knew almost as much as Dinah, and who, even while she thought of her, was coming up the narrow stairs. Marian heard her put her dripping umbrella beside the door, but for her life she could not move. If she should be disappointed after all, she said, and she tried to see how many she could count before she knew for certain.

"A letter—oh, have you a letter for me?" she attempted to say, when Mrs. Burt came in, but she could not articulate a word, and the good lady, wishing to tease her a little, leisurely took off her overshoes, hung up her shawl, wiped her damp bonnet with a handkerchief, and looked at the dumplings and then said, as indifferently as if the happiness of a young life was not to be crushed by what she had in her pocket, "it rains awfully down street!"

"I know—but the letter—was there a letter?" and Marian's blue eyes looked dark with excitement. "Yes, child, there was, but where it was mailed I don't know. 'Tis directed to me, and is from Kentucky, but I can't make out the post mark mor'n the dead. It's some kind of Forks, but the postmaster will never set the Hudson on fire with his writing."

"Forks of Elkhorn," cried Marian, snatching at the letter. "It's Frederic's superscription, too, and dated ever so many days ago. Dear Frederic, he didn't wait a minute before he wrote," and she pressed to her lips the handwriting of Isabel Huntington!

The envelope was torn open—the enclosed sheet was withdrawn, but about it there was a strangely familiar look. Was there a film before Marian's eyes? Was she growing blind, or did she recognize her own letter—the one she had sent to Redstone Hall? It was the same—for it said "Dear Frederic" at the top, and "Marian" at the bottom! And he had returned it to her unanswered—not a word—not a line—nothing but silence, as cold, as hard and as terrible as the feeling settling down on Marian's heart. But yes—there was one line—only one, and it read—oh, horror, could it be that he would mock her thus—that he would tear out her bleeding heart and trample it beneath his feet, by offering her this cruel insult.

"*Isabel Huntington is now the mistress of Redstone Hall.*"

This was the drop in the brimming bucket, and if she had suffered death when the great sorrow came upon her once before, she suffered more now a hundred fold. In her ignorance she fancied they were married, for how else could Isabel be mistress there, and she comprehended at once the shame—the disgrace such a proceeding would bring to Frederic, and the wrong, the dishonor, the insult it brought to her. There was a look of anguish in her eye and a painful contraction of the muscles about her mouth. There were purple spots upon her flesh, which seemed wasting away while she sat there, and a note of agony, rarely heard by human ear, was in her voice, as she cried, "No, no, no—it is too soon—too soon—anything but that," and the little Marian who, half an hour before, had heard the ticking of the clock and listened to the rain, lay in the arms of Mrs. Burt, a white, motionless thing, unconscious of pain, unconscious of everything. She had suffered all she could suffer, and henceforth no sorrow which could come to her would eat into her heart's core as this last one had done.

Mrs. Burt thought she was dead, as did those who came at her loud call, but the old physician said there was life, adding, as he looked at the blue pinched lips and shrunken face: "The more's the pity, for she has had some awful blow, and if she lives she'll probably be a raving maniac."

Poor Marian! As time passed on the physician's words seemed likely to be verified. For days she lay in the same death-like stupor, and when at last she roused from it, 'twas only to tear her hair and rave in wild delirium. At first, Mrs. Burt, who had examined the letter, thought of writing to Frederic and telling him the result of his cruel message, the truth of which she did not believe; but she seldom acted without advice, so she wrote first to Ben, who came quickly, crying like a very child, and wringing his great rough hands when he saw the swaying, tossing form upon the bed and knew that it was Marian.

"No, mother," he said, "we won't write. It's a lie the villain told her, but we will let him be till she's dead. God will find him fast enough, the rascal!" and Ben struck his fist upon the bureau as if he would like to take the management of Frederic into his own hands.

It was a long and terrible sickness which came to Marian, and when the delirium was on, the very elements of her nature seemed changed. For her hair she conceived an intense loathing; and clutching at her long tresses, she would tear them from her head and shake them from her fingers, whispering scornfully:

"Go, you vile red things! He hates you, and so do I."

"Better shave the hull concern and not let her yank it out like that," said Ben; and when she became more and more ungovernable, he passed his arms around her and held fast her little hands, while her head was shorn of the locks once so displeasing to Frederic Raymond.

Ben's taste, however, was different, and putting them reverently together, he dropped great tears upon them, and then laid them carefully away, thinking: "'Twill be something to look at when she's gone. Poor little picked bird," he would say as he watched by her side and listened to her moaning cries for home, "you'll be out of your misery afore long, and go to a'nough sight better hum than Red stun Hall; but I hev my doubts 'bout meetin' him there. Poor little girl, if you hadn't been born a lady and I hadn't been born a fool, and we'd been brung up together, mabby you wouldn't be a lyin' here a biting your tongue and wringin' your hands, with your head shaved slick and clean," and the sweat dropped from Ben's face, as he thought of what under widely different circumstances might have been. "But it can't be now," he said, "for even if she wan't jined to this villain she loves so much, she's as far above Ben Burt as the stars in Heaven."

This, however, did not lessen Ben's attentions in the least, or stay his tears when he thought that she would die. "She should be buried in Greenwood," he said; "he'd got more'n two hundred dollars in the bank at Ware, all arnt honest, with hard work; and if there was such a thing as a stun forty feet high she should have it, and he'd get som o' them that scribbled for a living to write a piece; there should be a big funeral, too—he could hire carriages as well as the best of 'em—and he'd have a procession so long that folks would stop and stare, and Frederic Raymond wouldn't be ashamed on't either, the *scalliwag*—he hoped when he and Isabel came to die they'd be pitched into the *canal* where the water was considerable kind o' dirty, too!"

This long speech relieved Ben somewhat, and fully determined to carry out his promise, he staid patiently by Marian, nor experienced one feeling of regret when he heard that, owing to his prolonged absence, his place in Ware had been given to another.

"Nobody cares," he said, "I can find something to do if it's nothin' but sawin' wood."

So he remained at home through all the winter days, and watched by the sick girl, who talked piteously of her home, of Alice, and *that man* who hated her so. She never spoke his name, but she sometimes begged of him to come and take her away where it didn't thunder all the time. The roar of the city disturbed her, and she frequently besought Ben to go and stop it so that she could sleep and be better in the morning; and Ben, had it been in his power, would have stayed the busy life around them, and let the weary, worn-out sufferer sleep. But this could not be, and so, day after day the heavy, incessant roar came through the curtained window into the darkened room, where Marian lay moaning in her pain. Once in her unconsciousness she folded meekly her thin hands and prayed, "Will God stop that noise and let me sleep just once?" then with an expression of childish trust upon her face, she said to those around her, "He *will* stop it to-morrow, I reckon."

And when the winter snows all were fallen, and the early March sun shone upon the kitchen walls, the *to-morrow* so much longed for came, and Marian woke at last to consciousness. She was out of danger, the physician said, though it might be long ere her health was fully restored. To Marian, this announcement brought but little joy. "She had hoped to die," she said, "and thus be out of the way." and then she spoke of Redstone Hall, asking if any tidings had come from there since the dreadful message she had received. There was none, for Isabel Huntington guarded her secret well, and Frederic Raymond knew nothing of the white, emaciated wreck which prayed each day that he might be happy with the companion he had chosen.

"If he had only waited," she said to Mrs. Burt and Ben, one day when she was able to be bolstered up in bed, "if he had waited and not taken her so soon, I shouldn't care so much, but its awful to think of his living with her after I wrote that letter."

"Marian," said Ben, a little impatiently, "I'm naturally a fool, so every body says, but I've sense enough to know that Mr. Raymond never went and married that woman so quick after you came away; 'tain't reasonable at all. Why, they'd mob him—tar and feather him—for you ain't dead, and he's no business with two wives."

Marian's face was whiter than ever when Ben finished speaking, and a bright red spot burned on her cheek as she gasped, "You didn't,—you can't believe she's there and not his wife. That would be worse than everything else."

"Of course I don't," returned Ben. "My 'pinion is that she ain't there at all, and he only writ that to make a clean finish of you, or 'tany rate, so't you wouldn't be coming back to bother him. He calkerlates to have her bimeby. I presume—say in seven years."

"Oh, I wish I knew," said Marian, and Ben replied, "Would you rest any easier nights if you did?"

"Yes, a heap," was the answer, and the great, blue eyes looked wistfully at Ben, as if anxious that he should clear up the mystery.

"You might write," suggested Mrs. Burt; but Marian shook her head, saying, "I wrote once, and you know my success."

"You certainly wouldn't go back," continued Mrs. Burt; and Marian answered indignantly, "Never! I am sure he hates me now, and I shall not trouble him again. Perhaps he thinks me mean because I read the letter intended for him, and so found it all out. But I thought it was mine until I read a ways, and then I *could not* stop. My eyes wouldn't leave the paper. Was it wrong in me, do you think?"

It is what anybody would have done," answered Mrs. Burt, and, changing the subject entirely, Marian rejoined, "Oh, I do wish I knew about this Isabel.'

For a time Ben sat thinking; then striking his hands together, he exclaimed, "I've got it, and it's jest the thing, too. I don't want no better fun than that. I've lost my place to Ware, and though I might get another, I've a notion to turn *peddler*. I allus thought I should like travellin' and seein' the world. I'll buy up a lot of jimcracks and take a bee line for Redstun Hall, and learn just how the matter stands. I can put on a little more of the Down East Yankee, if you think I hain't got enough, and I'll pull the wool over their eyes. What do you say, wee one?"

"Oh, I wish you would," said Marian, adding in the same breath, "what will you do, if you find him the husband of Isabel?"

"Do!" he repeated. "String 'em both up by the neck on one string. What do you 'spect I'd do? Honest, though," he continued, as he saw her look of alarm; "if she *is* his wife, which ain't at all likely, 'tis because he s'posed you're dead, but he knows better now, and I shall tell the neighbors that you're alive and breathin', and they can do with him what they choose—and if they ain't married, nor ain't nothin', I'll just do what you say."

"Come back, and don't tell Frederic you ever saw or heard of me," said Marian. "I shall not live a great while, and even if I do, I'd rather not trouble him. It would only make him hate me worse, and that I couldn't bear. He knows now where I am, and if he ever wants me, he will come. Don't tell him, nor any one, a word of me, Ben, but do go, for I long to hear from home."

To Mrs. Burt this project seemed a wild and foolish one, but she rarely opposed her son, and when se saw that he was determined, she said nothing, but helped him all she could.

"You'll be wantin' to send some jimcrack to that blind gal, I guess," he said to Marian one day, and she replied, "I wish I could, but I havn't anything, and besides you mustn't tell her of me."

"Don't you worry," answered Ben. "I've passed my word, and I never broke it yet. I can manage to give her somethin' and make it seem natural. What do you say to makin' her a bracelet out o' them curls of yourn that we shaved off?"

"That red hair! Frederic would know it at once," and Marian shook her head ruefully. but Ben persisted. "'Twould look real pretty, just like gingerbread when 'twas braided tight," and bringing out the curls, he selected the longest one, and hurried off.

The result proved his words correct, for when a few

days after he brought home the little bracelet, which was fastened with a neat golden clasp, Marian exclaimed with delight at the soft beauty of her hair:

"Darling Alice," she cried, kissing the tiny ornament, "I wish she could know that my lips have touched it—that it once grew on my head—but it wouldn't be best. She couldn't keep the secret, and you mustn't tell."

"Don't worry, I say," returned Ben. "I've got an idee in my brains for a wonder, and I'm jest as 'fraid of tellin' as you be. So cheer up a bit and grow fat, while I'm gone, for I want you to be well when I come back, so as to go to school and get to be a great scholar, that Mr. Raymond won't be ashamed on when the right time comes," and Ben spoke as cheerfully as if within his heart there was no grave where during the weary nights when he watched with Marian he buried his love for her, and vowed to think of her only as a cherished sister.

Marian smiled pleasantly upon him, watching him with interest as he made up his pack, consisting of laces, ribbons, muslin, handkerchiefs, combs and jewelry, a little real, and a good deal brass, "for the niggers," he said. Many were the charges she gave him concerning the blacks, telling him which ones to notice particularly, so as to report to her.

"Jehosiphat!" he exclaimed at last, "how many is there? I shall never remember in the world," and taking out a piece of paper, he wrote upon it, "Dinah, Hetty, Lid, Victory, Uncle Phil, Josh, and the big dog. There!" said he, reading over the list, "if I don't bring you news of every one, my name ain't Ben Burt. I'll wiggle myself inter their good feelin's and get 'em to talkin' of you, see if I don't."

Marian had the utmost confidence in Ben's success, and though she knew she should be lonely when he was gone, she was glad when, at last, the morning came for him to leave them. Ben, too, was equally delighted, for the novelty lent a double charm to the project; and, bidding his mother and Marian good-by, he gathered up his large boxes, and whistling a lively tune, by way of keeping up his spirits, started for Kentucky.

CHAPTER XII.

THE YANKEE PEDDLER.

The warm, balmy April day was drawing to a close, and the rays of the setting sun shone like burnished gold on the western windows of Redstone Hall. It was very pleasant there now, for the early spring flowers were all in blossom, the grass was growing fresh and green upon the lawn, and the creeping vines were clinging lovingly to the time-worn pillars, or climbing up the massive walls of dark red stone, which gave the place its name. The old negroes had returned from their labors, and were lounging about their cabins, while the younger portion looked wistfully in at the kitchen door, where Dinah and Hetty were busy in preparing supper. On the back piazza several dogs were lying, and as their quick ears caught the sound of a gate in the distance, the whole pack started up and went tearing down the avenue, followed by the furious yell of Bruno, who tried in vain to escape from his confinement.

"Thar's somebody comin'," said Dinah, shading her eyes with her hand, and looking toward the highway; "somebody with somethin' on his back. You, Josh, go after them dogs, afore they skeer him to death."

Stuttering out some unintelligible speech, Josh started in the direction the dogs had gone, and soon came up to a tall six-footer, who, with short pantaloons, a swallow-tailed coat, stove-pipe hat, sharp-pointed collar, red necktie, and two huge boxes on his back, presented a rather ludicrous appearance to the boy, and a rather displeasing one to the dogs., who growled angrily, as if they would pounce upon him at once. The club, however, with which he had armed himself kept them at bay, until Josh succeeded in quieting them down.

"Ra-ally, now," began our friend Ben, who vainly imagined it necessary to *put on* a little, by way of proving himself a genuine Yankee—"ra-ally, now boot-black, what's the use of keepin' sich a 'tarnal lot o' dogs to worry a decent chap like me."

It was Josh's misfortune to stammer much more when at all excited, and to this interrogatory he began, "Caw-caw-caw-cause ma-ma-mars wa-wa-want——"

"Great Heaven!" interrupted the Yankee, setting down his pack and eyeing the stuttering negro as if he had been the last curiosity from Barnum's—"*will* you tell a fellow what kind of language you speak."

"Spe-pe-pe-pects sa-sa-same ye-e-e you do," returned the negro, failing wholly to enlighten Ben, who rejoined indignantly, "You go to grass with your lingo;" and, gathering up his boxes, he started for the house, accompanied by Josh and the dogs, the first of which made several ineffectual attempts at conversation.

"Some nateral born fool," muttered Ben, thinking to himself that he would like to examine the boy's mouth and see what ailed it.

After a few minutes they entered the yard, and came up to the other blacks, who were curiously watching the new comer. Seating himself upon the steps and crossing one leg over the other, Ben swung his cowhide boot forward and back, and greeted them with, "wall, uncles, and *ants*, and cousins, how do you dew, and how do you find yourselves this afternoon?"

"Jest tolerable, thanky," answered uncle Phil, and Ben continued, "wall, health is a great blessing to them that hain't got it. Do you calkerlate that I could stay here to night? I've got lots o' gewgaws," pointing to his boxes —" hankerchers, pins, ear-rings and a red and yeller gownd that'll jest suit you, old gall," nodding to Dinah, who muttered gruffly, "if he calls me *old* what'll he say to Hetty?"

Ben saw he had made a mistake, for black women no more care to be old than their fairer sisters, and he tried to make amends by complimenting the indignant lady until she was somewhat mollified, when he asked again if he could stay all night?

"You, Josh," said Uncle Phil, "go and tell yer master to come here."

"Whew-ew," whistled Ben, "if you're goin' to send that stutterin' critter, I may as well be joggin', for no human can make out his rigmarole."

But Ben was mistaken. Josh's dialect was well understood by Frederic, who came as requested, and, standing in the door, gazed inquisitively at the singular looking object seated upon his steps, and apparently oblivious to everything save the *sliver* he was trying to extract from his thumb with a large pin, ejaculating occasionally, "gaul darn the pesky thing."

Nothing, however, escaped the keen grey eyes which from time to time peered out from beneath the stove-pipe hat. Already Ben had seen that Redstone Hall was a most beautiful spot, and he did not blame Frederic for disliking to give it up. He had selected Dinah and Phil from the other blacks, and had said that the baby, who, with a small white dog, was disputing its right to a piece of fat bacon and a chicken bone, was Victoria Eugenia. *Josh* he identified by his name, and he was wondering at Marian's taste in caring to hear from *him*, when Frederic appeared, and all else was forgotten in his eagerness to inspect the man "who could make a gal bite her tongue in two and yank her hair out by the roots, all for the love of him."

Frederic seemed in no hurry to commence a conversation, and during the minute that he stood there without speaking, Ben had ample time to take him in from his brown hair and graceful mustache down to his polished boots.

"Got up in considerable kind of good style," was Ben's mental comment, as he watched the young man carelessly scraping his finger nail with a pen-knife.

"Did you wish to see me?" Frederic said at last, and with another thrust at the sliver, Ben stuck his pin upon his coat sleeve, and reversing the position of his legs, replied, "wall, if you're the boss, I guess I dew; I'm Ben Butterworth from down East, and I've got belated, and bein' there ain't no taverns near I want to stay all night, and pay in money or notions. Got a lot on 'em, besides some tip top muslin collars for your wife, Mrs., what do you call her?" and the gray eyes glistened themselves upon the face, which for a single instant was white as marble—then the hot blood came rushing back, and Frederic replied, "there is no wife here, sir, but you can stay all night if you please. Will you walk in?" and he led the way to the sitting-room, followed by Ben, who had obtained what to him was the most important information of all.

The night was chilly, and in the grate a cheerful coal fire was burning, casting its ruddy light upon the face of a little girl, who, seated upon a stool, with her hair combed back from her sweet face, her waxen hands folded together and her strange brown eyes fixed upon the coals as if she were looking at something far beyond them, seemed to Ben what he had fancied angels in heaven to be. It was not needful for Mr. Raymond to say, "Alice, here is a peddler come to stay all night," for Ben knew it was the blind girl, and his heart gave a great throb when he saw her sitting there so beautiful, so helpless, and so lonely, too, for he almost knew that she was thinking of Marian, and he longed to take her in his arms and tell her of the lost one.

Motioning him to a chair, Frederic went out, leaving them together. For some minutes there was perfect silence, while Ben sat looking at her and trying hard to keep from crying. It seemed terrible to him that one so young should be blind, and he wanted to tell her so, but he dared not, and he sat so still that Alice began to think she was alone, and, resuming her former thoughts, whispered softly to herself, "oh, I wish she would come back."

"Blessed baby," Ben had almost ejaculated, but he checked himself in time, and said instead, "little gal."

Alice started, and turning her ear, seemed waiting for him to speak again, which he did soon.

"Little gal, will you come and sit in my lap?"

His voice was gentle and kind, but Alice did not care to be thus free with a stranger, so she replied, "I reckon I won't do that, but I'll sit nearer to you," and she moved her stool so close by him that her head almost rested on his lap.

"You must 'scuse me," she said, "if I don't act like other children do—I'm blind."

Very tenderly he smoothed her silken hair, and as he did so, she felt something drop upon her forehead. It was a tear, and wiping it away, she said:

"Man, be you hungry and tired, or what makes you c y?"

"I'm cryin' for you, poor, unfortunate lamb;" and the tender-hearted Ben sobbed out aloud.

"Oh, I wouldn't, I wouldn't," said the distressed ch'ld—"I'm used to it. I don't mind it now."

The ice was fairly broken, and a bond of sympathy established between the two.

"He must be a good man," Alice thought; and when he began to question her of her home and friends, she replied to him readily.

"You haven't no mother, nor sister, nor a'nt, nor nothin', but Mr. Raymond and Dinah," said Ben, after they had talked awhile. " Ain't there no white women in the house but you?"

" Yes, Mrs. Huntington and Isabel. She's my governess," answered Alice; and, conscious of a pang, Ben continued:

" Mr. Raymond sent for 'em, I s'pose?"

" No," returned Alice. " They came without sending for—came to visit, and he hired them to stay. Mrs. Huntington keeps house."

At this point in the conversation there was a rustling of garments in the hall, and a splendid, queenly creature swept into the room, bringing with her such an air of superiority that Ben involuntarily hitched nearer to the wall, as if to get out of sight.

" Je-ru-sa-lem! ain't she a dasher?" was his mental exclamation; and, in spite of himself, he followed her movements with an admiring glance.

" Taking a chair, she drew it to the fire, and, without deigning to notice the stranger, she said, rather reprovingly,

" Alice, come here."

The child obeyed, and Ben, determined not to be ignored entirely, said:

" Pretty well this evenin', miss?"

" How, sir?" and the black eyes flashed haughtily upon him.

Nothing abashed, he continued: " As't you if you're pretty well, but no matter, I know you to be by your looks. I've got a lot of finery that I know you want." And on opening his boxes, he spread out upon the carpet the collars and under-sleeves, which had been bought with a view to this very night. Very disdainfully Isabel turned away, saying she never traded with peddlers.

" I wonder if you don't," returned Ben, with imperturbable gravity. " Wall, now, seein' it's me, buy somethin', dew. Here's a bracelet that can't be beat," and he held up to view Marian's soft hair, which, in the bright firelight, looked singularly beautiful.

Isabel did unbend a little now. There was no sham about that, she knew, and, taking it in her hand, she tried to clasp it on her round, white arm; but it would not come together. It was not made for her!

"It isn't large enough," said she; "it must have been intended for some child."

"Shouldn't wonder if you'd hit the nail right on the head," returned Ben, and taking the bracelet he continued, "Mebby 'twas meant for this wee one—who knows?" and he fastened it on Alice's slender wrist. "Fits to a T," said he, "and you have it, too. Them clasps is little hearts, do you see?"

Frederic now entered the room, and holding up her arm, Alice said, "Look, is it pretty?"

"Yes, very," he replied, bending down to examine it, while Ben watched him narrowly, wondering how he would feel if he knew from whose tresses that braid was made.

"Harnsome color, ain't it, Square?" he said, holding Alice's hand a little more to the light, and continuing, "Now there's them that don't like red hair, but I swan I've seen some that wan't so bad. Now when it curls kinder—wall, like a gimblet, you know. I've got a gal to hum I call my sister, and her hair's as nigh this color as two peas, or it was afore 'twas shaved. She's been awful sick with the heart disorder, and fever, and I tell you, Square, if you'd o' seen her pitchin' and divin', and rollin' from one end of the bed to t'other, bitin' her tongue and yankin' out her hair by han'fuls, I rather guess you'd felt kinder streaked. It made a calf of me, though I didn't feel so bad then as when she got weaker, and lay so still that we held a feather to her lips to see if she breathed."

"Oh, did she die?" asked Alice, who had been an attentive listener.

"No," answered Ben, "she didn't, and the thankfullest prayer I ever prayed was the one I made in the buttery, behind the door, when the doctor said she would get well."

Supper was announced, and putting up his muslins, Ben followed his host to the dining-room. Alice, too, was at the table, the bracelet still upon her wrist, for she liked the feeling of it. "And she did so wish it was hers"

"I shall have to buy it for you, I reckon," said Frederic, and he inquired its price.

"Wall, now," returned Ben, "if 'twas any body but the little gal, I should say five dollars, but bein' it's hers, I'd kinder like to give it to her."

This, however, Frederic would not suffer. Alice would not keep it, he said, unless he paid for it, and he put a half eagle into the hand of the child, who offered it to Ben. For a moment, the latter hesitated, then thinking to himself, "Darnt it all, what's the use. If Marian goes to school, as I mean she shall, she'll need a lot of money, and what I get out o' him is clear gain," he pocketed the piece, and the bracelet belonged to Alice.

After supper, Ben sat down by the fire in the dining-room, hoping the family would leave him with Alice, and this they did ere long, Isabel going to the piano, and Frederic to the library to answer letters, while Mrs. Huntington gave some directions for breakfast. These directions were merely nominal, however, for Dinah, to all intents and purposes, was mistress of the household, and she came in to see to the supper dishes, which were soon cleared away, and Ben, as he wished, was alone with Alice. The bracelet seemed to be a connecting link between them, for Alice was not in the least shy of him now, and when he asked her again to sit in his lap, she did so readily.

"That Miss Isabel is a dreadful han'some gal," he began; "I should s'pose Mr. Raymond would fall in love with her."

No answer from Alice, whose sightless eyes looked steadily into the fire.

"Mebby he *is* in love with her."

No answer yet, and mentally chiding himself

for his stupidity in not striking the right vein, Ben continued:

"I wonder he hain't married afore this. He must be as much as twenty-five or six years old, and so han' some too!"

"He *has* been married," and the little face of the speaker did not move a muscle.

"Now you don't say it," returned Ben. "A widower, hey? How long sence he was married?"

"A few months," and the long eye-lashes quivered in the firelight just a little.

"I want to know—died so soon—poor critter. Tell me about her, dew. You didn't know her long, so I s'pose you couldn't love her a great sight?"

The brown eyes flashed up into Ben's face, and the blood rushed to Alice's cheek, as she replied "Me not love Marian! Oh, I loved her so much!"

The right chord was touched at last, and in her own way Alice told the sad story—how Marian had left them on her bridal night, and though they searched for her everywhere, both in the river and through the country, no trace of her could be found, and the conviction was forced upon them that she was dead.

"Je-ru-sa-lem! I never thought of that!" was Ben's involuntary exclamation; but it conveyed no meaning to Alice, and when he asked if they still believed her dead, she answered:

"I don't quite believe Frederic does. I don't, any way. I used to, though, but now it seems just like she would come back," and turning her face more fully toward him, Alice told how she had loved the lost one, and how each day she prayed that she might come home to them again.

"I don't know as she was pretty," she said, "but she was so sweet, so good, and I'm so lonesome without her," and down Alice's cheeks the big tears rolled, while Ben's kept company with them and fell upon her hands.

"Man, don't you cry a heap?" she asked, shaking the

round drops off and wondering why a perfect stranger should care so much for Marian.

"I'm so plaguy tender-hearted that I can't help it," was Ben's apology, as he blew his nose vigorously upon his blue cotton handkerchief.

For a time longer he talked with her, treasuring up blessed words of comfort for the distant Marian, and learning also that Alice was sure Frederic would never marry again until certain of Marian's death. He might like Isabel, she admitted, but he would not dare make her his wife till he knew for true what had become of Marian.

"And he does know it, the scented up puppy," thought Ben. "He jest writ her that last insultin' thing to kill her out and out; but he didn't come it, and till he knows he did, he dassent do nothin'."

This reasoning was very satisfactory to Ben, who, having learned from Alice all that he could, began to think it was time to cultivate the negroes, and putting the child from his knee, he said "he guessed he'd go out and see the slaves—mebby they'd like to trade a little, and he must be off in the mornin'."

Accordingly he started for the kitchen, where his character had been pretty thoroughly dissected. A negro from a neighboring plantation had dropped in on a gossiping visit, and as was very natural, the conversation had turned upon the peddler, whose peculiar appearance had attracted much attention at the different places where he had stopped. Particularly was this the case at the house the black man Henry lived.

"He done ask a heap of questions about us colored folks," said Henry; "how many was there of us, how old was we, and what was we worth, and when marster axed him did he want to buy, he said "no, but way off whar he lived he allus spoke in meetin', and them folks was mighty tickled to hear suffin' 'bout niggers.' Ole Miss say how't she done b'lieve he's an abolution come to run some on us off,' case he look like one o' them chaps down in the penitentiary."

"Oh. Lord," ejaculated Dinah, involuntarily hitching her chair nearer to Victoria Eugenia, who lay in her cradle.

Old Hetty, too, took alarm at once, and glancing nervously at her own grandchild Dudley, a little boy two years of age, who was stretched, upon the floor, "she hoped to goodness he wouldn't carry off Dud."

"Jest the ones he'll pick for. He could hide a dozen on em in them big boxes," said Henry, and feeling pleased at the interest he had awakened in the two old ladies he proceeded to relate the stories he had heard "'bout them fetched Yankees meddlin' with what didn't consarn 'em,' and he advised Dinah and Hetty both not to let the peddler get sight of the children for fear of what might happen.

At this point Ben came out of the house with his huge boxes. He was first discovered by Josh, who, delighted with the fun, pointed mysteriously toward him and stuttered, "Da-da-da 'e co-co-comes."

"The Lord help us," said Dinah and quick as thought she seized the sleeping Victoria Eugenia and thrust her into the churn as the nearest place of concealment.

The awakened baby gave a screech bnt Dinah stopped its mouth with a piece of the licorice she always carried in her pocket with her tobacco box and pipe. Meantime Hetty, determined not to be outdone, caught up Dud, and, opening the meal chest, tumbled him in, telling him in fierce whispers "not to stir nor wink, for thar was a man comin' to cotch him."

Snatching a newspaper which lay on the floor, she rolled it together and placed it under the lid, so as to allow the youngster a breathing place. This done, she resumed her seat just as Ben appeared, who, throwing down his pack, accosted her with—

"Wall, a'nt, got your chores done? 'Cause if you have I want to trade a little. I won't be hard on you," he continued, as he saw the forbidding expression of her face. "I'll dicker cheap and take most any kind o' dud for pay."

Dicker and chores were Greek to old Hetty, but she fully comprehended the word Dud. He meant her DUD — the one in the meal chest—and she grasped the handle of the frying pan, so as to be ready for what might follow next.

" Let me show you some breastpins," said Ben, looking round for a chair.

They were all occupied, and as the mischievous Josh pointed to the chest, Ben crossed over, and ere Hetty was aware of his intention, seated himself quite as a matter of course. But not long, for Hetty's dusky fist flourished in the air, and, more than all, the smothered cry of " Granny, granny, he done sot on me," which came from beneath him, landed him on the other side of the room, where he struck against the churn; whereupon, Victoria Eugenia set up another yell, which sent him back to the spot where Josh's cowhides were performing various evolutions by way of showing his delight.

" Thunder !" ejaculated Ben,looking first at the skirts of his swallow-tail, then at the chest, from which Dud was emerging, covered with meal, and then at the churn, over the top of which a pair of little black hands and a piece of licorice were visible, "what's the meaning of all this ?"

No explanation whatever was vouchsafed, and, to this day, Ben does not know the reason why those negroes were stowed away in such novel hiding places.

When the excitement had somewhat subsided, Ben returned to his first intention, behaving so civilly that the fears of the negroes gave way, and Dinah was so well pleased with purchasing a brass pin at half price that Ben ventured, at last to say:

" That little gal, Alice, has been tellin' me about Mr. Raymond's marriage. Unlucky, wasn't he ? Shouldn't wonder though, if he had a kind of hankerin' after that black-eyed miss. She's han'some as a picter."

Dinah needed but this to loosen her tongue. She

had long before made up her mind that "Isabel was no kind o' 'count;" and once the two had come to open hostilities, Isabel accusing Dinah of being a "lazy, gossiping nigger," while Dinah, in return, had told her "she warn't no better 'n she should be stickin' 'round after Mars. Frederic, when nobody knew whether Miss Marian was dead, or not."

This indignity was reported to Frederic, who reproved old Dinah, sharply; whereupon, she turned toward him, and, to use her favorite expression, "gin him a piece of her mind."

After this it was generally understood that between Dinah and Isabel here existed no very amicable state of feeling, and when Ben spoke of the latter, the former exploded at once.

"'Twas a burnin' shame," she said, "and it mortified her een-a-most to death to see the trollop a tryin' to set to marster, when nobody know'd for sartin if his fust wife was dead,"

"Marster's jest as fast as she," interposed Hetty, who seldom agreed with Dinah.

A contemptous sneer curled Dinah's lip as she said to Ben, in a whisper:

"Don't b'lieve none o' her trash. Them Higginses allus would lie. I hain't never seen Marster Frederic do a single thing out o' the way, 'cept to look at her, jest as Phil used to look at me when he was sparkin'. I don't think that was very 'spectable in him, to be sure, but looks don't signify. He dassen't marry her till he knows for sartin t'other one is dead. He done told Alice so, and she told me;" and then Dinah launched out into praises of the lost Marian, exalting her so highly that Ben tossed into her lap a pair of earrings which she had greatly admired.

"Take them," said he, "for standin' up for that poor runaway. I like to hear one woman stick to another."

Dinah cast an exulting glance at Hetty, who, nothing daunted, came forward and said:

"Miss Marian was as likely a gal as thar was in Kentuck, and she, for one, should be as glad to see her back as some o' them that made sich a fuss about it."

"Playin' 'possum," whispered Dinah. "Them Higginses is up to that."

Ben probably thought so too, for he paid no attention to Hetty, who, highly indignant started for Isabel, and told her "how Dinah and that fetch-ed peddler done spilt her character entirely."

"Leave the room," was Isabel's haughty answer. "I am above what a poor negro and an ignorant Yankee can say."

"For the dear Lord's sake," muttered the discomfited Hetty; "wonder if she ain't a Yankee her own self. 'Spects how she done forgot whar she was raised," and Hetty returned to the kitchen a warmer adherent of Marian than Dinah had ever been.

She, too, was very talkative now, and before nine o'clock Ben had learned all that he expected to learn, and much more. He had ascertained that no one had the slightest suspicion of the reason why Marian went away; that both Frederic and Isabel seemed unhappy; that Dinah and Hetty, too, believed "thar was somethin' warin' on thar minds;" that Frederic was discontented, and talked seriously of leaving Redstone Hall in care of an overseer, and moving, in the Autumn to to his residence on the Hudson; that Hetty hoped he would, and Dinah hoped he wouldn't, "'case if he did, it would be next to impossible to get a stroke o' work out o' them lazy Higginses."

"I've got all I come for, I b'lieve," was Ben's mental comment, as he left the kitchen and returned to the dining room, where he found Frederic alone. "I'll poke his ribs a little," he thought, and helping himself to a chair, he began:

"Wall, Square, I've been out seein' your niggers. Got a fine lot on 'em, and I shouldn't wonder if you was wo'th considerable. Willed to you by your dad, or was it a kind of a dowry come by your wife? You're a widower, they say;" and the gray eyes looked out at their corners, as Ben thought, "That'll make him squirm, I guess."

Frederic turned very white, but his voice was natural as he replied:

"My father was called the richest man in the county, and I was his only child."

"Ah, yes, come to you that way," answered Ben, continuing after a moment. "There's a big house up on the Hudson—to Yonkers—that's been shet up and rented at odd spells for a good while, and somebody told me it belonged to a Colonel Raymond, who lived South. Mabby that's yourn?"

"It is," returned Frederic, "and I expect now to go there in the Fall."

"I want to know. I shouldn't s'pose you could be hired to leave this place."

"I couldn't be hired to stay. There are too many sad memories connected with it," was Frederic's answer, and he paced the floor hurriedly, while Ben continued: Mabby you'll be takin' a new wife there?"

Frederic's cheek flushed as he replied:

"If I ever marry again, it will not be in years. Would you like to go to bed, sir?"

Ben took the hint and replying, "I don't care if I dew," followed the negro, who came at Frederic's call, up to his room, a pleasant, comfortable chamber, overlooking the river and the surrounding country.

"Golly, this is grand!" said Ben, examining the different articles of furniture, as if he had never seen anything like it before.

The negro, who was Lyd's husband, made no reply, but, hurrying down stairs to his mother-in-law, he told her, "Thar was somethin' mighty queer about that man, and if they all found themselves alive in the mornin,' he should be thankful."

Unmindful of breast-pin and ear-rings, Dinah became again alarmed, and, bidding Joe see that Victoria Eugenia was safe, she gathered up the forks and spoons, and rolling them in a towel, tucked them inside her straw tick, saying: "I reckon it'll make him sweat some to hist me and Phil on to the floor;" which was quite probable, considering that the united weight of the worthy couple was somewhat over three hundred!

The morning dawned at last, and, with her fears abated, Dinah washed the silver, made the coffee, broiled the steak and fried the corn-meal batter-cakes, which last were at first respectfully declined by Ben, who admitted that they "might be fust-rate, but he didn't b'lieve they'd set well on his stomach."

Hetty, who was waiting upon the table, quickly divined the reason, and whispered to him: "Lord bless you, take some; I done sifted the meal!"

This argument was conclusive, and helping himself to the light, steaming cakes, Ben thought, "I may as well eat 'em, for 'taint no wus, nor as bad as them Irish gals does to hum, only I happened to see it!"

Breakfast being over, he offered to settle his bill, which he found was nothing.

"Now, ra-ally, Square," he said, as Frederic refused to take pay, "I allus hearn that Kentuckians was mighty free-hearted, but I didn't 'spect you to give me my livin'. I'm much obleeged to you, though, and I shall have more left to eddicate that little sister I was tellin' you 'bout. I mean to give her tip-top larnin', and mebby sometime she'll come here to teach this wee one," and he laid his hand on Alice's hair.

The little girl smiled up in his face, and said, "Come again and peddle here, won't you?"

"Wouldn't wonder if I turned up amongst you some day," was his answer; and bidding the family good-bye, he went out into Bruno's kennel, for until this minute he had forgotten that the dog was to be remembered.

"Keep away from dar," called out Uncle Phil, while Bruno growled savagely and bounded against the bars as if anxious to pounce upon the intruder.

"I've seen enough of him," thought Ben, and shaking hands with Uncle Phil, he walked rapidly down the avenue and out into the highway.

Marian, he knew, was anxious to hear of his success, and not willing to keep her waiting longer than was necessary, he determined to return at once. Accordingly, while the unsuspecting inmates of Redstone Hall were discussing his late visit and singular appearence, he was on his way to the depot, where he took the first train for Frankfort, and was soon sailing down the Kentucky toward home.

CHAPTER XIII.

PLANS.

MARIAN was sitting by the window of her little room, looking out into the busy street below, and thinking how differently New York seemed to her now from what it did that dreary day when she wandered down Broadway, and wished that she could die. She was getting accustomed to the city roar, and the sounds which annoyed her so much at first did not trouble her as they once had done. Still there was the same old pain at her heart—a restless, longing desire to hear from home, and know if what she feared were true. She had counted the days of Ben's absence, and she knew it was almost time for his return. She did not expect him to-day, however, and she paid no attention to the heavy footstep upon the stairs, neither did she hear the creaking of the door; but when Mrs. Burt exclaimed, "Benjamin Franklin! where did you come from?" she started, and in an instant held both his hands in hers.

Wistfully, eagerly she looked up into his face, longing, yet dreading, to ask the important question.

"Have you been there?" she managed to say at last; and Ben replied, "Yes, chicken, I have, I've been to Redstun Hall, and seen the hull tribe on 'em That Josh is a case. Couldn't understand him no more than if he spoke a furrin tongue."

"But Frederic—did you see him, and is he—oh, Ben, do tell me—what you know I want to hear?" and Marian trembled with excitement.

"Wall, I will," answered Ben, dropping into a chair, and coming to the point at once. "Frederic ain't married to Isabel, nor ain't a-goin' to be, either."

"What made him write me that lie?" was Marian's next question, asked so mournfully that Ben replied:

"A body'd s'pose you was sorry it warn't the truth he writ."

"I am glad it is not true," returned Marian, "but it hurts me so to lose confidence in one I love. How does Frederic look?"

"White as a sheet and poor as a crow," said Ben. "It's a wearin' on him, depend on't. But she—I tell you she's a dasher, with the blackest eyes and hair I ever seen."

"Who?" fairly screamed Marian. "Who? Not Isabel? Oh, Ben, is Isabel there?" And Marian grew as white as Ben had described Frederic to be.

"Yes she is," returned Ben. "She's pretendin' to teach that blind gal, but Frederic ain't makin' love to her—no such thing. So don't go to faintin' away, and I'll begin at the beginning and tell you the hull story."

Thus re-assured, Marian composed herself and listened, while Ben narrated every particular of his recent visit to Redstone Hall.

"I stopped at some of the houses in the neighborhood," said he, "but I never as't a question about the Raymonds, for fear of bein' mistrusted. Come to think on't, though, I did inquire the road, and they sent me through corn fields, and hemp fields, and mercy knows what; such a way as they have livin' in the lots? But I kinder like it. Seems like a story, them big housen way off among the trees, with the whitewashed cabins round 'em lookin' for all the world like a camp-meetin' in the woods——"

"Yes, yes," interrupted Marian; "but Frederic—won't you ever reach him?"

"Not till I tell you about the dogs, and that jaw-breakin' chap they call Josh, with his cow hides, big as a scow-boat, I'll bet," was Ben's answer; and finding it useless to hurry him, Marian summoned all her patience and waited while he waded through his introduction to the blacks, his attempt to be more of a Yankee than he really was, his sliver in his thumb, and, finally his addressing Frederic as Square and inquiring for his wife!

Marian was all attention now, and held her breath, lest she should lose a single word. When he came to Isabel, and described her glowing, sparkling beauty, she trembled in every joint, and felt as if she were turning to stone; but when he spoke of Alice, and the sweet, loving words she had said of the lost one, the cold, hard feeling passed away, and, covering her face with her hands, she wept aloud. Everything which Ben had seen or heard he told, omitting not a single point, but lengthening out his story with surmises and suspicions of his own.

"Alice and Dinah both," said he, "told me Frederic wouldn't marry till they knew for certain you was dead, and as he does know for certain, you can calkerlate on that Isabel's bein' an old maid for all of him."

"I never supposed they'd think me drowned when I dropped my glove and handkerchief," said Marian. "Did they inquire at the depot."

"Yes—so Alice said," returned Ben, "and nobody knew nothin' of you; so it was nateral they should think you drownded: but, no matter, it makes it more like a novel, and now I'll tell you jest what 'tis, wee one, I don't mean no offense, and you must take it all in good part. You are a great deal better than Isabel, I know; but, as fur as looks and manners is concerned, you can't hold a candle to her, and a body knowin' nothing about either would naterally say she was most befittin' Redstun Hall; but, tell 'em to wait a spell. You hain't got your growth yet, and you are gettin' betterlookin' every day. That sickness made a wonderful change in you, and shavin' your hair was jest the thing. It's comin' out darker, as it always does, and in less than a year I'll bet my hat on its bein' a beautiful auburn. You must chirk up and grow fat, for I'm goin' to send you to school, and have you take lessons on the pianner, and learn French and everything, so that by the time you're twenty you'll be the best educated and han'somest gal in the city, and then when the right time comes, if Providence don't contrive to fetch you two together, Ben Burt will. I shall keep my eye on him, and if he's gettin' too thick with Isabel, I'll drop a sly hint in his ear. They're goin' to move up on to the Hudson to the old place—did I tell you?—and mebby you'll run afoul of him in the street some day."

"Oh, I hope not—at least, not yet—not till the time you speak of," said Marian, who had listened eagerly to Ben's suggestion, and already felt that there was hope for her in the future. She would study so hard, she thought, and learn so fast, and if she only could be thought handsome, or even decent-looking, she would be satisfied, but that was impossible, she feared.

She did not know that, as Ben had said, the severe illness through which she had passed had laid the foundation for a softer, more refined style of beauty than she would otherwise have reached. Her entire constitution seemed to have undergone a change, and now, with hope to buoy her up, she grew stronger, healthier, and, as a natural consequence, handsomer each day. She could not erase from her memory the insult Frederic had offered her, by writing what she believed he did, but her affection for him was strong enough to overlook even that, and she was willing to wait and labor years if at the end of that time she could hope to win his love.

Whatever Ben undertook he was sure to accomplish in the shortest possible time, and before starting upon another peddling excursion, the name of "MARIAN GREY" was enrolled among the list of pupils who attended Madam Harcourt's school. At first she was subject to many annoyances, for, as was quite natural, her companions inquired concerning her standing, and when they learned that her aunt was a sewing woman, and that the queer, awkward fellow who came with her the first day was her cousin and a peddler, they treated her slightingly, and laughed at her plain dress. But Marian did not care. One thought—one feeling alone actuated her; to make herself something of which Frederic Raymond should not be ashamed was her aim, and for this she studied early and late, winning golden laurels in the opinion of her teachers, and coming ere long to be respected and loved by her companions, who little suspected that she was the heiress of untold wealth.

Thus the Summer and a part of the Autumn passed away, and when the semi-annual examination came, Marian Grey stood first in all her classes, acquitting herself so creditably and receiving so much praise, that Ben, who chanced to be present, was perfectly overjoyed, and evinced his pleasure by shedding tears, his usual way of expressing feeling.

From this time forward Marian's progress was rapid, until even she herself wondered how it were possible for her to learn so fast when she had formerly cared so little for books. Hope, and a joyful anticipation of what would possibly be hers in the future, kept her up and helped her to endure the mental labors which might otherwise have overtaxed her strength. Gradually, too, the old soreness at her heart wore away, and she recovered in a measure her former light-heartedness, until at last her merry laugh was often heard ringing out loud and clear just as it used to do at home in days gone by. Very anxiously Ben watched her, and when on his return from his excursions he found her, as he always did, improved in looks and spirits, he rubbed his hands together and whispered to himself, "She'll set up for a beauty, yet, and no mistake. That hair of hern is growin' a splendid color."

He did not always express these thoughts to Marian, but the little mirror which hung on the wall in her room sometimes whispered to her that the face reflected there was not the same which had looked at her so mournfully on that memorable night when she had left her pillow to see what her points of ugliness were! The one which she had thought the crowning defect of all had certainly disappeared. Her red curls were gone, and in their places was growing a mass of soft wavy hair, which reminded her of the auburn tress she had so much admired and prized, because it was her mother's. She had no means of knowing how nearly they were alike, for the ringlet was far away, but by comparing her present short curls with those which had been shorn from her head, she saw there was a difference, and she felt a pardonable pride in brushing and cultivating her young hair, which well repaid her labor, growing very rapidly and curling anout her forehead in small, round rings, which were far from unbecoming.

Toward the last of November, Ben, who found his peddling profitable, took a trip through Western New York, and did not return until February, when, somewhat to his mother's annoyance, he brought a sick stranger with him. He had taken the cars at Albany, where he met with the stranger, who offered him a part of his seat and made himself so generally agreeable that Ben's susceptible heart warmed toward him at once, and when at last, as they drew near New York, the man showed signs of being seriously ill, Ben's sympathy was roused, and learning that he had no friends in the city, he urged him so strongly to accompany him home for the night, at least, that his invition was accepted, and the more readily, perhaps, as the stranger's pocket had been picked in Albany, and he had nothing left except his ticket to New York. This reason was not very satisfactory to Mrs. Burt, who from the first had disliked their visitor's appearance. He was a powerfully built young man, with black bushy hair, and restless, rolling eyes, which seemed ever on the alert to discover something not intended for them to see. His face wore a hard, dissipated look; and when Mrs. Burt saw how soon after seating himself before the warm fie, he fell asleep, she rightly conjectured that a fit of drunkenness had been the cause of his illness. Still, he was their guest, and she would not treat him uncivilly, so she bade her son to take him to his room, where he lay in the same deep, stupid sleep, breathing so loudly that he could be plainly heard in the adjoining room, where Marian and Ben were talking of the house at Yonkers which was not finished yet, and would not be ready for the family until sometime in May.

Suddenly the loud breathing in the bed-room ceased —the stranger was waking up; but Ben and Marian paid no heed, and talked on as freely as if there were no greedy ears drinking in each word they said—no wild-eyed man leaning on his elbow and putting together, link by link, the chain of mystery until it was as clear to him as noonday. The first sentence which he heard distinctly sobered him at once. It was Marian who spoke, and the words she said were, "I wonder if Isabel Huntington will come with Frederic to Yonkers."

"Isabel!" the stranger gasped. "What do they know of her?" and sitting up in bed, he listened until he learned what they knew of her, and learned, too, that the young girl whom Ben Burt called his cousin was the runaway bride from Redstone Hall.

Fiercely the black eyes flashed through the darkness, and the fists smote angrily together as the stranger hoarsely whispered:

"The time I've waited for has come at last, and the proud lady shall be humbled in the very dust!"

It was Rudolph McVicar who thus threatened evil to Isabel Huntington. He had loved her once, but her scornful refusal of him, even after she was his promised wife, had turned his love to hate, and he had sworn to avenge the wrong should a good chance ever occur. He knew that she was in Kentucky—a teacher at Redstone Hall—and for a time he had expected to hear of her marriage with the heir, but this intelligence did not come, and weary of New Haven, he at last made a trip to New Orleans, determining on his way back to stop for a time in the neighborhood of Redstone Hall, and if possible learn the reason why Isabel had not yet succeeded in securing Frederic Raymond. On the boat in which he took passage on his return were three or four young people from Franklin county, and among them Anges Gibson and her brother. They were a very merry party, and at once attracted the attention of Rudolph, who, learning that they were from the vicinity of Frankfort, hovered around them, hoping that by some chance he might hear them speak of Isabel. Nor was he disappointed; for one afternoon when they were assembled upon the upper deck, one of their number who lived in Lexington, and who had been absent in California for nearly two years, inquired after Frederic Raymond, whom he had formerly known at school.

"Why," returned the loquacious Agnes, "did no one write that news to you?" and oblivious entirely of Rudolph McVicar, who at a little distance was listening attentively, she told the story of Frederic's strange marriage and its sad denouement. Isabel, too, was freely discussed, Miss Agnes saying that Mr. Raymond would undoubtedly marry her, could he know that Marian was dead, but as there were some who entertained doubts upon that point he would hardly dare take any decisive step until uncertainty was made sure.

"When Miss Huntington first came to Redstone Hall," continued Agnes, "she took no pains whatever to conceal her preference for Mr. Raymond; but latterly a change has come over her, and she hardly appears like the same girl. There seems to be something on her mind, though what it is I have never been able to learn, which is a little strange, considering that she tells me everything."

Not a word of all this story was lost by McVicar. There was no reason now for his leaving the boat at Louisville. He knew why Isabel was not a bride, and secretly exulting as he thought of her weary restlessness, he kept on his way till he reached Albany, where a debauch of a few days was succeeded by the sickness which had awakened the sympathy of the tender-hearted Ben, and induced the latter to offer him shelter for the night. He was glad of it, now—glad that he had met with Ben, for by that means he had discovered the hiding-place of Frederic Raymond's wife. He did not know of her fortune, but he knew that she was Marian Lindsey; that accidentally, as he supposed, she had stumbled upon Mrs. Burt and Ben, who were keeping her secret from the world, and that was enough for him. That Isabel had something to do with her he was sure, and long after the conversation in the next room had ceased, he lay awake thinking what use he should make of his knowledge, and still not betray those who had befriended him.

Rudolph McVicar was an adept in cunning, and before the morning dawned he had formed a plan by which he hoped to crush the haughty Isabel. Assuming an air of indifference to everything around him, he sauntered out to breakfast, and pretended to eat, while his eyes rested almost constantly on Marian. She was very young, he thought, and far prettier than Agnes Gibson had represented her to be. She was changing in her looks, he said, and two or three years would ripen her into a beautiful woman of whom Frederic Raymond would be proud. Much he wished he knew why she had left Redstone Hall, but as this knowledge was beyond his reach, he contented himself with knowing who she was, and after breakfast was over, he thanked his new acquaintances for their hospitality, and went out into the city, going first to a pawnbroker's, where he left his watch, receiving in exchange money enough to defray his expenses in the city for several days.

That night, in a private room at the St. Nicholas, he sat alone, bending over a letter, which, when finished, bore a very fair resemblance to an uneducated woman's handwriting, and which read as follows:

M. Raymond—I now take my pen in hand to inform you that A young Woman, calling herself Marian lindsey has ben staying with me awhile And she said you was her Husband what she came of and left you for I don't know and I spose its none of my Biznes all I have to do is to tell you that she died wun week ago come sunday with the cankerrash and she made me Promise to rite and tell you she was ded and that she forgives you all your Sins and hope you wouldn't wate long before you marred agen it would of done your Hart good to hear her taulk like a Sante as she did. I should of writ soonner only her sicknes hindered me about gettin reddy for a journey ime goin to take my only Brother lives in scotland and ime goin out to live with him i was most reddy when Marian took sick if she had lived she was coming back to you I bleave and now that shes ded ime going rite of in the —— which sales tomorrough nite else ide ask you to come down and see where she died and all about it. i made her as comfitable as I could and hopin you wouldnt take it to hard for Deth is the Lot of all i am your most Humble Servant Sarah Green.

"There," soliloquized Rudolph, reading over the letter. "That covers the whole ground, and still gives him no clue in case he should come to New York. The ——— does sail the very day I have named, and though 'Sarah Green' may not be among her passengers, it answers my purpose quite as well. I believe I've steered clear of all doubtful points which might lead him to suspect it a forgery. He knows Marian would not attempt to deceive him thus, and he will, undoubtedly, think old Mrs. Green some good soul, who dosed the patient with saffron tea, and then saw her decently interred! He'll have a nice time hunting up her grave if he should undertake that. But he won't—he'll be pleased enough to know that he is free, for by all accounts he didn't love her much, and in less than six weeks he'll be engaged to Isabel. But I'll be on their track. I'll watch them narrowly, and when the day is set, and the guests are there, one will go unbidden to the marriage feast, and the story that uninvited guest can tell will humble the proud beauty to the dust. He will tell her that this letter was a forgery, and Sarah Green a myth: that Marian Lindsey lives, and Frederic Raymond, if he takes another wife, can be indicted for bigamy; and when he sees her eyes flash fire, and her cheek grow pale with rage and disappointment, Rudolph McVicar will be avenged."

This, then, was the plan which Rudolph had formed, and, without wavering for an instant in his purpose, he sealed the letter, and directing it to Frederic, sent it on its way, going himself the next morning to New Haven, where he had some money deposited in the bank. This he withdrew, and after a few days started for Lexington, where he intended to remain and watch the proceedings at Redstone Hall, until the denouement of his plot.

CHAPTER XIV.

THE EFFECT.

Not quite one year has passed away since the warm Spring night when Ben Burt first strolled leisurely up the long avenue leading to Redstone Hall. It was April, then, and the early flowers were in bloom, but now the chill March winds are blowing, and the brown stocks of the tall rose-tree brush against the window, from which a single light streams out into the darkness. It is the window of the little library where we have seen Frederic before, and where we meet him once again. He has changed somewhat since we saw him last, and there is upon his face a sad, thoughtful expression, as if far down in his heart there were a haunting memory which would follow him through all time, and embitter every hour.

Little by little, step by step, he had come to hate the wealth which had tempted him to sin—to loathe the beautiful home he once loved so well—and this had prompted him to leave it and go back to the old house on the river, where his early boyhood was passed. There were not so many mournful memories clustering around that spot, he thought, and if he once were there, he might perhaps forget the past, and be happy again. He would open an office in the city, and if possible earn his own living, so as not to spend more of Marian's fortune than was necessary. He could not tell why he wished to save it. He only knew that he could not bear to use it, and he roused himself at last, determining to do something for himself. This plan of moving to the Hudson was opposed by Isabel, who liked the easy, luxurious life she led at Redstone Hall; but, for once, Frederic would not listen to her, and he had made his arrangements to leave Kentucky in May, at which time his house would be in readiness to receive him. Isabel would go with him, of course—she was necessary to him now, though, faithful to the promise made to little Alice, he had never talked to her of love. And she was glad that he had not; for, with the knowledge she possessed, she would not have dared to listen to his suit, and she often questioned herself as to what the end would be.

One year or more of the dreary seven was gone, but the future looked almost hopeless to her, and she was sometimes tempted to go away and leave the dangerous game at which she was so hazardously playing. Still, when she seriously contemplated such a proceeding, she shrunk from it—for, even though she were never Frederic's wife, she would rather remain where she was, and see that no other came to dispute the little claim she had. All her assurance was gone, and in her dread lest Frederic should say the words she must not hear, she assumed toward him a half distant, half bashful manner, far more attractive than a bolder course of conduct would have been, and Frederic, while watching her in this new phase of character, struggled manfully against the feeling which sometimes prompted him to break his promise to the blind girl. She was faulty, he knew—far more so than he had once imagined—but she was brilliant, beautiful, accomplished, and he thought that he loved her.

But not of her was he thinking that chill March night when he sat alone in the library watching the flickering of the lamp, and listening to the evening wind, as it shook the bushes beneath his window. It was Marian's seventeenth birth-day, and he was thinking of her, wondering what she would have been had she lived to see this day. She was surely dead, he thought, or some tidings of her would have come to him ere this, and when he remembered how gentle, how pure and self-denying her short life had been, he said involuntarily, "Poor Marian—she deserved a better fate, and should she come back to me again I would prove to her that I am not all unworthy of her love."

There was a shuffling tread in the hall, and Josh appeared bringing several letters. One bore the Louisville post-mark—one was from New Orleans—one from Lexington, and one from Sarah Green!

"Who writes to me from New York?" was Ferderic's mental query, and tearing open the wrapper he drew nearer to him the lamp and read, while there crept over him a nameless terror as if even while he was thinking of the lost, the grave had opened at his feet and shown him where she lay; not in the moaning river—not in the deep, dark woods, nor on the western prairies, as he had sometimes feared, but far away in the great city, where there was no one to pity—no eye to weep for her save that of the rude woman who had written him the letter.

There Marian had suffered and died for him. His Marian—his young girl-wife! He could call her so now, and he did, saying it softly, reverently, as we speak always of the departed, while the tears he was not ashamed to weep, dropped upon the soiled sheet. He did not think of doubting it. There was no reason why he should, and his heart went out after the dead as it had never gone after the living. It seemed to him so terrible that she should die among strangers, so far from home; and he wondered much how she ever chanced to get there. She had remembered him to the last, "forgiving all his sins," the woman said, and knowing how much those few words meant, he said again, "Poor Marian," just as the door opened and Alice came slowly in.

There was a grand party that night at the house of Lawyer Gibson, and at Isabel's request Alice had come to ask how long before the carriage would be ready. Dinah had told her that Frederic was in the library, but he sat so still she thought he was not there, and she said inquiringly, "Frederic?"

"Yes, darling," was his answer in a tone which startled the sensitive child, for she detected in it a sound of tears, and hurrying to his side she passed her hand over his face to assure herself that she heard aright.

"Has something dreadful happened?" she asked, as she felt the moisture on his eye-lids.

Taking her on his lap, and laying his burning cheek against her cool forehead, Frederic said to her very tenderly and low:

"Alice, poor Marian is dead! Here is the letter which came to tell us," and he placed it in her hand. There was a sudden upward flashing of the brown eyes, and then their soft light was quenched in tears, as, burying her face in the young man's bosom, the blind girl sobbed, "Oh, no, no, Frederic, no."

For several minutes she wept passionately, while her little frame shook with strong emotion. Then lifting up her head and reaching toward the spot where she knew the letter lay, she said:

"Read it to me, Frederic," and he did read, pausing occasionally as he was interrupted by her low moaning cry.

"Is that all?" she asked, when he had finished. "Didn't you leave out a word?"

"Not one," was his reply, and with quivering lips the heart-broken child continued, "Marian sent no message for poor blind Alice to remember—she never thought of me who loved her so much. Why didn't she, Frederic?" and the sightless eyes looked beseechingly at him as if he could explain the mystery.

Poor child! Rudolph McVicar did not know how strong was the affection between those two young girls, or he would surely have sent a message to one who seemed almost a part of Marian herself, and it was this very omission which finally led the close reasoning child to doubt the truth of the letter. But she did not doubt it now. Marian was really dead to her, and for a long time she sat with Frederic, saying nothing, but by her silence manifesting to him how great was her grief at this sudden bereavement.

At last remembering her errand, she told him why she had come, and asked what she should say to Isabel.

"Tell her I shall not go," he said, "but she need not remain at home for that. The carriage can be ready at any time, and Alice will tell her the rest? You'll do it better than I."

Alice would rather that some one else should carry to Isabel tidings which she felt intuitively would be received with more pleasure than pain, but if Frederic requested it of her she would do it, and she started to return. To her the night and the day were the same, and ordinarily it mattered not whether there were lamps in the hall or not, but now, as she passed from the library into the adjoining room, there came over her a feeling of such utter loneliness and desolation that she turned back and said to Frederic:

"Will you go with me up the stairs, for now that Marian is dead, the night is darker than it ever was before."

He appreciated her feelings, and taking her by the hand, led her to the door of Isabel's room. Very impatiently Isabel had waited for her, wishing to know what hour Frederic intended starting, and if there would be time for Luce, her waiting maid, to curl her long, black hair. Accidentally she had overheard a gentleman say that if she wore curls she would be the most beautiful woman in Kentucky, and as he was to be present at the party she determined to prove his assertion.

"I hope that young one stays well," she said, angrily, as the moments went by, and at last, as Alice did not come, she bade Luce put the iron in the fire, and commence her operations.

The negress accordingly obeyed the orders, and six

long curls were streaming down the lady's back, while a seventh was wound around the hissing iron in close proximity to her ear, when Alice came in, and hurrying up to her side, began:

"Oh, Miss Huntington, poor, dear Marian wasn't dead all the time they thought she was. She was in New York, with Mrs. ——"

She did not finish the sentence; for, feeling certain that her treachery was about to be disclosed, the guilty Isabel jumped so suddenly as to bring the hot iron directly across her ear and a portion of her forehead. Maddened with the pain, and a dread of impending disgrace, she struck the innocent girl a blow which sent her reeling across the floor.

"Oh, Lordy!" exclaimed Luce, untwisting the hair so rapidly that a portion of it was torn from the head —"oh, Lordy! Miss Isabel, Alice never tached you;" and, throwing the iron upon the hearth, she hurried to the prostrate child, who had thrown herself upon the lounge and was sobbing so loud and hysterically that Isabel herself was alarmed, and while bathing her blistered ear, tried to stammer out some apology for what she had done.

"I supposed you carelessly ran against me," she said; "and it hurt me so I didn't know what I was doing. Pray, don't cry that way. You'll raise the house;" and she took hold of Alice's shoulder.

"I wish she would," muttered Luce; and, stooping down, she whispered: "Screech louder, so as to fotch Marster Frederic, and tell him jest how she done sarved you!"

But nothing could be further from Alice's mind than crying for effect. It was not so much the indignity she had suffered, nor yet the pain of the blow which made her weep so bitterly. It was rather the utter sense of desolation, the feeling that her last hope had drifted away with the certainty of Marian's death, and for a time she wept on passionately; while Isabel, with a hurricane in her bosom, walked the floor, wondering if her perfidy would ever be discovered, and feeling that she cared but little now whether it were, or not. Suspense was terrible, and when the violence of Alice's sobs had subsided, she said to her:

"Where is Marian, and when is she coming home?"

"Oh, never, never!" answered the child. "She can't come back, for she's dead now, Marian is;" and Alice covered her face again with her hands.

"Dead!" exclaimed Isabel, in a far different voice from that in which she had spoken before. "What do you mean?" and passing her arm very caressingly around the little figure lying on the lounge, she continued: "I am sorry I struck you, Alice. I didn't know what I was doing, and you must forgive me, will you, darling? There, dry your eyes, and tell me all about poor Marian. When did she die, and where?"

As well as she could for her tears, Alice told what she knew, and satisfied that she was in no way implicated, Isabel became still more amiable, even speaking pleasantly to Luce and telling her she might do what she pleased the remainder of the evening.

"Of course I shouldn't think of attending the party now, even if I were not so dreadfully burned. Poor Frederic! how badly he must feel!"

"He does," said Alice, "and he cried, too."

Isabel curled her proud lip contemptuously, and dipping her handkerchief again in the water, she applied it to her blistered ear, thinking to herself that he would probably be easily consoled. It would be proper, too, for her to commence the consoling process at once, by expressing her sympathy; and leaving Alice alone she went to the library where Frederic still was sitting, so absorbed in his own sad reflections that he did not observe her approach until she said, "Alice tells me you have heard from Marian," then he started suddenly, and turning toward her, answered, "Yes, you can read what is written here if you like," and he passed her McVicar's letter.

It did seem to Isabel that there was something familiar about the writing, particularly in the formation of the capitals, but she suspected no fraud, and accepted the whole as coming from Sarah Green.

"This is some new acquaintance Marian picked up," she thought. "The woman speaks of having known her but a short time. Probably she left Mrs. Daniel Burt and stumbled upon Sarah Green," and with an exultant smile upon her beautiful face, she put the letter down, and laying her hand very lightly on Frederic's shoulder, said, "I am sorry for you, Frederic, though it is better, of course, to know just what did become of the poor girl."

Frederic could not tell why it was that Isabel's words of sympathy grated harshly on his ear. He only knew that they did, and he was glad when she left him alone, telling him she should not, of course, attend the party, and saying in reply to his question as to what ailed her ear, that Luce, who was curling her hair, carelessly burned it.

"By the way," she continued, "when I felt the hot iron, I jumped and throwing out my hand accidentally hit Alice on her head, and, if you'll believe me, the sensitive child thinks I intended it, and has almost cried herself sick."

This falsehood she deemed necessary, in case the truth of the matter should ever reach Frederic through another channel, and feeling confident that she was safe in every respect, and that the prize she so much coveted was nearly won, she left him and sought her mother's chamber.

In the kitchen the news of Marian's certain death was received with noisy demonstrations—old Dinah and Hetty trying hard to outdo each other, and see which should shed the most and the biggest tears. The woollen aprons of both were brought into constant requisition, while Hetty rang so many changes upon the virtues of the departed that Uncle Phil became disgusted, and said "for his part he'd hearn enough 'bout dead folks. He liked Miss Marian as well as anybody, but he did up his mournin' them times that he wet hisself to the skin a tryin' to fish her out of the river. He thought his heart would bust then, though he knew all the time she wasn't thar, and he told 'em so, too. He knew she'd run away to New York, and he allus s'posed they'd hear she died summers at the South. He wan't disappointed. He could tell by his feelin's when anything was gwine to happen, and for more'n a week back he'd had it on his mind that Miss Marian was dead—they couldn't fool him!" and satisfied that he had impressed his audience with a sense of his foreknowledge, Uncle Phil pulled off his boots and started for bed, leaving Dinah and Hetty to discuss the matter at their leisure and speculate upon the probable result.

"I can tell you," said Dinah, "it won't be no time at all afore Marster'll be settin' to that Isabel, and if he does, I 'clar for't I'll run away, or hire out, see if I don't. I ain't a goin' to be sassed by none of yer low flung truck and hev 'em carryin' the keys. She may jest go back whar she come from, and I'll tell her so, too. I'll gin her a piece of my mind."

"She is gwine back," suggested Hetty, who, faithful to the memory of Miss Beatrice, admired Isabel on account of a fancied resemblance between the two. "Don't you mind how Marster is a gwine to move up to somewhar?"

"That's nothin'," returned Dinah. "They'll come back in the Fall, but I shan't be here. I'll hire myself out, and you kin be the head a spell."

This prospect was not an unpleasant one to Hetty, who looked with a jealous eye upon Dinah's rather superior position, and as a sure means of attaining the object of her ambition and becoming in turn the favorite, she warmly espoused the cause of Isabel, and waged many a battle of words with Dinah, who took no pains to conceal her dislike. Thus two or three weeks went by, and as nothing occurred to cause Dinah immediate alarm, her fears gradually subsided, until at last she forgot them altogether, while even Marian ceased to be a daily subject of conversation.

To Frederic reality was more endurable than suspense, for he could look the future in the face and think what he would do. He was free to marry Isabel, he believed; but, as was quite natural, he cared less about it now than when there was an obstacle in his way. There was no danger of losing her, he was sure, and he could wait as long as he pleased! Once he thought of going to New York to make some inquiries, and if possible find Marian's grave, but when he reflected that Sarah Green was on the ocean, even before her letter reached Kentucky, he decided to defer the matter until their removal to Yonkers, which was to take place about the middle of May. Isabel, too, had her own views upon the subject. There no longer existed a reason why Frederic should not address her, and in her estimation nothing could be more proper than to christen the new home with a bride. So she bent all her energies to the task, smiling her sweetest smile, saying her softest words, and playing the amiable lady to perfection. But it availed her nothing, and she determined at last upon a bolder movement.

Finding Frederic alone in the parlor, one day, she said:

"I suppose it will not affect you materially if mother and I leave when you remove to Yonkers. Agnes Gibson, you know, is soon to be married, and she has invited me to go with her to Florida, where, she says, I can procure a good situation as music-teacher, and mother wishes to go back to New Haven."

The announcement, and the coolness with which it was made, startled Frederic, and he replied, rather anxiously:

"I have never contemplated a separation. I shall need your mother there more than I do here, for I shall not have Dinah."

"Perhaps you can persuade her to stay, but I think it best for me to go," returned Isabel, delighted with her success.

Frederic Raymond did not wish Isabel to leave him, and, after a moment, he said:

"Why must you go, Isabel? Do you wish for a larger salary? Are you tired of us—of me?" And the last words were spoken hesitatingly, as if he doubted the propriety of his saying them.

"Oh, Frederic!" and in the soft, black eyes raised for an instant to his face, and then modestly withdrawn, there was certainly a tear! "Oh, Frederic!" was all she said, and Frederic felt constrained to answer: "What is it, Isabel? Why do you wish to go?"

"I don't—I don't," she answered, passionately; "but respect for myself demands it. People are already talking about my living here with you; and now poor Marian is dead and you are a widower, it will be tenfold worse. I wish they would let us alone, for I have been so happy here and am so much attached to Alice. It will almost break my heart to leave her!"

Isabel Huntington was wondrously beautiful then, and Frederic Raymond was sorely tempted to bid her stay, not as Alice's governess, nor yet as the daughter of his housekeeper, but as his wife and mistress of his house. Several times he tried to speak, and at last, crossing over to where she sat, he began—"Isabel, I have never heard that people were talking of you; there is no reason why they should, but if they are I can devise a method of stopping it and still keeping you with us. I have never spoken to you of—" love, he was going to say, and the graceful head was already bent to catch the sound, when a little voice chimed in, "Please, Frederic, I am here," and looking up they saw before them Alice.

She had entered unobserved and was standing just within the door, where she heard what Frederic said. Intuitively she felt what would follow next, and scarcely knowing what she did, she had apprised them of her presence.

"The brat!" was Isabel's mental comment, while Frederic was sensible of a feeling of relief, as if he had suddenly wakened from a spell, or been saved from some great peril. For several moments Isabel sat, hoping Alice would leave the room, but she did not, and in no very amiable mood the lady was herself constrained to go, by a call from her mother, who wished to see her on some trivial matter.

When she was gone, Alice groped her way to the sofa, and climbing upon it said to Frederic, "Won't you read me that letter again which Mrs. Green wrote to you?"

He complied with her request, and when he had finished, the child continued, "If Marian had really died, wouldn't she have sent some message to me, and wouldn't that woman have told us how she happened to be way off there, and all about it?"

"*If Marian really died!*" repeated Frederic. "Do you doubt it?"

"Yes," returned the child, "Marian loved me most as well as she did you, and she surely would have talked of me and sent me some word; then, too, is there much difference between scarlet fever and canker-rash? Don't some folks call it by both names?"

"I believe they do," said Frederic, wondering to what all this was tending.

"Marian had the scarlet fever, and I, too, just after I came here," was Alice's next remark. "You were at college, but I remember it, and so does Dinah, for I asked her a little while ago. Can folks have it twice?" and the blind eyes looked up at Frederic, as if sure that this last argument at least were proof conclusive of Marian's existence.

"Sometimes, but not often," answered Frederic, the shadow of a doubt creeping into his own mind.

"And if they do," persisted Alice, who had been consulting with Dinah—"if they do, they seldom have it hard enough to die, so Dinah says; and I don't believe that was a good, true letter. Somebody wrote it, to be wicked. Marian is alive, I almost know."

"Must you see her dead body, to be convinced?" asked Frederic, a little impatiently; and Alice rejoined:

"No, no; but somehow it don't seem right for you to—to—oh, Frederic!" and, bursting into tears, she came at once to the root of the whole matter.

She had thought a great deal about the letter, wondering why Marian had failed to speak of her, and at last rejecting it as an impossibility. Suddenly, too, she remembered that once, when she and Marian were sick, she heard some of the neighbors speak of their disease as scarlet fever, while others called it the canker-rash; and all united in saying they could have it but once. This had led to inquiries of Dinah, and had finally resulted in her conviction that Marian might possibly be living. Full of this new idea, she had hastened to Frederic, and accidentally overheard what he was saying to Isabel. She comprehended it, too, and knew that but for her unexpected presence he would, perhaps, have asked the lady to be his wife, and she felt again as if Marian were there urging her to stand once more between Frederic and temptation. All this she told to him, and the proud, haughty man, who would have spurned a like interference from any other source, listened patiently to the pleadings of the childish voice, which said to him so earnestly:

"Don't let Isabel be your wife!"

"What objection have you to her?" he asked; and when she replied, "She isn't good," he questioned her further as to the cause of her dislike—"was there really a reason, or was it mere prejudice?"

"I try to like her," said Alice, "and sometimes I do real well, but she don't act alone with me like she does when you are round. She'll be just as cross as fury, and if you come in, she'll smooth my hair and call me 'little pet.'"

"Does she ever strike you?" asked Frederic, feeling a desire to hear Alice's version of that story.

Instantly tears came in Alice's eyes, and she replied, "Only once—and she said she didn't mean that—but, Frederic, she did," and in her own way Alice told the story, which sounded to Mr. Raymond more like the truth than the one he had heard from Isabel. Gradually the conviction was forcing itself upon him that Isabel was not exactly what she seemed. Still he could not suddenly shake off the chain which bound him, and when Alice said to him in her odd, straightforward way, "Don't finish what you were saying to Isabel until you've been to New York and found if the letter is true," he answered, "Fie, Alice, you are unreasonable to ask such a thing of me. Marian is dead. I have no doubt of it, and I am free from the promise made to you more than a year since."

"May be she isn't," was Alice's reply, "and if she is, we shall both feel better, if you go and see. Go, Frederic, do. It won't take long, and if you find she is really dead, I'll never speak another naughty word of Isabel, but try to love her just as I want to love your wife. Will you go, Frederic? I heard you say you ought to see the house before we moved, and Yonkers is close to New York, isn't it?"

This last argument was more convincing than any which Alice had offered, for Frederic had left the entire management of repairs to one whom he knew understood such matters better than himself, consequently he had not been there at all, and he had several times spoken of going up to see that all was right. Particularly would he wish to do this if he took thither a bride in May, and to Alice's suggestion he replied, "I might, perhaps, do that for the sake of gratifying you."

"Oh, if you only would!" answered Alice. "You'll find her somewhere—I know you will—and then you'll be so glad you went."

Frederic was not quite so sure of that, but it was

safe to go, and while Isabel had been communicating to her mother what he had been saying to her, and asking if it were not almost a proposal, he was deciding to start for New York immediately. Alice's reasons for doubting the authenticity of the letter seemed more and more plausible the longer he thought of them, and at supper that night he astonished both Mrs. Huntington and daughter by saying that he was going North in a few days, and he wished the former to see that his wardrobe was in a proper condition for traveling. Isabel's face grew dark as night, and the wrathful expression of her eyes was noticable even to him. "There is a good deal of temper there," was his mental comment, while Isabel feigned some trivial excuse and left the room to hide the anger she knew was visible upon her face. He had commenced proposing to her, she was sure, and he should not leave Redstone Hall until he explained himself more fully. Still it would not be proper for her to broach the subject—her mother must do that. It was a parent's duty to see that her daughter's feelings were not trifled with, and by dint of cajolery, entreaties and threats, she induced the old lady to have a talk with Frederic, and ask him what his intentions were.

Mrs. Huntington was not very lucid in her remarks, and without exactly knowing what she meant, Frederic replied at random that he was in earnest in all he had said to Isabel about her remaining there, that he did not wish her to go away for she seemed one of the family, and that he would speak with her further upon the subject when he came back. This was not very definite, but Mrs. Huntington brushed it up a little ere repeating it to Isabel, who readily accepted it as an intimation that after his return, he intended asking her directly to be his wife. Accordingly she told Agnes Gibson confidentially what her expectations were, and Agnes told it confidentially to several others, who had each a confidential friend, and so in course of a few days it was generally understood that Redstone Hall was to have another mistress. Agnes in particular was very busy disseminating news, hoping by this means to turn the public gossip from herself and the white-haired man, or rather the plantation in Florida, which she was soon to marry. In spite of her protestations to the contrary people would say that *money* and not *love* actuated her choice, and she was glad of anything which would give her a little rest. So she repeated Isabel's story again and again, charging each and every one never to mention it and consulting between-times with her bosom friend as to what her arrangements were, and suggesting that they be married on the same day and so make the same tour. On the subject of bridal presents Agnes had a kind of mania, and knowing this, some of her friends, who lived at a distance and could not be present at the ceremony, sent their's in advance—several of them as a matter of course deciding upon the same thing, so that in Agnes' private drawer there were now deposited *three fish knives and forks*, all of which were the young lady's particular aversion. She would dispose of one of them at all hazards, she thought, and receive more than an equivalent in return, so she began to pave the way for a costly bridal present from the future Mrs. Frederic Raymond, by hinting of an elegant *fish knife and fork*, which in its satin-lined box would look handsomely upon the table, and Isabel, though detesting the article and thinking she should prefer almost anything else, said she was delighted, and when her friend came home from the south, she should invite her to dinner certainly once a week.

This arrangement wae generally understood, as were many others of a similar nature, until at last even the bridal dress was selected, and people said it was making in Lexington, where Frederic was well known, and where the story of his supposed engagement circulated rapidly, reaching to the second-rate hotel where Rudolph McVicar was a boarder. Exultingly his wild eyes flashed, and when he heard, as he did, that the wedding was fixed for the 20th of May, which he knew was Isabel's birthday, he counted the hours which must elapse ere the moment of his triumph came. And while he waited thus, and rumor, with her lying tongue, told each day some fresh falsehood of "that marriage in high life," Frederic Raymond went on his way, and with each milestone passed, drew nearer and nearer to the lost one—the Marian who would stand between him and Isabel.

CHAPTER XV.

THE HOUSE ON THE RIVER.

"MARIAN," said Ben, one pleasant April morning, "Frederic's house is finished in tip-top style, and if you say so, we'll go out and take a look. It will do you good to see the old place once more and know just how things are fixed."

"Oh, I'd like it so much," returned Marian, "but what if I should fall upon Frederic?"

"No danger," answered Ben; "the man who has charge of everything told me he wasn't comin' till May, and the old woman who is tendin' to things knows I have seen Mr. Raymond, for I told her so, and she won't think nothin'; so clap on your clothes in a jiff, for we've barely time to reach the cars."

Marian did not hesitate long ere deciding to go, and in a few moments they were in the street. As they were passing the ——— Hotel, Ben suddenly left her, and running up the steps spoke to one of the servants with whom he was acquainted. Returning ere long, he said, by way of apology, "I was in there last night to see Jim, and he told me there was a man took sick with a ravin' fever, pretty much like you had when you bit your tongue most in two."

Marian shuddered involuntarily, and without knowing why, felt a deep interest in the stranger, thinking how terrible it was to be sick and alone in a crowded, noisy hotel.

"Is he better?" she asked, and Ben replied, "No,

ten times wus—he'll die most likely. But hurry up—here's the omnibus we want," and in the excitement of securing a seat, they both forgot the sick man.

The trip to Yonkers was a pleasant one, for to Marian it seemed like going home, and when, after reaching the station, they entered the lumbering stage and wound slowly up the long, steep hill, she recognized many familiar way marks, and drawing her vail over her face, wept silently as she remembered all she had passed through since the night when Col. Raymond first took her up that same long hill, and told her by the way, of his boy Frederic, who would be delighted with a sister. The fond old man was dead now, and she, the little girl he had loved so much, was a sad lonely woman, going back to visit the spot which had been so handsomely fitted up without a thought of her.

The house itself was greatly changed, but the view it commanded of the river and the scenery beyond was the same, and leaning against a pillar Marian tried to fancy that she was a child again and listening for the bold footsteps of the handsome, teasing boy, once her terror and her pride. But all in vain she listened: the well-remembered foot-fall did not come: the handsome boy was not there, and even had he been, she would scarcely have recognized him in the haughty, elegant young man, her husband. Yes, he was her husband, and she repeated the name to herself, and when at last Ben touched her on the shoulder, saying, "I have told Miss Russell my sister was here, and she says you can go over the house," she started as if waking from a dream.

"Let us go through the garden first," she said, as she led the way to the maple tree where summers before che had built her little play-house, and where on the bark, just as high as his head then came, the name of Frederic was cut.

Far below it, and at a point which her red curls had reached, there was another name—her own—and

Frederic's jack-knife had made that, too, while she stood by and said to him, "I wish I was Marian Raymond, instead of Marian Lindsey."

How distinctly she remembered the characteristic reply:

"If you should happen to be my wife, you would be Marian Raymond; but pshaw, I shall marry a great deal prettier woman than you will ever be, and you may live with us if you want to, and take care of the children. I mean to have a lot!"

She had not thought of this speech in years, but it come back to her vividly now, as did many other things which had occurred there long ago. Within the house everything was changed, but they had no trouble in identifying the different rooms, and she lingered long in the one she felt sure was intended for Frederic himself, sitting in the chair where she knew he would often sit, and wondering if, while sitting there, he would ever think of her. Perhaps he might be afraid of meeting her accidentally in New York, and so he would seldom come there; or, if he did, it would be after dark, or when she was not in the street, and thus she should possibly never see him, as she hoped to do. The thought was a sad one, and never before had the gulf between herself and Frederic seemed so utterly impassible as on that April morning when, in his room and his arm chair, the girl-wife sat and questioned the dark future of what it had in store for her.

Once she was half tempted to leave some momento—something which would tell him she had been there. Sne spurned the idea as soon as formed. She would not intrude herself upon him a second time, and rising at last, she arranged the furniture more to her taste, changed the position of a picture, moved the mirror into a perfect angle, set Frederic's chair before the window looking out upon the river, and then, standing in the door, fancied that she saw him, with his handsome face turned to the light, and his rich brown hair shading his white brow. At his feet, and not far away was a little stool, and if she could only sit there once, resting her head upon his knee and hear him speaking to her kindly, affectionately, she felt that she would gladly die, and leave to another the caresses she could never hope to receive.

Isabel's chamber was visited next, and Marian's would have been less than a woman's nature could she have looked, without a pang, upon the costly furniture and rare ornaments which had been gathered there. In the disposal of the furniture there was a lack of taste—a decidedly Mrs. Russell air; but Marian had no wish to interfere. There was something sickening in the very atmosphere of her rival's apartment, and with a long, deep sigh, she turned away. Opening the door of an adjoining chamber, she stood for a moment motionless, while her lips moved nervously, for she knew that this was Alice's room. It was smaller than the others, and with its neat white furniture, seemed well adapted to the pure, sinless child who was to occupy it. Here too, she tarried long, gazing, through blinded tears, upon the little rocking-chair just fitted to Alice's form, looping up the soft lace custains, brushing the dust from the marble mantle, and patting lovingly the snowy pillows, for the sake of the fair head which would rest there some night.

"There are no flowers here," said she, glancing at the tiny vases on the stand. "Alice is fond of flowers, and though they will be withered ere she comes, she will be sure to find them, and who knows but their faint perfume may remind her of me," and going out into the garden she gathered some hyacinths and violets which she made into boquets and placed them in the vases, and bidding the old woman change the water every day, until they began to fade, and then leave them to dry until the blind girl came. "Ben told me of her; he once staid at Redstone Hall all night," she said, in answer to the woman's inquiring look. "He says she is a sweet young creature, and I thought flowers might please her."

"Fresh ones would," returned Mrs. Russell "but them that's withered ain't no use. S'pose I fling 'em away when they get old and put in some new the day she comes?"

"No, no, not for the world, leave them as they are," and Marian spoke so earnestly that the old lady promised compliance with her request.

"Be you that Yankee peddler's sister," she asked, as she followed Marian down the stairs. "If you be, nater cut up a curis caper with one or t'other of you, for you ain't no more alike than nothin'."

"I believe I do not resemble him much," was Marian's evasive answer, as with a farewell glance at the old place, she bade Mrs. Russell good-by and went with Ben to the gate where the stage was waiting to take them back to the depot.

It was dark when they reached New York, and as they passed the ——— Hotel a second time, Marian spoke of the sick man, and wondered how he was.

"I might go in and see," said Ben, "but it's so late I guess I won't, particularly as he's nothin' to us."

"But he's something to somebody," returned Marian, and as she followed on after Ben, her thoughts turned continually upon him, wondering if he had a mother —a sister—or a wife. and if they knew how sick he was.

While thus reflecting they reached home, where they found Mrs. Burt entertaining a visitor—a Martha Gibbs, who for some time had been at the ——— Hotel, in the capacity of chamber-maid, but who was to leave there the next day. Martha's parents lived in the same New England village where Mrs. Burt had formerly resided, and the two thus became acquainted, Martha making Mrs. Burt the depository of all her little secrets and receiving in return much motherly advice. She was to be married soon, and though her destination was a log house in the West, and her bridal *trousseau* consisted merely of three dresses—a silk, a delaine and a calico—it was an affair of great consequence to her, and she had come as usual to talk it over with Mrs. Burt, feeling glad at the absence of Ben and Marian, the latter of whom she supposed was an orphan neice of her friend's husband. The return of the young people operated as a restraint upon her, and changing the conversation, she spoke at last of a sick man who was up in the third story in one of the rooms of which she had the charge.

"He had the typhoid fever," she said, "and was raving distracted with his head. They wanted some good experienced person to take care of him, and had asked her to stay, she seemed so handy, but she couldn't. John wouldn't put their wedding off, she knew, and she must go, though she did pity the poor young man—he raved and took on so, asking them if anybody had seen *Marian*, or knew where she was buried!"

Up to this point Marian had listened, because she knew it was the same man of whom Ben had told her in the morning; but now the pulsations of her heart stopped, her head grew dizzy, her brain whirled, and she was conscious of nothing except that Ben made a hurried movement and then passed his arm around her, while he held a cup of water to her lips, sprinkling some upon her face, and saying, in a natural voice, "Don't you want a drink? My walk made me awful dry."

It was dark in the room, for the lamp was not yet lighted, and thus Martha did not see the side-play going on. She only knew that Ben was offering Marian some water; but Mrs. Burt understood it, and, when sure that Marian would not faint, she said:

"Where did the young man come from, and what is his name? Do you know?"

"He registered himself as *F. Raymond, Franklin County, Kentucky*," returned the girl; "and that's the bother of it. Nobody knows where to direct a letter to his friends. But how I have staid. I must go this minute," and greatly to the relief of the family, Martha took her leave.

Scarcely had the door closed after her, when Marian was on her knees, and, with her head in Mrs. Burt's lap, was begging of her to offer her services as nurse to Frederic Raymond!

"He must not die there alone," she cried. "Say you will go, or my heart will burst. They know Martha for a trusty girl, and they will take you on her recommendation. Help me, Ben, to persuade her," she continued, appealing to the young man, who had not yet spoken upon the subject.

He had been thinking of it, however, and as he could see no particular objection, he said, at last:

"May as well go, I guess. It won't do no hurt, any how, and mebby it'll be the means of savin' his life. You can tell Martha how't you s'pose he'll pay a good price for nussin', and she'll think it's the money you are after."

This suggestion was so warmly seconded by Marian, that Mrs. Burt finally consented to seeing Martha, and asking her what she thought of the plan. Accordingly, early the next morning, she sought an interview with the young woman, inquiring, first, how the stranger was, and then, continuing—

"What do you think of my turning nurse awhile and taking care of him? I am used to such folks, and I presume the gentleman is plenty able to pay."

She had dragged this last in rather bunglingly, but it answered every purpose, for Martha, who knew her thrifty habits, understood at once that money was the inducement, and she replied, "Of course he is. His watch is worth two hundred dollars, to say nothing of a diamond pin. I for one shall be glad to have you come, for I am going away some time to-day, and there'll be nobody in particular to take care of him. I'll speak about it right away."

The result of this speaking was that Mrs. Burt's

offered services were readily accepted, for Martha was known to be an honest, faithful girl, and any one whom she recommended must, of course, be respectable and trusty. By some chance, however, there was a misunderstanding about the name, which was first construed into Burton and then into Merton, and as Martha, who alone could rectify the error, left that afternoon, the few who knew of the sick man and his nurse, spoke of the latter as a "Mrs. Merton, from the country, probably." So when at night Mrs. Burt appeared and announce herself as ready to assume her duties, she was surprised at hearing herself addressed by her new name, and she was about to correct it when she thought, "It doesn't matter what I'm called, and perhaps on the whole, I'd rather not be known by my real name. I don't believe much in goin' out nussin' any way, and I guess I'll let 'em call me what they want to."

She accordingly made no explanation, but followed the servant girl up three long flights of stairs, and turning down a narrow hall, stood ere long at the door of the sick room.

CHAPTER XVI.

THE FEVER.

Night and day Frederic Raymond had traveled, never allowing himself a minute's rest, nor even stopping at Yonkers, so intent was he upon reaching New York and finding, if possible, some clue to Marian. It was a hopeless task, for he had no starting point—nothing which could guide him in the least, save the name of Sarah Green, and even that was not in the Directory, while to inquire for her former place of residence, was as preposterous as Marian's inquiry for Mrs. Daniel Burt! Still, whatever he could do he did, traversing street after street, threading alley after alley, asking again and again of the squalid heads thrust from the dingy windows, if Sarah Green had ever lived in that locality, and receiving always the same impudent stare and short answer, "No."

Once, in another and worse part of the city, he fancied he had found her, and that she had not sailed for Scotland as she had written, for they had told him that "Sal Green lived up in the fourth story," and climbing the crazy stairs, he knocked at the low, dark door, shuddering involuntarily and experiencing a feeling of mortified pride as he thought it possible that Marian—his wife—had toiled up that weary way to die. The door was opened by a blear-eyed, hard-faced woman, who started at sight of the elegant stranger, and to his civil questions replied rather gruffly, "Yes, I'm Sal Green, I s'pose, or Sarah, jest which you choose to call me, but the likes of Marian Lindsey never came near me," and glancing around the dirty, wretched room, Frederic was glad that it was so. He would rather not find her, or hear tidings of her, than to know that she had lived and died in such a place as this, and with a sickening sensation he was turning away, when the woman, who was blessed with a remarkable memory and never forgot anything to which her attention was particularly directed, said to him, "You say it's a year last Fall sence she left home."

"Yes, yes," he replied eagerly, and she continued, "You say she dressed in black, and wore a great long vail?"

"The same, the same," he cried, advancing into the room and thrusting a bill into the long hand, "oh, my good woman, have you seen her, and where is she now?"

"The Lord knows, mebby, but I don't," answered the woman, who was identical with the one who had so frightened Marian by watching her on that day when she sat in front of Trinity and wished that she could die, "I don't know as I ever seen her at all," she continued, "but a year ago last November such a girl as you described, with long curls that looked red in the sunshine, sat on the steps way down by Trinity and cried so hard that I noticed her, and knew she warn't a beggar by her dress. It was gettin' dark, and I was goin' to speak to her when Joe Black came up and asked her what ailed her, or somethin'. He ain't none of the likeliest," and a grim smile flitted over the visage of the wrinkled hag.

"Oh, Heaven," cried Frederic, pressing his hands to his head, as if to crush the horrid fear. "God save her from that fate. Is this all you know? Can't you tell me any more? I'll give you half my fortune if you'll bring back my poor, lost Marian, just as she was when she left me."

The offer was a generous one, and Sal was tempted for a moment to tell him some big lie, and thus receive a companion to the bill she clutched so greedily, but the agonizing expression of his white face kindled a spark of pity within her bosom, and she replied, "I did not finish tellin' you that while Joe was talking and had seemingly persuaded her to go with him, a tall chap that I never seen before knocked him flat, and took the girl with him, and that's why I remember it so well."

"Who was he, this tall man? Where did he go?" and Frederic wiped from his forehead the great drops of sweat forced out by terrible fear.

"I told you I never seen him before," was Sally's answer, "but he had a good face—a milk and water face—as if he never plotted no mischief in his life. She's safe with him, I'm sure. I'd trust my daughter with him, if I had one, and know he wouldn't harm her. He spoke to her tender-like, and she looked glad, I thought."

Frederic felt that this information was better than none, for it was certain it was Marian whom the woman had seen, and, in a measure comforted by her assurance of Ben Burt's honesty, he bade her good morning, and walked away.

At last, worn out and discouraged, he returned to his hotel, where he lay now burning with fever, and, in his delirium, calling sometimes for Isabel, sometimes for Alice, and again for faithful Dinah, but never asking why Marian did not come. She was dead, and he only begged of those around him to take her away from Joe Black, or show him where her grave was made, so he could go home and tell the blind girl he had seen it. Every ray of light which it was possible to shut out had been excluded from the room, for he had complained much of his eyes, and when Mrs. Burt entered, she could discover only the outline of a ghastly face resting upon the pillows, scarcely whiter than itself. It was a serious case, the attending physician said, and so she thought when she looked into his wild, bright eyes, and felt his rapid pulse. To her he put the same question he had asked nearly of every one:

"Do you know where Marian is?"

"Marian!" she repeated, feeling a little uncertain how to answer.

"Humor him! say you do!" whispered the physician, who was just taking his leave. And very truthfully Mrs. Burt replied:

"Yes, I know where she is! She will come to you to-morrow."

"No!" he answered mournfully. "The dead never come back, and it must not be, either. Isabel is coming then, and the two can't meet together here, for—. Come nearer, woman, while I tell you I loved Isabel the best, and that's what made the trouble. She is beautiful, but Marian was good—and do you know Marian was the Heiress of Redstone Hall; but I'm not going to use her money."

"Yes, I know," returned Mrs. Burt, trying to quiet him, but in vain.

He would talk—sometimes of Marian, and sometimes of Sarah Green, and the dreary room where he had been.

"It made Marian tired," he said, "to climb those broken stairs—tired, just as he was now. But she was resting so quietly in Heaven. and the April sun was shining on her grave. It was a little grave—a child's grave, as it were—for Marian was not so tall nor so old as Isabel."

In this way he rambled on, and it was not until the morning dawned that he fell into a heavy sleep, and Mrs. Burt had leisure to reflect upon the novel position in which she found herself.

"It was foolish in me to give up to them children," she said, "but now that I am here, I'll make the best of it, and do as well as I can. Marian shan't come, though! It would kill her dead to hear him going on."

Mrs. Burt was a little rash in making this assertion,

for even while she spoke, Marian was in the reception-room below, inquiring for the woman who took care of Mr. Raymond. Not once during the long night had she eyelids closed in sleep, and with the early morning she had started for the hotel, leaving Ben to get his breakfast as he could.

"Say Marian Grey wishes to see her," she said, in answer to the inquiry as to what name the servant was to take to No. ———

"My goodness!" exclaimed Mrs. Burt; "why didn't Ben keep her at home?" and, gliding down the stairs, she tried to persuade Marian to return.

But when she saw the firm, determined expression in the young girl's eye, she knew it was useless to reason with her, and saying, rather pettishly, "You mu t expect to hear some cuttin' things," she bade her follow up the stairs. Frederic still lay sleeping, his face turned partly to one side, and his hand resting beneath his head. His rich brown hair, now damp with heavy moisture, was pushed back from his white forehead, which, gleaming through the dusky darkness, first showed to Marian where he lay. The gas light hurt his eyes, and the lamp, which was kept continually burning, was so placed that its dim light did not fall on him, and a near approach was necessary to tell her just how he looked. He was fearfully changed, and, with a bitter moan, she laid her head beside him on the pillow, so that her short curls mingled with his darker locks, and she felt his hot breath on her cheek.

"Frederic—dear Frederic!" she said, and at the sound of her voice he moved uneasily, as if about to waken.

"Come away, come away," whispered Mrs. Burt. "He may know you, and a sudden start would kill him."

But Marian was deaf to all else save the whispered words dropping from the sick man's lips. They were of home, of Alice, of the library, and oh, joy! could it be she heard aright—did he speak of her? Was it

Marian he said? Yes, *it was Marian*, and with a cry of delight, which started Mrs. Burt to her feet, and penetrated even to the ear of the unconscious Frederic, she pressed her lips upon the very spot which they had touched before on that night when she gave him her first kiss. Slowly his eyes unclosed, but the wildness was still there, and Mrs. Burt, who stood anxiously watching him, felt glad that it was so. Slowly they wandered about the room, resting first upon the door, then on the chandelier, then on the ceiling above, and dropping finally lower, until at last they met and were riveted upon Marian, who, with clasped hands, stood breathlessly awaiting the result.

"Will he know her? Does he know her?" was the mental query of Mrs. Burt; while Marian's fast-breathing heart asked the same question eagerly. There was a wavering, a fierce struggle between delirium and reason, and then, with a faint smile, he said:

"Did you kiss me just now?" and he pointed to the spot upon his forehead.

Marian nodded, for she could not speak, and he continued:

"Marian kissed me there, too! Little Marian, who went away, and it has burned and burned into my veins until it set my brain on fire. Nobody has kissed me since, but Alice. Did you know Alice, girl?"

"Yes," answered Marian, keen disappointment swelling within her bosom and forcing the great tears from her eyes.

She had almost believed he would recognize her, but he did not; and sinking down by his side, she buried her face in the bed clothes, and sobbed aloud.

"Don't cry, little girl," he said, evidently disturbed at the sight of her tears. "I cried when I thought Marian was dead, but that seems so long ago."

"Oh Frederic—" and forgetful of everything, Marian sprang to her feet. "Oh, Frederic, is it true? Did you cry for me?"

At the sound of his own name the sick man looked

bewildered, while reason seemed struggling again to assert its rights, and penetrate the misty fog by which it was enveloped. Very earnestly he looked at the young girl, who returned his gaze with one in which was concentrated all the yearning love and tenderness, she had cherished for him so long.

"Are you Marian?" he asked, and in an instant the excited girl wound her arms around his neck, and laying her cheek against his own, replied:

"Yes, Frederic yes. Don't you know me, your poor lost Marian?"

Very caressingly he passed his hand over her short silken curls—pushed them back from her forehead—examined them more closely, and then whispered mournfully,

"No, you are not Marian. This is not her hair. But I like you," he continued, as he felt her tears drop on his face; "and I wish you to stay with me, and when the pain comes back charm it away with your soft hands. They are little hands," and he took them between his own, "but not so small as Marian's were when I held one in my hand and promised I would love her. It seemed like some tiny rose leaf, and I could have crushed it easily, but I did not; I only crushed her heart, and she fled from me forever, for 'twas a lie I told her," and his voice sunk to a lower tone. "I didn't love her then—I don't know as I love her now, for Isabel is so beautiful. Did you ever see Isabel, girl?"

"Oh, Frederic," groaned Marian, and wresting her hands from his gaasp, she tottered to a chair, while he looked after her wistfully.

"Will she go away?" he said to Mrs. Burt. "Will she leave me alone, when she knows Alice is not here nor Isabel? I wish Isabel would come, don't you?"

There was another moan of anguish, and, rolling his bright eyes in the direction of the arm chair, the poor man whispered:

"Hark! that's the sound I heard the night Marian

went away! I thought then 'twas the wind, but I knew afterwards that it was she, when her soul parted with her body, and it's followed me ever since. There is not a spot at Redstone Hall that is not haunted with that cry. I've heard it at midnight, at noon-day—in the storm and in the rushing river—where we thought she was buried. All but Alice—she knew she wasn't, and she sent me here to look. She don't like Isabel, and is afraid I'll marry her. Maybe I shall, sometime! Who knows?"

And he laughed in delirious glee.

"Heaven keep me, too, from going mad?" cried Marian. "Oh! why did I come here?"

"I told you not to all the time," was Mrs. Burt's consolatory remark; which, however was lost on Marian, who, seizing her bonnet and shawl, rushed from the room, unmindful of the out-stretched arms which seemed imploring her to stay.

The fresh morning air revived her fainting strength, but did not cool the feverish agony at her heart, and she sped onward, until she reached her home, where she surprised Ben at his solitary breakfast, which he had prepared himself.

"Oh! Ben, Ben!" she cried, coming so suddenly upon him that he upset the coffee-pot into which he was pouring some hot water. "Would it be wicked for you to kill me dead, or for me to kill myself?"

"What's to pay now?" asked Ben, using the skirt of his coat for a holder in picking up the steaming coffee-pot.

Very hastily Marian related her adventures in the sick room, telling how Frederic had talked of marrying Isabel before her very face.

"Crazy as a loon," returned Ben. "I shouldn't think nothin' of that. You say he talked as though he thought you was dead, and of course he don't know what he's sayin'. Have they writ to his folks?"

"Yes," returned Marian, who had made a similar inquiry of Mrs Burt. "They directed a letter to

'Frederic Raymond's friends, Franklin County, Kentucky,' but that may not reach them in a long time."

"Wouldn't it be a Christian act," returned Ben "for us, who know jest who he is, to telegraph to that critter, and have her come? By all accounts he wants to see her, and it may do him good."

Marian felt that it would be right, and, though it cost her a pang, she said, at last:

"Yes, Ben, you may telegraph; but what name will you append?"

"Benjamin Butterworth, of course," he replied. "They'll remember the peddler, and think it nateral I should feel an interest." And leaving Marian to take charge of the breakfast table, he started for the office.

Meantime the sick room was the scene of much excitement--Frederic raving furiously, and asking for "the girl with the soft hands and silken hair." Sometimes he called her Marian, and begged of them to bring her back, promising not to make her cry again.

"There is a mystery connected with this Marian he talks so much about," said the physician, who was present, "and he seems to fancy a resemblance between her and the girl who left here this morning. What may I call her name?"

"Marian, my daughter," came involuntarily from Mrs. Burt, whose mental rejoinder was, "God forgive me for that lie, if it was one. Names and things is gettin' so 'twisted up that it takes more than me to straighten 'em!"

"Well, then," continued the physician, "suppose you send for her. It will never do for him to get so excited. He is wearing out too fast."

"I will go for her myself," said Mrs. Burt, who fancied some persuasion might be necessary ere Marian could be induced to return.

But she was mistaken, for when told that Frederic's life depended upon his being kept quiet, and his being kept quiet depended upon her presence, Marian con sented, and nerved herself to hear him talk, as she knew he would, of her rival.

"If he lives, I will be satisfied," she thought, "even though he never did or can love me," and with a strong, brave heart, she went back again to the sick man, who welcomed her joyfully, and folding his feeble arms around her neck, stroked again her hair, as he said, "You will not leave me, Marian, till Isabel is here. Then you may go—back to the grave I cannot find, and we will go home together."

Marian could not answer him, neither was it necessary that she should. He was satisfied to have her there, and with her sitting at his side, and holding his hand in hers, he became as gentle as a child. Occasionally he called her "little girl," but oftener "Marian," and when he said that name, he always smoothed her hair, as if he pitied her, and knew he had done her a wrong. And Marian felt each day more and more that the wound she hoped had partly healed was bleeding afresh with a new pain, for while he talked of Marian as a mother talks of an unfortunate child, he spoke of Isabel with all a lover's pride, and each word was a dagger to the heart of the patient watcher, who sat beside him day and night, until her eyes were heavy, and her cheeks were pale with her unbroken vigils.

"Do you then love this Isabel so much?" she said to him one day, and sinking his voice to a whisper he replied, "Yes, and I love you, too, though not like her, because I loved her first."

"And Marian?" questioned the young girl, "Don't you love her?"

Oh, how eagerly she waited for the answer, which when it came almost broke her heart.

"Not as I ought to—not as I have prayed that I might, and not as I should, perhaps, if she hadn't been to me what she is. Poor child," he continued, brushing away the tears which rolled like rain down Marian's cheeks, "poor child, are you crying for Marian?"

"Yes—yes, for Marian—for poor heart-broken me;" and the wretched girl buried her face in the pillow beside him, for he held her firmly by the wrist, and she could not get away.

In this manner several days went by, and over the intellect so obscured there shone no ray of reason, while the girlish face grew whiter and whiter each morning light, and at last the physician said that she must rest, or her strength would be exhausted.

"Let me stay a little longer," she pleaded—"stay at least until Miss Huntington arrives."

"Miss who?" asked the doctor. "Do you then know his family?"

"A friend of mine knows them," answered Marian, a deep flush stealing over her cheek.

"I hope, then, they will reward you well," continued the physician. "The young man would have died but for you. It is remarkable what control you have over him."

But Marian wished for no reward. It was sufficient for her to know that she had been instrumental in saving his life, even though she had saved it for Isabel. The physician said that Frederic was better, and that afternoon, seated in the large arm-chair, she fell into a refreshing sleep, from which she was finally aroused by Mrs. Burt, who bending over her, whispered in her ear:

"Wake up. She's come—she's here—Miss Huntington!"

There was magic in that name, and it roused the sleeping girl at once, sending a quiver of pain through her heart, for her post she knew was to be given to another. Not both of them could watch by Frederic, and she, who in all the world had the best right to stay, must go; but not until she had looked upon her rival and had seen once the face which Frederic called so beautiful. This done, she would go away and die, if it were possible, and stand no longer between Frederic and the bride he so much desired. She did not understand why he had so often spoken of herself as being dead, when he knew that she was not. It was a vagary of his brain, she said—he had had many since she came there, and she hoped he would sometimes talk of her to Isabel, just as he had talked of Isabel to her. There was a hurried consultation between herself and Mrs. Burt, with regard to their future proceedings, and it was finally decided that the latter should remain a few days longer, and so report the progress of affairs to Marian, who, of course, must go away. This arrangement being made they sat down and rather impatiently waited for the coming of Isabel, who was in her room resting after her tiresome journey.

"Oh how can she wait so long?" thought Marian, glancing at Frederic, who was sleeping now more quietly than he had done before for a long time.

She did not know Isabel Huntington, and she could not begin to guess how thoroughly selfish she was, nor how that selfishness was manifest in every movement. The letter, which at last had gone to Frahkfort, was received the same day with the telegram, and as a natural consequence, threw the inmates of Redstone Hall into great excitement. Particularly was this the case with Isabel, who unmindful of everything, wrang her hands despairingly, crying out, "Oh! what shall I do if he dies?"

"Do!" repeated Dinah, forgetting her own grief in her disgust. "For the Lord's sake, can't you do what you allus did? Go back whar you come from, you and your mother, in course."

Isabel deigned no reply to this remark, but hurried to her chamber, where she commenced the packing of her trunk

"Wouldn't it look better for me to go?" suggested Mrs. Huntington, and Isabel answered:

"Certainly not, the telegram was directed to me. No one knows me in New York, and I don't care what folks say here. If he lives I shall be his wife, of course, else why should he send for me. It's perfectly natural that I should go." And thinking to herself that she would rather Frederic should die than to live for another, she completed her hasty preparations, and was on her way to the depot before the household had time to realize what they were doing.

In passing the house of Lawyer Gibson she could not forbear stopping a moment to communicate the sad news to her particular friend, who, while condoling with her, thought to herself, "He does care more for her than I supposed, or he would not have not sent for her."

"When will you come back?" she asked, and Isabel replied, "Not until he is better or worse. Oh, Agnes, what if he should die. Imagine Mr. Rivers at the point of death and you will know just how I feel."

"Certainly, very, indeed," was the meaningless answer of Agnes, who, as the day of her bridal drew near, began to fancy that she might be easily consoled in case anything should come between herself and the white haired Floridan. "Perhaps you will be married before you return," she suggested, and Isabel, who had thought of the same possibility, replied, "Don't, pray, speak of such a thing—it seems terrible when Frederic is so sick."

"You won't cotch the cars if you ain't keerful," chimed in Uncle Phil, and kissing each other a most affectionate good-by, the young ladies parted, Agnes thinking to herself, "I reckon I wouldn't go off to New York after a man who hadn't really proposed—but then it's just like her," while Isabel's mental comment was, "It's time Agnes was married, for she's really beginning to look old; I wouldn't have my grandfather though!"

So much for girlish friendships!

Distressed and anxious as Isabel seemed, it was no part of her intention to travel nights, for that would give her a sallow, jaded look; so she made the journey leisurely, and even after her arrival, took time to rest and beautify ere presenting herself to Frederic. She had ascertained that he was better, and had the best of care, so she remained quietly in her chamber an hour or so, and it was not until after dark that she bade the servant show her the way to the sick room.

"I will tell them you are coming," suggested the polite attendant, and, going on before her, he said to Mrs. Burt that "Miss Huntington would like to come in."

In the farthest corner in the room, where the shadows were the deepest, and where she would be the least observed, sat Marian, her hands clasped tightly together, her head bent forward, and her eyes fixed intently upon the door through which her rival would enter. Frederic was awake, and, missing her from her post, was about asking for her, when Isabel appeared, looking so fresh, so glowing, so beautiful, that for an instant Marian forgot everything in her admiration of the queenly creature, who, bowing civilly to Mrs. Burt, glided to the bedside, and sank upon her knees, gracefully—very gracefully—just as she had done at a private rehearsal in her own room! Tighter the little hands were clasped together, and the head which had dropped before was erect now, as Marian watched eagerly for what would follow next.

"Dear Frederic," said Isabel, and over the white face in the arm-chair the hot blood rushed in torrents for it seemed almost an insult to hear him thus addressed—"Dear Frederic, do you know me? I am Isabel:" and, unmindful of Mrs. Burt, or yet of the motionless figure sitting near, she kissed his burning forehead, and said again; "Do you know me?"

The nails were marking dark rings now in the tender flesh, while the blue eyes flashed until they grew almost as black as Isabel's, and still Marian did not move. She could not, until she heard what answer would be given. As the physician had predicted, Frederic was better since his refreshing sleep, and through the misty vail enshrouding his reason a glimmer of light was shining. The voice was a familiar one, and though it partly bewildered him, he knew who it was that bent so fondly over him. It was somebody from home, and with a thrill of pleasure akin to what one feels when meeting a fellow countryman far away on a foreign shore, he twined his arms around her neck, and said to her joyfully: "You are Isabel, and you've come to make me well."

Isabel was about to speak again, when a low sob startled her, and, turning in the direction from whence it came, she met a fierce, burning gaze which riveted her as by some magnetism to the spot, and for a moment the two looked intently into each other's eyes. Isabel and Marian, the one stamping indelibly upon her memory the lineaments of a face which had stolen and kept a heart which should have been her own, while the other wondered much at the strange white face which even through the darkness seemed quivering with pain.

Purposely Mrs. Burt stepped between them, and thus the spell was broken, Isabel turning again to Frederic, while Marian, unlocking her stiff fingers, grasped her bonnet and glided from the room so silently that Isabel knew not she was gone until she turned her head and found the chair empty.

"Who was that?" she said to Mrs. Burt—"that young girl who just went out?"

"My daughter," answered Mrs. Burt, again mentally asking forgiveness for the falsehood told, and thinking to herself, "Mercy knows it ain't my nater to lie, but when a body gets mixed up in such a scrape as this, I'd like to see 'em help it!"

After the first lucid interval, Frederic relapsed again into his former delirious mood, but did not ask for Marian. He seemed satisfied that Isabel was there, and he fell asleep again, resting so quietly that when it was eleven Isabel arose and said, "He is doing so well I believe I will retire. I never sat up with a sick person in my life, and should be very little assistance to you. That daughter of yours is somewhere around, I suppose, and will come if you need help."

Mrs. Burt nodded, thinking how different was this conduct from that of the unselfish Marian, who had watched night after night without giving herself the rest she absolutely needed. Isabel, on the contrary, had no idea of impairing her beauty, or bringing discomfort to herself by spending many hours at a time in that close, unwholesome atmosphere, and while Marian in her humble apartment was weeping bitterly, she was dreaming of returning to Kentucky as a bride. Frederic could scarcely do less than reward her kindness by marrying her as soon as he was able. She could take care of him so much better, she thought, and ere she fell asleep she had arranged it all in her own mind, and had fancied her mother's surprise at receiving a letter signed by her new name, "Isabel H. Raymond." She would retain the "H," she said. She always liked to see it, and she hoped Agnes Gibson, if she persisted in that foolish fancy of the fish-knife, would have it marked in this way!

It was long after daylight ere she awoke, and when she did her first thought was of her pleasant dream and her second of the girl she had seen the night before. "How white she was," she said, as she made her elaborate toilet, "and how those eyes of hers glared at me, as if I had no business here. Maybe she has fallen in love while taking care of him;" and Isabel laughed aloud at the very idea of a nursing woman's daughter being in love with the fastidious Frederic! Once she thought of Mrs. Daniel Burt, wondering where she lived, and half wishing she could find her, and, herself unknown, could question her of Marian.

"Maybe this Mrs. Merton knows something of her," she said, and thinking she would ask her if a good opportunity should occur, she gave an extra brush to her glossy hair, looked in a small hand mirror to see that the braids at the back of her head were right, threw open her wrapper a little more to show her flounced cambric skirt, and then went to the breakfast room, where three attendants, attracted by her style and the prospect of a fee, bowed obsequiously and asked what she would have. This occupied nearly another hour, and it was almost ten ere she presented herself to Mrs. Burt, who was growing very faint and weary.

At the physicain's request more light had been admitted into the room, and Frederic, who was much better this morning, recognized Isabel at once. He had a faint remembrance of having seen her the previous night, but it needed Mrs. Burt's assertion to con-confirm his conjecture, and he greeted her now as if meeting her for the first time. Many questions he asked of the people at home, and how they had learned of his illness.

"We received a letter and a telegram both," said Isabel, continuing, "You remember that booby peddler who sold Alice the bracelet and frightened the negroes so? Well, he must have telegraphed, for his name was signed to the dispatch, 'Benjamin Butterworth.'"

Mrs. Burt was very much occupied with something near the table, and Frederic did not notice her confusion as he replied, "He was a kind-hearted man, I thought, but I wonder how he heard of my illness, and where he is now. Mrs. Merton, has a certain Ben Butterworth inquired for me since I was sick?"

"I know nobody by that name," returned Mrs. Burt, and without stopping to think that her question might lead to some inquiries from Frederic, Isabel rejoined, "Well, do you know a Mrs. Daniel Burt?"

"Mrs. Daniel Burt!" repeated Frederic, as if trying to recall something far back in the past, while the lady in question started so suddenly as to drop the cup of hot water she held in her hand.

Stooping down to pick up the cup, she said something about its having burned her, and added, "I ain't much acquainted in the city, and never know my next door neighbors."

"Mrs. Daniel Burt," Frederic said again, "I have surely heard that name before. Who is she, Isabel?"

It was Isabel's turn now to answer evasively; but being more accustomed to dissimulate than her companion, she replied, quite as a matter of course, "You may have heard mother speak of her in New Haven. I used to know her when I was a little girl, and I believe she lives in New York. She was a very good, but common kind of woman, and one with whom I should not care to associate, though mother, I dare say, would be glad to hear from her."

"The impudent trollop," muttered Mrs. Burt, marvelling at the conversation, and wondering which was trying to deceive the other, Frederic or Isabel. "The former couldn't hoodwink her," she said, "even if he did Isabel. She understood it all, and he knew who Mrs. Daniel Burt was just as well as she did, for even if he had forgotten that she once lived with his father, Marian's letter had refreshed his memory, and he was only 'putting on' for the sake of misleading Isabel. But where in the world did that jade know her!" that was a puzzle, and settling it in her own mind that there were two of the same name, she left the room and went down to her breakfast.

During the day not a word was said of Marian. Isabel was evidently too much pleased with Frederic's delight at seeing her to think of anything else, while Mrs. Burt did not consider it necessary to speak of her. Frederic, too, for a time had forgotten her, but as the day drew near its close, he relapsed into a thoughtful mood, replying to Isabel's frequent remarks either in monosyllables or not at all. As the darkness increased he seemed to be listening intently, and when a step was heard upon the stairs or in the hall without, his face would light up with eager expectation and then be as suddenly overcast as the footstep passed his door. Gradually there was creeping into his mind a vague remembrance of something or somebody, which for many days had been there with him, gliding so noiselessly about the room that he had almost fancied it trod upon the air, and he could scarcely tell whether it were a spirit or a human being like himself. Little by little the outline so dimly discerned assumed a form, and the form was that of a young girl—a very fair young girl, with sweet blue eyes, and soft, baby hands, which had held his aching head and smoothed his tangled hair, oh, so many times. Her voice too, was low and gentle, and reminding him of some sad strain of music heard long, long ago. It seemed to him, too, that she called him Frederic, dropping hot tears upon his face. But where was she now? Why did't she come again, and who was she—that little blue-eyed girl? For a time the vision faded and all was confused again, but the reality came back ere long, and listening eagerly for something which never came, he thought and thought until great drops of sweat stood thickly upon his brow; and Isabel, wiping them away, became alarmed at the wildness of his eye and the rapid beating of his pulse. A powerful anodyne was adminstered, and he slept at last a fitful feverish sleep, which however, did him good, and in the morning he was better than he had been before.

Mrs. Burt, who had watched him carefully, knew that the danger was past, and that afternoon she left him with Isabel, while she went home, where she found Marian seriously ill, with Ben taking care of her in his kind but awkward manner.

"Did Frederic remember me? Does he know I have been there?" were Marian's first questions, and when Mrs. Burt replied in the negative, she turned away whispering, mournfully, "It is just as well."

"He is doing well," said Mrs. Burt, "and as you need me more than he does now, I shall come home and let that Isabel take care of him. It wont hur't her any, the jade. She can telegraph for her mother if she chooses."

Accordingly, she returned to the sick-room, where she found Frederic asleep and Isabel reading a novel.

To her announcement of leaving, the latter made no objection. She was rather pleased than otherwise, for, as Frederic grew stronger, the presence of a third person, and a stranger, too, might be disagreeable. She would telegraph for her mother, of course, as she did not think it quite proper to stay there alone. But her mother was under her control; she could dispose of her at any time, so she merely stopped her reading long enough to say, "Very well, you can go if you like. How much is your charge?"

Mrs. Burt did not hesitate to tell her; and Isabel, who had taken care of Frederic's purse, paid her, and then resumed her book, while Mrs. Burt, with a farewell glance at her patient, went from the room, without a word of explanation as to where she could be found in case they wished to find her.

It was dark when Frederic awoke, and it was so still around him that he believed himself alone.

"They have all left me," he said; "Mrs. Merton, Isabel, and that other one, that being of mystery—who was she—who could she have been?" and shutting his eyes, he tried to bring her before him just as he had often seen her bending o'er his pillow.

He knew now that it was not a phantom of his brain, but a reality. There had been a young girl there, and when the world without was darkest, and he was drifting far down the river of death, her voice had called him back, and her hands had held him up so that he did not sink in the deep, angry waters. There were tears many times upon her face, he remembered, and once he had wiped them away, asking why she cried. It was a pretty face, he said, a very pretty face, and the sunny eyes of blue seemed shining on him even now, while the memory of her gentle acts was very, very sweet, thrilling him with an undefined emotion, and awakening within his bosom a germ of the undying love he was yet to feel for the mysterious stranger. She had called him Frederic, too, while he had called her Marian. She had answered to that came, she asked him of Isabel, and—oh, Heaven!" he cried, starting quickly and clasping both hands upon his head. Like a thunderbolt it burst upon him, and for an instant his brain seemed all on fire. "It was Marian!—it was Marian!" he essayed to say, but his lips refused to move, and when Isabel, startled by his sudden movement, struck a light and came to his bed-side, she saw that he had fainted!

In great alarm she summoned help, begging of those who came to go at once for Mrs. Merton. But no one knew of the woman's place of residence, and as she had failed to inquire, it was a hopeless matter. Slowly Frederic came back to consciousness, and when he was again alone with Isabel he said to her, "Where is that woman who took care of me?"

"She is gone," said Isabel. "Gone to her home."

"Gone," he repeated. "When did she go, and why?"

Isabel told him the particulars of Mrs. Burt's going, and he continued:

"Was there no one else here when you came? No young girl with soft blue eyes?" and he looked eagerly at her.

"Yes," she replied. "There was a queer acting thing sitting in the arm-chair the night I first came in—"

"Who was she, and where is she now?" he asked, and Isabel answered, "I am sure I don't know where she is, for she vanished like a ghost."

"Yes, yes; but who was she? Did she have no name?" and Frederic clutched Isabel's arm nervously.

"Mrs. Merton told me it was her daughter—that is all I know," said Isabel; and in a tone of disappointment he continued:

"Will you tell me just how she looked, and how she acted when you first saw her?"

"One would suppose you deeply interested in your nurse's daughter;" and the glittering black eyes flashed scornfully upon Frederic, who replied:

"I am interested, for she saved my life. Tell me, won't you, how she looked?"

"Well, then," returned Isabel pettishly, "she was about fifteen, I think—certainly not older than that. Her face was very white, with big, blue eyes, which glared at me like a wild beast's; and what is queerer than all, she actually sobbed when I, or rather you kissed me; perhaps you have forgotten that you did?"

He had forgotten it, for the best of reasons, but he did not contradict her, so intent was he upon listening to her story.

"I had not observed her particularly before; but when I heard that sound I turned to look at her, while she stared at me as impudently as if I had no business here. That woman stepped between us purposely I know, for she seemed excited; and when I saw the arm-chair again the girl was gone."

Thus far everything, except the probable age, had confirmed his suspicions; but there was one question more—an all-important one—and with trembling eagerness he asked:

"What of her hair? Did you notice that?"

"It was brown, I think," said Isabel—"short in her neck and curly round her forehead. I should say her hair was rather handsome."

With a sigh of disappointment Frederic turned upon his pillow, saying to her:

"That will do—I've heard enough."

Isabel's last words had brought back to his mind something which he had forgotten until now—the girl's hair was short, and he remembered distinctly twining the soft rings around his fingers. They were not long, red curls, like those described by Sally Green. It wasn't Marian's hair—it wasn't Marian at all; and in his weakness his tears dropped silently upon the pillow, for the disappointment was terrible. All that night and the following day he was haunted with thoughts of the young girl, and at last, determin ing to see her again and know if she were like Marian, he said to Isabel:

"Send for Mrs. Merton. I wish to talk with her."

"It is an impossibility," returned Isabel: "for, when she left us, I carelessly neglected to ask where she lived——"

"Inquire below, then," persisted Frederic. "Somebody will certainly know, and I must find her."

Isabel complied with his request, and soon returned with the information that no one knew aught of Mrs. Merton's whereabouts, though it was generally believed that she came from the country, and at the time of coming to the hotel was visiting friends in the city.

"Find her friends, then," continued Frederic, growing more and more excited and impatient.

This, too, was impossible, for everything pertaining to Mrs. Merton was mere conjecture. No one could tell where she lived, or whither she had gone; and the sick man lamented the circumstance so often that Isabel more than once lost her temper entirely, wondering why he should be so very anxious about a woman who had been well paid for her services—"yes, more than paid, for her price was a most exorbitant one."

Meantime, Mrs. Huntington, who, on the receipt of Isabel's telegram, had started immediately, arrived, laden with trunks, bandboxes, and bags, for the old lady was rather dressy, and fancied a large hotel a good place to show her new clothes. On learning that Frederic was very much better, and that she had been sent for merely on the score of propriety, she seemed somewhat out of humor—"Not that she wanted Frederic to die," she said, "and she was glad of course that he was getting well, but she didn't like to be scared the way she was; a telegram always made her stomach tremble so that she didn't get over it in a week; she had traveled day and night to get there, and didn't know what she could have done if she hadn't met Rudolph McVicar in Cincinnati."

"Rudolph!" exclaimed Isabel. "Pray, where is he now?"

"Here in this very hotel," returned her mother. "He came with me all the way, and seemed greatly interested in you, asking a thousand questions about when you expected to be married. Said he supposed Frederic's illness would postpone it awhile, and when I told him you wan't even engaged as I knew of, he looked disappointed. I believe Rudolph has reformed!"

"The wretch!" muttered Isabel, who rightly guessed that Rudolph's interest was only feigned.

He had heard of her sudden departure for New York, and had heard also (Agnes Gibson being the source whence the information came) that she might, perhaps, be married as soon as Frederic was able to sit up. Accordingly, he had himself started northward, stumbling upon Mrs. Huntington in Cincinnati, and coming with her to New York, where he stopped at the same hotel, intending to remain there and wait for the result. He did not care to meet Isabel face to face, while she was quite as anxious to avoid an interview with him; and after a few days she ceased to be troubled about him at all. Frederic absorbed all her thoughts, he appeared so differently from what he used to do—talking but little either to herself or her mother, and lying nearly all the day with his eyes shut, though she knew he was not asleep; and she tried in vain to fathom the subject of his reflections. But he guarded that secret well, and day after day he thought on, living over again the first weeks of his sickness in that chamber, until at last the conviction was fixed upon his mind that, spite of the short hair, spite of the probable age, spite of the story about Mrs. Merton's daughter, or yet the letter from Sarah Green, that young girl who had watched with him so long and then disappeared so mysteriously, was none other than Marian—his wife. He did not shudder now when he repeated that last word to himself. It sounded pleasantly, for he knew it was connected with the sweet, womanly love which had saved him from death. The brown hair which Isabel had mentioned he rejected as an impossibility. It had undoubtedly looked dark to her, but it was red still, though worn short in her neck, for he remembered that distinctly. Sarah Green's letter was a forgery—Alice's prediction was true, and Marian still lived.

But where was she now? Why had she left him so abruptly? and would he ever find her? Yes, he would, he said. He would spare no time, no pains, no money in the search; and when he found her he would love and cherish her as she deserved. He was beginning to love her now, and he wondered at his infatuation for Isabel, whose real character was becoming more and more apparent to him. His changed demeanor made her cross and fretful; while Alice Gibson's letter, asking when she was to be married, and saying people there expected her to return a bride, only increased her ill-humor, which manifested itself several times toward her mother, in Frederic's presence.

At last, in a fit of desperation, she wrote to Agnes Gibson that she never expected to be married—certainly not to Frederic Raymond—and if every young lady matrimonially inclined should nurse her intended husband through a course of fever, she guessed they would become disgusted with mankind generally, and that man in particular! This done, Isabel felt better—so much better indeed that she resolved upon another trial to bring about her desired object, and one day, about two weeks after her mother's arrival, she said to Frederic:

"Now that you are nearly well, I believe I shall go to New Haven, and, after a little, mother will come, too. I shall remain there, I think, though mother, I suppose, will keep house for you this year, as she has engaged to do."

To this suggestion Frederic did not reply just as she thought he would.

"It was a good idea," he said, "for her to visit her old home, and he presumed she would enjoy it." Then he added, very faintly: "Alice will need a teacher here quite as much as in Kentucky, and you can retain your situation if you choose."

Isabel bit her lip, and her black eyes flashed angrily as she replied:

"I am tired of teaching only one pupil, for there is nothing to interest me, and I am all worn out, too."

She did look pale, and, touched with pity, Frederic said to her, very kindly:

"You do seem weary, Isabel. You have been confined with me too long, and I think you had better go at once. I will run down to see you, if possible, before I return to Kentucky."

This gave her hope, and, drying her eyes, which were filled with tears, Isabel chatted pleasantly with him about his future plans, which had been somewhat disarranged by his unexpected illness. He could not now hope to be settled at Riverside, as he called his new home, until some time in June—perhaps not so soon—but he would let her know, he said, in time to meet him there.

A day or two after this conversation, Isabel started for New Haven, whither in the course of a week she was followed by both her mother and Rudolph, the latter of whom was determined not to lose sight of her until sure that the engagement, which he somewhat doubted, did not in reality exist.

CHAPTER XVII.

THE SEARCH.

WHEN the carriage containing Mrs. Huntington rolled away from the hotel, Frederic, who was standing upon the steps, experienced a feeling of relief in knowing that, as far as personal acquaintances were concerned, he was now alone and free to commence his search for Marian. Each day the conviction had been strengtnened that she was alive—that she had been with him a few weeks before—and now every energy should be devoted to finding her. Once he thought of advertising, but she might not see the paper, and as he rather shrank from making his affairs thus public, he abandoned the project, determining, however, to leave no other means untried; he would hunt the city over, inquire at every house, and then scour the surrounding country. It might be months, or it might be years, ere this were accomplished; but accomplish it he would, and with a brave, hopeful heart, he started out, taking first a list of all the Mertons in the Directory, then searching out and making of them the most minute inquiries, except, indeed, in cases where he knew, by the nature of their surroundings, that none of their household had officiated in the capacity of nurse. The woman who had taken care of him was poor and uneducated, and he confined himself mostly to that class of people.

But all in vain. No familiar face ever came at his call. Nobody knew her whom he sought—no one had heard of Marian Lindsey, and at last he thought of Sally Green, determining to visit her again, and, if possible, learn something more of the girl she had described. Perhaps she could direct him to Joe Black, who might know the tall man last seen with Marian. The place was easily found, and the dangerous stairs creaked again to his eager tread. Sal knew him at once, and tucking her grizzly hair beneath her dirty cap, waited to hear his errand, which was soon told. Could she give him any further information of that young girl, had she ever heard of her since his last visit there, and would she tell him where to find Joe Black?—he might know who the man was, and thus throw some light on the mystery.

"Bless your heart," answered the woman, "Joe died three weeks ago with the delirium tremens, so what you git out of him won't help you much. I told you all I knew before; or no, come to think on't, I seen 'em go into a Third avenue car, and that makes me think the feller lived up town. But law, you may as well hunt for a needle in a haystack as to hunt for a lost gal in New York. You may git out all the police you've a mind to, and then you ain't no better off. Ten to one they are wus than them that's hidin' her, if they do wear brass buttons and feel so big," and Sal shook her brawny arm threateningly at some imaginary officers of justice.

With a feeling of disgust, Frederic turned away, and, retracing his steps, came at last to the Park, where he entered a Third avenue car, though why he did so he scarcely knew. He did not expect to find her there, but he felt a satisfaction in thinking she had once been over that route—perhaps in that very car—and he looked curiously in the faces of his fellow-passengers as they entered and left. Wistfully, too, he glanced out at the houses they were passing, saying to himself: "Is it there Marian lives, or there?" and once when they stopped for some one to alight, his eye wandered down the opposite street, resting at last upon a window high up in a huge block of buildings. There was nothing peculiar about that window—nothing to attract attention, unless it were the neat white fringed curtain which shaded it, or the rose geranium which in its little earthen pot seemed to indicate that the inmates of that tenement retained a love for flowers and country fashions, even amid the smoke and the dust of the city. Frederic saw the white curtain, and it reminded him of the one which years ago hung in his bedroom at the old place on the river. He saw the geranium, too, and the figure which bent over it to pluck the withered leaf. Then the car moved on, and to the weary man sitting in the corner there came no voice to tell how near he had been to the lost one, for that window was Mrs. Burt's, and the bending figure—Marian.

He had seen her—he had passed within a few rods of her and she could have heard him had he shouted aloud, but for all the good that this did him she might have been miles and miles away, for he never dreamed of the truth, and day after day he continued his search, while the excitement, the fatigue, and the constant disappointment, told fearfully upon his constitution. Still he would not give it up, and every morning he went forth with hope renewed, only to return at night weary, discouraged, and sometimes almost despairing of success.

Once, at the close of a rainy afternoon, he entered again a Third avenue car, which would leave him not very far from his hotel. It had been a day of unusual fatigue with him, and utterly exhausted, he sank into the corner seat, while passenger after passenger crowded in, their damp overcoats and dripping umbrellas filling the vehicle with a sickly steam, which affected him unpleasantly, causing him to lean his aching head upon his hand, and so shut out what was going on around him. They were full at last—every seat, every standing point was taken, and still the conductor said there was room for another, as he passed in a delicate young girl, who modestly drew her vail over her face to avoid the gaze of the men, some of whom stared rather rudely at her. Just after she came in, Frederic looked up, but the thick folds of the vail told no tales of the sudden paling of the lip, the flushing of her cheek, and the quiver of the eye-lids. Neither did the violent trembling of her body, nor the quick pressure of her hand upon her side convey to him other impression than that she was tired—faint, he thought—and touching his next neighbor with his elbow, he compelled him to move along a few inches, while he did the same, and so made room for the girl between himself and the door.

"Sit here, Miss," he said, and he turned partly toward her, as if to shield her from the crowd, for he felt intuitively that she was not like them.

Her hands, which chanced to be ungloved and grasped the handle of her basket, were small, very small, and about the joints were little laughing dimples, looking very tempting to Frederic Raymond, who was a passionate admirer of pretty hands, and who now felt a strong desire to clasp the tiny snowflakes just within his reach.

Involuntarily he thought of those which had so lately held his feverish head; they must have been much like the little ones holding so fast the basket, and he wished that chance had brought Marian there instead of the young girl sitting so still beside him. A strange sensation thrilled him at the very idea of meeting her thus, while his heart beat fast, but never said to him that it was Marian herself! Why didn't it? He asked himself that question a thousand times in after years, saying he should know her again, but he had no suspicion of it now, though when they stopped at the same street down which he once had looked at the open window, and when the seat beside him was empty, he did experience a sense of loneliness—a feeling as if a part of himself had gone with the young girl. Suddenly remembering that in his abstraction he had come higher up than he wished to do, he also alighted, and standing upon the muddy pavement, looked after the tripping figure moving so rapidly toward the window where the geranium was blossoming, and where a light was shining now. It disappeared at last, and mentally chiding him for stopping in the rain to watch a perfect stranger, Frederic turned back in the direction of his hotel, while the girl, who had so awakened his interest, rushed up the narrow stairs, and bounded into the room where Mrs. Burt was sitting, exclaimed :

"I've seen him! I've sat beside him in the same car!"

"Why didn't you fetch him home, then?" asked Ben, who had returned that afternoon from a short excursion in the country.

Marian's face crimsoned at this question, and in a hard, unnatural voice she replied :

"He didn't wish to come. He didn't even pretend to recognize me, though he gave me a seat, and I knew him so quick."

"Had that brown dud over your face, I s'pose," returned Ben, casting a rueful glance at the vail. "Nobody can tell who a woman is, now-a-days. Why didn't you pull it off and claim him for your husband, and make him pay your fare?"

"Oh, Ben," said Marian, "you certainly wouldn't have me degrade myself like that! Frederic knew who I was, I am sure, for I saw him so plain—but he does not wish to find me. He never asked for me since I left his sick room. All he cared for was Isabel, and I wish it were possible for him to marry her."

"You don't wish any such thing," answered Ben, and in the same cold, hard tone Marian continued :

"I do. I thought so to-night when I sat beside him and looked into his face. I loved him once as much as one can love another, and because I loved him thus I came away, thinking in my ignorance that he might be happy with Isabel ; and when I saw that advertisement, I wrote, asking if I might go back again. The result of the letter you know. He insulted me cruelly. He told me a falsehood, and still I was not cured. When I thought him dying in the hotel, I went and staid with him till the other came: but, after I was gone, he never spoke of me, and he even professed not to know Mrs. Daniel Burt, asking who she was, when he knew as well as I, for I told him who she was, and he directed my letter to her. I never used to think he was deceitful, but I know it now, and I almost hate him for it."

"Tut, tut. No you don't," chimed in Ben; and Marian growing still more excited, continued, "Well, if I don't, I will. I have run after him all I ever shall, and now if we are reconciled he must make the first concessions!"

"Whew-ew," whistled Ben, thinking to himself, "Ain't the little critter spunky, though!" and feeling rather amused than otherwise, he watched Marian as she paced the floor, her blue eyes flashing angrily and her whole face indicative of strong excitement.

She fully believed that Frederic knew her, simply because she recognized him, and his failing to ac knowledge the recognition filled her with indignation and determination to forget him if it were possible. Ah, little did she dream then of the lonely man, who, in the same room where she so recently had been, sat with bowed head, and thought of her until the distant bells tolled the hour of midnight.

It was now three weeks since he commenced his search, and he was beginning to despair of success. His presence he knew was needed in Kentucky, where Alice had been left alone with the negroes, and where his arrangements for moving were not yet completed. His house on the river was waiting for him, the people wondering why he didn't come, and as he sat thinking it all over, he resolved at last to go home and bring Alice to Riverside—to send for Mrs. Huntington as had previously been arranged, and then begin the search again. Of Isabel too, he thought, remembering his hasty promise of going to New Haven, but this he could not do. So he penned her a few lines, telling her how it was impossible for him to come, and saying that on his return to Riverside with Alice, he should expect to find her mother and herself waiting to receive him.

"I cannot do less than this," he said. "Isabel has been with me a long time, and though I do not feel toward her as I did, I pity her; for I am afraid she likes me better than she should. I have given her encouragement, too; but when I come back, I will talk with her candidly. I will tell her how it is, and offer her a home with me as long as she shall choose to stay. I will be to her a brother; and when Marian is found, the two shall be like sisters, until some man who has not a wife already takes Isabel from my hands."

Thus deciding, Frederic wrote to Alice, telling her when he should probably be home, and saying he should stop for a day or so at Yonkers. This done, he retired to rest, dreaming strange dreams of Marian and the girl who sat beside him. They were one and the same, he thought; and he was raising the brown vail to see, when he awoke to consciousness, and experienced a feeling of disappointment in finding his dream untrue.

That morning a vague, uneasy feeling prompted him to stroll slowly down the street whither the young girl had gone the previous night. The window in the third story was open again, and the geranium was standing there still, its broad leaves growing fresher and greener in the sunshine which shone warm upon the window sill, where a beautiful kitten lay, apparently asleep. Frederic saw it all, and for an instant felt a thrill of fear lest the cat should fall and be killed on the pavement below. But a second glance assured him of its safety—for, half buried in its long, silk fur, was a small white hand, a hand like Marian's and that of the girl with the thick brown vail. "Its owner was the mistress of the kitten," he said; and the top of her head was just visible, for she sat reading upon a little stool, and utterly unconscious of the stranger who, on the opposite side in the street, cast many and wistful glances in that direction, not because he fancied that she was there, nor yet for any explainable reason, except that the fringed curtain reminded him of his boyhood; and he knew the occupant of that room had once lived in the country, and bleached her linen on the sweet, clean grass, which grew by the running brook.

"Marian," said Mrs. Burt, "who is that tall man going down the street? He's been looking this way ever so much. Isn't it——"

She did not need to repeat the name, for Marian saw who it was, and her fingers buried themselves so deeply in the fat sides of the kitten that the little animal fancied the play rather too rude for comfort, and, spitting at her mistress pertly bounded upon the floor.

"It's Frederic!" cried Marian. "Maybe he's coming here, for he has crossed the street below, and is coming up this side." And in her joy Marian forgot the harsh things she had said of him only the night before.

But in vain Marian waited for the step upon the stairs—the loud knock upon the door—neither of them came, and leaning from the window she watched him through her tears until he passed from sight.

That afternoon, as Frederic was sauntering leisurely down the street in the direction of the depot—for he intended going to Yonkers that night—he stumbled upon Ben, whose characteristic exclamation was, "Wall, Square, glad to see you out agin, but I didn't b'lieve I ever should when I sent word to that gal. She come, I s'pose?"

"Yes," returned Frederic, "and I am grateful to you for your kindness in telegraphing to my friends. How did you know I was sick?"

"Oh, I'm allus 'round," said Ben. "Know one of them boys at the hotel, and he told me. I s'posed you'd die, and I should of come to see you mabby, only I had to go off peddlin'. Bizness afore pleasure, you know."

This remark seemed to imply that Frederic's dying would have been a source of pleasure to the Yankee, but the young man knew that he did intend it, and the two walked on together—Ben plying his companion with questions, and learning that both Isabel and Mrs. Huntington were now in New Haven, but would probably go to Riverside when Frederic returned from Kentucky.

"That's a grand place," said Ben; "fixed up in tip-top style, too. I took my sister out to see it, and she thought 'twas pretty slick. Wouldn't wonder if you're goin' to marry that black haired gal, by the looks of things?" and Ben's gray eyes peered sideways at Frederic, who replied, "I certainly have no such intentions."

"You don't say it," returned Ben. "I shouldn't of took the trouble to send for her if I hadn't s'posed you was kinder courtin'. My sister thought you was, and she or'to know, bein' she's been through the mill!"

Frederic winced under Ben's pointed remarks, and as a means of changing the conversation, said, "If I am not mistaken, you spoke of your sister when in Kentucky, and Alice became quite interested. I've heard her mention the girl several times. What is her name?"

"Do look at that hoss—flat on the pavement. He's a goner," Ben exclaimed, by way of gaining a little time.

Frederic's attention was immediatly diverted from Ben, who thought to himself, "I'll try him with half the truth, and if he's any ways bright he'll guess the rest."

So when, to use Ben's words, the noble quadruped was "safely landed on t'other side of Jordan where there wan't no omnibus drivers, no cars, no canal boats, no cartmen, no gals to pound their backs into pummice, no wimmen, nor ministers to yank their mouths, nor nothin' but a lot as big as the United States with the Missippi runnin' through it, and nothin' to do but kick up their heels and eat clover," Ben came back to Frederic's question, and said, "You as't my sister's name. They tried hard to call her *Mary Ann*, I s'pose. My way of thinkin' 'taint neither one nor t'other, though mabby you'll like it—MARIAN; 'taint a common name. Did you ever hear it afore?"

"Marian!" gasped Frederic, turning instantly pale, while a strange, undefinable feeling swept over him—a feeling hat he had never been so near finding her as now.

"Excuse me, Square," said Ben, whose keen eyes lost not a single change in the expression of Frederic's face. "I'm such a blunderin' critter! That little blind gal told me your fust wife was Marian, and I or'to known better than harrer your feelings with the name."

"Never mind," returned Frederic, faintly, "but tell me of your sister—and now I think of it, you said once you were from down east, which I supposed referred to one of the New England states, Vermont perhaps?"

"Did use to live in Massachusetts," replied Ben. "But can't a feller move?"

Frederic admitted that he could, and Ben continued, "I or'to told you, I s'pose, that Marian ain't my own flesh and blood—she's adopted, that's all. But I love her jest the same. Her name is Marian Grey," and Ben looked earnestly at Frederic, thinking to himself, "Won't he take the hint when he knows, or had or'to know that her mother was a Grey."

But hints were lost on Frederic. He had no suspicion of the truth, and Ben proceeded, "All her kin is dead, and as mother hadn't no daughter she took this orphan, and I'm workin' hard to give her a good schoolin'. She can play the pianner like fury, and talks the French grammar most as well as I do the English!"

This brought a smile to Frederic's face, and he did not for a moment think of doubting Ben's word.

"You seem very proud of your sister," he said, at last, "and as I owe you something for caring for me and telegraphing to my friends, let me show my gratitude by giving you something for this Marian Grey. What shall it be? Is she fond of jewelry? Most young girls are."

Ben stuck his hands in his trousers pocket and seemed to be thinking; then, removing his hands he replied, "Mabby you'll think it sassy, but there is somethin' that would please us both. I told her about you when I came from Kentucky, and she cried like a baby over that blind gal. Then, when you was sick, she felt worried agin, beg your pardon, Square, but I told her you was han'some. Jest give us your picter, if it ain't bigger than my thumb, and would it be asking too much for you when you git home to send me the blind gal's. She's an angel, and I should feel so good to have her face in my pocket. You can direct to Ben Butterworth—but law, you won't, I know you won't."

"Why not?" asked Frederic, laughing at the novel request. "Mine you shall surely have, and Alice's also, if she consents. Come with me now, for we are opposite a daguerrean gallery."

The result of this was that in a short time Ben held in his hand a correct likeness of Frederic, which was of priceless value to him, because he knew how highly it would be prized by her for whom alone he had requested it.

As they passed out into the street again, Frederic said to him rather abruptly, "Do you know Sarah Green?"

"No," answed Ben, and Frederic continued,

"Do you know Mrs. Merton?"

Ben started a little, and then repeating the name replied, "Ain't acquainted with that name neither. Who is she?"

"She took care of me," returned Frederic, "and I would like to find her, and thank her for her kind ness."

"I shouldn't s'pose she could of took care of you alone, sick as you was," said Ben, waiting eagerly for the answer, which, had it been what he desired, might lead to the unfolding of the mystery.

But Frederic shrank from making Ben his confidant. "It was hard for her till Miss Huntington came."

"Blast Miss Huntington," thought Ben, now thoroughly satisfied that his companion did not care to discover Marian, or he would certainly say something about her.

Both she and his mother were sure that he knew she had been with him in his sickness, and if he really wished to find her he would speak of her as well as of Mrs. Merton.

"But he don't," thought Ben. "He don't care a straw for her, and she's right when she says she won't run after him any more. He don't like Isabel none too well, and I raally b'lieve the man is crazy."

This settled the matter satisfactorily with Ben, who accompanied Frederic to the depot, waiting there until the departure of the train.

"Give my regrets to that Josh, and the rest of the niggers, and don't on no account forget the picter," were his last words, as he quitted the car, and then hurried home impatient to show Marian his surprise.

He found her sitting by the open window—a listless, dreamy look in her blue eyes, and a sad expression upon her face, which said that her thoughts were far away in the South-land, where Nature had decked her beautiful home with all the glories of the merry month of May and the first bright days of June. Roses were blooming there now, she knew, and she thought of the bush she had planted beneath the library window, wondering if that were in bloom, and if its fragrance ever reminded the dear ones of her. Did Alice twine the buds amid her soft hair, just as she used to do, and call them Marian's buds, saying they were sweeter than all the rest?

"Darling Alice," she murmured, "I shall never see her again:" and her tears were dropping upon her lap just as Ben came in, and began:

"Wall, wee one, I've seen the Square, and talked with him of you."

"Oh, Ben, Ben!"—and Marian's face was spotted with her excitement—"what made you? What did he say? and where is he?"

"Gone home," answered Ben; "but he had this took on purpose for you;" and he tossed the picture into her lap.

"It is—it is Frederic. Oh, Mrs. Burt, it is," and Marian's lip touched the glass, from which the face of Frederic Raymond looked kindly out upon her.

It was thinner than when she used to know it, but fuller, stronger-looking than when it lay among the tumbled pillows. The eyes, too, were hollow, and not so bright, while it seemed to her that the rich brown hair was not so thrifty as of old. But it was Frederic still, her Frederic, and she pressed it again to her lips, while her heart thrilled with the joyful thought that he remembered her, and had sent her this priceless token. But why had he gone home without her—why had he left her there alone if he really cared for finding her? Slowly, as a cloud obscures a summer sky, a shadow crept over her face—a shadow of doubt—of distrust. There was something she had not heard, and with quivering lip she said to Ben, "What does it mean? You have not told me why he sent it."

It was cruel to deceive her as he had done, and so Ben thought when he saw the heaving of her chest, the pressure of her hands, and more than all, the whiteness of her face, as he told her why Frederic sent to her that picture; that it was not taken for Marian Lindsey, but rather for Marian Grey, adopted sister of Benjamin Butterworth.

"He does not wish to find me," said Marian when

Ben had finished speaking. "We shall never be reconciled, and it is just as well, perhaps."

"I think so, too," rejoined Ben, "or at any rate I'd let him rest a spell, and learn everything there is in books for woman-kind to learn. You shall go to college, if you say so, and bimeby, when the old Nick himself wouldn't know you, I'll get you a chance to teach that blind gal, and he'll fall in love with his own wife; see if he don't," and Ben stroked the curls within his reach very caressingly, thinking to himself, "I won't tell her now 'bout Alice's picter, 'cause it may not come, but I'll cheer her up the best way that I can. 'She grows handsome every day of her life," and as this, in Ben's estimation, was the one thing of all others to be desired by Marian, he could not forbear complimenting her aloud upon her rapid improvement in looks.

"Thank you," she answered, smiling very faintly, for to her, beauty or accomplishments were of little avail if in the end Frederic's love were not secured.

Anon, however, hope whispered to her that it might be, and again she opened the daguerreotype, catching a glow of encouragement from the eyes which looked so kindly at her, as if they fain would tell her of the weary days the original of that picture had spent in searching for her, or how, even now, amid the noise and dust of the crowded cars, he sat, wholly unmindful of what was passing around, never looking at the beautiful blue river without, or yet at the motley passengers within, but with his hat drawn over his eyes and his shawl across his lap, he thought of her alone, except indeed occasionally when there would intrude itself upon him the remembrance of the girl with the brown vail, or a thought of Marian Grey!

CHAPTER XVIII.

HOME AGAIN.

FREDERIC was coming home again—"Marster Frederic," who, as Dinah said, "had been so near to kingdom-come that he could hear the *himes* they sung on Sundays."

Joyfully the blacks told to each other the glad news, which was an incentive for them all to bestir themselves as they had not done before during the whole period of their master's absence. Old Dinah, whose mind turned naturally upon eatables, busied herself in conjuring up some new and harmless relish for the invalid, while Uncle Phil spent all the whole day in rubbing down the horses and rubbing up the carriage with which he intended meeting his master at Frankfort. Josh, too, caught the general spirit, and remembering how much his master was wont to chide him for his slovenly appearance, he cast rueful glances at his sorry coat and red cowhides, wishing to goodness he had some "clothes to honor the 'casion with."

"I m-m-might sh-sh-shine these up a little," he said, examining his boots, and, purloining a tallow candle from Hetty's cupboard, he set himself to the task, succeeding so well that he was almost certain of commendation.

A coat of uncle Phil's was borrowed next, and though it hung like a tent cloth about Josh's lank proportions, the effect was entirely satisfactory to the boy, who had a consciousness of having done all that could reasonably be expected of him.

In the house Alice was not idle. From the earliest dawn she had been up, for there was something on her mind which kept her wakeful and restless. Frederic's letters, which were read to her by the wife of the overseer, who lived near by, had told her of the blue-eyed girl who had been with him in his sickness, and in one letter, written ere he had given up the search, he had said, while referring to the girl: "Darling Alice, I am so glad you sent me here, for I hope to bring you a great and joyful surprise."

Not the least mention did he make of Marian, but Alice understood at once that he meant her. Marian and the blue-eyed girl were the same, and he would bring her back to them again. She was certain of it, and though in his last letter, dated at Riverside, and apprising them of his intended return, he had not alluded to the subject, it made no difference with her. He wished really to surprise her, she thought, and seeking out Dinah, she said to her, rather cautiously, for she would let no one into her secret:

"Supposing Frederic had never been married to Marian, but had gone now after a bride—I don't mean Isabel," she said, as she felt the defiant expression of Dinah's face—"but somebody else—somebody real nice. Supposing, I say, he was going to bring her home, which room do you think he would wish her to have?"

"The best chamber, in course," answered Dinah—"the one whar the 'hogany bedstead and silk quilt is. You wouldn't go to puttin' Marster Frederic's wife off with poor truck, I hope. But what made you ask that question? What have you hearn?"

"Nothing in particular," answered Alice, "only it would be nice if he should bring somebody with him, and I want to fix the room just as though I knew he would. May Lid sweep and dust it for me?"

For a moment Dinah looked at her as if she thought

her crazy. Then thinking to herself, "it'll 'muse her a spell any way, and I may as well humor her whim," she replied. "Sakes alive, yes, and I'll ar the bed. Thar haint nobody slep' in't sence Marian run away, 'cept Miss Agnes one night and that trollop, Isabel, who consulted me by sayin' how't they done clarmbered onto a table afore they could get inter bed, 'twas so high. Ain't used to feathers whar she was raised, I reckon, and if you'll b'lieve it, she said how't she allus slep' on har afore she come here! Pretty stuff that must be to lie on; but Lord, them Yankees is mostly as poor as poverty, and don't know no differ."

Having relieved herself of this speech, which involved both her opinion of Yankees in general and Isabel in particular, the old lady proceeded to business, first *arin'* the bed, as she said, and then making it higher, if possible, than it was made on the night when Isabel so injured her feelings by laughing at its hight. Lid's services were next brought into requisition; and when the chamber was swept and dusted, the arrangement of the furniture was left entirely to Alice, who felt that what she did was right, and wished so much that she could see just how Marian's favorite chair looked standing by the window, from which the gorgeous sunsets Marian so much admired could be plainly seen. Just opposite, and on the other side of the window, Frederic's easy chair was placed—the one in which he always sat when tired, and where Alice fancied he would now delight to sit with Marian, so near that he could look into her eyes and tell her that he was glad to have her there. He was beginning to love her Alice knew by the tone of his letters; and her heart thrilled with joy as she thought of the happiness in store for them all. She would not be lonely now in her own pleasant chamber, for it was so near to Marian's. She could leave the doors open between, and that would be so much nicer than having black Ellen sleeping on the floor.

Dear little Alice! She built bright castles in the air

that summer day, and they were as real to her as if Frederic had written, "Marian is found, and coming home with me."

"She loved a great many flowers around her," she said, and groping her way down the stairs and out into the yard, she gathered from the tree beneath the library window a profusion of buds and half opened roses, which she arranged into bouquets, and placed in vases for Marian, just as Marian had gathered flowers for her from the garden far away on the river.

It was done at last; and very inviting that pleasant, airy apartment looked with its handsome furniture, its bright carpet and muslin curtains of snowy white, to say nothing of the towering bed. There were flowers on the mantle, flowers on the table, flowers in the window, flowers everywhere, and their sweet perfume filled the air with a delicious fragrance which Dinah declared was "a heap sight better than that scent Miss Isabel used to put on her hankercher and fan. Ugh, that fan!" and Dinah's nose was elevated at the very thought of Isabel's sandal-wood fan which had been her special abhorrence.

"Isn't it most time for Uncle Phil to start?" asked Alice, when Dinah had finished fixing the room.

"Yes, high time," answered Dinah, "but Phil is so slow. I'll jest hurry him up," and followed by Alice she descended the stairs, meeting in the lower hall with Lyd, who held in her hand a brown envelope, which she passed to Alice, saying "One dem letters what come like lightnin' on the telegraph. A boy done brung it."

"A telegram," cried Alice, feeling at first alarmed. "Go for Mrs. Warren to read it."

But the overseer's wife was absent, as was also her husband, and neither the blacks nor Alice knew what to do.

"There isn't more than a line and a half," said Alice, passing her finger over the paper and feeling the thick sand which had been sifted upon it. "I presume something has detained Frederic, and he has sent word that he will not be here to-day."

"Let me see dat ar," said Phil, who liked to impress his companions with a sense of his superior wisdom, and, adjusting his iron-bowed specs, he took the letter, which in reality was Greek to him.

After an immense amount of wry faces and loud whispering he said:

"Yes, honey, you're correct, though Marster Frederic has sich an onery hand-write that it takes me a a heap of time to make it out. It reads, 'Somethin' has detained Frederic, and he has sent word that he'll be here to-morry.'" And, with the utmost gravity, Phil took off his specs, and was walking away with the air of one who has done something his companions could never hope to do, when Hetty called out.

"Wonder if he 'spects us to swaller dat ar, and think he kin read, when he jest done said over what Miss Alice say. Can't fool dis chile."

This insinuation Uncle Phil felt constrained to answer, and with an injured air he replied:

"Kin read, too, for don't you mind how't Miss Alice say. 'Won't be here to day,' and it's writ on the paper, 'Comin' to-morry.'" And, fully satisfied that he had convinced his audience, Uncle Phil hastened off, ere Hetty had time for further argument. So certain was Phil that Alice's surmises were correct and the telegram interpreted aright, and so anxious withal to prove himself sure, that he would not go to Frankfort, as he proposed doing.

"There was no use on't," he said. "Marster wouldn't be thar till to-morry," and he whiled away the afternoon at leisure.

But alas for Uncle Phil. Mrs. Warren had made a mistake in Frederic's last letter, the young man writing he should be home on the15th, whereas she had read it the 17th; afterward, Frederic had decided to leave Riverside one day earlier, and he telegraphed from

Cincinnati for Phil to meet him. Finding neither carriage nor servant in waiting, he hired a conveyance, and about four o'clock P. M. from every cabin door there came the joyful cry—

"Marster Frederic has come."

"Told you so," said Hetty, with an exultant glance at Uncle Phil, who wisely made no reply, but hastened with the rest to tell his master, "How d'ye?"

"How is it that some one did not meet me?" Frederic asked, after the first noisy outbreak had somewhat subsided. "Didn't you get the despatch?"

The negroes looked at Phil, who stammered out—

"Yes, we done got it, but dem ole iron specs of mine is mighty nigh wore out—can't see in 'em at all, and I read 'to-morry' instead of 'to-day.'"

The loud shout which followed this excuse enlightened Frederic as to the true state of the case, and he, too, joined in the laugh, telling the crest-fallen Phil that "he should surely have a new pair of silver specs which would read 'to-day' instead of 'to-morry.'"

"But where is Alice?" he continued. "Why don't she come to greet me?"

"Sure 'nough," returned Dinah. "Whar can she be, when she was so fierce to have you come? Reckon she's up in the best charmber she's been fixin' up for somethin', she wouldn't tell what."

"I'll go and see," said Frederic, starting in quest of the little girl, who, as Dinah had conjectured, was in the front chamber—the one prepared with so much care for Marian.

She had been sitting by the window when she heard the sound of wheels coming up the avenue.—Then the joyful cry of "Marster's comin'," came to her quick ear, and, starting up, she bent her head to listen for another voice—a voice she had not heard for many a weary month. But she listened in vain, for Marian was not there. Gradually she became convinced of the fact, and, laying her face on the window-sill, she was weeping bitterly when Frederic came in.

Pausing for a moment in the door, he glanced around, first at the well remembered chair, then at the books upon the table, then at the flowers, and then he knew why all this had been done.

"I would that it might have been so," he thought, and going to the weeping Alice he lifted up her head and pushing her hair from her forehead, whispered to her softly, "Darling, was it for Marian you gathered all these flowers?"

"Yes, Frederic, for Marian," and Alice sobbed aloud.

Taking her in his lap, Frederic replied, "Did you think I would bring her home?"

"Yes, I thought you had found her, and I was so glad. What made you write me that?"

"Alice I did find her," returned Frederic; "I have seen her, I have talked with her. Marian is alive."

At these words, so decidedly spoken, the blind eyes flashed up into Frederic's face eagerly, wistfully, as if they fain would burst their vail of darkness and see if he told her truly.

"Is it true? Oh, Frederic, you are not deceiving me? I can't bear any more disappointment," and Alice's face and lips were as white as ashes, as she proceeded further to question Frederic, who told her of the blue-eyed girl who, just as he was treading the brink of the river of death, had come to him and called him back to life by her kind acts and words of love.

"She had a sweet, childish face," said he, "fairer, sweeter than Marian's when she went away—but Marian must have changed; for I knew that this was she."

Then he told her of her sudden disappearance when Isabel came—of his fruitless efforts to find her, and how while searching for her, he had met another girl, whose hands reminded him of those which he had felt so many times upon his brow.

"Wasn't that Marian?" said Alice, who had forgotten her grief in listening.

There was a mournful pathos in the tone of his voice, and it emboldened Alice to ask another question.

"Frederic," she began, and her little hand played with his hair, as it always did when she was uncertain as to how her remarks would be received, "Frederic, ain't you loving Marian a heap more than you did when she went away?"

Frederic did not hesitate a moment ere replying, "Yes, darling, I am, for that young girl crept away down into my heart where Marian ought to have been, before I asked her to be my wife; and I shall find her too. I only stopped long enough to come home for you. The house is ready at Riverside, and your room is charming."

"Will Isabel be there?" was Alice's next inquiry, and Frederic answered by telling her all he knew of the matter.

He did not say he was beginning to understand her and consequently to like her less, but Alice inferred as much, and with this fear removed from her mind, she could endure patiently to become again a pupil of Miss Huntington. For a long time they talked together, wondering who wrote the letler purporting to have come from Sarah Green, and why it had been written. Then Frederic told her of the peddler Ben, and of his sister, *Marian Grey*, who, at that moment, had his daguerreotype in her keeping. . Of Marian Grey Alice did not say to him "She is our Marian," for she had not such a thought, but she seemed interested both in her and in Ben, and when told that the latter had asked for her picture she consented at once, saying he should have it as soon as they were settled at Riverside.

"I would not tell any one that Marian was with me," said Frederic, as their conversation drew to a close; "I had rather the subject should not be discussed until I really find her and bring her home; then we will set apart a day of general thanksgiving."

To this suggestion Alice readily assented, and as the

supper bell just then rang, and the two went together to the delicious repast, which Dinah had prepared with unusual care, insisting the while that "thar was nothin' fit for nobody to eat."

Frederic, however, whose appetite was increasing each day, convinced her to the contrary, and while watching him as he did justice to her viands, the old negress thought to herself, "'Clar for't, how he does eat. I should know he come from Yankee land. You can allus tell 'em, the way they crams, when they get whar thar is somethin'."

The news of Frederic's return spread rapidly, and that night he received calls from several of his neighbors, together with an invitation to Agnes Gibson's wedding, which was to take place in a few days. In the invitation Alice was included, and though Dinah demurred, saying that "trundle-bed truck or'to stay at home," Alice ventured to differ from her, and at the appointed time went with Frederic to the party, which was splendid in all its parts, having been got up with a direct reference to the newspaper articles which were sure to be published concerning it. Agnes, of course, was charming in white satin, point lace, orange flowers, flowing vail, and all other *et ceteras* which complete the dress of a fashonable bride. And the bridegroom—poor old man—looked very well in his new suit of broadcloth, even if his knees did shake—not from fear, however, but as one of the guests remarked, "Because it was a way they'd had for several years!' The top of his head was bald, it is true, and his hair' as white as snow, but for every silver thread Agnes knew there was a golden eagle in his purse, and this consoled her somewhat, though it did not prevent her from watching jealously to see if any one was talking of the palsied man, her husband. Her expected present from Isabel had never come, and the three *fish knives*, ranged in a row, looked as if two of them, at least, were rather more ornamental than useful, as did also the four card baskets, and three gold thimbles, which occupied a conspicuous plece. To Frederic, Agnes was especially gracious, asking him numberless questions concerning her "dear friend," and saying "she hoped to meet her in her travels, as they were going North and were intending to spend the Summer at Saratoga, Newport, and Nahant. I thought once you would be taking your bridal tour about this time," she said to him, when several were standing near.

"I assure you I had no such idea," was Frederic's reply, and Agnes continued, "Indeed I supposed you were engaged, of course."

"Then you supposed wrong," he answered, glad of this public opportunity to contradict a story he knew had gained a wide circulation. "I esteem Miss Huntington as a friend and distant relative, but I certainly have no intention whatever of making her my wife."

Frequently, during the evening, he was asked if he had found any clue to Sarah Green or her letter; and as he could in all sincerity reply in the negative, no one guessed that instead of Sarah Green he had found his wife—only, however to lose her again.

"But he would find her," he said to himself, and as he looked at the ill-matched bride and groom, he could not forebear wishing that it were himself and Marian. He would stay by her now, he thought, and when it grew dark in the parlor instead of suffering her to go away alone and read the fatal letter, he would draw her to his side, and telling her of its contents, would sue for her forgiveness, and offer to her love in return for the fraud imposed upon her.

It was a pleasant picture Frederic drew that night of what his bridal might have been, and so absorbed was he in it that when, as they were going home, Alice with a yawn said to him, "Wasn't it so tiresome hearing those young folks say such foolish things to each other, and hearing the old ones talk about their servants?" he replied, "why no, child, I spent a most delightful evening."

"I—don't—see—how you could," was the drowsy

answer, and in a moment more Alice lay upon the carriage cushions fast asleep!

It was nearly three weeks after this party ere Frederic's arrangements for leaving Kentucky were entirely completed, and it was not until the latter part of July that he finally started for his new home. The lamentations of the negroes were noisy in the extreme, though far more moderate than they would have been if their master had not said that it was very probable he should return in the Autumn, and merely make Riverside a Summer residence. If he found Marian he should come back, of course, he thought, but he did not deem it best to raise hopes which might never be realized, so he said nothing of her to the blacks who supposed of course she was dead.

The parting between Dinah and Alice was a bitter one, the former hugging the little girl to her bosom and wondering how "Marster Frederic 'spected a child what had never waited on itself even to fotch a drop of water, could get along way off dar whar thar warn't nary nigger nor nothin' but a pack o' low flung Irish. Order 'em 'round," she said to Alice, wiping her eyes with her checked apron, "order 'em round jist like they warn't white. Make 'em think you be somebody. Say your pra'rs evey night—war your white cambric wrappers in the mornin', and don't on no count catch any poor folksy's marners 'mong them Yankees for I shouldn't get my nateral sleep o' nights, till you got shet of 'em, and—" lowering her voice, "if so be that you tell any of the quality 'bout us blacks, s'posin you you kinder set me 'bove Hetty and them Higginses, bein' that I the same as nussed you."

To nearly all these requirements Alice promised compliance, and then, as the carriage was waiting, she followed Frederic down to the gate, and soon both were lost to the sight of the tearful group which from the piazza of Redstone Hall, gazed wistfully after them.

It was at the close of a sultry Summer day when

the travelers reached Riverside, where they found Mrs. Huntington waiting to receive them. Frederic had written, apprising her of the time when he should probably arrive, and asking her to be there if possible. Something, too, he had said of Isabel, but that young lady was not in the most amiable mood, and as she was comfortably domesticated with another distant relative, she declined going to Frederic until he came to some understanding, or at least manifested a greater desire to have her with him than his recent letters indicated. Accordingly her mother went alone, and Frederic was not sorry, while Alice was delighted. Everything seemed so bright and airy, she said, just as though a load were taken from them, and like a bird she flitted about the house, for she needed to pass through a room but once ere she was familiar with its location, and could find it easily. With her own cozy chamber she was especially pleased, and in less than half an hour her little hands had examined every article of furniture, even to the vases which held the withered blossoms gathered so long ago.

"Somebody must have put these here for me," she said, and then her mind went back to the morning when she, too, had gathered flowers for her expected friend, and she wondered much who had done a similar service for her.

"It's me," returned Mrs. Russell, who was still staying at Riverside. "Now I wonder if you found them dried-up things so soon," she continued, advancing into room. "I should of hove them out, only that the girl who fixed 'em made me promise to leave 'em till you came. 'Pears like she b'lieved you'd think more on 'em for knowin' that she picked 'em."

"Girl! Mrs. Russell. What girl?" and Alice's eyes lighted up, for she thonght at once of Marian, who would know of course about the house, and as she would naturally wish to see it, she had come some day and left these flowers, which would be so dear to her if she found her suspicions correct. "Who was the girl?" she asked again, and Mrs. Russell replied:

"I don't remember her name, but she went all over the house, fixing things in Mr. Raymond's room, which I didn't think was very marnerly, bein' that 'twa'n't none o' hern. Then she come in here and set ever so long before she picked these posys, which she told me not to throw away."

"Yes, it was Marian," came involuntarily from Alice's lips, while the woman, catching at the name rejoined:

"That sounds like what he called her—that tall spooky chap, her brother—Ben something. She said he had seen you at the South."

"Oh, Ben Butterworth. It was his adopted sister;" and Alice turned away, feeling greatly disappointed that *Marian Grey*, and not Marian Lindsey, had arranged those flowers for her.

This allusion to Ben reminded Alice of his request for her picture, and one morning, when Frederic was going to New York, she asked to go with him and sit for her daguerreotype. There was no reason why she should not, and in an hour or two, she was listening, half stunned, to the noise and uproar of the city.

"Oh, Frederic," she cried, holding fast to his hand, as they made their way up town—"oh, Frederic, I wonder Marian didn't get crazy and die. I'm sure I should. I'm almost distracted now. Where are all those people and carts going that I hear running by us so fast, and what makes them keep pushing me so hard. Oh, dear, I wish I hadn't come!" and as some one just then jostled her more rudely than usual, Alice began to cry.

"Never mind," said Freredric soothingly, "we are almost there, and we will take a carriage back. Folks can't push you then;" and in stooping down to comfort the little girl, he failed to see the graceful figure passing so near him that the hem of her dress fluttered against his boot.

They had come upon each other so suddenly that there was not time for the brown vail to be dropped, neither was it needful, for so absorbed was Frederic with his charge that he neither knew nor dreamed how near to *Marian Lindsey* he had been.

Alice's tears being dried, they kept on their way, and when the picture was taken, Frederic did it up and directing it to Ben Butterworth, sent it to the office, then calling a carriage, he took Alice, as he had promised, all over the great city. And Alice enjoyed it very much, laying back on the soft cushions, and knowing that no one could touch her of all the noisy throng she heard so distinctly, but could not see. It was a day long talked of by the blind girl, and she asked Mrs. Huntington to write a description of it to the negroes, who she knew fancied that Louisville was the largest city in the world.

Not long after this, something which Mrs. Huntington said about her daughter determined Frederic to visit her and make the explanation which he felt it his duty to make, for he knew he had given her some reason to think he intended asking her to be his wife He accordingly feigned some excuse for going to New Haven, and one morning found himself at the door where Isabel was stopping.

"Give her this," he said, handing his card to the servant who carried it at once to the delighted young lady.

"Frederic Raymond," read Isabel. "Oh, yes. Tell him I'll be down in a moment," and she proceeded to arrange her hair a little more becomingly, and made several changes in her dress, so that the one minute was nearly fifteen ere she started for the parlor, where Frederic was rather dreading her coming, for he scarcely knew what he wished to say.

Half timidly she greeted him as a bashful maiden is supposed to meet her lover, and seating herself at a respectful distance from him, she asked numberless questions concerning his health, her numberless friends in Kentucky, her mother, and dear little Alice, who, she presumed, did not miss her much.

"Your mother's presence reminds us of you very often, of course," returned Frederic, "but you know we can get accustomed to almost anything, and Alice seems very happy."

"Yes," sighed Isabel. "You will all forget me, I suppose, even to mother—but for me I have not been quite contented since I left Kentucky. I thought it tiresome to teach, and perhaps was sometimes impatient and unreasonable, but I have often wished myself back again. I don't seem to be living for anything now," and Isabel's black eyes studied the pattern of the carpet quite industriously.

This long speech called for a reply, and Frederic said, "You would not care to come back again, would you?"

"Why, yes," returned Isabel; "I would rather do that than nothing."

For a time there was silence, while Frederic fidgeted in his chair and Isabel fidgeted in hers, until at last the former said:

"I owe you an explanation, Isabel, and I have come to make it. Do you remember our conversation in the parlor, and to what it was apparently tending, when we were interrupted by Alice?"

"Yes," replied Isabel, "and I have thought of it so often, wondering if you were in earnest, or if you were merely trifling with my feelings."

"I certainly had no intention of trifling with you," returned Frederic: "neither do I know as I was really in earnest. At all events it is fortunate for us both that Alice came in as she did;" and having said so much, Frederic could now look calmly upon a face which changed from a serene Summer sky to a dark, lightning-laden thunder-cloud as he told her the story he had came to tell.

In her terrible disappointment, Isabel so far forgot herself as to lose her temper entirely, and Frederic, while listening to her as she railed at him for what she called his perfidy, wondered how he ever could have thought her womanly or good.

"It was false that Marian was living, and had taken care of him when sick," she said. "He could not impose that story upon her, and he only wished to do it because he fancied that he was in some way pledged to her and wished for an excuse, but he might have saved himself the trouble, for even had Alice not appeared she should have told him No. She liked him once, she would admit, but there was nothing like living beneath the same roof to make one person tire of another, and even if she were not disgusted with him before, she should have become so while taking care of him in New York, and so she wrote to Agnes Gibson, who, she heard, had spread the news that she was engaged, though she had no authority for doing so, but it was just like the tattling mischief-maker!"

"Are you through?" Frederic coolly asked, when she had finished speaking. "If you are I will consider our interview at an end."

Isabel did not reply and he arose to go, saying to her as he reached the door, "I did not come here to quarrel with you, Bell, I wish still to be your friend, and if you are ever in trouble come to me as to a brother. Marian will, I trust, be with me then; but she will be kind to you, for 'tis her nature."

"Plague on that Marian," was Isabel's unlady-like thought as the door closed after Frederic. "I wonder how many times she's coming to life! How I wanted to charge him with his meanness in marrying her fortune, but as that is a secret between the two, he would have suspected me of treachery. The villain! I believe I hate him—and only to think how those folks in Kentucky will laugh. But it's all Agnes' doings. She inveigled more out of me than there was to tell, and then repeated it to suit herself. The jade! I hope she's happy with that old man"—and at this point Isabel broke down in a flood of tears, in the midst of which the door bell rang again, and hurrying up the stairs she listened to the names, which this time were "Mr. and Mrs. Rivers," (Agnes and her husband) and they asked for her.

Drying her tears, and bathing her eyes until the redness was gone, Isabel went down to meet the "tattling mischief-maker," embracing her very affectionately, and telling her how delighted she was to see her again, and how well she was looking.

"Then why do you not embark on the sea of matrimony yourself, if you think it such a beautifier," said Agnes.

"Me?" returned Isabel, with a toss of her head; "I thought I wrote you that I had given up that foolish fancy."

"Indeed, so you did," said Agnes, "but I had forgotten it, and when I saw Mr. Raymond at the Tontine, where we are stopping, I supposed of course he had come to see you, and I said to Mr. Rivers it really was too bad, for from what he said at our wedding I fancied there was nothing in it, and had made up my mind to take you with us to Florida, as I once talked of doing. Husband's sister wants a teacher for her children, don't she, dear?"

Mr. Rivers was about to answer in the affirmative, but ere he could speak Isabel chimed in, "Oh, you kind, thoughtful soul. Let me go with you now; do. Nothing could please me more. I have missed your society so much, and am so unhappy here!" and in the black eyes there was certainly a tear, which instantly touched the heart of the sympathetic old man who anticipated his wife's reply, by saying, "Certainly you shall go, if you like. You'll be company for Mrs. Rivers, and if I am in my dotage, as some say, I've sense enough to know that she can't be contented all the time with her grandfather. Eh, Aggie?" and chucked his bride under the chin.

"Disgusting!" thought Isabel.

"Old fool!" thought Agnes, who was really rather

pleased with the idea of having Isabel go with her to her new home, for though she did not love her dear friend, she rather enjoyed her company, and she felt that anybody was acceptable who would stand as a third person between herself and the grandfather she had chosen.

The more she thought of the plan the better she was pleased with it, and before parting the whole was amicably adjusted. Early in October, Isabel was to join her friend in Kentucky, and go with her from thence to Florida, where she was either to remain with Mrs. Rivers, or to teach in the family of Mrs. McGregor, Mr. Rivers' sister. The former was what Isabel intended to do, for she thoroughly disliked teaching, and if she could live without it, she would. Still she did not so express herself to her visitors, and she appeared so gracious and so grateful withal, that the heart of the bridegroom was wholly won, and after his return to their hotel, he extolled her so highly that Agnes began to pout, a circumstance which pleased her fatherly spouse, inasmuch as it augured more affection for himself than he had supposed her to possess.

The story of Isabel's intended trip to Florida was not long in reaching Rupolph McVicar, who had been wondering why something didn't occur, and if he were really to be disappointed after all.

"I wasted that paper and ink for nothing," was his mental comment when he heard from her own lips that Isabel was going; for, presuming upon his former acquaintance, he finally ventured to call upon her, demeaning himself so well that, like her mother, Isabel began to think he had reformed.

Still there was an expression in his eye which she did not like, and when at last he left her, she experienced a feeling of relief, as if a spell had been removed. After her recent interview with Frederic she would not go to his house, so her mother went to New Haven, staying with her daughter a week and then returning to Riverside, while Isabel started for Kentucky, where, as she had expected, she met with Mr. and Mrs. Rivers, and was soon on her way to Florida.

When sure that Isabel was gone, and that Sarah Green's letter had indeed been written in vain, Rudolph, who cared nothing now whether Marian were ever discovered to her husband or not, went to New York and embarked on a whaling voyage, as he had long thought of doing, fancying that the roving life of a seaman would suit his restless nature.

And now, with Rudolph on the sea, with Isabel in Florida, with Marian at school, and Frederic at Riverside, we draw a vail over the different characters of our story, nor lift it again until three years have passed away, bringing changes to all, but to none a greater change than to the so-called Marian Grey.

CHAPTER XIX.

THE GOVERNESS.

It was a bright September afternoon, and the dense foliage of the trees looked as fresh and green as when watered by the Summer showers, save here and there a faded leaf came rustling to the ground, whispering to those at whose feet it fell of the Winter which was hastening on, and whose breath even now was on the northern seas. Softly the Autumnal sunlight fell upon the earth, and the birds sang as gayly in the trees as if there were no hearts bereaved—no small, low rooms where all was darkness and gloom—no humble procession winding slowly through the crowded streets and out into the country, where, in a new-made grave, a mother's love was buried, while the mourners, two in number, a young man and a girl, held each other's hand in token that they were bound together by a common sorrow. Not a word was said by either; and when the solemn burial rite was over, they returned as silently to the carriage, then were driven back to their desolate home—the tenement where Frederic Raymond had watched the curtained window and the geranium growing there.

For many days that window had been darkened, just as it was when Marian Grey lay there with the fever in her veins; but it was open now, and the west wind came stealing in, purifying the room from the faint sickening smell of coffins and of death, for the Destroyer had been there. And when the mourners came back from the grave in the country, one threw himself upon the lounge, and burying his face in the cushions, sobbed aloud:

"Oh, Marian, it's terrible to be an orphan and have no mother."

"Yes, Ben, 'tis terrible," and Marian's tears dropped on the hair of the honest-hearted Ben.

Up to this hour he had restrained his grief, but now that he was alone with Marian, he wept on until the sun went down and the night shadows were creeping into the room. Then lifting up his head, he said, "It is so dark—so dismal now—and the hardest of all is the givin' up our dear old home where mother lived so long, and the thinkin' maybe you'll forget me when you live with that grand lady."

"Forget you! Oh, Ben, I never can forget how much you have done for me, denying yourself everything for my sake," said Marian, while Ben continued, "Nor won't you be ashamed of me neither, if I should come sometimes to see you? I should die if I could not once in a while look into your eyes; and you'll let me come, won't you, Marian?"

"Of course I will," she replied, continuing after a moment, "It is not certain yet that I go to Mrs. Sheldon's. I have not answered her last letter because—You know what we talked about before your mother died!"

"Yes, yes, I know," returned Ben, "but I had forgot it—my heart was so full other things. I'll go out there to-morrow. I'd rather you should teach at Rverside, even if you'd never heard of Frederic, than go to that grand lady, who might think, because you was a governess, that you wan't fit to live in the same house."

"I have no fears of that," said Marian. "Mrs. Harcourt says she is an estimable woman; but still, I too, would rather go to Riverside, if I were sure Frederic would not know me. Do you think there is any danger?"

"No," was Ben's decided answer, and in this opinion Marian herself concurred, for she knew that she had changed so much that none who saw her when first she came to Mrs. Burt's would recognize her now.

About three months before the night of which we are writing, she had been graduated at Mrs. Harcourt's school with every possible honor, both as a musician and a scholar. There had never been her equal there before, Mrs. Harcourt said, and when her friend, Mrs. Sheldon, who lived in Springfield Mass., applied to her for a family pupil, she warmly recommended her favorite pupil, Marian Grey, frankly stating, however, that she was of humble origin—that her adopted mother or aunt was a poor sewing woman, and her adopted brother a peddler. This, however, made no difference with Mrs. Sheldon, and several letters had passed between herself and Marian, who would have accepted the liberal offer at once, but for a lingering hope that Ben would carry out his favorite plan, and procure her a situation as teacher at Riverside. She had forgotten what she once said about learning to hate Frederic, and the possibility of living again beneath the some roof with him made her heart beat faster than its wont. She had occasionally met him in the street, and once she was sure his eye had rested upon her in passing, but she knew by its expression that she was not recognized, and when Ben suggested offering her services as Alice's governess she readily consented.

During these years Ben had not lost sight of Frederic's movements, though it so chanced that they had met but twice, once just after the receipt of Alice's picture, which had been greeted by Marian with a shower of kisses and tears, and once the previous Autumn, when Frederic was about returning to Kentucky, for, with his changed feelings toward Marian, Mr. Raymond felt less delicacy in using her money—less aversion to Redstone Hall, where his presence was really needed, for a portion of the year at least, and which he intended making his Winter residence.

But he was at Riverside now, and Ben was about going there to see what arrangements could be made, when his mother's sudden death caused both himself and Marian to forget the subject until the night after the burial, when, without a moment forgetting the dead or the dreary blank her absence made, they talked together of the future, and decided that on the morrow Ben should go to Riverside and see if there were room in Frederic's house for Marian Grey. The morning came, and at an early hour Ben started, bidding Marian keep up her spirits as he was sure of bringing her good tidings.

Frederic was sitting in his arm chair, which stood near the window, just where Marian had placed it three years and a half ago. Not that it had never been moved since that April morning, for, freed from old Dinah's surveillance, Mrs. Huntington, who was still at Riverside, proved herself a pattern housekeeper, and the chair had probably been moved a thousand times to make room for the broom and brush, but it was in its old place now, and Frederic was sitting in it, thinking of Marian and his hitherto fruitless efforts at finding her. He was beginning to get discouraged, and still each time he went to the city he thought "perhaps I may meet her to-day," and each night, as the hour for his return drew near, Alice waited upon the piazza when the weather was fine, and by the window when it was cold, listening intently for another step than Frederic's—a step which never came, and then Alice grew less hopeful, while Marian seemed farther and farther away as month after month went by bringing no tidings of her. Frederic knew that she must necessarily have changed somewhat from the Marian of old, for she was a woman now, but he should readily recognise her, he said. He should know her by her peculiar *hair*, if by no other token. So when his eye once rested on a face of surpassing sweetness, shaded by curls of soft chestnut hair, which in the sunlight wore a rich red tinge, he felt a glow like that which one experiences in gazing for a single instant on some picture of rare lovelinness; then the picture faded, the graceful figure glided by, and there was nothing left to tell how, by stretching forth his hand, he might have grasped his long lost Marian. Moments there were when she seemed near to him, almost within his reach, and such a moment was the one when Mrs. Huntington announced *Ben Butterworth*, whom he had not seen for a long time.

Involuntarily he started up, half expecting his visitor had come to tell him something of her. But when he saw the crape upon Ben's hat, and the sorrow on his face, he forgot Marian in his anxiety to know what had happened.

"My mother's dead," said Ben, and the strong man, six feet high, sobbed like a little child, bringing back to Frederic's mind the noiseless room, the oddly shaped box, the still, white face, and tolling bell, which were all he could distinctly remember of the day when he, too, said to a boy like himself, "My mother's dead."

These three words. Alas, how full of anguish is their utterance, and how their repetition will call up an answering throb in the heart of every one who has ever said in bitterness of grief, "My mother's dead."

Frederic felt it instantly, and it prompted him to take again the rough hand, which he pressed warmly in token of his sympathy.

"He *is* a good man," thought Ben, wiping his tears away; and after a few choking coughs and brief explanations as to how and when, he came at once to the object of his visit.

"He should peddle now just as he used to do, of course, but wimmen wan't so lucky, and all Marian could do was to teach. He had given her a tip-top larnin', though she had earnt some on't herself by sewin'. She had got a paper thing, too, with a blue ribin, from Miss Harcourt, who praised her up to the skies. In short, if Mr. Raymond had not any teacher for Alice, wouldn't he take Marian Grey?" and Ben twirled his hat nervously, while he waited for the answer.

"I wish you had applied to me sooner," said Frederic, "for in that case I would have taken her, but a Mrs. Jones, from Boston, came on only a week ago, so you see I am supplied. I am very sorry, for I feel an interest in Miss Grey, and will use my influence to procure her a situation."

"Thank you; there's a place she can have, but I wanted her to come here," returned Ben, who was greatly disappointed and began to cry again.

Frederic was somewhat amused, besides being considerably disturbed, and after looking at the child-man for a moment, he continued:

"Mrs. Jones is engaged for one year only, and if at the end of that time Miss Grey still wishes to come, I pledge you my word that she shall do so."

This brought comfort at once. One year was not very long to wait, and by that time Marian would certainly be past recognition, and as all Ben's wishes and plans centered upon one thing, to wit: Mr. Raymond's falling in love with his unknown wife, he was readily consoled, and wiping his eyes, he said apologetically, as it were, "I'm dreadful tender-hearted, and since I've been an orphan it's ten times wus. So you must excuse my actin' like a baby. Where's Alice?"

Frederic called the little girl, who, childlike, waited to put on her bracelet, "so as to show the man that she still wore it and liked it very much." She seemed greatly pleased at meeting Ben again, asking him why he had not been there before, and if he had received her picture.

"Yes, wee one," said he, taking her round white arm in his hand and touching the bracelet. "I should have writ, only that ain't in my line much, and I don't always spell jest right, but we got the picter, and Marian was so pleased she cried."

"What made her?" said Alice, wonderingly. "She don't know me."

"But she knows you're blind, for I told her," was Ben's quick reply, which was quite satisfactory to Alice, who by this time had detected a note of sadness in his voice, and she asked what was the matter.

To her also Ben replied, "My mother's dead," and the mature little girl understood at once the dreary loneliness that a mother's death must bring even to the heart of a big man like Ben. Immediately, too, she thought of Marian Grey, and asked "What she would do?"

"I come out to see if your pa—no, beg your pardon—to see if the Square didn't want her to hear you say your lessons," was Ben's answer, and Alice exclaimed, "Oh, Frederic. Let her come. I know I shall like her better than Mrs. Jones, for she's young and pretty, I am sure. May she come?"

"Alice," said Frederic, "Mrs. Jones has an aged mother and two little children dependent upon her earnings, and, should I send her away, the disappointment would be very great. Next year, if we all live, Miss Grey shall come, and with this you must be satisfied."

Alice saw at once that he was right, and she gave up the point, merely remarking that "a year was a heap of a while."

"No, 'tain't," said Ben, who each moment was becoming more and more reconciled to the arrangement.

One year's daily intercourse with fashionable people, he thought, would be of invaluable service to Marian, and as he wished her to be perfect both in looks and manners when he presented her to Frederic Raymond, he was well satisfied to wait, and he returned to New York with a light, hopeful heart. Marian, on the contrary, was slightly disappointed, for like Alice, a year seemed to her a long, long time. Still there was no alternative, and she wrote to Mrs. Sheldon that she would come as early as the first day of October. It was hard to break up their old home, but it was necessary, they knew, and with sad hearts they disposed of the furniture, gave up the rooms, and then, when the appointed time came, Marian started for her new home, accompanied by Ben, who went rather unwillingly.

"We ain't no more alike than ile and water," he said, when she first suggested his going, "and they won't think as much of you for seein' me."

But Marian insisted, and Ben went with her, mentally resolving to say but little, as by this means he fancied "he would be less likely to show how big a doit he was!"

CHAPTER XX.

WILL GORDON.

Mrs. Sheldon's residence was a most delightful spot, reminding Marian a little of Redstone Hall, and as she passed up its nicely graveled walk and stepped upon its broad piazza, she felt that she could be very happy there, provided she met with sympathizing friends. Any doubts she might have had upon this subject were speedily dispelled by the appearance of Mrs. Sheldon, in whose face there was something very familiar; and it was not long ere Marian identified her as the lady who had spoken so kindly to her in the car between Albany and New York, asking her what was the matter, and if she had friends in the city. This put Marian at once at her ease, and her admiration for her employer increased each moment, particularly when she saw how gracious she was to Ben, who true to his resolution, scarcely spoke except to answer Mrs. Sheldon's questions and to decline her invitation to dinner.

"I should never get through that in the world without some blunder," he thought, and as the dinner-bell was ringing, he took his leave, crying like a child when he parted with Marian, who was scarcely less affected than himself.

Going to the depot, he sauntered into the ladies' room, where he found a group of young girls, who were waiting the arrival of a friend, and who, meantime, were ready for any fun which might come up. Ben instantly attracted their attention, and one who seemed to be the leader of the party, began to quiz him, asking "where he lived, and if he had ever been so far from home before?"

Ben understood the drift of her remarks at once, and with imperturbable gravity, replied:

"I come from down East, where they raise sich as me, and this is the fust time I was ever out of Tanton, which allus was my native town!"

Then, taking his tobacco box from his pocket, he passed it to an elegant-looking man, whom he readily divined to be the brother of the girl, saying to him:

"Have a chaw, captain? I'd just as lief you would as not."

As he heard the loud laugh which this speech called forth, he continued, without the shadow of a smile:

"I had—'strue's I live, for I ain't none o' your tight critters. Nobody ever said that of Ben Bur—Ben Butterwith," he added, hastily, for until Marian was discovered to Frederic, he thought it best to retain the latter name.

"Ben Butterworth," repeated the young girl in an aside to her brother—"Why, Will, didn't sister Mary tell us that was the adopted brother or cousin of her new governess? You know Miss Grey mentioned his name in one of her letters."

"Yes, sir," said Ben, ere Will had time to reply. "If by Mary you mean Miss Sheldon, I'm the chap. Brought my sister there to-day, to be her school-ma'am, and I don't want you to run over her neither, 'cause you'll be sorry bimeby. That was all gammon I told you about never being away from home before, for I've seen considerable of the world."

The cars from Boston were by this time rolling in at the depot, and without replying to Ben's remark, the young lady went out to look for her friend.

That night, just after dark, Mrs. Sheldon's door bell rang, and her brother and sister came in, the latter dressed in the extreme of fashion, and bearing about her an air which seemed to indicate that she had long been accustomed to receive the homage of those around her. Seating herself on the sofa, she began, "Well, Mary, Will and I have come over to see this wonderful prodigy. Mother was here, you know, this afternoon, and she came home half wild on the subject of Miss Grey, insisting that I should call directly, and so like a dutiful daughter I have obeyed, though I must confess that the sight of Ben Butterworth, whom we met at the depot, did not greatly prepossess me in her favor."

"They are not at all alike," said Mrs. Sheldon, "neither are they in any way related. Miss Grey is highly educated, and has the sweetest face I ever saw. She has some secret trouble, too, I'm sure, and she reminds me of a beautiful picture over which a vail is thrown, softening, and at the same time heightening its beauty."

"Really," said Will, rousing up, "some romance connected with her. Do bring her out at once."

Mrs. Sheldon left the room, and going up to Marian's chamber, knocked at the door. A low voice bade her come in, and she entered just in time to see Marian hide away the daguerreotype of Frederic, at which she had been looking.

"My brother and sister are in the parlor and have asked for you," she said.

"I will come down in a moment," returned Marian, who wished a little time to dry her tears, for she had been weeping over the pictures of Frederic and Alice, both of which she had in her possession.

Accordingly, when Mrs. Sheldon was gone, she bathed her face until the stains had disappeared; then smoothing her collar and brushing her wavy hair, she descended to the parlor, where Ellen Gordon sat prepared to criticise, and William Gordon sat prepared for almost anything, though not for the vision which greeted his view when Marian Grey appeared before him. The dazzling purity of her complexion contrasted well with her black dress, and the natural bloom upon her cheek was increased by her embarrassment, while her eyes dropped modestly beneath the long-fringed lashes, which Ellen noticed at once, because they were the one coveted beauty which had been denied to herself.

"Jupiter!" was Will's mental comment. "Mary didn't exaggerate in the least, and Nell will have to yield the palm at once."

Something like this passed through Ellen's mind, but though on the whole a frank, right-minded girl, she was resolved upon finding fault with the stranger, simply because her mother and sister had said so much in her praise.

"She is vulgar, I know," she thought, and she watched narrowly for something which should betray her low birth, but she waited in vain.

Marian was perfectly lady-like in her manners; her language was well chosen; her voice soft and low; and ere she had been with her half an hour, Ellen secretly acknowledged her superiority to most of the young ladies of her acquaintance, and she regretted that she, too, had not been educated at Mrs. Harcourt's school, if such manners as Miss Grey's were common there.

At Mrs. Sheldon's request, Marian took her seat at the piano, and then Ellen hoped to criticise; but here again she was at fault, for Marian was a brilliant performer, keeping perfect time, and playing with the most exquisite taste.

As she was turning over the leaves of the music book after the close of the first piece, Will said to his sister:

"By the way, Nell, I had a letter from Fred to-day and he says he will be delighted to get you that music the first time he goes to the city."

Marian started just as she had done that afternoon when Mrs. Sheldon called her youngest boy Fred. Still there was no reason why she should do so. Frederic was a common name, and she kept on turning the leaves, while Ellen replied, "What else did he write, and when is he going south?"

Marian's hand was stayed now, and she listened eagerly for the answer, which was "Sometime in November, and he has invited me to go with him, but I hardly think I shall. He's lonesome, he says, and can find no trace of his run-away wife. So, there's a shadow of a chance for you Nell."

The hand which held the leaf suspended, came down with a crash upon the keys of the piano, but Ellen thought it was an accident, if she thought of it at all; and she replied, "Fie, just as though I would have a man before I knew for certain that his wife was dead. I admire Mr. Raymond very much, and if he had not been so foolish as to marry that child, I can't say that he would not have made an impression, for he is the finest-looking and most agreeable gentleman I ever met. Isn't it strange where that girl went, and what she went for? Hasn't he ever told you anything that would explain it?"

Up to this point Marian had sat immovable, listening eagerly and wondering where these people had known Frederic Raymond. Then, as something far back in the past flashed upon her mind, she turned, and looking in the young man's face, knew who he was and that they had met before. His name had seemed familiar from the first, and she knew that he was the Will Gordon who had been Frederic's chum in college, and had once spent a vacation at Redstone Hall. He had predicted that she would be a handsome woman, and Frederic had said she could not with such hair. She remembered it all distinctly, but any effect it might then have had upon her was lost in her anxiety to hear the answer to Ellen's question.

"Fred generally keeps his matters to himself, but I know as much as this: He didn't love that Miss Lindsey any too well when he married her, but he has admitted to me since that his feelings toward her had undergone a change, and he would give almost anything to find her. He is certain that she was with him when he was sick in New York, and since that time he has sought for her everywhere."

William Gordon had no idea of the effect his words produced upon the figure which, on the music stool, sat as motionless as if it had been a block of marble. During all the long, dreary years of exile from home there had not come to her so cheering a ray of hope as this, and the bright bloom deepened on her cheek, while the joy which danced in her deep blue eyes made them look almost black beneath the heavy lashes. Frederic was beginning to love her—he had acknowledged as much to Mr. Gordon, and her heart bounded forward to the time when she should see him face to face, and hear him tell her so with his own lips. Little now she heeded Ellen's next remark, "I presume it would be just the same even if he were to find her. He is a great admirer of beauty, and she, I believe, was very ordinary looking."

"Not remarkably so," returned Will. "She was thin-faced and had red hair, but I remember thinking she might make a handsome woman—"

"With red hair! Oh, Will!" and the blacktressed Ellen laughed at the very idea.

A sudden movement on Marian's part made Will recollect her, and he hastened to apologise for his apparent forgetfulness of her presence.

"You will please excuse us," he said, "for discussing an affair in which you, of course, can have no interest."

"Certainly," she replied, while around the corners of her mouth were little laughing dimples, which told no tales to the young man, who continued: "Will you give us some more music? I admire your style of playing."

Marian was in a mood for anything, and turning to the piano she dashed off into a merry, spirited thing, to which Will's feet kept time, while Ellen looked on amazed at the white fingers which flew like lightning over the keys, seemingly never resting for an instant upon any one of them, but lighting here and there with a rapidity she never before seen equalled. It was the outpouring of Marian's heart, and the tune she played was a song of jubilee for the glad tidings she had heard. Ere she had half finished, Will Gordon was at her side, gazing wonderingly into her face, which sparkled and glowed with her excitemënt.

"She is strangely beautiful," he thought, and so he said to Ellen when they were walking home together.

"She looks very well," returned Ellen, "but I trust you will not feel it your duty to fall in love with her on that account. Wouldn't it be ridiculous though, for you, who profess never to have felt the least affection for any woman, to yield at once to Mary's governess?"

"Mary's governess is no ordinary person," answered Will. "How like the mischief she made those fingers go in that last piece. I never saw anything like it;" and he tried in vain to whistle a few bars of the lively strain.

That night three men dreamed of Marian—Will Gordon in his bachelor apartments, which he had said should never be invaded with a female's wardrobe—Ben Burt in his room at the Lovejoy Hotel—and Frederic Raymond in his cheerful home upon the Hudson. But to Marian, sleeping so quietly in her chamber there came a thought of only one, and that one Frederic Raymond, whose picture lay beneath her pillow. She had never placed it there until to-night, for she had felt that she had no right to do so. But Mr. Gordon's words had effected a change. He said that Frederic was begining to love her at last—that he had sought for her without success—that he would give almost anything to find her. It is true she could not reconcile all this with her preconceived opinion: but she had no wish to doubt it, and she accepted it as truth, thinking it was probably a very recent thing with him, this searching after and loving her.

Very rapidly and pleasantly to Marian did the first few weeks of her sojourn with Mrs. Sheldon pass away. She was interested in her pupils, two bright-faced little girls, and doubly interested in their brother, the brown-eyed *Fred*, whose real name she learned was Frederic Raymond, he having been called, Mrs. Sheldon said, after Williams particular friend, who spent his winters in Kentucky, and his Summers at Riverside, a delightful place on the Hudson. Frederic Raymond was a frequent subject of conversation in Mrs. Sheldon's family, and once, after Marian had been there four or five months, and Will, as usual, was spending an evening there, the matter was discussed at length, while Marian, sitting partly in the shade, so that the working of her features could not be seen, dropped stitch after stitch in the cloud she was crotcheting, and finally stopped altogether as the conversation proceeded.

"I am positive," said Mrs. Sheldon, "that I saw Mrs. Raymond in the cars, between Albany and Newburg. It was four years ago, last Autumn, and about that time she came away. There was a very young girl sitting before me, dressed in black, with long red curls, and she looked as if she had wept all her tears away, though they fell like rain when I spoke to her and asked her what was the matter. I remember her particularly from her question, 'Is New York a heap noisier than Albany or Buffalo?'"

"That 'heap' is purely Southern," interrupted Will, while his sister continued:

"She said she had but one friend in the world, and that one was in New York. I remember, too, that one of her hands was ungloved. It was so white and small, and she used it so often to brush her tears away."

Here Will glanced involuntarily at the beautiful little hands busy with the cloud. It might have been fancy, but he thought they trembled, and so he closed the register and opened a door, thinking the heat of of the room might have made Miss Grey nervous—and he was growing very careful of her comfort!

Poor Will!

Returning to his seat, he replied to his sister's remark, "That was undoubtedly Marian Lindsey. Did you speak of it to Frederic?"

"No," said Mrs. Sheldon, "I have always thought he disliked talking of her to me, and that makes me think there is something wrong—that he did her an injury."

"Every man who marries without love injures the woman he makes his wife," said Will, "and Frederic does not profess to have loved her then. His father drew him into this match, and for some inexplicable reason Fred consented, when all the time he loved that Isabel Huntington. But he has recovered from that infatuation, and I am glad of it, for I never liked her, and had the thing been possible, I should say she poisoned him against this Marian. Why, Miss Grey, you are actually shivering," he added, as he saw the violent trembling of Marian's body, and this time he opened the register and shut the door, offering to go for a shawl, and asking where she had taken such a cold.

"It's only a slight chill—it will soon pass off," she said, and as Mrs. Sheldon was just then called from the room, Will drew his chair a little nearer to Marian and continued:

"This Raymond affair must be irksome to you, who know nothing about it."

"Oh, no," said Marian faintly. "I am greatly interested, particularly in the girl-wife. Can't he find her? Seems as though he might. Perhaps though, he don't really care."

"Yes, he does," interrupted Will. "He disliked her once, but I believe he feels differently toward her now. His hobby in college was a handsome wife, but he has learned that beauty alone is worthless, and he would gladly take Marian back."

"Red hair and all?" asked Marian, mischievously, and Will replied, "Yes, I believe he's even made up his mind to the red hair. I didn't objcct to it myself, and I once saw this girl."

"Redstone Hall is a beautiful spot, I believe," said Marian, briefly stating thai Ben had once been there in his travels, and had since met Mr. Raymond in New York.

"Then you know the family," said Will, in some surprise.

"I know *of* them," returned Marian, "for Ben was so much interested in the blind girl that after his return he talked of little else."

"You have never seen them youself, of course," and taking this fact for granted, Will proceeded to give her a most minute description of Redstone Hall, of its master, and of herself as she was when he visited Kentucky.

Frederic's marriage was then touched upon. Will telling how angry his chum used to be when he received a letter on the subject from his father.

"We were studying law together," he said, "and, as we were room-mates in college, it was quite natural that we should confide in each other; so he used to tell me of his father's project, and almost *swear* he wouldn't do it. I never was more astonished than when I heard he was to be married in a few days. 'It's all over with me,' he wrote, 'I can't help it!" and he signed himself 'Your wretched Fred!' But what are you crying for, Miss Grey? You certainly are. What is the matter?"

"I am crying for her—for poor Marian Lindsey!" was the answer; and Marian's tears flowed faster.

Will Gordon was distressed at the sight of woman's tears, but particularly at the sight of Marian Grey's, and he tried to console her by saying he was sure Mr. Raymond would sometime find his wife, and they all would be the happier for what they both had suffered. Involuntarily he had touched the right chord, for, in listening to his predictions of future good, which should come to Frederic Raymond's wife, Marian Grey ceased to weep, and when, ere his departure, Will asked her for for some music, she gave him one of those stirring pieces she always played when her heart was running over with happy anticipations!

Will Gordon was older than Frederic Raymond, and an examination of the family Bible would have shown him to be thirty. Quite a bachèlor, his sister Ellen said, and she marveled that he had lived thus long without taking to himself a wife. But Will was very fastidious in his ideas of females, and though he had traveled much, both in Europe and his own country, he had never seen a face which could hold his fancy for a moment, until the sunny blue eyes of Marian Grey shone upon him and thawed the ice which had laid about his heart so many years. Even then he did not quite understand the feeling, or know how it was that night after night he found himself locked out at home, while morning after morning his sister Ellen scolded him for staying out so late, wondering what attraction he could find at Mary's, when he knew as well as she that he would never disgrace the Gordon family by marrying a *governess*, and a peddler's adopted sister, too! Will hardly thought he should either. He didn't quite know what ailed him, and in a letter written to Frederic, who was now in Kentucky, he gave an analysis of his feelings, after having first told him that Marian Grey was the adopted sister of a Yankee peddler, who had once visited Redstone Hall, and who, he was sure, Frederic would remember for his oddities.

"I wish you could see this girl," he wrote, "I'd like to have your opinion, for I know you are a *connoisseur* in everything pertaining to female charms, but I am sure you never in all your life saw anything like Marian Grey. I never did, and I have seen the proudest court beauties in Europe—but nobody like her. And yet it is not so much the exceeding fairness of her complexion, or the perfect regularity of her features, as it is the indescribably fascinating something which demands your pity as well as your admiration. There is that about her mouth, and in her smile, which seems to say that she has suffered as few have ever done, and that from this suffering she has risen purified, beautified, and if I may be allowed a term which my good mother would call wicked in the extreme, *glorified* as it were!

"Just picture to yourself a graceful, airy figure, five feet four inches high—then clothe it in black, and adapt every article of dress exactly to her form and style, then imagine a rose-bud face, which I cannot describe, with the deepest, saddest, brightest, merriest, sunniest, laughing blue eyes you ever saw. You see there is a slight contradiction of words, but every one by turns will apply to her eyes of blue. Then her hair—oh, Fred, words fail me here. It's a mixture of everything—brown, black, yellow, and red. Yes, red—I mean it, for it has decidedly a reddish hue in the sunshine. By gas-light it is brown, and by daylight a most beautiful chesnut or auburn—rippling all over her head in glossy waves, and curling about her forehead and neck.

"Beautiful—beautiful Marian! Yes, I will call her Marian here on paper, with no one to see it but you. 'Tis a sweet, feminine name, Fred;—the name, too, of your lost wife. I told her that story the other night, and she cried great tears, which looked like pearls upon her cheek.

"Do write soon, and give me your advice—though what I want of it is more than I can tell. I only know that I feel strangely about the region of my waistbands, and every time I see Miss Grey, I feel a heap worse, as you folks say. She is of low origin, I know, and this would make a difference with a man as proud as you, but I don't care. Marian Grey has bewitched me, I verily believe, until I am—I don't know what.

"Do write, Fred, and tell me what I am, and what to do. But pray don't preface your letter with long-winded remarks about marrying my equal—looking higher than a peddler's sister, and all that nonsense, for it will be lost on me. I never can get higher than Marian's blue eyes unless indeed I reached her hair, at which point I should certainly yield, and go over to the enemy at once."

This letter reached Frederic one rainy afternoon, when he had nothing to do but to read it, laugh over it, reflect upon and answer it. Will Gordon's description of Marian Grey thrilled him with a strange feeling of pleasure, imperceptibly sending his thoughts after another Marian, and involuntarily he said, aloud, "If she had been like this picture Will has drawn, I should not be here so lonely and desolate."

Frederic Raymond was prouder far than Will Gordon, and his feelings at first rebelled against his friend's taking for a bride the sister of unpolished, uneducated Ben. "But it is his own matter," he said; "I see plainly that he is in love, so I will write at once and tell him what is the 'trouble'"

Accordingly he commenced a letter, in which after expressing his happiness that his college friend had not persisted in shutting his eyes to all female charms, he wrote:

"I should prefer your wife to be somewhat nearer your equal in point of family, it is true, but your description of Marian Grey won my heart entirely, and you have my consent to offer yourself at once. By so doing, you will probably deprive Alice of her governess and me of a pleasant companion, for I had made an arrangement with Ben to have Miss Grey with us next year. But no matter for that. Woo and win her just the same, and Heaven grant you a happier future than my past has been.

"'Beautiful! beautiful Marian!' you said, and without knowing why, my heart responded to it. She is beautiful, I am sure, and your description of her is just what I would like to apply to my own wife—my lost Marian! You see I have withdrawn my allegiance from black-haired dark-eyed maidens, and gone over to laughing blue eyes and auburn tresses.

"By the way, speaking of the dark eyed maidens reminds me that Agnes Gibson's husband is dead, and she is sole heiress of all his fortune, except a legacy which he left to Miss Huntington, who lived in his family at the time of his death. Poor old man! Rumor says he led a sorry life with both of them, but at the last his young wife cajoled him into making his will, and was really kind to him. She is at her father's now, and Miss Huntington is there also. I called upon them yesterday, and have hardly recovered yet from the chilling reception I met with from the latter.

"But pardon me, Will, for this digression, when I was to write of nothing save Marian Grey. The name reminded me of my own wife, and that, as a matter of course, suggested Isabel. Give my compliments to Miss Grey, and tell her that, under the circumstances, I release her from her engagement with myself, and that, if she is a sensible girl, as I suppose she is, she will not keep you on your knees longer than necessary. Let me hear of your success or failure, and, on no account, forget to invite me to the wedding. It is possible I may be obliged to come North on business, in the course of a few weeks, and, if so, I shall certainly call on you for the sake of seeing this wonderful Marian Grey. "Yours truly,

"F. Raymond."

CHAPTER XXI.

WILL'S WOOING.

THE silver tea-set and damask cloth had been removed from Mrs. Gordon's supper-table. The heavy curtains of brocatelle were dropped before the windows; a cheerful fire was burning in the grate, for Mrs. Gordon eschewed both furnaces and stoves; the gas burned brightly in the chandelier, casting a softened light throughout the room, and rendering more distinct the gay flowers on the carpet. The lady-mother, a fair type of a thrifty New England woman, had donned her spectacles, and from a huge pile of socks was selecting those which needed a near acquaintance with the needle, and lamenting over her son's propensity at wearing out his toes!

The son, meantime, half lay, half sat upon the sofa, listlessly drumming with his fingers, and feeling glad that Ellen was not there, and wondering how he should begin to tell his mother what he so much wished her to know.

"I should suppose she might see it," he thought—"might know how much I am in love with Marian, for I used to be always talking about her, and now I never mention her, it makes my heart thump so if I try to speak her name. Nell will make a fuss, perhaps, for she thinks so much of family: but Marian is family enough for me. Mary likes her, and I guess mother does. I mean to ask her."

"Mother?"

"What, William?" and the good lady ran her hand into a sock with a shockingly large rent in the heel.

No woman can be very gracious with such an open prospect, and, as Will saw the scowl on his mother's face, he regretted that he had spoken at this inauspicious moment.

"I'll wait till she finds one not quite as dilapidated as that," he thought, and when the question was repeated, "What, William?" he replied, "Is Nell coming home to-night?"

"I believe so. I wish she was here now to help me, for I shall never get these mended. What makes you wear out your socks so fast?"

"I don't know, I'm sure, unless it's beating time to Miss Grey's lively music. Don't she play like the mischief, though?"

Mrs. Gordon did not answer, and Will continued, "Let me help you mend. I used to in college and in Europe, too, and if I never marry,"—here Will's voice trembled a little—"I shall need to know how. Thread me a darning needle, won't you?"

Mrs. Gordon laughingly compiled with his request, and the fashionable Will Gordon was soon deep in the mysteries of sock-darning, an accomplishment in which he had before had some experience. Very rapidly his mother's amiability increased, until at last he ventured to say, "Let me see, how old am I?"

"Thirty, last August, just twenty years younger than I am."

"Then, when you were at my age you had a boy ten years old. I wonder how I should feel in a like predicament."

"I'm afraid you'll never know," and Mrs. Gordon commenced on a fresh sock.

"Mother, how would you to have me marry and settle down?" Will continued, after a moment's silence, and his mother replied, "Well enough, provided I liked your wife."

"You don't suppose I'd marry one you didn't like,

I hope. Just look, can you beat that?" and he held up what he fancied to be a neatly darned sock, which, spite of its bungling appearance, received so much praise, that he felt emboldened to proceed.

Taking Frederic's letter from his pocket he passed it to his mother, asking her to read it, and give him her opinion.

"You know I never can make out Mr. Raymond's writing," said Mrs. Gordon, "so pray read it yourself."

But this Will could not do, and he insisted until his mother took the letter and began to read, while he forgot to darn, so intent was he upon watching the expression of her face. At first it turned very red, then white, and then the great drops of perspiration stood upon her forehead, for she felt as every mother does, when they first learn that their only boy is about yielding to another the love they have claimed so long.

"Have you spoken to Marian?" she asked, giving him back the letter, but not resuming her work.

"No," was his answer: and she continued, "Then I wouldn't."

"Why not?" he asked, in some alarm; and with a tremor in her voice, his mother replied, "I've nothing against Marian, but we are so happy together, and it would kill me to have you go away."

"Is that all?" and in his delight Will ran the darning-needle under his thumb nail; "I needn't go away. I can bring her home, and you won't have to mend my socks any more. Those back chambers are seldom used, and—"

"Back chambers!" exclaimed Mrs. Gordon. "I guess if you bring a wife here, you'll occupy the parlor chamber and bedroom. I was going to re-paper them in the Spring, and I think on the whole I'll refurnish it entirely, for you might sometimes have calls up there."

"You charming woman," cried Will, kissing his mother, whose consent he understood to be fully won.

He knew she had always admired Miss Grey, but he

expected more opposition than this, and in his delight he would have gone to see Marian at once, were it not that he had heard she was absent that evening. For an hour or more he talked with his mother of his plans, and when at last Ellen came in, she, too, was let into the secret. Of course, she rebelled at first, for her family pride was very strong, and the peddler Ben, was a serious objection. But when she saw how earnest her brother was, and that her mother, too, had espoused his cause, she condescended to say:

"I suppose you might do worse, though folks will wonder at your taste in marrying Mary's governess."

"Let them wonder, then," said Will. "They dare not slight my wife, you know," and then he drew a pleasing picture of the next Summer, when, with his mother, Marian and Ellen, he would visit the White Mountains and Montreal.

"Why not go to Europe?" suggested Ellen. "Mr. Sheldon talks of going in August, and if you must marry this girl, you may as well go, too."

"Well spoken for yourself, little puss," returned Will; "but it's a grand idea, and I'll make arrangements with Tom as soon as I have seen Marian. Maybe she'll refuse me," and Will turned pale at the very idea.

"No danger," was Ellen's comment, while her mother thought the same, for in her estimation no one in their right mind could refuse her noble boy.

It was a long night to Will, and the next day longer still, for joyful hope and harrowing fears tormented his mind, and when at last it was dark, and he had turned his face toward Mr. Sheldon's, he half determined to go back. But he didn't, and with his usual easy, off-hand manner, he entered his sister's sitting-room. Though bound to secrecy, Ellen had told the news to Mrs. Sheldon, who, of course, had told her husband; and soon after Will's arrival, the two found some excuse for leaving him alone with Marian Grey.

Marian liked William Gordon very much—partly

because he was Frederic's friend, and partly because she knew him to be a most affectionate brother and dutiful son—two rare qualities in a traveled and fashionable man. She was always pleased to see him, and she welcomed him now as usual, without observing his evident embarrassment when at last they were alone. There were no stockings to be darned, and he did not know how to commence, until he remembered Frederic's letter. It had helped him with his mother—it might aid him now—and after fidgeting awhile in his chair, he said:

"I heard from Mr. Raymond yesterday."

"Indeed!" and Marian's voice betrayed more interest than the word would indicate.

"He wrote that you were engaged to him—"

"I engaged to Frederic Raymond!" and Marian started so suddenly that she pulled her needle out from the worsted garment she was knitting.

"Engaged to teach, I mean," returned Will. "I'll show you what he wrote when you pick up those stitches. What do you call that queer-shaped thing?"

"A Sontag, or Hug-me-tight," said Marian, while Will involuntarily exclaimed, "Oh, I wish I could—see Fred, he's such a good fellow," he hastened to add, as he saw Marian's wondering glance.

But the beginning and end of the sentence were too far apart to belong to each other, and there was a moment's awkward silence, which was broken at last by Marian, who, resolving to take no notice of the strange speech, said:

"What did Mr. Raymond write of me?"

"I'll show you just a little," and Will pointed out the sentence commencing with "Give my respects to Miss Grey," etc.

The sight of the well-remembered handwriting affected Marian sensibly; but when she came to the last part, and began to understand to what it all was tending, her head grew dizzy and her brain whirled for a moment. Then an intense pity for Will Gordon filled her soul, for looking upward she met the glance of his eyes, and saw therein how much she was beloved.

"No, no, Mr. Gordon!" she cried, putting her hands to her ears as he began to say: "Dear Marian." "You must not call me so; it is wicked for you to do it—wicked for me to listen. I am not what I seem."

And she burst into tears, weeping so bitterly that in his efforts to soothe her, Will well nigh carried out the wish which had been finished up with "seeing Frederic Raymond."

Her not being what she seemed, he fancied might refer to something connected with her birth, and he hastened to assure her that no circumstance whatever could change his feelings, or prevent him from wishing her to be his wife.

"Won't you, Marian?" he said, holding her in his arm so she could not escape. "I have never loved before. I always said I could not, until I saw you; and then everything was changed. I have told my mother, darling, and Ellen, too. They are ready to receive you, if you will go. Look at me, and say you will come to my home, which will never again be so bright to me without you. Won't my darling answer me?" he continued, while she sobbed so violently as to render speaking impossible. "I am sorry if my words distressed you so," he added, resting her head upon his bosom, and fondly smoothing her hair.

"I am distressed for you," Marian at last found voice to say. "Oh, Mr. Gordon, I should be most wretched if I thought I had encouraged you in this! But I have not, I am sure. I like you very, very much, but I *cannot be your wife!*"

"Marian, are you in earnest?" And on Will Gordon's manly face was a look never seen there before.

He did not know until now how much he loved the beautiful young girl he held so closely to his side. All the affections of his heart had centered themselves, as it were, upon her, and he could not give her up. She had been so kind to him—had welcomed him ever with her sweetest smile—had seemed sorry at his departure—and was not this encouragement? He had taken it as such, and ere she could reply to the question: "Are you in earnest?" he added:

"I have thought, from your manner, that I was not indifferent to you, else I had never told you of my love. Oh, Marian, if you desert me now, I shall wish that I could die!"

Marian struggled until she released herself from his embrace, and, standing before him, she replied:

"I never dreamed that you thought of me, save as a friend, and if I have encouraged you, it was because —you reminded me of another. Oh, Mr. Gordon, must I tell you that long before I came here, I had learned to love some other man—hopelessly, it is true, for he does not care for me; but that can make no difference. Had I never seen him—never known of him—I might—I *would* have been your wife, for I know that you are noble and good; but 'tis too late—too late!"

He did not need to ask her now if she were in earnest; for, looking up into her truthful, clear blue eyes, he knew there was no hope for him, and bowing his head upon the arm of the sofa, he groaned aloud, while the heaving of his chest showed how much he suffered, and how manfully he strove to keep his feelings down. Mournfully Marian gazed upon him, wishing she had never come there, if by coming she had brought this hour of anguish to him. Half timidly she laid her hand upon his head, for she wished to comfort him; and, as he felt the touch of her fingers, he started, while an expression of joy lighted up his face, only to pass away again as he saw the same unloving look in her eye.

"If I could comfort you," she said, "I would gladly do it; but I cannot. You will forget me in time, Mr. Gordon, and be as happy as you were before you knew me."

He shook his head despairingly. "No one could

forget you; and the man who stands between us must be a monster not to requite your love. Who is he, Marian?' or is it not for me to know?"

"I would rather you should not—it can do no good," was Marian's reply; and then Will Gordon pleaded with her to think again ere she told him so decidedly no. She might outlive that other love. She ought to, certainly, if 'twere a hopeless one; and if she only gave him half a heart, he would be content until he won the whole. They would go to Europe in Autumn; and beneath the sunny skies of Italy she would learn to love him, he knew. "Won't you, Marian?" and in the tone of his voice there was a word of eager, fearful, yearning love.

"I can't—I can't; it is utterly impossible!" was the decided answer; and, without another word, Will Gordon rose and passed, with a breaking heart, from the room he had entered so full of hope and pleasing anticipations.

The fire burned just as brightly in the grate at home as it had done the night before; the gas-light fell as softly on the roses in the carpet, and on his mother's face there was a placid, expectant look, as he came in. But it quickly vanished when she saw how he pale he was, and how he crouched down into his easy chair, as if he fain would hide from every one the pain gnawing at his heart. There had never been a secret between Mrs. Gordon and her son, for in some respects the man of thirty was as much a child as ever; and when his mother, coming to his side, parted the damp hair from his forehead, and looked into his eyes, saying:

"What is it, William? Has Marian Grey refused my boy?'" he told her all. How Marian Grey had given her love to another, and that henceforth the world to him would be a dreary blank.

It was, indeed, a terrible disappointment, and as the days wore on, it told fearfully upon William's health, until at last the mother sought an interview with Marian Grey, beseeching her to think again.

"You can be happy with William," she said, "and I had prepared myself to love you as a daughter. Do, I beseech of you, give me some hope to carry back to my poor boy?"

"I cannot—I cannot!"

And, laying her head in the motherly lap of Mrs. Gordon, Marian wept bitterly—half tempted, more than once, to tell her the whole truth.

But this she did not do, and she wept on, while Mrs. Gordon's tears kept company with her own.

"Don't you like my Willian?" she asked, unconsciously playing with the bright hair resting on her lap.

"Yes—very, very much; but I loved another first." And this was all the satisfaction Marian could give.

Mrs. Sheldon next tried her powers of persuasion, pleading for herself quite as much as for her brother, for she loved the young girl dearly, and would gladly have called her sister. But naught which she could say had the least effect, and *Ellen* determined to see what she could do. She had been very indignant at first, to think a poor teacher should refuse her brother, and something of this spirit manifested itself during her interview with Marian.

"I am astonished at you," she said; "for, though we have ever treated you as our equal, you must know that in point of family you are not, and my brother has done what few young men in his standing would have done. Why, there never was a gentleman in Springfield whom the girls accounted a better match than William, unless it were Mr. Raymond from Kentucky, and they only gave him the preference because he lives South, and possibly has a wife somewhere. So they could not get him, if they wished to. Now, if you were in love with *him*, and he were not already married, I should not think so strangely of your conduct, for he may be Will's superior in some respects;

but I cannot conceive of your refusing him for any common man such as would be likely to address you."

Marian did not think it necessary to reply in substance to this long speech, neither did she, by word or look, resent Ellen's overbearing manner; but she answered, as she always did:

"I would marry your brother, if I could; but I cannot."

"Then I trust you will have a pleasant time teaching all your days," said Ellen, as she slammed the door behind her, and went to report her success.

All this trouble and excitement wore upon Marian, and after a time she became too ill to leave her room, where she kept her bed, sometimes fancying it all a dream—sometimes resolving to tell the people who she was, and always weeping over the grief she had brought to William Gordon, who, during her illness, showed how noble and good he was by caring for her as tenderly as if she had indeed been his promised bride. He did not see her, but he made his presence felt in a thousand different ways, and when they told him how her tears would drop upon the fresh bouquets he sent her from the green-house every morning, he would turn away to keep his own from falling.

One night, toward the last of March, as he sat with his mother in the same room where he first told her of his love for Marian Grey, the door-bell rang, and a moment after, to his great surprise, Frederic Raymond walked into the room. William had forgotten what his friend had said about the possibility of his coming north earlier than usual, and he was so much astonished that for some moments he did not appear like himself.

"You know I wrote that business might bring me to Albany," said Frederic, "and that if I came so far I should visit you."

"Oh, yes, I remember now," returned William, the color mounting to his forehead as he recalled the nature of the last letter written to Frederic, who, from his manner, guessed that something was wrong, and forbore questioning him until they retired to their room for the night.

"Fred," said William, after they had talked awhile on indifferent subjects, "Fred," and Will's feet went up into a chair, for even a man who has been refused feels better, and can tell it better, with his heels a little elevated, "Fred, it's all over with me, and it makes no difference now whether the sun rises in the east or in the west."

"I suspected as much," returned Frederic, "from your failing to write and from the length of your face. What is the matter? You didn't coax hard enough, I reckon, and I shall have to undertake it for you. How would you like that? I dare say I should be more successful," and Frederic's smile was much like the Frederic of other days, when he and Will were college friends together.

"I said everything a man could say, but the chief difficulty is that she *don't* love *me* and *does* love another," returned Will, at the same time repeating to his companion as much of his experience as he thought proper.

"A discouraging beginning, I confess," said Frederic; "but perhaps she will relent."

"No she won't," returned Will; "she is just as decided now as she was that night. I have exhausted all my persuasion; mother has coaxed, so has Mary, so has Nell, and all to no purpose. Marian Grey can never be my wife. If it were not for this other love, though, I would not give it up."

"Who is the favored one?" Frederic asked, and his friend replied, "Some rascal, I dare say, for she says it is a hopeless attachment on her part, and that makes it all the worse. Now if I knew the man was worthy of her, I should not feel so badly. If it were *you*, for instance, or somebody like you, I'd try to be satisfied, knowing she was quite as well off as she would be with me," and Will's feet went up to the top of the chair as he thought how magnanimous he would be were it Frederic Raymond who was beloved by Marian Grey.

"I am sorry for you," said Frederic—"sorry that you, too, must walk under a cloud, as I am doing. We little thought, when we were boys, that we should both be called to bear a heavy burden; but thus has it proved. Mine came sooner than yours, and it seems to me 'tis the hardest of the two to bear."

"Fred, you don't know what you are saying. Your grief cannot be as great as mine, for I *love* Marian Grey as man never loved before, and when she told me 'No,' and I knew she meant it, I felt as if she were tearing out my very heartstrings. *You* acknowledge that you never loved your wife; but you married her for—I don't know *what* you married for ——"

"*For* MONEY!" And the word dropped slowly from Frederic's lips.

"*For money?*" repeated Will. "She had no money—this Marian Lindsey. She was a poor orphan, I always thought. Will you tell me what you mean?"

"I have never told a living being why I made that girl my wife," said Frederic; "but I can trust you, I know, and I have sometimes thought I might feel better if some one shared my secret. Still, I would rather not explain to you *how* Marian was the heiress of Redstone Hall, for that concerns the dead; but heiress she was, not only of all that, but of all the lands and houses said to belong to the Raymond estate in Kentucky; not a cent of it was mine; and, rather than give it up, I married her without one particle of love—married her, too, when she did not know of her fortune, but supposed herself dependent upon me."

"Oh, Frederic, did you thus wrong that girl? I never thought you capable of such an act. I knew you did not love her, but the rest ——. It hurts me to think you did it, and that you still live on her money."

"Hush, Will!" And Frederic bowed his head for very shame. "I deserve your censure, I know, but if my sin was great—great has been my punishment. Look at me, Will. I am not the light hearted man you parted with six years ago upon the college green; for, since that dreadful night when I first knew poor Marian had fled, and thought she was in the river, I have not had a single moment of perfect peace or freedom from remorse. I have not spent more of her money either than I could help. Bad as I am, I shrink from that. Redstone Hall grew hateful to me—it was haunted with so many bitter memories of her, and was, besides, the place where I sinned against her a second time by daring to think of another—of Isabel. You remember her?"

"Fred Raymond!" and in his indignation, Will's feet came down from the top of the chair, "you did not aggravate your guilt by talking of love to *her?*"

"No, no," groaned Frederic, "I did not, though Heaven only knows the fierce struggle it cost me to see her there every day, and know I must not say one word to her of love. I left Redstone Hall at last, as you know. Left it because it was Marian's and Riverside was my father's, before Marian came to us; so it did not seem quite so much like spending her money, for I did try to be a man and earn my own living. They did not get on well without me in Kentucky. They needed me there a part of the time, at least; and when, at last, I began to feel differently toward Marian, I felt less delicacy about her fortune, and I have spent my winters at Redstone Hall, where the negroes and the neighbors around all suppose Marian dead, for I have never told them that she was with me in New York. Isabel knows it, but for some reason she has kept it to herself; and I am glad, for I would rather people should not talk of it until she is really found. I have sought for her so long and unsuccessfully that I'm growing discouraged now."

"If you knew that she was dead, would you marry Isabel?" asked Will; and Frederic replied,

"Never!'

Then, in a reverent tone, as if speaking of one above him in purity and innocence, he told how the little blind girl had stood between him and temptation, holding up his hands when they were weakest, and keeping his feet from falling. "But that desire is over. I can look Isabel Huntington calm in the face and experience no sensation, save that of relief, to think I have escaped her. With the legacy left her by Mr. Rivers, and the little means her mother had, she has bought a small house near Riverside; so I shall have them for neighbors every Summer. But I do not care. I have no love now for Isabel. It all died out when I was sick, and centered itself upon that little sweet-faced girl, who, I know, was Marian, though I cannot find her. If I could, Will, I'd willingly part with every cent of money I call mine, and work for my daily bread. Labor would not seem a hardship, if I knew that when my toil was done, there was a darling wife waiting for me at home—a wife like what I hope my Marian is, and like what your Marian Grey may be."

"Not mine, Frederic. There is in all the world no Marian for me," said Will.

"Nor for me, perhaps," was the sad response, and in the dim firelight, the two mournful faces looked wistfully at each other, as if asking the sympathy neither had to give.

And there they sat until the clock in the room below, struck the hour of midnight. Two weary heart-broken men, in the pride of their early manhood, sat talking each to the other, one of "*My* Marian," and one of "Mine;" but never, never dreaming that the beautiful Marian Grey, so much beloved by William Gordon, was the lost Marian so greatly mourned by Frederic Raymond.

CHAPTER XXII.

THE BIRTHDAY.

Mrs. Gordon's breakfast bell rang several times next morning ere the young men made their appearance, for, as a natural consequence, the late hours of the previous night had been followed by protracted slumbers. As they were making their hasty toilet, Frederic said to Will:

"This is Marian's twentieth birthday."

"Is it possible?" returned Will. "It seems but yesterday since I saw her, a little girl in pantalets, with long curls streaming down her back. I liked her very much, she seemed so kind, so considerate of every one's comfort; and I remember telling you once that she would be a handsome woman, while you said—'Never, with that hair!'"

"Neither can she," rejoined Frederic. "She may be rather pretty. Yes, I am sure she is pretty, for the face which bent over my pillow was not an ugly one; but I still insist that a woman with red hair cannot be handsome."

"Tastes differ," returned Will. "Now, I'll venture to say Miss Grey's hair was red when she was a child. It is not very far from it now, in the sunlight; and everybody speaks of her hair as her crowning beauty."

"I wish I could see her," said Frederic; "for, as she will not be your wife, I suppose she will be Alice's governess. And it is quite proper that I should have an interview with her, and talk the matter over. Will you call with me this evening?"

"Certainly," returned Will; "for, though it will afford me more pain than pleasure to meet her, I will not be so foolish as to avoid her."

Breakfast being over, the young men started for a walk down town, going by Mrs. Sheldon's house, of course, although it was entirely out of their way. But neither thought of this, and they passed it on the opposite side of the street; so that Will could, unobserved, point out Marian's room to Frederic.

"That's it," he said—"the one with the blinds thrown open. There she has often sat, I suppose, thinking of the villain who stands between me and happiness. The rascal! I tell you, Fred, I wish I had him as near to me as you are!" and Will Gordon fancied how, in such a case, he would treat a man who did not love Marian Grey!

Frederic made no answer, for his eyes were fixed intently upon the window, hoping to catch a glimpse of one who was fast becoming an object of interest even to him. But he looked in vain, for Marian had not yet risen. Pale, weary and weak, she reclined among her pillows, her fair hair falling about her face in beautiful disorder, and her eyes turned also toward the window, not because she knew that Frederic was looking in that direction, but because the morning sun was shining there, and she was watching it as it danced upon the curtain of bright crimson.

"I have seen the suns of twenty years," she thought, "and I am growing old so fast. I wonder if Frederic would know me now."

At this moment, Mrs. Sheldon came in, and advancing toward the window, looked down into the street. Catching a view of her brother and his friend, she exclaimed:

"Frederic Raymond! I wonder when he came?"

"What? Where? Who is it?" Marian asked, quickly, at the same time raising herself upon her elbow, and looking wistfully in the direction Frederic had gone.

"Mr. Raymond, Will's friend, from Kentucky," returned Mrs. Sheldon. "He must have come last night?" and as little Fred just then called to her from without, she left the room.

When she was alone, Marian buried her face in the bed-clothes, and murmured:

"Oh, if I could only see him! I long so to test his powers of recognition, and see if he would know me."

She almost hoped he would, and claim her for his wife, as this, she fancied, might cure Will Gordon sooner than aught else which could be done. She was sure they would talk of her, for Frederic had bidden Will propose, and he would naturally ask the result of that proposal. Will would say she had refused him because she loved another, and would not something whisper to her husband that "the other" was himself—that Marian Grey was his Marian—the Marian of Redstone Hall—and he would come to her that very day, perhaps, and all the morning she waited anxiously for a step she was certain she would know, though it might not be as elastic and bounding as of old, ere she had trammeled it with a heavy weight. She listened nervously for its full, rich tones, asking for her, in the parlor below. But she listened in vain and the restless excitement brought on a severe headache, which rendered it impossible for her to leave the room, even if he came. This Mrs. Sheldon greatly lamented, for she had invited the young men to tea, and while accepting her invitation, Will had asked if Miss Grey would not be able to spend a part of the evening with them.

"She is to be Fred's governess, you know," he said, "and he naturally wishes to make her acquaintance."

This request Mrs. Sheldon made known to Marian, who asked, eagerly, if "to-morrow would not do as well?"

"It might," returned Mrs. Sheldon, "were it not that he leaves on the early train."

Marian sighed deeply, and turning upon her pillow

tried to sleep, hoping thus to lose the throbbing pain in her head—but it would not be lost; and when, as it was growing dark, she heard the sound of feet upon the gravelled walk, and knew whose feet they were, it ached as it had not done before during the entire day. She heard them as they entered the lower hall, and fancied she saw Frederic place his hat and shawl upon the stand, and pass his fingers through his hair ere he entered the parlor, which was directly beneath her room. She knew when he was there, for she heard his well-remembered voice speaking to the children, and covering her face with her hands she wept aloud to think she should not see him.

Meantime, in the parlor below, little Fred had climbed into his uncle's lap and commenced a rather embarrassing conversation. Somehow Will reminded him of Marian, for the two were associated together in his mind; and he said, rather as a piece of news: "Miss Day is sick—up stairs she is; and when I told her you was comin' she *vomucked* and cried so hard!"

Frederic could not help laughing, and, emboldened by this proof of appreciation, the child continued: "What made her cry, Uncle Will? I asked her didn't she want you to come, and she say yes. Don't she like you?"

"I guess not," said Will, trying himself to laugh, while Frederic, pitying his embarrassment, strove to divert the little fellow's mind by asking about the sled he saw upon the steps as he came in.

This had the desired effect, for a sled was of more consequence to Fred than Miss Grey's tears, and he prattled on about it until his nurse came to take him from the room. After he was gone Mr. Raymond spoke of Miss Grey, asking if he should not have the pleasure of seeing her.

"She is suffering from a nervous headache," returned Mrs. Sheldon, "and cannot come down, for which I am very sorry, as I wish you to hear her play."

"I do not care so much for that," returned Frederic, "as for seeing her, so as to carry back a good account to Alice. Do tell me, Mrs. Sheldon, is she really as beautiful, and fascinating, and accomplished as report would make her out to be?"

"I should say she would fully warrant any praise you may have heard of her," returned Mrs. Sheldon, "although her beauty is not of the brilliant style. She is very modest and gentle in her appearance, and there is in her eyes and in her smile something so very sad and plaintive, that I often feel like crying when I look at her, for I know she must have suffered some great trouble, young as she is."

Involuntarily Frederic and William glanced at each other, for they knew what that trouble was, and the latter felt as if he would like to take vengeance on the man who could be indifferent to love like that of Marian Grey!

After a moment, Mrs. Sheldon continued:

"There has been something said, I believe, about her going to you next September, but I warn you now that I shall use every possible effort to keep her. We sail for Europe in August, you know, and she will be of invaluable service to me then, as she speaks French and German so readily. The tour, too, will do her good, and you must not be surprised to hear that she cannot come to Riverside."

Mr. Raymond was too polite to oppose Mrs. Sheldon openly, but he had become too deeply interested in Marian Grey to give her up without a struggle, and when alone again with Will, in the chamber of the latter, he broached the subject, asking his companion if he thought there was any probability of Miss Grey's disappointing him.

"I mean to write her a note," he said, and sitting down by Will's writing desk he took up a sheet of gilt edged paper and commenced, "My dear Marian."

"Pshaw!" he exclaimed, "what am I thinking about?" and tearing up the sheet he threw it into the grate and commenced again, addressing her this time as "Miss Grey."

He considered her services engaged to himself, he said, and should expect her at Riverside early in September. She could come sooner if she liked, for Mrs. Jones was to leave the first of August.

"That European trip may tempt her," he thought, and he added, "I am glad to learn from Mrs. Sheldon that you are such a proficient in German and French, for I have serious thoughts of visiting the Old World myself ere long, and as Alice, of course, will go with me, we shall prize your company all the more on account of these accomplishments."

This note he gave to Will, who said, "Perhaps I shall try again, and if I succeed, I suppose you will give her up to me."

"Yes," answered Frederic, "I'll give way for Will Gordon's wife, but for no one else," and there the conversation ceased concerning Marian Grey; nor was it resumed again, for early the next morning he started for New York, as he intended stopping at Riverside ere he returned to Kentucky.

True to his trust, Will gave the note to Marian the first time that he met her, after she was well enough to come down stairs as usual.

"It is from Mr. Raymond," he said, and Marian's face was scarlet as she took it and looked into his eye with an eager, searching glance, to see if he knew her secret."

But he did not, and with spirits which began to ebb, she broke the seal and read the few brief lines, half smiling as she thought how very formal and business-like they were. But it was Frederic's hand-writing, and when sure Will did not see her she pressed it to her lips.

"What you do that for?" asked little Fred, whose sharp eyes saw everything not intended for them to see.

"Sh—sh," said Marian; but the child persisted. "Say, what you *tiss* that letter for?"

Will Gordon was standing with his back to her, but, at this strange question, he turned quickly and fastened his eyes on Marian's face, as if he would fathom her inmost soul.

"There's something there," she said, passing the note again over her lips as if she would brush the "something" away.

This explanation was wholly satisfactory to Fred, who, with childish simplicity, asked, "Did you get it?"

But Will was not quite certain, and for several days he puzzled his brain with wondering whether "Marian Grey really did kiss Frederic Raymond's note or not." If so, why did she? She could not be in love with a man she had never seen. She was not weak enough for that, and at last rejecting it as an impossibility and accepting the troublesome "something" as a reality, his mind became at rest upon that subject.

CHAPTER XXIII.

MARIAN RAYMOND.

VERY rapidly the Spring passed away, enlivened once by a short visit from Ben, who, having purchased an entire new suit of clothes for the occasion, looked and appeared unusually well, talking but little until he was alone with Marian, when his tongue was loosed, and he told her all he had come to tell.

He had been to Riverside, he said, and Mrs. Russell, who was still there and was to be the future housekeeper, was very gracious to him, on account of his being the adopted brother of their next governess, Miss Grey.

"She showed me your chamber," said he, "and it's the very one they fixed up so nice for Isabel. Nobody has ever used it, for Miss Jones slep' in a little room at the end of the hall. Frederic has had a door cut from Alice's chamber into yourn, 'cause he said how't you and she would want to be near to each other, he knew. And I'll tell you what, when you git there, it seems to me you'll be as nigh Heaven as you'll ever git in this world. Mrs. Huntington has bought a little cottage close by Frederic's," he continued, "and she's livin' there with Isabel, who has got to be an heir——"

"An heiress!" repeated Marian. "Whose, pray?"

"Don't know," returned Ben, "only that old man she went to Florida with is dead, and he willed her some. I don't know how much, but law, she'll spend it in no time. Mrs. Russell said her lace curtains cost an awful sight, though she b'lieved they was bought second-hand, in New York. I walked by there afoot to see 'em, and between you and me they are yallerer than saffern. My advice to her is that she bile 'em up in ashes and water, jest as mother used to bile up my shirts that I wore in the factory. It'll whiten 'em quickest of anything, and if I's you I'd kinder tell her so—friendly like, you know—'cause it don't look well for decent folks to have such dirty things a hangin' to their winders!"

Marian smiled at Ben's simplicity, telling him that "the chief value of the curtains consisted probably in their soiled, yellow appearance."

"Whew," whistled Ben, "I wish mother'd had a little more larnin', for if she'd known it was genteel to be dirty, mabby she wouldn't have broke her back a scrubbin', when there warn't no use on't."

Isabel's curtains having been discussed at length, and herself described as Ben saw her "struttin' through the streets," he arose to go, telling Marian he should not probably see her again until he visited her in the Autumn at Riverside.

"I guess I wouldn't let it all out at once," said he, "but wait and let Frederic sweat. It'll do him good, and he isn't paid yet for all he's made you suffer. I ain't no Universaler, but I do like to see folks catch it as they go 'long."

Once Marian thought to tell him of William Gordon's unfortunate attachment, particularly as he was loud in his praises of the young man; but upon second reflections she decided to keep that matter to herself, hoping that the subject would never be mentioned to her again. And in this her wishes seemed to be realized, for as the weeks after Ben's departure went by, William began to be more like himself than he had been before since her refusal of him. He came often to Mrs. Sheldon's, sang with her sometimes as of old, and she fancied he was losing his love for her. But she was mistaken, for it was strengthening with each hour's interview. The very hopelessness of his passion rendered it more intense, it would seem, until at last, unable longer to remain where she was, and know she could never be his, he went from home, nor returned again until near the middle of August, when he found Mrs. Sheldon's house in a state of great confusion. Furniture was being covered or packed away, rooms shut up, and windows fastened down, while his sister was in that state of feminine bliss when every chair is filled with new dresses, save two, and those two are occupied by the makers of said dresses.

Mr. and Mrs. Sheldon were going to Europe. They would sail in about two weeks, and as Marian had positively declined to accompany them, they had engaged another governess, who was to meet them in New York. It was decided that Marian should remain a few days with Mrs. Gordon, and then go to Riverside, where her coming was anxiously expected both by Frederic and Alice. This arrangement was highly satisfactory to Will, who anticipated much happiness in having her wholly to himself for a week. There would be no sister Ellen, with curious, prying eyes, for she was going with Mrs. Sheldon as far as New York—no little girls always in the way—no funny Fred, to see and tell of everything—nobody, in short, but his good mother, who he knew would often leave him alone with Marian.

During his absence from home he had thought much upon the subject, and had resolved to make one more trial at least. She might be eventually won, and if so, he should care but little for the efforts made to win her. With this upon his mind, he felt rather relieved than otherwise when the family at last were gone, and Marian was an inmate of his mother's house. Both Mr. and Mrs. Sheldon had urged him to accompany them, and he had made arrangements to do so in case he found Marian still firm in her refusal. They were intending to stop for a few days in New York, and he could easily join them the day on which the ship was advertised to sail. He should know his fate before that time, he thought, and he strove in various ways to obtain an interview with Marian, who, divining his intention, was unusually reserved in her demeanor toward him, and if by chance she found herself with him alone, she invariably formed some excuse to leave the room, so that Will began at last to lose all hope, and to think seriously of joining his sister as the surest means of forgetting Marian Grey.

"She does not care for me," he said to his mother, one night after Marian had retired. "I believe she rather dislikes me than otherwise. I think on the whole I shall go, and if so, I must start in the morning, for the vessel sails to-morrow night."

To this his mother made no objection, for though she would be very lonely without him, she was accustomed to rely upon herself, so she rather encouraged him than otherwise, thinking it would do him good. Accordingly, next morning, when Marian came down to breakfast, she was surprised to hear of Will's intended departure.

"Oh, I am sorry," she said, involuntarily, for Will Gordon had a strong place in her affections, and knew not what danger might befall him on the deep.

Breakfast being over, there remained to Will but half an hour, and as a part of this was necessarily spent with the servants, and in preparations for his journey, he had at the last but a few moments in which to say his farewell words to Marian. She was in the back parlor, his mother said, and there he found her weeping, for she felt that her friends were leaving her one by one, and though in a few days she was going back to her husband and her home, she knew not what the result would be. Will's sudden determination to visit Europe affected her unpleasantly, for she felt that she was in some way connected with it, and she was conscious of a feeling of loneliness, such as she had not experienced before since she first came to Mrs. Sheldon's.

"Are you weeping?" said Will, when he saw her with her head bowed down upon the arm of the sofa.

Marian did not answer, and with newly awakened hope Will drew nearer and seated himself beside her. "It might be that he was mistaken, after all," he thought. "Her tears would seem to indicate as much. Girls were strange beings, everybody said," and passing his arm around the weeping Marian, he whispered: "Do you like me, then?"

"Yes, very, very much," she answered, "and now that you are going away, and I may never see you again, I am so sorry I ever caused you a moment's pain."

"I needn't go, Marian," William said, drawing her close to him. "I will stay, oh, so gladly, if you bid me do so. But it must be for *you*. Shall I, Marian? May I stay?" and again Will Gordon poured into her ear deep burning words of love—entreating her to be his wife—to forget that other love so unworthy of her, and to give herself to him, who would cherish her so tenderly. Then he told her how the thought that she did not love him had made him go away, when he would so much rather remain where she was, if he could know she wished it. "Answer me, Marian," he said, "for time hastens, and if you tell me no again, I must be gone. Never man loved and worshipped his wife as I will love and worship you. Speak and tell me yes."

Will paused for her reply, and looking into her face, which she had turned towards him, he thought he read a confirmation of his hopes, but the first words she uttered wrung his heart with cruel disappointment.

"I cannot be your wife," she said. "I mean it, Mr. Gordon, I cannot, and oh, it would be wicked not to tell you. Can I trust you? Will you keep my secret safe, as I have kept it almost six long years?"

There was some insufferable barrier between them, and William Gordon felt it, as trembling in every limb, he answered, "Whatever you intrust to me shall not be betrayed."

"Then, listen," she said, "and say if you will bid me marry you. I told you I was not what I seemed, and I am not. People, perhaps, call me young, but to myself I seem old, I have suffered so much and all my womanhood has been wasted, as it were, in tears. I told you once that before coming here I had given to another the love for which you sued, and I told you truly; but Mr. Gordon, there was more to tell; that other one, who loves me not, or who, if he does, has never manifested it to me by word or deed, is *my own husband!*"

"Oh, Marian, Marian, this indeed is death itself!" groaned Will, for though he had said there was no hope, it seemed to him now that he had never believed or realized it, as when he heard the dreadful words, "my own husband."

"Do not despise me for deceiving you," Marian continued. "If I had thought you could have seen aught to desire in me, a poor, humble girl, I might, perhaps, have warned you in time, though how could I tell you, a stranger, that I was an unloved wife?"

"Where is he—that man?" Will asked, for he could not say "your husband," and his lip quivered with something akin to the pain one feels when he hears the cold earth rattling into the grave where he has buried his fondest pride.

Marian's confession was a death-blow to all Will had dared to hope, and he asked for the husband more as a matter of form than because he really cared to know.

"Mr. Gordon," said Marian, rising to her feet, and standing with her face turned fully toward him, "*Must* I tell you more? I thought I needed only to speak of a *husband* and you would guess the rest. Don't you know me? Have we never met before?"

Wistfully, anxiously William gazed at her, scanning her features one by one, while a dim vision of something back in the past floated before him, but assumed no tangible form, and shaking his head, he answered: "Never, to my knowledge."

"Look again. Is not my face a familiar one? Did you never see it before? Not here—not in New England—but far away, where the Summer comes earlier and the Winter is not so long. Is there not something about me—something in my person, or my voice, which carries you back to an old house on the river where you once met a little curly-haired girl?"

She did not need to say more. Little by little it had come to him, and, starting to his feet, he caught her hand, exclaiming, "Great Heaven! *The lost wife of Frederic Raymond!*"

"Yes," she answered, "the lost Marian of Redstone Hall," and leaning her head upon his arm, she burst into tears, for he seemed to her like a brother now, while she to him—

He could not think of her as a sister yet—he loved her too well for that; but still his feelings toward her had changed in the great shock with which he recognized her. She could never be his Marian, he knew, neither did he desire it. And for a moment he stood speechless, wholly overwhelmed with astonishment and wonder. Then he said, "Marian Raymond, why are you here?"

"Why?" she repeated bitterly. "You may well ask why. Hated by him who should care for me, what could I do but go away into the unknown world, and throw myself upon its charities, which in my case have not been cold or selfish. God bless the noble-hearted Ben, and the sainted woman, his mother, who did not cast me off when I went to them, homeless, friendless, and heart-broken."

In her excitement, Marian clasped her hands together, and the blue of her eye grew deeper, darker, as she paid this tribute of gratitude to those who had been her friends indeed. Involuntarily, Will Gordon, too, responded to the words, "God bless the noble-hearted

Ben," for, looking at the beautiful girl before him, he felt that what she was she owed to the self-denying, unwearied efforts of the uncultivated but generous Ben.

"Marian," he said again, "you must go home. Go to your husband. He is waiting for you. He has sought for you long; he has expiated his sin. Go, Marian, go——"

"I am going," she answered, "and if I only knew he wanted me—wanted his wife——"

"He does want you," interrupted Will. "He has told me so many a time,"

Marian was about to reply, when Mrs. Gordon appeared, warning her son that the carriage was at the door; and with a hurried farewell to Marian and his mother, Will hastened off, whispering to the former, "I shall write to you when on the sea—"

"And keep my secret safe. I would rather divulge it myself," she added.

He nodded in the affirmative, and was soon on his way to the depot, so bewildered with what he had heard, that he scarcely knew whether it were reality or a dream. Gradually, however, it became clear to him, and he remembered many things which confirmed the strange story he had heard.

Greatly he wished to write to Frederic, and tell him that Marian Grey was his wife, but he would not break his promise, and he was wondering how he could hasten the discovery, when, as the cars left the depot at Hartford, a broad hand was laid upon his shoulder, and a voice which sounded familiar, said, "Wall, captain, bein' we're so full, I guess you'll have to make room for me, or else I'll have to set with that gal whose hoops take up the hull concern."

"Ben Butterworth," Will exclaimed, turning his face toward the speaker, who recognized him at once.

"Wall," he began, as he took the seat Will readily shared with him, "I didn't 'spose 'twas you. How do you do, and how's Marian? Has she gone to Riverside yet?"

"No," returned Will, and looking Ben directly in the face, he continued, "How much of Miss Grey's history do you know?"

"Mor'n I shall tell, I'll bet. How much do you know?" and Ben set his hat a little more on one side of his head.

"More than you suppose, perhaps," returned Will. "And if you, too, are posted, I'd like to talk the matter over, but if not, I shall betray no secrets."

"I swan, I b'lieve you do know," said Ben. "Did she tell you?"

Will nodded, and Ben continued, "She wrote to me that you knew Mr. Raymond, and liked him, too; I guess he ain't a very bad chap after all, is he?"

The ice was fairly broken now, and both Will and Ben settled themselves for a long conversation. Will did not think it betrayed Marian's confidence to talk of her with one who understood her affairs so much better than himself, and ere they reached New York, he had heard the whole story—heard how Ben had stumbled upon her in New York, and taken her to his home without knowing aught of her, except that she was friendless and alone—how the mother, now resting in her grave, had cared for the orphan girl, and how Ben, too, had done for her what he could.

"'Twan't much any way," he said, "and I never minded it an atom, for 'twas a pleasure to arn money for her schoolin'."

And Ben spoke truly, for it never occurred to him that he had denied himself as few men would have done—toiling early and late, through sunshine and storm, wearing the old coat long after it was threadbare, and sometimes, when peddling, eating but two meals a day, by way of saving for Marian. Of all this he did not speak to his companion. He did not even think of it, or, if he did, he felt that he was more than paid in seeing Marian what she was. Accidentally, he said that his name was really Ben Burt, and that he should be glad when the time came for him to be called thus again.

"When will that be?" asked Will, and Ben replied by unfolding to him his long cherished plan of having Frederic make love to his own wife.

"You might write to him, I s'pose," he said, "but that would spile all my fun, and I'd rather let the thing work itself out. He's bound to fall in love with her. He can't help it, and I don't see how *you* could. Mabby you did." And Ben's grey eyes looked quizzically at his companion, who colored deeply as he replied merely to the first part of Ben's remark. "I certainly will not interfere in the matter, though before meeting you I was wondering how I could do so, and not betray Marian's confidence. I am sure now it will all come right at last, and you ought to be permitted to bring it round in your own way, for you have been a true friend to her, and I dare say she loves you as a brother."

This was touching Ben on a tender point, for his old affection for Marian was not quite dead yet, and Will's last words brought back to him memories of those dreary winter nights, when in his way he had battled with the love he knew he must not cherish for Marian Grey. He fidgetted in his seat, got up and looked under him, sat down again and looked out of the window, and repeated to himself a part of the multiplication table, by way of keeping from crying.

"Bless her, she's an angel," he managed at last to say, adding, as he met the inquiring glance of Will: "It's my misfortin' to be oncommon tender-hearted, and when I git to thinkin' of somethin' that concerns nobody but me, I can't keep from cryin' no way you can fix it," and two undeniable tears rolled down his cheeks and dropped from the end of his nose.

"He, too," sighed Will Gordon, and as he thought how much more the uncouth man beside him had done for Marian Grey than either Frederic or himself, and that he really had the greatest claim to her gratitude and love, his heart warmed toward Yankee Ben as to a long tried friend, and he resolved to leave for him a substantial token of his regard.

"Why don't you settle down, as a grocer, in some small country town?" he asked, as they came near the city.

"I have thought of that," said Ben, "for I'm gettin' kinder tired of travelin' now that there ain't no home for me to go to once in so often. I think I should like to be a grocery man first rate, and weigh out saleratus and bar soap to the old wimmen. Wouldn't they flock in, though, to see me, I'm so odd! But 'taint no use to think on't for I hain't the money now, though, mabby I shall have it bimeby. My expenses ain't as great as they was."

By this time they had reached the depot, and Will, who knew they must part there, said to him, "How long do you stay in New York?"

"Not long," returned Ben, "I've only come to recruit my stock a little."

"Go to the Post-Office before you leave," was Will's reply, as he stepped from the platform and was lost in the crowd.

"What did he mean?" thought Ben. "Nobody writes to me but Marian, and I ain't expectin' nothin' from her, but I guess I may as well go."

Accordingly, the next night, when Will Gordon, with little Fred in his arms, was looking out upon the sea, Ben wended his way to the office, inquiring first for Ben Butterworth and then for Ben Burt. There was a letter for the latter, and it contained a draft for three hundred dollars, together with the following lines:

"You and I have suffered alke, and in each of our hearts there is a hidden grave. I saw it in the tears you shed when talking to me of Marian Grey. Heaven bless you, Ben Burt, for all you have been to her.

She is one of the fairest, best, of God's creation, but she was not meant for you nor me; and we must learn to go our way without her. You have done for her more, perhaps, than either Mr. Raymond or myself would have done in the same circumstances, and thus far you are more worthy of her esteem. You will please accept the inclosed as a token that I appreciate your self-denying labors for Marian Grey. Use it for that grocery we talked about, if you choose, or for any purpose you like. If you have any delicacy just consider it a loan to be paid when you are a richer man than I am. You cannot return it, of course, for when you receive it I shall be gone.

"Yours, in haste, WILLIAM GORDON."

This letter was a mystery to Ben, who read it again and again, dwelling long upon the words, "You and I suffered alike, and in each of our hearts there is a hidden grave."

"That hits me exactly," he said, "though I never thought of callin' that hole in my heart a grave—but 'taint nothin' else, for I buried somethin' in it, and the tender brotherly feelin' I've felt for Marian ever since was the grave stun I set up in memory of what had been. But what does he know about it, though why shouldn't he, for no mortal man can look in Marian's face and not feel kinder cold and hystericky-like at the pit of his stomach! Yes, he's in love with her, and that's the way she came to tell who she was. Poor Bill! poor Bill! I know how to pity him to a dot," and Ben heaved a deep sigh as he finished this long soliloquy.

The money next diverted his attention, but no puzzling on his part could explain to him satisfactorily why it had been sent.

"S'posin' he was grateful," he said, "he needn't give me three hundred dollars for nothin', but bein' he has, I may as well use it to start in business, though I shall pay it back, of course," and when alone in his room at the Hotel where he stopped, he wrote upon a bit of paper.

"NEW YORK, August 30 18—

"For vally rec. I promise to pay Bill Gordon, or bearer, the sum of three hundred dollars with use from date.

"BENJAMIN BURT."

This note he put carefully away in his old leathern wallet, where it was as safe and as sure of being paid as if it had been in William Gordon's hands instead of his.

Meantime Marian at Mrs. Gordon's was half regretting that she had told her secret to William, and greatly lamenting that they had been interrupted ere she knew just how much Frederic wished to find her. That his feelings toward her had changed, she was sure, but she would know by word and deed that he loved her ere she revealed herself to him, and the dark mystery of that cruel letter must be explained before she could respect him as she had once done. And now but a few days remained ere she should see him face to face, for she was going to Riverside very soon. Some acquaintance of hers were going west by way of New York, and she decided to accompany them, though by soing doing she would reach Riverside one day earlier than she was expected.

"It would make no difference of course," she said, and she waited impatiently for the appointed morning.

It came at last and long before the hour for starting she was ready, the dancing joy in her eyes, and her apparent eagerness to go being sadly at variance with the expression of Mrs. Gordon's face, for the good lady loved the gentle girl and grieved to part with her.

"I am sorry to leave you," Marian said, when the last moment came, "but I am so glad I am going, too, sometime, perhaps, you may know why and then you will not blame me."

She could not shed a tear although she had become greatly attached to her Springfield home, and her excitement continued unabated until she reached New York, where they stopped for the night. There were several hours of daylight left, and stealing away from her friends she took a Third Avenue car and went up to their old house where strangers were living now. She did not care to go in, for the dingy, uncurtained windows looked far from inviting, and she passed slowly down the other side of the street, musing upon all that had passed since the night when she first climbed those narrow stairs, and asked a mother's care from Mrs. Burt. She did not think then that she would ever be as happy as she was to-day with the uncertainty of meeting Frederic to-morrow. It seemed a great while to wait, and as Ben had once numbered the weeks in seven years, so she now counted the hours, which must elapse ere she felt the pressure of Frederic's hand—for he would shake hands with her of course, and he would look into her face, for he had heard much of her both from Will Gordon and Ben. Would he be disappointed? Would he think her pretty? Would he know her? And Alice—what would she say? Marian dreaded this test more than all the rest, for she felt that there was danger in the instinct of the blind girl. Slowly she retraced her steps and returning to the Astor, sought her own room, informing her friends that she was weary and would rest.

"Five hours more," was her first thought when she awoke next morning, from a sounder sleep than she had supposed it possible to enjoy when under such excitement. Ere long it was four hours more, then three, then two, then one, and then the cars stopped at the depôt at Yonkers. Two trunks marked "M. G." stood upon the platform, and near them a figure in black, bowing to her friends, who leaned from the car window, and holding in her hands a satchel, a silk umbrella, two checks, her purse, and a book, for Marian possessed the weakness of her sex, and in traveling always carried the usual amount of baggage.

"To Riverside," she said, when asked where she wished to go, and she looked around as if half expecting a familiar face.

But she looked in vain, and in a few moments she was comfortably seated in the lumbering stage, which once before had carried her up that long hill. Eagerly she strained her eyes to catch the first view of the house; and when at last it came in sight, she was too intent upon it to observe the showily-dressed young lady tripping along upon the walk, and holding her skirts with her thumb and finger so as to show her dainty slipper.

But if Marian did not see Isabel, Isabel saw her. It was not usual for the stage to come up at that hour of the day, and as it passed her by, Isabel turned to see where it was going.

"To Riverside," she exclaimed, as she saw it draw up to the gate. "It must be the new governess," and as there was no house very near, she stopped to inspect the stranger as well as she could at that distance. "Black," she said, as Marian stepped upon the ground; "But I might have known it, for regular built teachers always wear black, I believe. She is rather tall, too. An umbrella, of course. I wonder she hasn't her blanket shawl and overshoes this hot day. Her bonnet is pretty, and that hem in her veil very wide. On the whole, she's quite genteel for a governess," and Isabel walked on while Marian went up the graveled walk, expecting at each step to meet with either Frederic or Alice.

She would rather it should be the latter, for in case of recognition, she knew she could bind the blind girl to secrecy for a time, but no one appeared, and about the house there was no sign of life, save a parrot, which, in its cage beneath a maple tree, screamed out wholly unintelligible words. The door was shut, and even after the driver had placed her trunks upon the piazza and gone, Marian stood there ringing the bell. The window to her right was open, and she knew it was the window of Frederic's room, but he was not sitting near it, and after a little she ventured to approach it and look in. It did not seem to have been occupied at all that day, for everything was arranged in perfect order as if broom and duster had recently done service there. Its prim, neat appearance affected Marian unpleasantly, as if it were the furerunner of some disappointment, and going back to the door she resolutely pulled the silver knob. The loud, sharp ring made her heart beat violently, and when she heard a heavy tread, not unlike a man's coming up the basement stairs, she thought, "What if it is Frederic himself? What shall I say?"

"It is Frederic," she continued, as the step came nearer, and she was wishing she could run away and hide, when the door was opened by Mrs. Russell, her feet encased in a pair of Mr. Raymond's cast-off shoes, which accounted for her heavy tread, and herself looking a little crest-fallen at the sight of her visitor, whom she recognized at once.

"Miss Grey, I b'lieve?" she said, dropping a low curtesy. "We wan't expectin' you till to-morrow; but walk in, and make yourself at home. You'll want to go to your room, I 'spose. Traveled all night, didn't you? You look pale, and I wouldn't wonder if you wanted to sleep most of the day. I never thought of such a thing as your comin' this mornin'. Dear me, what shall I do?"

This was said in an under-tone, but it caught the ear of Marian, who, now that she had a chance to speak, asked for Mr. Raymond, timidly, as if fearful that with his name her sacret might slip out.

"Bless you!" returned Mrs. Russell, "both of 'em went to New York early this morning, and won't be home till dark, maybe, and that's why I feel so. I don't know how to entertain you as they do, and Miss Alice has been reckoning on giving you a good impression. I'm so sorry you've—they've gone, I mean. I wan't expecting to get any dinner to-day, and was having such a nice time, sewin' on my new dress;" and, with the last, the whole cause of the old lady's uneasiness was divulged.

In the absence of Frederic and Alice, she had counted upon a day of leisure, which Marian's arrival had seriously interrupted.

"I beg you not to trouble yourself for me," said Marian, who readily understood the matter. "I never care for a regular dinner: indeed, I may not be hungry at all."

The old lady's face brightened perceptibly, and she replied:

"Oh, I don't mind a cup of tea, and the like o' that; but to brile or stew this hot day ain't so pleasant, when a person is fleshy, as I am. I'll get you something, though; and now you go up stairs to your room, the one at the right hand, with the white furniture, and the silver jigger, that let's the water into that marble dish. We live in style, I tell you; and Mr. Raymond is a gentleman, if there ever was one—only he wants meat three times a day, just as he has in Kentucky. Thinks, I 'spose, it don't hurt me any more to sweat over the fire, than it does that Dinah, Alice talks so much about. Yes, that's the door—right there;" and Mrs. Russell went back to the making of her dress, while Marian sought her chamber, feeling rather disappointed at the absence of both Frederic and Alice, whose object in visiting New York, that day, will be explained in the succeeding chapter, and will necessarily take us backward for a little in our story.

CHAPTER XXIII.

FREDERIC AND ALICE VISIT MARIAN'S OLD HOME.

"FREDERIC," said Alice, about six weeks before Marian's arrival at Riverside, "who hired that Mrs. Merton to take care of you when you were sick at the hotel?"

"The proprietor, I suppose," returned Frederic.

Alice continued:

"But who told him of her?"

"I don't know," said Frederic. "She was from the country, I believe."

"Yes, yes," returned Alice; "but some person must have recommended her, and if you can ascertain who that person was, you may find Mrs. Merton, and learn something of Marian."

"I wonder I never thought of that before," said Frederic, adding, "that if Alice had her sight he believed she would have discovered Marian ere this."

"I know I should," was her answer; and after a little further conversation, it was decided that Frederic should go to New York, and learn, if possible, who first suggested Mrs. Merton as a nurse.

This was not so easy a matter as he had imagined it to be, for though Frederic himself was well remembered at the hotel, where he was now a frequent guest, scarcely any one could recall Mrs. Merton distinctly, and no one seemed to know how she came there, until a servant, who had been in the house a long time, spoke of Martha Gibbs, and then the proprietor suddenly remembered that she had recommended Mrs. Merton as being a friend of hers.

"But who is Martha Gibbs, and where is she now?" Frederic asked; and the servant replied that

"Her home used to be in Woodstock, Conn.;" and with this item of information Frederic wrote to her friends, inquiring where she was.

To this letter there came ere long an answer, saying that Mrs. John Jennings lived in ———, a small town in the interior of Iowa. Accordingly the next mail westward from Yonkers carried a letter to said Mrs. Jennings, asking where the woman lived who had nursed Mr. Raymond through that dangerous fever. This being done, Frederic and Alice waited impatiently for a reply, which was long in coming, for Mr. Jennings' log tenement was several miles from the post-office, where he seldom called, and it was more than a week ere the letter reached him. Even then it found him so engrossed in the arrival of his first-born son and heir, that for two or three days longer it lay unopened in the clock-case, ere he thought to look at it.

"I don't know what it means, I'm sure," he said, taking it to his wife, who, having never heard of the death of her old friend, replied, "Why, he wants to know where Mrs. Burt lives. Just write on a piece of paper: 'East — – street, No. —, third story; turn to your right; door at the head of the stairs.' I wonder if he's never been there yet?"

John was not an elaborate correspondent, and he simply wrote down his better half's direction, saying nothing whatever of Mrs. Burt herself, and thus conveying to Frederic no idea that Merton was not the real name.

"A letter from Iowa," said Frederic to Alice, as he came in from the office, on the very night when Marian was walking slowly past what was once her home. "I have the street and number, and to-morrow I am going there."

"And I am going, too," cried Alice. Won't Marian be surprised to see us both. I hope she'll come to the door herself; and Frederic, if she does, you'll kiss her, won't you, and act like you was glad, for if you don't, maybe she won't come back with us."

"I will do right," answered Frederic, adding in a low tone, "Perhaps she will not be there."

"Yes, she will," was Alice's positive reply, "or if she's not, somebody can tell us where she is. Only to think, we shall see her to-morrow. I do wish it would hurry, and I'm glad Miss Grey is not coming until the day after. It will be so nice to have them both here. Do you suppose they'll like each other, Marian and Miss Grey?"

"I dare say they will," returned Frederic, smiling at the little girl's enthusiasm, and hoping she might not be disappointed.

Anon, a shadow clouded Alice's face, and observing it, Frederic passed his hand over her hair, saying, "What is it, birdie?"

"Frederic," said Alice, creeping closely to the side of the young man, "Isn't Miss Grey very beautiful?"

"Mr. Gordon and Ben say so," returned Frederic, and Alice continued:

"Don't be angry with me, but you loved Isabel the best because she was the handsomest, and now you won't love Miss Grey better than Marian, will you, and you'll be Marian's husband right off, won't you?"

"When Marian comes here, it will be as my wife," said Frederic, and with this answer Alice was satisfied.

"I wish it would grow dark faster," she said, for she could tell when it was night; and Frederic, while listening to the many different ways she conjured up for them to meet Marian, became almost as impatient as herself for the morrow, when his renewed hopes might, perhaps, be realized.

The breakfast next morning was hurried through, for neither Alice nor Frederic could eat, and Mrs. Russell, when she saw how much was left untouched, congratulated herself upon its answering for the hired man's dinner, and thus giving her a nice long time for sewing.

"It isn't a bit likely Miss Grey will come to-day," said Alice, as she followed Frederic to the carriage; and, confident of this, they gave Miss Grey no further thought, but went on their way in search of Marian. When they reached New York, Frederic, who had some business to transact, left Alice in the parlor at the Astor, where she sat with her face to the window, just as though she could see the passers-by; and, as she sat there, a party who were leaving glanced hastily in, all seeing the little figure by the window, and *one* thinking to herself, "She wears her hair combed back, as Alice used to do!"

Then the group passed on, while over the face of the blind girl there flitted for an instant a wondering, bewildering expression, for her quick ear had caught the sound of a voice which, it seemed to her, she had heard before—not there—not in New York—but far away, at Redstone Hall. What was it? Who was it? She bent her head to listen, hoping to hear it again, but it came no more, for Marian Grey had left the house, and was passing up Broadway. It was not long ere Frederic returned, and, taking Alice's hand, he led her into the street, and entered a Third avenue car.

"We are on the right track, I think," he said; "for it was this way she went with the man described by Sarah Green."

Alice gave a sigh of relief, and, leaning against Frederic, rather enjoyed the pleasant motion of the car, although she wished it would go faster.

"Won't we ever get there?" she asked, as they plodded slowly on, stopping often to take in a passenger, or set one down.

"Yes, by and by," said Frederic, encouragingly. "I am not quite certain of the street, myself, but I shall know it when I see the name, of course;" and he looked anxiously out as they passed along. "Here it is!" he cried, at last; and, seizing Alice's arm, he rather dragged than led her from the car, and out upon the crossing. "Why," he exclaimed, gazing eagerly around him, "I have been here before—down this very street;" and his eye wandered involuntarily in the direction of the window where once the white-fringed curtain hung.

It was gone now, as was the rose geranium. The kitten, too, was gone, and the small hand resting on it; while in their place appeared the heads of two or three dirty children, looking across the way, and making wry faces at similar dirty children in the window opposite. Frederic saw all this, and it affected him unpleasantly, causing him to feel as if he had parted from some old friend. But no; where was that? It must be in this locality; and he wondered how one accustomed to the luxuries of Redstone Hall could live in this place so long.

"I've found it!" he said, as his eye caught the number; and now, that he believed himself near to what he had sought so long, he was more impatient than Alice herself.

He could not wait for her uncertain footsteps, and pale with excitement, he caught her in his arms and hurried up the narrow stairs, which many a time had creaked to Marian's tread. The third story was reached at last, and he stood panting by the door, where Mr. Jennings had said that he must stop. It was open, and the greasy, uncarpeted floor, of which he caught a glimpse, looked cheerless and uninviting, but it did not keep him back a moment, and he advanced into the room, which, by the three heads at the window, he knew was the same where the white curtain once had hung, and where now the glaring August sunlight came pouring in, unbroken and unsubdued.

At the sight of a stranger one of the heads turned toward him and a little voice said:

"Ma's out washin', she is, and won't be home till night."

There was a cold, heavy feeling of disappointment settling round Frederic's heart, for nothing there seemed at all like what he remembered of the neat, tidy Mrs. Merton, but he nerved himself to ask:

"What is your mother's name?"

"Bunce, and my pa is in the Tombs," was the reply.

"How long have you lived here?" was the next question, asked with a colder, heavier heart.

"Next Christmas a year," said the little girl, and catching Frederic's arm, Alice whispered,

"Do let's go out into the open air."

But Frederic did not move—there was a spell upon him, and for several moments it kept him there in the very room where Marian had wept so many tears for him, and where, in her desolation, she had asked that she might die when the greatest sorrow she had ever known came upon her—the sorrow brought by Isabel's cruel letter. There close to where he stood was the door of the little room where for weeks and months she had lain, tossing in her feverish pain, while over her Ben Burt kept his tireless watch, nor asked for greater reward than to know that she would live. And was there nothing to tell him of all this—nothing to whisper that the one he sought had been there once, but was waiting for him now in his own home! No, there was nothing but dark, cheerless poverty staring him in the face, and with a sigh he turned away, and knocking at other doors, asked for the former occupants of those front rooms. Nearly all the present tenants had moved there since Mrs. Burt's death, and none knew aught of her save one rather decent-looking woman, who said "she remembered the folks well, though they held their heads above the likes of her. She'd seen them comin' in and out and had peeked into their room, so she knew they was well to do."

"Was their name Merton? and did a young girl

live with them?" asked Frederic; and the woman replied:

"Merton sounds some like it, though I'd sooner say 'twas *Burton*, or something like that. I never even so much as passed the time of day with 'em, for I tell you they felt above me; but the girl was a jewel—so trim and genteel like."

"That was Marian," whispered Alice; and Frederic continued:

"Where are they now?"

"Bless you," returned the woman. "One on 'em is in Heaven, and the Lord only knows where t'other one went to."

Alice's hand, which lay in Frederic's, was clutched with a painful grasp; and the perspiration gathered about the young man's white lips as he stammered out:

"Which one is dead? Not the girl? You dare not tell me that?"

"I dare if it was so," returned the woman; "but 'twant; 'twas the old one—the one I took to be the mother; though I have heard a story about the girl's comin' here long time ago, before I moved here. I was away when the woman died, and when I got back the rooms was empty, and the boy and girl was gone; nobody knows where; and I haint seen 'em since."

Frederic was too much interested in Marian to hear anything else, and he paid no attention to her mention of a boy. Marian was all he wished to find, but it was in vain that he questioned and cross-questioned the woman. She had given all the information she could; and with an increased feeling of disappointment he left her, glancing once more into the room where he was sure Marian had lived. Alice, too, was willing to stop there now; and when Frederic told her of the geranium and the kitten he had once seen in the window, a smile mingled with her tears, and she wished she had them now, especially the kitten! She did not know that the matronly-looking cat, which, behind the broken stove, was purring sleepily, was the same Maltese kitten Marian had fondled so often. At the time of leaving she had given it to an acquaintance near by, but pussy preferred her old haunts, and returning to them, persisted in remaining there until the arrival of the new comers, who took her in, and she now daily shared the meagre fare of the three children by the window. Intuitively, as it were, she felt that Alice was a lover of her race, and she came towards her, purring loudly, and rubbing against her side.

"Lands sake," exclaimed the woman. "Here's the very cat the young girl used to tend so much. I know it by the white spot between its eyes. I found it mewing and making an awful noise by the door when I came back; and though I ain't none of your cat women, I flung it a bone or two till them folks came, and the children kept it to torment, I 'spect, just as young ones will. I see one of 'em with a string round its neck t'other day a chokin' it most to death."

"Oh, Frederic," and Alice's face expressed what she wished to say, while she caught up the animal in her arms.

Frederic understood her, and speaking to the oldest of the children, he said, "Will you give me your cat?"

"No, no," the three set up at once, and Alice whispered, "Buy her, Frederic, won't you?"

"Will you let me have her for fifty cents?" he asked, showing the silver coin.

"No, no," and the youngest began to cry.

"Give more," said Alice, and Frederic continued, "Fifty cents a piece, then. You can buy a great many cakes and crackers with it"—

"And candy," suggested Alice.

The youngest began to show signs of relenting, as did the second, but the third persisted in saying "No."

"Offer her more," was whispered in a low voice, and glancing around the poorly furnished room, Frederic took out his purse and said, "You shall have a dollar a piece, but part of it must be saved for your mother,—besides that, this little girl is blind," and he laid his hand on Alice's head.

This last argument would have been sufficient without the dollar, for it touched a chord of pity in the heart of that child of poverty, and coming closer to Alice she looked at her curiously, saying, "Can't you see a bit more'n I can with my eyes shut?" and she closed her own by way of experimenting.

"Not a bit," returned Alice, "but I love kitty just the same, because she used to belong to a dear friend of mine. May I have her?"

"Ye-es," came half reluctantly from the lips of the child, as she extended her hand for the money.

"Oh, I'm so glad," said Alice when they were at a safe distance from the house. "I was afraid they'd take it back," and she held fast to the kitten, which made no effort to escape, but lay in her arms, singing occasionally as if well pleased with the exchange.

This, however, Frederic knew would not continue until they reached home, and stepping into a shop which they were passing, he bought a covered basket, in which the cat was placed and the lid secured, a proceeding not altogether satisfactory to the prisoner. Alice, too, was equally distressed, and when she learned that Frederic could not go home until night, she insisted upon his getting her a room at the Astor, where she could let her treasure out without fear of its escaping. Frederic complied with her request, and in her delight with her new pet, she half forgot how disappointed she had been in the result of their visit. But not so with Frederic. He felt it keenly, for never had his hopes of finding Marian been raised to a higher pitch than that morning, and even now he could not give it up. Leaving Alice at the hotel he went back again to the street and made the most minute inquiries, but all to no purpose. He could not obtain the least clue to her, and he retraced his steps with a feeling that she was as really lost to him as if Sarah Green's letter had been true and Marian resting in her grave.

"Why had that letter been written?" he asked himself again and again.

Somebody knew of Marian, and there was a mystery connected with it—a mystery of wrong it might me. Perhaps she could not come back, even though she wanted to, and his pulses quickened with painful rapidity as he thought of all the imaginary terrors which might surround the lost one. It was indeed a sad reflection, and his spirits were unusually depressed, when just before sunset he took Alice by one hand, the basket in the other, and started for home.

"I didn't think we should come back alone," said Alice, when at last they reached the depot at Yonkers, and she was lifted into the carriage waiting for them. "It's dreadful we couldn't find her, but I am so glad we've got the cat;" and she guarded the basket carefully, as if it had contained the diamonds of India.

Frederic did not care to talk, and folding his arms, he leaned moodily back in his carriage, evincing no interest in anything until as they drew near home, the driver said to Alice:

"Guess who's come?"

"Oh, I don't know—Dinah, may be," was Alice's reply, and then Frederic smiled at the preposterous idea.

"No; guess again," said the driver. "Somebody as handsome as a doll."

"Miss Grey!" cried Alice, almost upsetting her basket in her delight.

Eagerly she questioned John, and then replied, "I'm so glad, though I was going to fix her room so nice to-morrow—but no matter, it's always pleasant up there. How lonesome she must have been all day with nothing but the garden, the books, and the piano."

"She has been homesick," I guess," said John, "for

I seen her cryin', I thought, out under a tree in the garden."

"Poor thing!" sighed Alice. "She won't be homesick any more when we get there; will she, Frederic? I wonder if she likes cats!" And as by this time they had stopped at their own gate, the little girl went running up the walk, shaking the basket prodigiously, and inciting its contents to such violent struggles that in the hall the lid came off, and bounding from its confinement, the cat ran into the parlor, where, trembling with fright, it crouched as for protection, at the feet of Marian Grey.

CHAPTER XXIV.

THE MEETING.

Notwithstanding Alice's fears the day had not been a long one to Marian, who had been so occupied in unpacking her trunks and in going over the house and grounds, as scarcely to heed the lapse of time, and she was surprised when, about sunset, she saw John drive from the yard, and knew he was going for his master. Not till then did she fully realize her position, and she sought her chamber to compose herself, for the dreaded trial, which each moment came nearer and nearer.

"Will Frederic know me?" she asked herself a dozen times, and as often answered no—but Alice, ah, Alice, there was danger to be apprehended from her, and Marian felt that she would far rather meet the scrutinizing gaze of Frederic Raymond's eyes than submit herself to the touch of the blind girl's fingers, or trust her voice to the blind girl's ear.

That might not have changed. She could not tell if it had, though she thought it very probable, for six years was a long, long time, and it was nearly that since she left Redstone Hall. She could not sustain a feigned voice, she knew, and there was no alternative save to wait the trial and abide the result of a recognition. She felt a pardonable pride in wishing to make a good impression upon Frederic, for he could see, and she spent a much longer time at her toilet than usual. Black was very becoming to her dazzling complexion, and the thin tissue she wore fitted her admirably, showing just enough of her neck, while the wide, loose sleeves displayed the whole of her well-shaped arm, which, from contrast, looked white and smooth as ivory. Hitherto she had curled her entire hair, but she did not dare to do so now, and she confined a part of it with a comb, while the remainder of it was suffered to curl as usual about her face and behind her ears. This changed her looks somewhat, but was still becoming, and as she saw in the mirror the reflection of her sweet young face and deep blue eyes there came a brighter glow to her cheek, for she knew that the cherished wish of her early girlhood had been fulfilled, and that Ben Burt was right when he called her beautiful.

The gas was lighted when she entered the parlor below, and turning it down a little, she took a book and seated herself somewhat in the shade. But the volume might as well have been wrong side up for any idea its contents conveyed to her, so absorbed was she in what was fast approaching, for she had heard the carriage stop at the gate, and felt the cold moisture starting out beneath her hair and on her hands.

"I will be calm," she said, and with one tremendous effort of the will she quieted the violent throbbings of her heart, and leaning on her elbow, pretended to be reading, though not a sound escaped her ear. She heard the little feet come running up the walk, and the heavy, manly tread following in the rear.

She heard the struggle in the hall between Alice and the cat, and when the latter bounded into the room and crouched down at her feet, she thought there was something familiar in that spot between the eyes. But it could not be, she said, though Alice's exclamation of "Do, Frederic, shut the door, so she cannot get away," seemed to intimate that pussy was a stranger there. Stooping down, she passed her hand caressingly over the animal's back, whispering, in a low tone, "Spotty, darling, is it you?"

Won by her voice, the cat sprang up on Marian's lap just as Frederic glanced hastily in.

"Your pet is safe," he said to Alice, whom he followed to the sitting-room, waiting there a moment, and then starting to meet Miss Grey.

She knew he was coming, counting every step, and without raising her eyes from the book she pretended to be reading, knew just when he crossed the threshold of the door. Removing her hand from her head, where it had been resting, she gently pushed the cat from her lap, and half rising to her feet, waited for the first words of greeting.

"Miss Grey, I believe;" and bowing low, Frederic Raymond advanced towards Marian, who now stood up, so that the blaze of the chandelier fell full upon her, revealing at once her face and form.

Had her very life depended upon it she could not have spoken then, for the stormy emotions the name "Miss Grey" called up, mastered her speech entirely. She knew he would thus address her, but it grated harshly on her ear to hear him call her so, and her heart yearned for the familiar name of Marian, though she had no reason to expect it from him.

"You are welcome to Riverside," he continued; "and I regret that your first day here should have been so lonely."

This gave her a little time, and conquering her weakness she extended her hand to take the one he offered. Hers was cold and clammy, and trembled like an imprisoned bird, as it lay in his broad, warm palm. For an instant he held it there, and gazed down into her sweet, childish face, which did not look wholly unfamiliar to him, while she herself seemed more like a friend than a total stranger. The tie between them, which naught but death could sever, and which was bound so closely around Marian's heart, brought to his own an answering throb, and when at last she spoke, assuring him that she had not been lonely in the least, he started, for there was something in the tone which moved him as a stranger oft is moved, when hearing in the calm, still night the air of "Home, Sweet Home." It carried him back to Redstone Hall, years and years ago, when in the moonlight he had played with his dusky companions upon the river brink. But Marian Lindsey had no portion of his thoughts at that first interview with Marian Grey, who ventured at last to look into his face just as he was looking into hers. Oh, how much like the Frederic of old he was, save that in his mature manhood he was finer, nobler looking, while the proud fire of his eye had given place to a milder, softer expression, and she felt intuitively that he was far more worthy of her love than when she knew him before.

Motioning her to a chair, he, too, sat down at a little distance and conversed with her pleasantly, as friend converses with friend, asking about her journey, making inquiries after Mrs. Sheldon's family, and experiencing a most unaccountable sensation when he saw how she blushed at the mention of William Gordon! Ben was next talked about, and Marian was growing eloquent in his praise, when suddenly a sight met her view which pretrified her powers of speech and sent the hot blood ebbing backward from her cheek and lip. In the hall without and where Frederic could not see her, the blind girl stood, her hands clasped and slightly raised, her lips apart, her eyes rolling, her head bent forward, and her ear turned toward the door, whence came the sound which had arrested her footsteps and chained her to the spot. She had started for the parlor and come thus far, when she, too, caught the tone which had affected even Frederic, and her head grew dizzy with the bewildering sound, for to her it brought memories of Marian. Had she come? Was she there with Frederic and Miss Grey? Eagerly she waited to hear the sound repeated, wondering why Miss Grey, too, did not join in the conversation. It came again, the old familiar strain, though tuned to a sadder note, for Marian had suffered much since last she talked with Alice, and it was perceptible even in her voice. Tighter and tighter the small hands pressed together—lower and lower bent the head, while a shade of disappointment flitted over the face of the listening child, for this time it did not seem quite so natural as at first, and she knew, too, that 'twas Miss Grey who spoke, for her subject was Ben Butterworth.

"What is it?" asked Frederic, observing that Miss Grey stopped suddenly in the midst of a remark.

Marian pointed toward the spot where Alice stood, but ere Frederic had time to step forward, the loud ring of the bell started Alice from an attitude which, had Frederic Raymond seen it, would surely have led to a discovery.

"The little girl, she acts so singular," said Marian, thinking she must make some explanation.

"She's blind, you know," was answered in a low tone, and going toward the hall, Frederic met with Alice just as a servant opened the outer door, and a stranger entered, asking for Mr. Raymond.

"In a moment," said Frederic, and leading Alice up to Marian, he continued, "Your teacher," and then left the two together.

For an instant there was perfect silence, and Marian knew the blind girl could hear the beating of her heart, while she in turn watched the wonder and perplexity written on the speaking face turned upward toward her own, the brown eyes riveted upon her, as if for once they had broken from their prison walls and could discern what was before them.

Oh! how Marian longed to take the little, helpless creature in her arms; to hug her, to kiss her, to cry over her, and tell her of the love which had never known one moment's abatement during the long years of their separation. But she dared not; and she sat gazing at her to see if she had changed since the night when she left her sleeping so quietly in their dear old room at home. She was now nearly thirteen, but her figure was so slight, and her features so child-like, that few would have guessed her more than nine, unless they judged by her mature, womanly mind. To Marian she seemed the same; and when, unable longer to restrain herself, she drew the child to her, and, kissing her forehead, said to her kindly,

"You are Alice, my pupil, I am sure. Alice what?"

"Alice Raymond," and the sightless eyes never moved for an instant from the questioner's face.

"Are you very nearly related to Mr. Raymond?" asked Marian; and Alice replied:

"Second cousin, that's all. But he has been more than a brother to me since—since—"

The perplexed, mystified look increased on Alice's face, and her gaze grew more intense as she continued: "Since Marian went away."

There was a moment's stillness, and then the hand which hitherto had rested on Marian's lap was raised until it reached the head, where it lay lightly, very lightly, though to Marian it seemed like the weight of a thousand pounds, and she felt every hair prickle at its root when the blind girl said to her:

"AIN'T YOU MARIAN?"

"Yes, Marian Grey. Didn't you know my first name?" was the answer, spoken so deliberately that Marian was astonished at herself.

There was a wavering then in the brown eyes, a quivering of the lids, and the great tears rolled down Alice's cheeks, for with this calm reply, uttered so naturally, the hope she had scarcely dared to cherish passed away, and she murmured sadly:

"It cannot be her."

"What makes you cry, darling?" asked Marian, choking back her own tears, which were just ready to flow, and which did gush forth in torrents, when Alice answered:

"Oh, I wish I wasn't blind to-night!"

This surely was a good cause for weeping and pressing the little one to her bosom, Marian wept over her passionately for a few moments; then, drying her eyes, she said:

"Why to-night more than any other time?"

"Because I want so much to know how you look," returned Alice; adding immediately: "May I feel of your face? It's the only way I have of seeing."

"Certainly," answered Marian; and the fingers wandered slowly, cautiously, over every feature, involuntarily caressing the fair, round cheek, but lingering longest on the hair—the beautiful hair—whose glossy waves were perceptible even to the touch.

"What color is it?" she asked, winding one of the curls around her finger.

"Some call it auburn, some chesnut, and some a mixture of both," was the reply, and Alice continued her investigations by mentally comparing its length with a standard she had in her own mind.

The two did not agree, for the curls she remembered were longer and far more wiry than the silken tresses of Miss Grey.

"How tall are you?" she suddenly asked, and Marian tried to laugh, although every nerve was thrilling with fear, for she knew she was passing through a dangerous test.

"Rather tall," she replied, standing up, "Yes, very tall, some would say. Put up your hand and see."

Alice did as she requested, and her tears came faster as she whispered mournfully. "You're the tallest."

"Did you think we had met before?" asked Marian, and then the sobs of the child burst forth unrestrained.

Burying her face in Marian's lap, she cried, "Yes—no—I don't know what I thought, only you don't seem to me like I supposed you would. You make me tremble so, and I keep thinking of somebody we lost long ago. At first your voice sounded so natural, that I knew most she was here, but you aint't even like her. You're taller and fatter, and handsomer, I reckon, and yet there is something about you that makes my heart beat so fast. Oh, I wish I could see what it is. What made God make me blind?"

Never before had Marian heard a murmur from the

lips of the unfortunate child, and it seemed to her cruel not to whisper words of comfort in her ear. But she could not do it yet, and so she kissed her tenderly, saying, "Did you love this other one so very much?"

"Yes, very, very much," was Alice's reply, "and it hurts me so to think we cannot find her. I thought we surely should to-day, for we went there, Frederic and I—went where she used to live, and she wasn't there. 'Twas a dreary place, and Frederic groaned out loud to think she ever lived there."

"Perhaps it didn't look so then," suggested Marian, who felt constrained to say a word in favor of her former home.

"Oh, I know it didn't," returned Alice, "for Frederic has been by there, though he didn't know it then, and he says it looked real nice, with the white curtain and the kitten asleep on the window sill. It's a cat now, and we brought it home."

"Her cat?" and Marian started eagerly.

"Yes," said Alice, "Frederic gave three dollars for it," and forgetting her late grief in this new interest, she told how they knew it was Marian's, and then as Miss Grey expressed a wish to see it, she started in quest of it, just as Frederic appeared, telling them tea was ready.

"I am afraid you will think we keep Lent here all the year round," he said, apologetically. "I was surprised to find that Mrs. Russell compelled you to fast until our return."

"It didn't matter," Marian relpied; though she had wondered a little at the non-appearance of supper, for Mrs. Russell, intent upon her dress, had no idea of "makin' two fusses," and she kept her visitor waiting until the return of Frederic, saying, "the supper would taste all the better when it did come."

Very willingly Marian followed Frederic to the dining-room, where everything was indicative of elegance and wealth.

"Mrs. Jones used to sit here; and I now give the

place to you," said Frederic, motioning to the seat by the tea-tray, and himself sitting down opposite, with Alice upon his right.

Marian became her new position well, and so Frederic thought, as he saw how gracefully her snowy fingers handled the silver urn, and how much at home she seemed. There was a strange fascination about her as she sat there at the head of his table, with the bright bloom on her cheek, and the dewy lustre in her beautiful blue eyes, which occasionally wandered toward the figure opposite, but as often fell beneath the curious gaze which they encountered. Frederic could not forbear looking at her, even though he saw that it embarrassed her—she was so fresh, so fair, so modest—while there was about her an indescribable something which he could not define, for though a stranger, as he supposed, she seemed near to him—so near that he almost felt he had a right to pass his arm around her, and kiss the girlish lips which Will Gordon had likened to a rose-bud.

"Poor Will," sighed, "he did lose a prize when he lost Marian Grey."

Involuntarily his mind went back to Redstone Hall, and to the time when another Marian sat opposite, and did for him the office this one was doing. The contrast between the two was great, but, with a nobleness worthy of the man, he thought "Marian Grey is far more beautiful, 'tis true, but Marian Lindsey was my wife."

Then he remembered the day when Isabel first sat at his board, and he had felt it a sin to look at her in all her queenly beauty. He had grown hard since then, for he could not think it wicked to look at Marian Grey, or deem it a wrong to the other one, and he feasted his eyes upon her until she arose from the table, and went, at Alice's request, to see the cat, which was safely confined in a candle box, "by way of taming her," Alice said.

"I think there's no need of that," returned Marian,

stroking her soft coat. "I am sure she will not run away. What do you propose calling her?"

"Marian, I reckon, only you might not want her named after *you*, and it wouldn't be, for it's the other one."

"I haven't the least objection," said Miss Grey, laughing, "only Marian will sound oddly. Suppose you call it 'Spottie,' there's a cunning white spot between its eyes."

"Yes, Alice, let that be the name," said a voice behind them, and turning, Marian saw Frederic, who had all the time been standing near and watching them as like two children they knelt together by the candle box and gave the cat its milk—Marian and Alice, side by side, just as they used to be of old—just as Frederic had seen them many a time.

The tableau was a familiar one, and so he felt it to be, though he could not divine the reason. The tall, beautiful girl before him bore no resemblance to the Marian of Redstone Hall, and still nothing she did seemed strange or new to him.

"I certainly have dreamed of her," he said, when lifting up her head she shook back from her face the clustering curls, and smiled on Alice as she used to do. "I have dreamed of her just as I sometimes dream of places, and see them afterward in waking."

This conclusion was entirely satisfactory, and he returned with the girls to the parlor, while "Spottie" followed after, hovering near to Marian, whose low spoken words and gentle caresses had reawakened the affection which had perhaps been dormant during the last year.

"Will you play for us, Miss Grey?" said Frederic, and without a word of apology, Marian seated herself at the piano, whose rich, mellow tones roused her enthusiasm at once, and she played more than usually well, while Alice stood by listening eagerly, and Frederic looked on, scarce heeding the stirring notes, so intent was he upon the dimpled hands which swept the keys so skillfully.

On the third finger there was a little cornelian ring, the first gift of Ben, and as he looked, he felt certain he had seen that ring and those hands before. But where? He tried to recall the time and the place. Stepping forward, he looked into her face, but that gave him no clue, only the ring and the hands were familiar. Suddenly he started, for he remembered the when and the where—remembered, too, that Alice, when told of the girl with the brown vail, had said to him, "Wan't that our Marian?"

He had accepted the suggestion as a possible one then, but he doubted it now, for if that maiden were Marian Grey, it certainly could not have been Marian Lindsey. The exquisite music ceased, and ere Alice had time for a word of comment, he asked abruptly: "Miss Grey, did you ever ride in the cars with me in New York?"

The question was a startling one, but Marian's face was turned from him, and he could not see the effort she made to answer him calmly.

"I think it very probable. I have been in the cars a great many times, and with a great many different people."

"Yes, but one rainy night, more than four years ago, did I not offer you a seat between myself and the door? You wore a brown vail, and carried a willow basket, if it were you. Something about your appearance has puzzled me all the evening, and I think I must have met you there. It was on the Third Avenue cars."

Marian trembled violently, but by constantly turning the leaves of her music book, she managed to conceal her agitation, and when Frederic ceased speaking, she answered in her natural tone, "Now that you recall the circumstances, I believe I do remember something about it, though you do not look as that man did. I imagined he had been sick, or was in trouble," and Marian's blue eyes turned sideways to witness, if possible, the effect of her words. But she was disappointed, for she could not see how white Frederic was for a single instant, but she felt it in his voice, as he replied:

"You are right. I had been sick, and was in great trouble."

"Wasn't that when you were looking for Marian?" Alice asked, and again the blue eye sought Frederic's face, turning this time so that they could see it.

"Yes, I was hunting for Marian," was the answer; and the deep sigh which accompanied the words brought a thrill of joy to the Marian hunted for, and she knew now, and from his own lips, too, that he had sought for her, nay, that he was looking for her even then, when in her anger she censured him for not recognizing her.

Little by little she was learning the truth just as it was; and when at a late hour she bade Frederic good night, and went to her own chamber, her heart was almost too full for utterance, for she felt that the long, dark night was over, and the dawn she had waited for so long was breaking at last around her. Intuitively, Alice, who had been permitted to sit up so long as she did, caught something of the same spirit. "It was almost as nice as if Marian really were there," she said; and she came twice to kiss her governess, while on her face was a most satisfied expression, as she nestled among her pillows and listened to the footsteps in the adjoining chamber where Marian made her nightly toilet.

"Oh, I wish she'd let me sleep with her," she thought. "It would be a heap more like having Marian back." And, when all was still, she stepped upon the floor and glided to the bedside of Marian, who was not aware of her approach until a voice whispered in her ear:

"May I stay here with you? I've been making believe that you was Marian—our Marian, I mean—and I want to sleep with you so much just as I used to do with her—may I?"

"Yes, darling," was the answer, as Marian folded

her arms lovingly around the neck of the blind girl, whose soft, warm cheek was pressed against her own.

And there, just as they were used to do in the old Kentucky home, ere sorrow had come to either, they lay side by side, Marian and Alice, the one dreaming sweet dreams of the Marian come back to her again; and the other, that to her the gates of Paradise were opened, and she saw the glory shining through, just as in Frederic Raymond's eyes she had seen the glimmer of the love-light which was yet to overshadow her and brighten her future pathway.

CHAPTER XXV.

LIFE AT RIVERSIDE.

It was a joyful waking which came to Marian next morning, and when fresh and glowing from her invigorating bath she descended to the piazza she was surprised at finding Frederic there before her, looking haggard and pale, as if the boon of sleep had been denied to him. After Marian and Alice had bidden him good night, he, too, had retired to his room, which was directly under theirs; and sitting in his arm-chair, he had listened to the footsteps above, readily distinguishing one from the other, and experiencing unconsciously a vague, delicious feeling of comfort in knowing that the long-talked of Marian Grey had come to him at last, and that she was even more beautiful than he had imagined her to be from Will Gordon's glowing description. He would keep her with him, too, he said, until the other one was found, if that should ever be: and then, as the footsteps and the murmur of voices in the chamber above him ceased, and all about the house was still, his heart went out after the other one, demanding of the solitude around to show him where she was—to lead him to her so that he could bring her back to the home where each day he was wanting her more and more. And the solitude thus questioned invariably carried his thoughts to *Marian Grey*, whose delicate, girlish beauty had made so strong an impression upon his mind. "How would the two compare?"

he asked. "Would not the governess far outshine the wife? Would not the contrast be a painful one?"

"No, no!" he said; "for, though Marian Lindsey were not as beautiful as Marian Grey, she was gentle, pure and good." And then, as he sought his pillow, he went back again in fancy to that feverish sick-room, and the tender love which alone had saved him from death; while mingled with this remembrance were confused thoughts of the vailed maiden in the corner of the car—of the geranium growing in the window, and of Marian Grey, who seemed a part of every thing—for, turn which way he would, her blue eyes were sure to shine upon him; and once, when, for a few moments, he fell into a troubled sleep, she said to him, "I am the Marian you seek."

Then this vision faded, and he saw a little grave, on whose humble stone was written, "The Heiress of Redstone Hall," and with a nervous start he woke, only to doze and dream again, until at last he was glad when the dawn came stealing across the misty river, and looked in at his window. The sun was not yet up when he arose, and going out upon the broad piazza, tried by walking to gain the rest the night had failed to bring. As he walked Spottie came purring to his side, rubbing against his feet and looking into his face as if she fain would tell him, if she could, that the lost one had returned, and was safe beneath his roof.

Frederic Raymond could not be said to care particularly for cats, but there was a charm connected with this one gambolling at his feet, and he did not deem it an unmanly act to stoop down and caress it for the sake of her who had often had it in her arms.

"Can you tell me nothing of your mistress," he said, aloud, for he thought himself alone.

Instantly the cat, whose ear had caught a sound he did not hear, bounded toward the door where Marian Grey was standing. Advancing toward her, Frederic said, "You must excuse me, Miss Grey. I am not often guilty of petting cats, but this one has a peculiar attraction for me, inasmuch as it once belonged to—to —to Mrs. Raymond," and Frederic felt vastly relieved to think he had actually spoken of his wife to Marian Grey, and called her Mrs. Raymond, too! He knew Will Gordon had told her the story, and when he saw how the color came and went upon her cheek, he fancied that it arose from the delicacy she would naturally feel in talking with him of his runaway wife. He was glad he had introduced the subject, and she should continue it or not, as she choose. Marian hardly knew how to reply, for though she longed to hear what he had to say of Mrs. Raymond, she scarcely dared trust herself to question him.

At last, however, she ventured to say, "Yes, Alice told me that it was once your wife's. She is dead, isn't she?"

Frederic started, and walking off a few paces, replied, "Marian dead! not that I know of! Did you ever hear that she was?" and he came back to Marian, looking at her so earnestly that she colored deeply, as she replied:

"Mr. Gordon told me something of her; and I had the impression that———"

She did not know how to finish the sentence, and she was glad to hear a little, uncertain step upon the stairs, as that was an excuse for her to break off abruptly, and go to Alice, who had come down in quest of her, expressing much surprise that she should rise so early and dress so quietly.

"Mrs. Jones used to make such a noise coughing and sneezing," she said, "that she always woke me, while Isabel never got up till breakfast was ready, and sometimes not then, when we were in Kentucky. Negroes were made to wait on her, she said. She'll be coming over here to call and see how you look. I heard her asking Mrs. Russell last week if you were pretty, and she said———"

"Never mind what she said," suggested Marian adding laughingly, "I have heard of Miss Huntington before. Will Gordon told me of her, and Ben, too. He saw her in Kentucky, you knew; so you see, I am tolerably well posted in your affairs;" and she turned towards Frederic, who was about to answer, when Alice, who had climbed into a chair, and was standing with her arm around the young man's neck, chimed in:

"If Mr. Gordon told you that Frederic liked her, it isn't so, for he don't; do you, Frederic?"

"I like all the ladies," was his reply; and the breakfast bell just then rang, the conversation ceased, and they entered the house together, Alice holding fast to Marian's hand, and dancing along like a joyous bird.

"You seem very happy this morning," said Frederic, smiling down upon the happy child.

"I am," she replied. "I'm most as happy as I should be if we had found Marian yesterday. Wouldn't it be splendid if this were really Marian, and wouldn't you be glad?"

Frederic Raymond did not say yes—he did not say anything; but as he looked at the figure in white presiding a second time so gracefully at his table, he fancied that it would not be a hard matter for any man to be glad if Marian Grey were his wife. Breakfast being over, Alice assumed the responsibility of showing her teacher the place.

"You were here once, I know," she said, "and left me those flowers, but you hadn't time then to see half. There's a tree down in the garden, where Frederic's name is cut in the bark, and Marian Lindsey's, too. You must see that;" and she led her off to the spot where John had seen her crying the day before. "I ain't going to study a bit for ever so long. Frederic says I needn't," said Alice. "I'm going to have a right nice time with you." And Marian was not sorry, for nothing could please her better than rambling with Alice over what was once her home.

Very rapidly the first few days passed away, and ere a week had gone by, Marian understood tolerably well the place which Marian Lindsey occupied in her husband's affections, and she needed not the letter received from William Gordon to tell her that the Frederic Raymond of to-day was not the same from whose presence she had once fled with a breaking heart. He was greatly changed, and if she had loved him in the early days of her girlhood, her heart clung to him now with an affection tenfold stronger than she had ever known before. From Alice, who was very communicative, she learned many things of which she little dreamed, when in New York she was hiding from her husband, and believing that he hated her. Alice liked nothing better than to talk of Marian, and one afternoon, when Frederic was in New York, and the two girls were sitting together in their pleasant chamber, she told her sad story in her own childish way, accepting her companion's tears, which fell like rain as tokens of sympathy for the lost one.

"Frederic cried just like he was a woman," she said, "when he came up from the river, cold, and wet, and sick, and told us they could not find her. I remember, too, how he groaned when I asked him what made her kill herself; she didn't, though," she added quickly, as she heard Marian's exclamation of horror at the very idea; "she wasn't even dead, but we thought she was, and we mourned for her so much. The house was like a funeral all the time till Isabel came."

"And how was it then?" Marian asked.

Alice did not reply immediately, and as Marian saw the shadow which flitted over her face, she pressed her hands together nervously, for she fancied that she knew what Redstone Hall was like when Isabel, her rival, came.

"You were telling me about the house after Miss Huntington's arrival," she rejoined, as Alice showed no signs of continuing the conversation, but sat with her eyes fixed upon the floor as if she were thinking of something far back in the past.

At Marian's remark she started, and with the same dreamy, perplexed look upon her face, replied:

"Perhaps I ought not to tell; but you seem so near to me that I don't believe Frederic would care. He's got over it, too, but he loved Isabel," and Alice's voice sank to a whisper, as if afraid the walls would hear. "He loved her a heap better than he did poor dear Marian, who somehow found it out that night, and rather than be his wife when he didn't want her, she ran away, you know."

"Yes, yes, I know," gasped Marian, while Alice, little dreaming how well she knew, continued, "And so when Isabel came, he couldn't help loving her some, I suppose, though Dinah thought he could, and she used to scold mightily when she heard her singing and playing, as she did all the time, so as to get Frederic in there," and Alice's tone and manner were so much like old Dinah and so highly expressive of her meaning, that Marian could not forbear smiling. "I talked to Frederic one night," said Alice, "and told him I didn't believe Marian was dead, and I reckon I made him think so, too, for he promised he would wait for her ten years."

"Will he marry then, if he does not find her?" Marian asked by way of calling out the little girl, who replied:

"I suppose he won't live all his life alone; at any rate, he said he wouldn't. Oh, Miss Grey!" and Alice started so quickly that Marian started, too; "I'd a heap rather Marian would be his wife than anybody, because he married her first; but if she don't come back, can't you guess what I wish would be?" and Alice wound her arms around the neck of Marian, who did guess, but could not embody her guessing in words.

"Did Mr. Raymond never hear from her?" she asked, and resuming her seat, Alice replied:

"Yes, and that's the mystery. One cold March night when Isabel was dressing for a party, and was just as cross as she could be, there came to him a letter from Sarah Green, saying she was dead and buried with canker-rash."

"Dead!" exclaimed Marian, starting quickly. "When? Where?"

"In New York," answered Alice; and Marian listened breathlessly to the story of her supposed decease, wondering, as Frederic had often done, whence the letter came, and why it had been sent.

"It must have been a plan of Ben's to see what he would do," she thought; and she listened again, with burning cheeks and beating heart, while Alice told of Frederic's grief when he read that she was dead.

"I know he cried," said Alice, "for there were tears on his face, and he sat so still, and held me so close to him that I could hear his heart thump so hard," and she illustrated by striking her tiny fist upon the table.

Then she told how sometime after she had interrupted Frederic in the parlor, just as he was asking Isabel to be his wife, and had almost convinced him again of Marian's existence.

"Blessed Alice," said Marian, involuntarily. "You have been Miss Lindsey's good angel, and kept her husband from falling."

"I couldn't help it," answered Alice. "I most knew she was alive; and I was so glad when he started for New York. I was sure he'd find her; and he did. She took care of him a few days and his voice sounded so low and sad when he told me of her, and how she left him when Isabel came. Your brother Ben—the nice man who gave me the bracelet—telegraphed for her to go; and you would suppose she was crazy—she flew around so, ordering the negroes, and knocking Dud down flat, because he couldn't run fast enough to get out of her way. That made Aunt Hetty, his grandmother, mad, and she yellowed Isabel's collar that she was ironing. If I hadn't been blind I should have cried myself so those dreadful days when we expected to hear Frederic was dead, for next to Marian I love him the best. He's real good to me now; and when I asked him once what made him pet me so much more than he used to, he said, 'Because our dear, lost Marian loved you, and you loved her.'"

"Did he say that? Did he call her his 'dear, lost Marian?'" and the eyes of the speaker sparkled with delight, while across her mind there flitted the half-formed resolution that before the sun had set Frederic Raymond should know the whole.

Ere Alice could answer this question, there was a loud ring at the door, and a servant brought to Miss Grey Isabel Huntington's card.

"I knew she'd call," said Alice. "She wants to see how you look; but I don't care, for Frederic says you're a heap the handsomest; I asked him last night after you quit playing, and had left the room."

The knowledge that Frederic Raymond preferred her face to that of Isabel, rendered Marian far more self-possessed than she would otherwise have been, as she went down to meet her visitor, whose call was prompted from mere curiosity, and not from any friendliness she felt towards Marian Grey. Isabel had heard much of Marian's beauty from those who met her since her arrival at Riverside, and she had come to see if rumor were correct. During the last three years she had not improved materially, for her disappointment in failing to win Frederic Raymond had soured a disposition never particularly amiable, and she was now a censorious, fault-finding woman of twenty-five, on the lookout for a husband, and trembling lest the dreaded age of thirty should find ner still unmarried. For Frederic Raymond she affected a feeling of contempt; insinuating that he was mean—that his property was not gained honestly; that she knew something which she could tell but shouldn't—all of which had but little effect in a place where he was so much better known than herself. And still, had Frederic Raymond evinced the slightest interest in her, she would gladly have met him more than half the way, for the love she really felt for him once had never died away. And even now she watched him often through blinding tears as he passed her cottage door. The story of Marian's existence she had repudiated at first and in the excitement of going south, and the incidents connected with her sojourn there, she had failed to speak of it even to Mrs. Rivers, choosing rather to make her friends believe that she had deliberately refused the owner of Redstone Hall. Recently, however, and since her arrival at Riverside, she had indirectly circulated the story, and Frederic had more than once been questioned as to its authenticity. Greatly to Isabel's chagrin he took no pains to conceal the fact, but frankly spoke of Mrs. Raymond, as a person who had been, and who he hoped was still a living reality. Very narrowly Isabel watched the proceedings at Riverside, and when she heard that Alice's new governess was in some way connected with the "gawky peddler," whom she remembered well, she sneered at her as a person of no refinement, marvelling greatly at the praises bestowed upon her. At last, curious to see for herself, she donned her richest robes, and now in the parlor at Riverside, sat awaiting the appearance of Miss Grey.

"Let her be what she will, Frederic can't marry her, and that's some consolation," she thought, just as a tripping footstep announced the approach of Marian, and, assuming her haughtiest manner, she arose, and bowed to Frederic Raymond's wife.

They had met before, but there was no token of recognition between them now, and as strangers they greeted each other, Marian's hand trembling slightly as she offered it to Isabel—for she knew that this was not their first meeting. Coldly, inquisitively and almost impudently, the haughty Isabel scrutinized the graceful creature, mentally acknowledging that she was beautiful, and hating her for it. With great effort Marian concealed her agitation, and answered carelessly the first few common-place remarks addressed to her, as to how she liked Riverside, and if this were her first visit there.

"No," she answered to this last question—"I came here once with Ben, who, you remember, was once at Redstone Hall."

"I could not well forget him. His odd Yankee ways furnished gossip for many a day among the negroes." And Isabel tossed her head scornfully, as if Ben Burt were a creature far beneath her notice.

After a little, she spoke of Mr. Raymond, asking Marian, finally, what she thought of him, and saying she supposed she knew he was a married man.

"I know he has been married, but is there any certainty that his wife is still living?" asked Marian, for the sake of hearing her visitor's remarks.

"Any certainty! Of course there is," said Isabel, experiencing at once a pang of jealousy lest the humble Marian Grey had dared to think of Frederic as a widower, and hence a marriageable man. "Of course she's living, though, I must say, he takes no great pains to find her. He did look for her a little, I believe, after he was sick in New York; but he did it more to divert his mind from a very mortifying disappointment than from any affection he felt for her, and it was this which prompted him to go to New York at all."

"What disappointment?" Marian asked, faintly, and, affecting to be embarrassed, Isabel replied:

"It would be unbecoming in *me* to say what the nature of it was, and I referred to it thoughtlessly. Pray, forget it, Miss Grey;" and she turned the leaves of a handsomely bound volume lying on the table with well feigned modesty.

Marian understood her at once, and was glad that Isabel was too intent upon an engraving to observe her agitation. Notwithstanding what Alice said, Frederic *had* offered himself to Isabel, and her refusal had sent him to New York, where he hoped to forget his mortification, and where sickness had overtaken him. In the kindness of her heart, Isabel had come to him, and the words of affection which she had heard her speak to Frederic were prompted by pity, rather than love, as she then supposed. And after Isabel had left him, he had looked for her merely by way of excitement, and not because he cared to find her. Such were the thoughts which flashed upon Marian's mind and destroyed at once her half-formed resolution of telling Frederic that night. She did not know Isabel, and she could not understand why she should be guilty of a falsehood to her—a perfect stranger.

"He is not learning to love me, after all," was the sad cry of her heart; and, when she spoke again, there was a plaintive tone in her voice, and Isabel wondered she had not observed before how mournful it was. And, as they sat talking, there came along the graveled walk a step familiar to them both, and the color deepened on their cheeks; while in the kindling light which shone in the eyes of blue, and flashed from the eyes of black, there was a spark of jealousy, as if each were reading the secret thoughts of the other.

Frederic had returned from the city earlier than was his custom, for he usually spent the entire day; but there was something now to draw him home besides the blind girl, and he was conscious of quickening his footsteps as he drew near his house, and of watching eagerly for the flutter of a mourning robe, or the sight of a sunny face, which, he knew, would smile a welcome. He heard her voice in the parlor, and ere he was aware of it, he stood in the presence of Isabel. Narrowly Marian watched him, marvelling somewhat at his perfect self-possession; for Isabel was to him an object of such indifference that he experienced far less emotion in meeting her than in speaking to Marian Grey, and asking if she had been lonely.

"You men are so vain," said Isabel, with a toss of her head, "and think we miss you so much. Now I'll venture to say Miss Grey has not thought of you in all day. Why should she?"

"Why shouldn't she?" asked Frederic, giving to Marian a smile which sent the hot blood tingling to her finger tips.

"'Why shouldn't she!'" returned Isabel—"just as though we, girls, ever think of married men. By the way, have you heard anything definite from Mrs. Raymond, since she left you so suddenly in New York, or have you given up the search?"

Marian pitied Frederic then, he turned so white; and she almost hated Isabel, as she saw the malicious triumph in her eye. Breathlessly, too, she awaited the answer, which was:

"I shall never abandon the search until I find her, or know certainly that she is dead. I went to the place where she used to live, not long ago."

"Indeed! What did you learn?" and a part of Isabel's assurance left her, for she felt that his searching for his wife was a reality with him; while Marian's heart grew hopeful and warm again, as she listened to Frederic Raymond telling Isabel Huntington of that dear old room which had been her home so long.

"I can't conceive what made her run away," said Isabel, fixing her large, glittering eyes upon Frederic, who coolly replied, "*I can*," and then turning to Marian he abruptly commenced a conversation upon an entirely different subject.

Biting her lip with vexation, Isabel arose to go, saying she should expect to see Miss Grey at her own house, and that she hoped she would sometimes bring Mr. Raymond with her.

"You need not be afraid to come," she continued, addressing herself to him, "for everybody knows you have a wife, consequently your coming will create no scandal concerning yourself and *mother!*" and with a hateful laugh she swept haughtily down the walk.

From this time forth Isabel was a frequent visitor at Riverside, where she always managed to say something which seriously affected Marian's peace of mind and led her to distrust the man who was beginning to feel far more interest in the Marian found than in the Marian lost. This the quick-sighted Isabel saw and while her bosom rankled with envy towards her rival, she exulted in the thought that love her as he might he dared not tell her of his love, for a barrier the living wife had built between the two. Though professing the utmost regard for Miss Grey she did not hesitate to speak against her when an opportunity occurred, but her shafts fell harmlessly, for where Marian was known she was esteemed and the wily woman gave up the contest at last and waited anxiously to see the end.

Towards the last of October, Ben, who was now a petty grocer in a New England village, came to Riverside for the first time since Marian's residence there. Never before had he appeared so happy, and his honest face was all aglow with his delight at seeing Marian at last where she belonged.

"You fit in like an odd scissor," he said to her when they were alone. "Ain't it most time to tell?"

"Not yet," returned Marian. "I would rather wait until I am back at Redstone Hall. We are going there next month, and then, too, I wish I knew how much of Isabel's insinuations to believe."

"Isabel be hanged," said Ben. "She lied I know, and mebby that letter was some of her devilment. Has she washed them curtains yit?"

Marian replied by telling him of the letter from Sarah Green and asking if he could explain it. But it was all a mystery to him, and he puzzled his brain with it for a long time, deciding at last that it might have come from some of her Kentucky acquaintance who chanced to be in New York, and sent it just for mischief.

"But they overshot the mark," said he. "You ain't dead by a great sight, and I b'lieve I'd let the cat out pretty soon. That makes me think you wrote that

Spottie was here. Where is the critter? 'Twould be good for sore eyes to see her again."

Marian went in quest of her, and on her return found Alice with Ben, who, in her presence, dared not manifest all that he felt at sight of his old friend. Taking the animal on his lap he looked at it for a moment with quivering chin; then stroking its soft fur, he said, with a prolongation of each syllable, which rendered the sound ludicrous, "*Gri-mal-kin*—poor *gri-mal-kin*," and a tear dropped on its back.

"What!" exclaimed Alice, coming to his side, "what did you call the kitty?"

"*Gri-mal-kin*," answered Ben, adding, by way of explanation, "that, I b'lieve, is the *Latin* for cat."

Marian could not forbear laughing aloud, and as Ben joined with her, it served to keep him from crying outright, as he otherwise might have done.

"What are you going to do with it when you go South?" he asked, and upon Alice's replying that they should leave it with Mrs. Russell, he proposed taking it instead and keeping it until Spring, when he could return it.

This suggestion was warmly seconded by Marian, and as Alice finally yielded the point, Ben carried Spottie off the next morning, promising the little girl that it should be well cared for in her absence. Alice shed a few tears at parting with her pet, but they were like April showers, and soon passed away in her joyful anticipations of a speedy removal to Kentucky, for Frederic was going earlier this season than usual, and the 10th of November was appointed for them to start. If they met with no delays they would reach Redstone Hall on the anniversary of Marian's bridal, and to her it seemed meet that on this day of all others she should return again to her old home, and she wondered if Frederic, too, would think of it or send one feeling of regret after his missing bride. He did remember it, for the November days were always fraught with me mories of the past. This year, however, there was a difference, for though he thought much of Marian Lindsey, it was not as he had thought of her before, and he was conscious of a most unaccountable sensation of satisfaction in knowing that even if she could not go with him to Kentucky, her place would be tolerably well filled by Marian Grey!

CHAPTER XXVI.

REDSTONE HALL.

NEWS had been received at Redstone Hall, that the family would be there on the 13th; but Frederic's coming home was a common occurrence now, and did not create as great a sensation among his servants as it once had done. Still it was an event of considerable importance, particularly as he was to bring with him a new governess, who, judging from his apparent anxiety to have everything in order, was a person of more distinction than the prosy Mrs. Jones, or even the brilliant Isabel. Old Dinah accordingly worked herself up to her usual pitch of excitement, and then, long before it was time, started off her spouse, who was to meet his master at Big Spring Station, and who waited there impatiently at least an hour ere the whistle and smoke in the distance announced the arrival of the train.

"We are here at last," said Frederic, when they stopped before the depot; and he touched the arm of Marian, who sat leaning against a window, her head bent down, and her thoughts in such a wild tumult that she scarcely comprehended what she was doing or where she was.

During the entire journey she had labored under the highest excitement, which manifested itself sometimes in snatches of merry songs, sometimes in laughter almost hysterical, and again when no one saw her, in floods of tears, which failed to cool her feverish impatience. It seemed to her she could not wait, and she counted every mile-stone, while her breath came faster and faster as she knew they were almost there. With a shudder she glanced at the clump of trees under whose shadow she had hidden six years before, and those who noticed her face as she passed out marvelled at its deathly pallor.

"Jest gone with consumption," was Phil's mental comment; and he wondered at the eager, curious glance which she gave to him. "'Spects she never seen a nigger before," he muttered; and as by this time the travelers were comfortably seated in the wide capacious carriage, he chirrupped to his horses, and they moved rapidly on toward Redstone Hall.

Marian did not try longer to conceal her delight, and Frederic watched her wonderingly, as with glowing cheeks and beaming eyes she looked first from one window and then from the other, the color deepening on her face and the pallor increasing about her mouth, as way-mark after way-mark was passed and recognized.

"You seem very much excited," he said to her at last; and, assuming as calm a manner as possible, she replied:

"For years back the one cherished object of my life was to visit Kentucky; and now that I am really here, I am so glad! oh, so glad!" and Frederic could see the gladness shining in her eyes, and making her so wondrously beautiful to look upon that he was sorry when the twilight shadows began to fall, and partially obscured his vision.

"There is the house," he said, pointing to the chimneys, just discernible above the trees.

But Marian had seen them first, and when as they turned a corner, the entire building came in view, she sank back upon the cushion, dizzy and sick with the thoughts which came crowding so fast upon her. The day had been soft and balmy, and mingled with the gathering darkness was the yellow, hazy light the sun of the Indiam summer often leaves upon the hills. The early mist lay white upon the river, while here and there a shower of leaves came rustling down from the tall trees, which grew in such profusion around the old stone house. And Marian saw everything — heard everything—and when the horses' hoofs struck upon the bridge, where once they fancied she had stood and plunged into eternity, an icy chill ran through her frame, depriving her of the power to speak or move. Through the dim twilight she saw the dusky forms gathered expectantly around the cabin doors—saw the full, rounded figure of Dinah on the piazza—saw the vine-wreathed pillar where six years ago that very night, she had leaned with a breaking heart, and wept her passionate adieu to the man, who, sitting opposite to her now, little dreamed of what was passing in her mind. In a distant hempfield she heard the song some negroes sang returning from their labor, and as she listened to the plaintive music, her tears began to flow, it seemed so natural—so much like the olden time.

Suddenly as they drew nearer and the song of the negroes ceased the stillness was broken by the deafening yell which Bruno, from his cage, sent up. His voice had been the last to bid the runaway good bye, and it was the first to welcome her back again. With a stifled sob of joy too deep for utterance, she drew her veil still closer over her face, and when at last they stopped and the light from the hall shone out upon her, she sat in the corner of the carriage motionless and still.

"Come, Miss Grey," said Frederic, when Alice had been safely deposited and was folded to Dinah's bosom, "Come, Miss Grey, are you sleeping?" and he touched the hand which lay cold and lifeless upon her lap. "She has fainted," he cried. "The journey and excitement have over-taxed her strength," and, taking her in his arms as if she had been a little child, he bore her into the house and up to her own chamber, for he rightly guessed that she would rather be there when she returned to consciousness.

Laying her upon the lounge, he removed her bonnet and veil, and then kneeling beside her, looked wistfully into her face, which in its helplessness seemed more beautiful than ever.

"Has she come to, yet?" asked the puffing Dinah, appearing at the door. "It's narves what ailed her, I reckon, and I told Lyd to put some delirian to the steep. That'll quiet her soonest of anything."

Frederic knew that his services were no longer needed, and after glancing about the room to see that everything was right, he went down stairs leaving Marian to the care of Dinah, who, as her patient began to show signs of returning consciousness, undressed her as soon as possible and placed her in the bed, herself sitting by and bathing her face and hands in camphor and cologne. The fainting fit had passed away, but it was succeeded by a feeling of such delicious languor that for a long time Marian lay perfectly still, thinking how nice it was to be again in her old room with Dinah sitting by, and once as the hard, black hand rested on her forehead, she took it between her own, murmuring involuntarily, "Dear Aunt Dinah, I thank you so much."

"Blessed lamb," whispered the old lady, "they told her my name, I 'spect. 'Pears like she's nigher to me than strangers mostly is," and she smoothed lovingly the bright hair floating over the pillow.

Twice that evening there came up the stairs a cautious step which stopped always at the door, and Dinah as often as she answered the gentle knock, came back to Marian and said, "It's marster axin' is you any wus."

"Tell him I am only tired, not sick," Marian would say, and turning on her pillow, she wept great tears of joy to think that Frederic should thus care for her.

At last, having drank the "delirian tea," more to please old Dinah than from any faith she had in its virtues, she fell into a quiet sleep, which was disturbed but twice, once when at nine o'clock Bruno was loosed from his confinement, and with a loud howl went rushing past the window, and once when Alice crept carefully to her side, holding her breath lest she should arouse her, and whispering low her nightly prayer. Then, indeed, Marian moved as if about to waken, and the blind girl thought she heard her say, "Darling Alice," but she was not sure, and she nestled down beside her, sleeping ere long the dreamless sleep which always came to her after a day of unusual fatigue.

The rosy dawn was just stealing into the room, next morning, when Marian awoke with a vague, uncertain feeling as to where she was, or what had happened. Ere long, however, she remembered it all; and, stepping upon the floor, she glided to the window, to feast her eyes once more upon her home. Before her lay the garden, and though the November frosts had marred its Summer glory, it was still beautiful to her; and, hastily dressing herself, she went forth to visit her olden haunts, strolling leisurely on until she reached a little Summer-house which had been built since she was there. Over the door were some pencil marks, in Frederic's hand-writing; and though the rains had partly washed the letters away, there were still enough remaining for her to know that "Marian Lindsey" had been written there.

"He has sometimes thought of me," she said; and she was about entering the arbor, when there rose upon the air a terrific yell, which, had she been an intruder, would have sent her flying from the spot. But she did not even tremble, and she awaited fearlessly the approach of the huge creature, which, bristling with rage, came tearing down the graveled walk, his eyeballs glowing like coals of fire, and his head lowered as if ready for attack.

Bruno was still on guard, and when, in the distance, he caught a sight of Marian, he started with a lion like bound, which soon brought him near to the brave girl, who calmly watched his coming, and, when he was close upon her, said to him:

"Good old Bruno! Don't you know me, Bruno?"

At the first sound of her voice, the fire left the mastiff's eye, for he, too, caught the tone which had once so startled Alice, and which puzzled Frederic every day; still, he was not quite assured, and he came rushing on, while she continued speaking gently to him. With a bound, half playful, half ferocious, he sprang upon her, and, catching him around the neck, she passed her hand caressingly over his shaggy mane, saying to him, softly,

"I am Marian, Bruno! Don't you know me?"

Then, indeed, he answered her—not with a human tongue, it is true; but she understood his language well, and by the low, peculiar cry of joy he gave as he crouched upon the ground, she knew that she was recognised. Of all who had loved her at Redstone Hall, none remembered her save the noble dog, who licked her face, her hair, her hands, her dress, her feet; while all the time his body quivered with the intense delight he could not speak.

At last as she knelt down beside him, and laid her cheek against his neck, he bent his head, and gave forth a deep, prolonged howl, which was answered at a little distance by a cry of horror, and turning quickly Marian saw Frederic hastening toward the spot, his face pale as ashes, and his whole appearance indicative of alarm. He had been roused from sleep by the yell which Bruno gave when he first caught sight of Marian, and ere he had time to think what it could be, Alice knocked at his door, exclaiming:

"Oh, Frederic, Miss Grey, I am sure, has gone into the garden, and Bruno is not yet secured. I heard him bark just like he did last year when he mangled black Andy so. What if he should tear Miss Grey?"

Frederic waited for no more, but dressing himself quickly he hastened out, sickening with fear, as he came upon the fresh tracks the dog had made when going down the walk. He saw Marian's dress, and through the lattice he caught a sight of Bruno.

"He has her down! He is drinking her life-blood!" he thought; and for an instant the pulsations of his heart stood still, nor did they resume their wonted beat even after he saw the attitude of Marian Grey, and his terrible watch-dog, Bruno.

"Marian!" he began, for he could not be formal then. "Marian! leave him, I entreat you. He is cruelly savage with strangers."

"But I have tamed him, you see," she answered, winding her arms still closer around his neck, while he licked again her face and hair.

Wonderingly Frederic looked on, and all the while there came to him no thought that the two had met before—that the hand patting so fondly Bruno's head had fed him many a time—and that amid all the changes which six years had made, the sagacious animal had recognized his mistress and playmate, Marian Lindsey.

"It must be that you can win all hearts," he said, watching her admiringly, and marvelling at her secret power.

Shaking back her sunny curls, and glancing upward into his face Marian answered involuntarily:

"No, not all. There is one I would have given worlds to win, but it cast me off, just when I needed comfort the most."

She spoke impulsively, and as she spoke there arose within her the wish that he, like Bruno, might know her then and there. But he did not. He only remembered what Will Gordon had said of her hopeless attachment and her apparent confession of the same to him, smote heavily upon his heart, though why he, a married man, should care he could not tell. He didn't really care, he thought; he only pitied her, and by way of encouragement he said, "Even that may yet be won;" and while he said it, there came over him a sensation of dreariness, as if the winning of that heart would necessarily take from him something which was becoming more and more essential to his happiness.

Their conversation was here interrupted by Josh, who was Bruno's keeper, and had come to chain him for the day. Marian knew him at once, though he had changed from the short, thick lad of twelve to the taller youth of seventeen; and when, as he saw her position with Bruno, he exclaimed, "Goo-goo-good Lord!" she turned her beaming face toward him and answered laughingly, "I have a secret for charming dogs."

Involuntarily Josh's old cloth cap came off, while over his countenance there flitted an expression as if that voice were not entirely strange to him. Touching his master's arm, and pointing to the kneeling maiden, he stammered out:

"Ha-ha-hain't I s-s-seen her afore?"

"I think not," answered Frederic, and with a doubtful shake of the head, Josh attempted to lead Bruno away.

But Bruno would not move, and he clung so obstinately to Marian that she arose, and patting his side, said playfully:

"I shall be obliged to go with him, I guess. Lead the way, boy."

With eyes protruding like saucers, Josh turned back, followed by Marian and Bruno, the latter of whom offered no resistance when his mistress bade him enter his kennel, though he made woundrous efforts to escape when he saw that she was leaving him.

"In the name of the Lord," exclaimed Hetty, shading her eyes with her hand, to be sure she was right, "if thar ain't the young lady shettin' up the dog. I never knowed the like o' that."

Then as Marian came towards the kitchen, she continued, "'Pears like I've seen her somewhar."

"Ye-ye-yes," chimed in Josh, who had walked faster than Marian. "Who-o-oo is she, Hetty?"

Marian by this time had reached the door, where

she stood smiling pleasantly upon the blacks, but not daring to call them by name until she saw Dinah, who curtesied low, and coming forward asked, "Is you better this mornin'?"

"Yes, quite well, thank you. Are these your companions?" said Marian, anxious for an opportunity to talk with her old friends.

"Yes, honey," answered Dinah. "This is Hetty, and this is Lyd, and this——"

She didn't finish the sentence, for Hetty, who had been earnestly scanning Marian's features, grasped her dress, saying, "Whar was you born?"

"Jest like them Higginses," muttered Dinah. "In course, Miss Grey don't want to be twitted with bein' a Yankee the fust thing."

But Hetty had no intentions of casting reflections upon the place of Marian's birth. Like Josh she had detected something familiar in the young girl's face, and twice she had swept her hand across her eyes to clear away the mist and see if possible what it was which puzzled her so much.

"I was born a great many miles from here," said Marian, and ere Hetty could reply, Josh, whose gaze had all the time been riveted upon her, stuttered out, "Sh-sh-she is-s-s-s like M-m-m-Miss Marian."

Yes, this was the likeness they had seen, but Marian would rather the first recognition should come from another source, and she hastened to reply, "Oh, Mrs. Raymond, you mean. Alice noticed it when I first went to Riverside. You suppose your young mistress dead, do you not?"

Instantly Dinah's woolen apron was called into use, while she said, "Yes, poor dear lamb, if thar's any truth in them Scripter sayin's, she's a burnin' and a shining light in de kingdom come." And the old negress launched forth into a long eulogy, in the midst of which Frederic appeared in quest of Marian.

"I am listening to praises of your wife," she said, and there was a mischievous triumph in her eye as she saw how his forehead flushed, for he was beginning to be slightly annoyed when she, as she often did, alluded to his wife.

Why need she thrust that memory continually upon him? Was it not enough for him to know that somewhere in the world there *was* a wife, and that he would rather hear any one else speak of her than the bright-haired Marian Grey.

"Dinah can be very eloquent at times," he said, "but come with me to Alice. She has been sadly frightened on your account," and he led the way to the piazza, where the blind girl was waiting for them.

Breakfast being over, Marian and Alice sought the parlor, where, instead of the old fashioned instrument which the former remembered as standing there, she found a new and beautifully carved piano.

"Frederic ordered this on purpose to please you," whispered Alice. "He said it was a shame for you to play on the other rattling thing."

This was sufficient to call out Marian's wildest strains, and as a matter of course the entire band of servants gathered about the door to listen just as they once had done when the performer was Isabel. As was quite natural, they yielded their preference to the last comer, old Hetty acknowledging that even "Miss Beatrice couldn't beat that."

It would seem that Marian Grey was destined to take all hearts by storm, for ere the day was done her virtues had been discussed in the kitchen and by the cabin fire, while even the gallant Josh, at his work in the hemp-field, attempted a song, which he meant to be laudatory of her charms, but as he was somewhat lacking in poetical talent, his music ran finally into the well known ballad of "Mary Ann," which suited his purpose quite as well.

Meantime, Marian, stealing away from Alice, quietly explored every nook and corner of the house, opening first the little box where she once had kept her mother's hair. It was just as she had left it, and kissing it reverently she placed it by the side of her silken locks, to see how they compared. It might be that the tress of the dead had faded somewhat, for there was certainly a richer, darker tinge to her own wavy hair, and bowing her head upon the bureau she dropped tears of thankfulness that her childhood's prayer had been more than answered. The library was visited next, and she seated herself again in the chair where she had sat when penning her last farewell to Frederic. Where was that letter now? She wished that she could see it, though she did not care to read it, and without any expectation of finding it she pressed what she knew was the secret spring to a private drawer. It yielded to her touch—the drawer came open, and there before her lay the letter—her letter—she knew it by its superscription, and by its tear-stained, soiled appearance. She had wept over it herself, but she knew full well her tears alone had never blurred and blotted it like this. Frederic's had mingled with them, and her heart was trembling with joy when another object caught her eye and quickened her rapid pulsations. Her glove! the little black kid glove she had dropped upon the bridge was there, wrapped in a sheet of paper, and with it the handkerchief!

"Frederic has saved them all," she whispered, shuddering involuntarily, for it seemed almost like looking into the grave, where he had buried these sad remembrances of her. He had preserved them carefully, she thought, and she continued her investigation, coming at last upon a daguerreotype of herself, taken when she was just fifteen.

"Oh, horror!" she cried, and sinking back in her chair, she laughed until the tears ran at the forlorn little face which looked upon her so demurely from the casing. "Frederic must enjoy looking at you vastly, and thinking you are his wife," she said, and she felt a thrill of pride in knowing that Marian Grey bore scarcely the slightest resemblance to that daguerreotype.

There was a similarity in the features and in the way the hair grew around the forehead, while the eyes were really alike. But the likeness extended no further, and she did not wonder that none, save Bruno, had recognized her. Returning the picture to its place, she was about to leave the room, when Frederic came in, appearing somewhat surprised to find her there, sitting in his chair as if she had a perfect right so to do. At first she was too much confused to apologize, but she managed at last to say:

"This cozy room attracted me, and I took the liberty to enter. You have a very fine library, I think; some of the books must have been your father's."

It was the books, of course, which she came to see, and sitting down opposite to her Frederic talked with her about them until she chanced to spy a portrait, put away behind the ponderous sofa, with its face turned to the wall.

"Whose is it?" she asked, directing Frederic's attention to it. "Whose is it, and why is it hidden there?"

Instantly the young man's face grew dark, and Marian trembled beneath the glance he bent upon her. Then the cold, hard look passed away, and he replied:

"It is an unfinished portrait of Mrs. Raymond, taken from a daguerreotype of her when she was only fifteen. But the artist did not understand his business, and it looks even worse than the original."

This last was spoken bitterly, and Marian felt the hot blood rising to her cheeks.

"I never even told Alice of it," he continued, "but put it away in here, where I hide all my secrets."

He glanced at the private drawer—so did Marian; but she was too intent upon seeing a portrait which could look worse than the daguerreotype to heed aught else, and she said, entreatingly, "Oh, Mr. Raymond, please let me see it, won't you? I lived in New York a long time, you know, and perhaps I may have met her, or even known her under some other name?

May I see it?" and she was advancing toward the sofa, when Frederic seized both her hands, and holding them in his, said, half hesitatingly, half mournfully: "Miss Grey, you must excuse me for refusing your request. Poor Marian was far from being handsome, nay, I sometimes thought her positively ugly. She is certainly so in the portrait, and a creature as highly gifted with beauty as you, might laugh at her plain features, but if you did—" He paused a moment, and Marian's eyelashes fell beneath his steady gaze—"And if you did," he continued, "I never could like you again, for she was my wife, and as such must be respected."

Marian could not tell why it was, but Frederic's words and manner affected her painfully. She half feared she had offended him by her eagerness to see the portrait, while mingled with this was a strange feeling of pity for poor, plain Marian Lindsey, as she probably looked upon the canvas, and a deep respect for Frederic, who would, if possible, protect her from even the semblance of insult. Her heart was already full, and, releasing her hands from Frederic's, she resumed her seat, and leaning her head upon the writing-desk, burst into tears, while Frederic paced the room, wondering what, under the circumstances, he was expected to do. He knew just how to soothe Alice, but Marian Grey was a different individual. He could not take her in his lap and kiss away her tears, but he could at least speak to her; and he did at last, laying his hand as near the little white one grasping the table edge as he dared, and saying, very gently:

"If I spoke harshly to you, Miss Grey, I am sorry—very sorry; I really did not intend to make you cry. I only felt that I could not bear to hear you, of all others, laugh at my poor Marian, and so refused your request. Will you forgive me?"

And by some chance, as he looked another way, his hand did touch hers, and held it, too! He did not think that an insult to the portrait at all, nor yet of the supposed original; for there was something in the way the snowy fingers twined themselves round his, which drove all other ideas from his mind, and for one brief instant he was supremely happy.

From the first he had thought of Marian Grey as a sweet, beautiful young creature, whom some man would one day delight to call his own; but the possibility of loving her himself had never occurred to him until now, when, like a flash of lightning, the conviction burst upon him that, spite of Marian Lindsey—spite of his marriage vow—spite of the humble origin which would once have shocked his pride—and spite of everything, Marian Grey had won a place in his heart from which he must dislodge her. But, how? He could not send her away, for she seemed a part of himself, and he could not live without her; but he would stifle his new-born love, he said, and as the best means of doing so, he would talk to her often of his wife as a person who certainly had an existence, and would some day come back to him; so, when Marian replied: "I feared you were angry with me, Mr. Raymond; I would not have asked to see the portrait had I supposed you really cared," he drew his chair at a respectful distance and said: "I cannot explain the matter to you, but if you knew the whole sad story of my marriage, and the circumstances which led to it, you would not wonder that I am somewhat sensitive upon the subject. I used to think beauty the principal thing I should require in a wife, but poor Marian had none of that, and were you to see the wretched likeness, you would receive altogether too unfavorable an impression of her; for, notwithstanding her plain face, she was far too good for me."

"Do you really think so?" was Marian's eager exclamation, while close behind it was the secret struggling hard to escape, but she forced it back, until such time as she should be convinced that Frederic loved her as Marian Grey, and would hail with delight the news that she was indeed his wife.

He seemed surprised at her question, but he answered, unhesitatingly:

"Yes; far too good for me."

"And do you really wish to find her?" was Marian's next question, which brought a flush to Frederic's face, and caused him to hesitate a little ere he replied.

Yesterday he would have said Yes, at once, but since coming into that library he had discovered that the finding of his wife would be less desirable than before. But it should not be so. He would crush every thought or feeling which detracted in the least from his late interest in Marian Lindsey, and with a great effort he said:

"I really wish to find her;" adding, as he saw a peculiar expression flit over Marian's face; "Wouldn't you, too, be better pleased if Redstone Hall had a mistress?"

"Yes, provided that mistress were your wife, Marian Lindsey," was the ready answer; and, looking into her face, Frederic was conscious of an uneasy sensation, for Miss Grey's words would indicate that the presence of his wife would give her real pleasure.

Of course, then, she did not care for him, as he cared for her; and why should she? He asked himself this question many a time after the chair opposite him was vacant, and she had left him there alone. Why should she, when she came to him with the knowledge that he was already bound to another. She might not have liked him perhaps had he been free, though, in that case, he could have won her love, and compelled her to forget the man who did not care for her. Taking the high-backed chair she had just vacated, he rested his elbow upon the table, and tried to fancy that Marian Lindsey had never crossed his path, and Marian Grey had never loved another. It was a pleasant picture he drew of himself were Marian Grey his wife, and his heart fairly bounded as he thought of her stealing to his side, and placing upon his arm those little soft white hands of hers, while her blue eyes looked into his own, and her rose-bud lips called him "Husband!" and, as he thought, it seemed to him more and more that it must one day be so. She would be his at last, and the sun of his domestic bliss would shine upon him all the brighter for the dreary darkness which had overshadowed him so long. From this dream of happiness there came ere long a waking, and burying his face in his hands he moaned aloud, "It cannot be, and the hardest part of all to bear is the wretched thought that but for my dastardly, unmanly act, it might, perhaps, have been—but now, never! never! Oh, Marian Grey! Marian Grey! I would that we had never met!"

"Frederic, didn't you hear me coming? I made a heap of noise," said a voice close to his side, and Alice's arm was thrown across his neck.

She had heard all he was saying, but she did not comprehend it until he muttered the name of Marian Grey, and then the truth flashed upon her.

"Poor Frederic," she said, soothingly, "I pity you so much, for though it is wicked, I am sure you cannot help it."

"Help what?" he asked, rather impatiently, for this one secret he hoped to bury from the whole world, but the blind girl had discovered it, and she answered unhesitatingly:

"Can't help loving Marian Grey. I've been fearful you would," she continued, as he made no reply. "I did not see how you could well help it, either, she is so beautiful and good, and every night I pray that if our own Marian is really dead God will let us know."

This was an entire change in Alice. Hitherto she had pleaded a living Marian—now she suggested one deceased, but Frederic repelled the thought at once.

"Marian was not dead," he said, "and though he admired Miss Grey, he had no right to love her. He didn't intend to, either, and if Alice had discovered anything, he trusted she would forget it."

And this was all the satisfaction he would give the

little girl, who, feeling that he would rather be alone, turned away, leaving him again with his unhappy thoughts.

That night he joined the young girls in the parlor and compelled himself to listen while Marian made the old walls echo with her ringing, merry music. But he would not look at her, nor watch her snowy fingers sweeping over the keys, lest they should make worse havoc with his heart-strings than they had already done. At an early hour he sought his chamber where the livelong night he fought manfully with the love which, now that he acknowledged its existence, grew rapidly in intensity and strength. It was not like the love he had felt for Isabel—it was deeper, purer, more absorbing, and what was stranger far than all, he could not feel that it was wicked, and he trembled when he thought how hardened he had become.

The next day, which was the Sabbath, he determined to see as little of Marian as possible, but when at the breakfast table she asked him in her usual frank, open-hearted way to go with her to church, he could not refuse, and he went, feeling a glow of pride at the sensation he knew she was creating, and wondering why she should be so excited.

"I cannot keep the secret much longer," Marian thought, as she looked upon the familiar faces of her friends, and longed to hear them call her by her real name. "I will at least tell Alice who I am, and if she can convince me that Frederic would be glad, I will perhaps explain to him."

When church was out, Mrs. Rivers, who still lived at her father's, pressed forward for an introduction, and after it was over, whispered a few words to Frederic, who replied, "Not in the least," so decidedly that Marian heard him, and wondered what Agnes' remark could have been. She was not long left in doubt, for as they were riding home, Frederic turned to her and said: "Mrs. Rivers thinks you look like my wife."

Marian's cheeks were scarlet, as she replied:

"Josh and Hetty thought so, too, and it is possible there may be a resemblance,"

"Not the slightest," returned Frederic, half vexed that any one should presume to liken the beautiful girl at his side to one as plain as he had always considered Marian Lindsey to be.

Leaning back in the carriage, he relapsed into a thoughtful mood, which was interrupted once by Marian's asking "if he believed he should know his wife in case he met her accidentally?"

"Know her? Yes—from all the world!" was the hasty answer; and, wrapping his shawl still closer about him, Frederic did not speak again until they stopped at their own door.

That night, as Marian sat with Alice in their chamber, she said to the little girl:

"If you could have any wish gratified which you chose to make, what would it be?"

For an instant Alice hesitated—then her eyes filled with tears, and, and winding her arms around her teacher's neck, she whispered:

"At first I thought I'd rather have my sight—but only for a moment—and then I wished, if Marian were not dead, she would come back to us, for I'm afraid Frederic is getting bad again, though he cannot help it, I'm sure."

"What do you mean?" Marian asked, and Alice replied:

"Don't you know? Can't you guess? Don't you hear it in his voice when he speaks to you?"

Marian made no response, and Alice continued:

"Frederic seems determined to love everybody better than Marian, and though I love you more than I can tell, I want her to come back so much."

"And if you knew she were coming, when would you rather it should be?" asked Marian, and Alice replied:

"Now—to-night; but as that is impossible, I'd be satisfied with Christmas. Yes, on the whole, I'd rather it would be then; I should call her our Christmas Gift, and it would be the dearest, sweetest one that I could have."

"Darling Alice," thought Marian, "your wish shall be gratified."

And, kissing the blind girl affectionately, she resolved that on the coming Christmas, one at least of the inmates of Redstone Hall should know that Marian Grey was only another name for the runaway Marian Lindsey.

CHAPTER XXVII.

TELLING ALICE.

One by one the bright November days went by and the hazy Indian Summer light faded from the Kentucky hills, where now the December sun was shining cold and clear. And as the weeks passed away, there hung over Redstone Hall a dark, portentous cloud, and they who had waited so eagerly the coming of the holidays trembled lest the merry Christmas song should prove a funeral dirge for the pet and darling of them all. Alice was dying, so the physician said, while Dinah, too, had prophesied that ere the New Year came the eyes which never in this world had looked upon the light would be opened to the glories of the better land.

For many weary days and nights the fever flame had burned in the young girl's veins, but it had left her now, and like a fragile lily she lay among her pillows, talking of Heaven and the grave as something very near to her. Noiselessly Marian trod across the floor, holding back her breath and speaking in soft whispers, lest she should disturb the little sufferer whose side she never for a moment left except to take the rest she absolutely needed. Frederic, too, often shared her vigils, feeling almost as anxious for one as for the other. Both were very dear to him, and Marian, as she witnessed his tender care of Alice, and his anxiety for herself lest her stength should be overtasked, felt more and more that he was worthy of her love. Alice, too, appreciated his goodness, as she had never done before, and once when he sat alone with her, and Marian was asleep, she passed her hand caressingly over his face and said:

"Dear Frederic, you have been so kind to me, that I am sure God has some good in store for you."

Then as she remembered what would probably be the greatest good to him, she continued, "I know what's in your heart, and I pity you so much, but there is light ahead; I've thought strange things, and dreamed strange dreams since I lay here so sick, and as I once was certain Marian was alive, so now I'm almost certain that she's dead."

"Hush, Alice, hush," said Frederic, laying his head upon the pillow beside her, but Alice did not heed him, and she continued—

"I never saw her in this world, and maybe I shan't know her right away, though next to mother, I reckon she'll be the first to welcome me to Heaven, if she's there, and I know she is, or we should have heard from her. I shall tell her of her old home, Frederic; tell her how we mourned for her when we thought that she was dead. I don't know what it was that made her go away, but I shall tell her you repented of the act, and how you looked for her so long, and that if you had found her you would have loved her, sure. That will not be a lie, will it, Frederic?"

"No, darling, no," was the faintly spoken answer, and Alice continued:

"Then, when I have explained all, I'll steal away from Heaven, just long enough to come and tell you she is there. You'll be in the library, maybe, and I reckon 'twill be dark, though if you'd any rather, I'll come in the daytime, and when you feel there's somebody near, somebody you can't see, you may know that it is me come to say that you are free to love the other Marian."

"Don't, Alice, don't," said Frederic, for it made his heart bleed afresh to hear her talk of what he had no hope would ever be.

But Alice's faith was stronger, and to Marian Grey she sometimes talked in a similar strain, saying "she knew she should meet the other one in Heaven," and Marian, while listening to her, felt that she must undeceive her. "It may possibly make her better," she thought, and when, at last, the Christmas eve had come, and it was her turn to watch that night, she determined to tell her, if she fancied that she had strength to bear it, One by one, the family servants retired, and when at last they were alone, Marian drew her chair close beside the bed, wondering how she should commence, and what effect it would have upon the little girl, who erelong awoke, and said to her:

"I've been dreaming of Marian, and I thought she looked like you do—but she don't of course; and I wonder how I'll know her from my mother, for she, too, was young when she died. If it were you, Miss Grey, I could tell you so easily, for I should look among the brightest angels there, and the one who sang the sweetest song and had the fairest face, would certainly be Marian Grey: but the other Marian—how shall I know her—think?"

Leaning forward so that her hot cheek touched the pale one of the sick girl, Marian said:

"Wouldn't you know her by her voice?"

"I'm afraid not," answered Alice; "I thought you were she at first when I heard you speak."

"How is it now, darling?" Marian asked, in a voice so tremulous that Alice started, and her white face flushed as she replied: "You are not like her now, except at times, and then—it's all so queer. There's a mystery about you, Miss Grey—and seems sometimes just like I didn't know what to think—you puzzle me so!"

"Shall I tell you, Alice? Have you strength to hear who and what I am?" Marian asked; and Alice answered eagerly;

"Yes—tell me—do?"

"And you'll promise not to faint, nor scream, nor reveal it to anybody, unless I say you may?"

"It must be something terrible to make me faint or scream!"

"Not terrible, dearest, but strange!" and sitting down upon the bed, Marian wound her arm around the little girl.

It was a hazardous thing the telling that secret then. but Marian did not realize what she was doing, and in as calm a voice as she could command, she began:

"People call me Marian Grey, but that is not my name!"

"Not Marian Grey!" and the brown eyes flashed wonderingly. "Who are you, then, Marian what?"

Marian did not reply to this question, but said instead: "I had seen you before that night at Riverside."

"Seen me where?" and the little fingers trembled with an indefinable dread of the shock which she instinctively felt was waiting for her.

"I had seen you many times," said Marian, "and that is why my voice is familiar. Put your hand upon my face again, and maybe you will know it."

"I can't, I can't! you frighten me so!" gasped Alice, and Marian continued:

"I must have changed much, for they who used to know me have never suspected that I am in their midst again—none but Bruno. Do you remember my power over him? Bruno and I were playmates together."

Marian paused and gazed earnestly at the child, who lay panting in her arms, her face upturned and the blind eyes fixed upon hers with an intensity she had never before seen equalled. In the deep stillness of the room she could hear the loud beating of Alice's heart, and see the bed-clothes rise and fall with every throb.

"Alice," she said at last, "don't you know me now?' and in her voice there was a world of yearning tenderness and love.

"*Yes*," and over the marble face there shone a smile of almost seraphic sweetness. "You are *Marian*—my Marian—Frederic's Marian—Dinah's Marian—*All of us Marian!*" and with a low, hysterical cry the blind girl crept close to the bosom of her long lost friend.

Stretching out her feeble arms she wound them round Marian's neck, and raising herself upon her elbow, kissed her lips, her cheek, her forehead, her hair, whispering all the time, "Blessed Marian—precious Marian—beautiful Marian—our Marian—Frederic's, and mine, and everybody's. Oh, I don't want to go to heaven now: I'd rather stay with you. Call him—call Frederic, quick, and tell him? Why haven't you told him before? Ho, Frederic, come here!" and the feeble voice raised to its highest pitch, went ringing through the room and penetrated even to the adjoining chamber, where, since Alice's illness, Frederic had slept.

"Alice," said Marian, "if you love me, you will not tell him now. I am not ready yet."

"What if I should die?" Alice asked, and Marian replied:

"You won't die. I almost know you won't. Promise, Alice, promise," she continued, as she heard Frederic's step in the hall without.

"How can I—how can I? It will choke me to death!" was Alice's answer, and the next moment Frederic had crossed the threshold of the door.

"What is it, Miss Grey?" he asked. "Didn't you call?"

Alice is rather excited, that's all," said Marian, "and you can go back. We do not wish to disturb you."

"Frederic," came a faint whisper from the bedside, and knowing that farther remonstrance was useless, Marian stood like a rock, while Frederic advanced toward the child, who lay with her head thrown back, the great tears rolling down her cheeks, and the great joy of what she had heard, shining out all over her little face.

"Did you want me, birdie?" he asked, but ere he had ceased speaking, Marian was at his side.

Alice knew that she was there, and she pressed both hands upon her lips to force back the secret she had been forbidden to divulge.

"Is she delirious?" Frederic asked, and shaking her head, Alice whispered: "No, no, but happy, so happy. Oh, Frederic, I don't want to die! Must I? If I take a heap of Doctor's stuff, will I get well, think?"

"I hope so," said Frederic, his suspicions of insanity rapidly increasing.

"Give me your hand," she continued, "and yours, too, Miss Grey."

Both were extended, and joining them together she said, "Love her, Frederic. Love her all you want to. You may—you may. It isn't wicked. Oh, Marian, Marian."

The last word was a whisper, and as it died away, Marian seized Frederic's arm, and said, beseechingly: "Please leave the room, Mr. Raymond. You see she is excited, and I can quiet her best alone. Will you go?"

The brown eyes looked reproachfully at her and entreatingly at him, but neither heeded the expression, and with a feeling that he scarcely understood what the whole proceeding meant, and why he had been called in if he must be summarily dismissed, Frederic went out, leaving Marian alone with Alice.

"Why didn't you let me tell him?" the latter asked, and Marian replied, "I shall tell him by and by: but I am not ready yet, and you must not betray me."

"I'll try," said Alice, "but 'tis so hard. I had to bite my tongue to keep the words from coming. Where have you beeen? Why didn't you come to us before. How came you so beautiful—so grand?" Alice asked, all in the same breath.

But Marian absolutely refused to answer the question until she had become quiet and been refreshed with sleep.

"All in good time, dearest," she said, "but you must rest now. You are wearing out too fast, and you know you do not want to die."

This was the right chord to touch, and it had the desired effect.

"Let me ask *one* question, and say *one* thing," said Alice, "and I won't talk another word till morning. When you are ready may *I* tell Frederic, if I ain't dead?"

"Yes, darling," was the ready answer, and winding her arms round Marian's neck, the blind girl continued: "Isn't it almost morning?"

"Yes, dear."

"And when it is, won't it be Christmas day?"

"Yes, but you have asked three questions, instead of one."

"I know—I know; but what I want to say is this: "I wished my Christmas gift might be Marian, and it is. Last year it was of a beautiful little pony, but you are worth ten hundred million ponies. Oh, I'm so glad—so glad," and on the childish face there was a look of perfect happiness.

Even after she shut her eyes and tried to sleep her lips continued to move, and Marian could hear the whispered words: "Our own Marian—our blessed Marian."

The excitement was too much for Alice, and when next morning the physician came, he pronounced her worse than she had been the previous night.

"But I ain't going tc die," said Alice resolutely; "I can't die now," and it was this very determination on her part which did more to save her life than all the doctor's drugs or Dinah's wonderful tears.

For many days she seemed hovering between life and death, while Marian never for a moment left her, and Alice was more quiet when she was sitting by, holding her feverish hand; she seemed to have lost all her desire to tell, for she never made any attempt so to do, though she persisted in calling her teacher Marian, and a look of pain always flitted over her face when she heard her addressed as Miss Grey. Sometimes she would start up, and winding her arms around her neck would whisper in her ear, "Are you Marian for sure—our Marian, I mean?"

"Yes, Marian Lindsey, sure," would be the answer, and the little girl would fall away again into a half unconscious state, a smile of joy wreathing her white lips, and an expression of peace resting on her face.

At last, just as the New Year's morning dawned, she woke from a deep, unbroken sleep, and Marian and Frederic, who watched beside her, knew that she was saved. There were weeks of convalescence, and Dinah often wondered at Alice's patience in staying so long and willingly in the chamber where she had suffered so much. But to Alice that sick room was a second paradise and Marian the bright angel whose presence made all the sunlight of her life.

Gradually as she could bear it, Marian told her everything which had come to her since she left Redstone Hall, and Alice's eyes grew strangely bright when she heard that the bracelet she had always prized so much was made from Marian's hair, and that Ben's visit to Kentucky was all a plan of his to see if Frederic were married.—Greatly was she shocked when she heard of the letter which had almost taken Marian's life.

"Frederic never did that cruel thing," she knew.

"But 'twas in his hand-writing," said Marian, "and until the mystery is cleared away, I cannot forgive him."

For a long time Alice sat absorbed in thought, then suddenly starting forward, she cried: "I know, Marian. I know now, Isabel did it. I'm sure she did. I remember it all so plain.

"Isabel," repeated Marian: "how could she? What do you mean?"

"Why," returned Alice, "You say you sent it a

few weeks after you went away, and I remember so well Frederic's going to Lexington one day, because that was the time it came to me that you were not dead. It was the first morning, too, that Isabel heard my lessons, and she scolded because I didn't remember quick, when I was thinking all the time of you, and my heart was aching so. For some reason, I can't tell what, I showed her that note you left for me. You remember it; don't you? It read:

"Darling Alice! Precious Alice: If my heart were not already broken, it would break in leaving you."

"Yes, yes; I remember," said Marian, and Alice continued:

"She said your hand-writing was queer, when she gave me back the note. That evening, Josh came back from Frankfort with a heap of letters for Frederic, and one of them I know was from you. I was standing out under the big maple tree thinking of you, when Isabel came and asked to take the note again, and I let her have it. Ever so long after, I started to go into the library, for I heard somebody rustling papers, and I didn't know but Dud was doing mischief. Just as I got to the door, I heard a voice like Isabel's only sounded scared like, exclaim, 'It is from her, but he shall never see it, never;' or something like that, and when I called to her she wouldn't answer me until I got close to her, and then she laughed as if she was choked, and said she was trying to frighten me. Marian, that *her* was you, and that *he* was Frederic. She copied his writing, and sent the letter back because she wanted Frederic herself."

"Could she do such a thing," said Marian more to herself than to Alice, who replied:

"She can do anything; for Dinah says she's one of the ——, I reckon that I'll skip that word in there, because it's almost swearing, but it means *Satan's unaccountables*," and Alice's voice dropped to a whisper at what she fancied to be profanity.

Marian could understand why Isabel should do such

a wicked thing even better than Alice, and after reflecting upon it for a time, she accepted it as a fact, and even suggested the possibility of Isabel's having been the author of the letter from Sarah Green.

"She was! she was!" cried Alice, starting to her feet! "It's just like her—for she thought Frederic would surely want to marry her then. I know she wrote it, and managed to get it to New York somehow;" and as is often the case poor Isabel was compelled to bear more than her share of the fraud, for Marian, too, believed that she had been in some way implicated with the letter from Sarah Green.

"And I may tell Frederic now—mayn't I?" said Alice. "Suppose we set to-morrow, when he's in the library among the letters. He'll wonder what I'm coming in there for, all wrapped up in shawls. But he'll know plenty quick, for it will be just like me to tell it all at once, and he will be so glad. Don't you wish it was to-morrow now?"

Marian could not say she did, for she had hoped for more decisive demonstration of affection on Frederic's part ere she revealed herself to him, but Alice was so anxious, and had waited so patiently, that she at last consented, and when at supper she met Frederic as usual, she was conscious of a different feeling towards him than she had ever experienced before. He seemed unusually dejected, though exceedingly kind to her, talking but little, it is true, but evincing, in various ways, the interest he felt in her, and even asking her to sit with him awhile ere returning to Alice's chamber. There was evidently something on his mind which he wished to say, but whatever it might have been, seven o'clock found it still unsaid, and as Alice retired at that hour, Marian arose to go.

"Must you leave me?" he said, rising too, and accompanying her to the door. "Yes, you must!" and Marian little guessed the meaning these three words implied.

She only felt that she was not indifferent to him—

that the story Alice was to tell him on the morrow would be received with a quiet kind of happiness at least—that he would not bid her go away as she once had done before—and with the little blind girl, she, too, began to think the morrow would never come.

CHAPTER XXVIII.

TELLING FREDERIC.

It was midnight, and from the windows of the library at Redstone Hall there shone a single light, its dim rays falling upon the haggard face of the weary man, who, since parting from Marian in the parlor, had sat there just as he was sitting now, unmindful of the lapse of time—unmindful of every thing save the fierce battle he was waging with himself. Hour by hour—day by day—week by week, had his love for Marian Grey increased, until now he could no more control it than he could stay the mighty torrent in its headlong course. It was all in vain that he kept or tried to keep Marian Lindsey continually before his mind, saying often to himself: "She is my wife—she is alive, and I must not love another."

He did not care for Marian Lindsey. He did not wish to find her now—he almost hoped he never should, though even that would avail him nothing, unless he knew to a certainty that she were really dead. Perhaps he never could know, and as he thought of the long, dreary years in which he must live on with that terrible uncertainty forever haunting him, he pressed his hands upon his burning forehead and cried aloud: "My punishment is greater than I can bear. Oh, Marian Grey, can it be that you, who might have been the angel of my life, were sent to avenge the wrongs of that other Marian?"

He knew it was wicked, this intense, absorbing passion for Marian Grey, but he could not feel it so, and he would have given half his possessions for the sake of abandoning himself for one brief hour to this love —for the sake of seeing her eyes of blue meet with the look he had so often fancied her giving to the man she loved. And she loved him! He was sure of it! He saw it those nights when he watched with her by Alice's bedside; he had seen it since in the sudden flushing of her cheek and the falling of her eyes when he approached. And it was this discovery which prompted him to the act he meditated. Not both of them could stay there, himself and Marian, for he would not that she should suffer more than need be. She had recovered from her first and early love; she would get over this, and if she were only happy, it didn't matter how desolate her going would leave him, for she must go, he said. He had come to that decision, sitting there alone, and it had wrung great drops of perspiration from his brow and moans of anguish from his lips. But it must be—there was no alternative, he thought, and in the chair where Marian Lindsey once had written her farewell, he wrote to Marian Lindsey's rival that Redstone Hall could be her home no longer.

"Think not that you have displeased me," he said, "for this is not why I send you from me. Both of us cannot stay, and though for Alice's sake I would gladly keep you here, it must not be. I am going to New Orleans, to be absent three or four weeks, and shall not expect to find you here on my return. You will need money, and I enclose a check for a thousand dollars. Don't refuse to take it, for I give it willingly, and though my conduct is sadly at variance with my words, you must believe me when I say that in all the world you have not so true a friend, as

"FREDERIC RAYMOND."

Many times he read this letter over, and it was not until long after midnight that he sought his pillow, only to toss from side to side with feverish unrest, and he was glad when at last Josh came in to make the fire, for by that token he knew it was morning.

"Tell Dinah I will breakfast in my room," he said, "and say to Phil that he must have the carriage ready early, for I am going to New-Orleans, and he will carry me to Frankfort."

"Ye-e-es, Sir," was Josh's answer, as he departed with the message.

"Marster have breakfast in his room, and a goin' to New-Orleans? In the Lord's name what's happened him?" exclaimed Dinah, and when Marian came down to her solitary meal, she repeated the story to her, asking if she could explain it.

"Marster's looked desput down in the mouth a long time back," she said. "What you 'spect 'tis?"

Marian could not tell; neither did she venture a suggestion, so fearful was she that Frederic's intended departure would interfere with the plan of which Alice had talked incessantly since daylight. Hastily finishing her breakfast, she hurried back to her chamber, whither the note had preceded her.

"Luce brought this to you from Frederic," said Alice, passing her the letter, "and she says he looks like he was crazy. Read it and see what he wants."

Marian accordingly tore open the envelope, and with blanched cheek and quivering lip read that she must go again from Redstone Hall, and worse than all, there was no tangible reason assigned for the cruel mandate. The check next caught her eye, and with a proud, haughty look upon her face, she tore it in fragments and scattered them upon the floor, for it seemed an idle mockery for him to offer what was already hers.

"What is it, Marian?" asked Alice, and recovering her composure Marian read to her what Frederic said, while Alice's face grew white as hers had done before.

"You go away!" she exclaimed, bounding upon the floor and feeling for the warm shawl which she wore when sitting up. "You won't do any such thing

You've as much right here as he has, and I'm going this minute to tell him so."

She had groped her way to the door and was just opening it when Marian held her back, saying:

"You must not go out undressed and barefooted as you are. The halls are cold. Wait here while I go and learn the reason of this sudden freak."

"But I want so much to tell him myself," said Alice, and Marian replied, "So you shall, I'll send Dinah up to dress you and then I will come for you when it's time."

This pacified Alice, who already began to feel faint with her exertions, and she crept back to bed, while Marian descended the stairs, going first to Dinah as she had promised, and then with a beating heart turning her steps toward the library. It was much like facing the wild beast in its lair, confronting Frederic in his present savage mood. He felt himself as if his reason were overturned, for the deliberate giving up of Marian Grey, and the feeling that he should probably never look upon her face again, had stirred, as it were, the very depths of his heart's blood, and in a state of mind bordering upon distraction, he was making the necessary preparations for his hasty journey, when a timid knock was heard outside the door.

"Who's there? I'm very busy," was his loud, imperious answer, but Marian was not to be thus baffled, and turning the knob, she entered without further ceremony, recoiling back a pace or two when she met the expression of Frederic's eye.

With his hands full of papers, which he was thrusting into his pocket, his hair disordered and his face white as ashes, he turned toward her, saying; "Why are you here, Miss Grey? Haven't you caused me pain enough already? Have you received my note?"

"I have," she answered, advancing still further into the room. "And I have come to ask you what it means. You have no right to dismiss me so suddenly without an explanation. How have I offended? You must tell me."

"I said you had not offended," he replied, "and further than that I can give no explanation."

"I shall not leave your house, nor yet this room until you do," was her decided answer, and with the air of one who meant what she said, Marian went so near to the excited man that he could have touched her had he chosen.

For an instant the two stood gazing at each other, Marian never wavering for an instant, while over Frederic's face there flitted alternately a look of wonder, admiration, and perplexity. Then that look passed away and was succeeded by an expression of the deep love he felt for beautiful girl standing so fearlessly before him.

"I cannot help it," he murmured at last, and tottering to the door, he turned the key; then returning to Marian, he compelled her to sit down beside him upon the sofa, and passing his arm around her, so that she could not escape, he began: "You say you will not leave the room until you know why I should send you from me. Be it so, then. It surely cannot be wrong for me to tell when you thus tempt me to the act; so, for one brief half-hour, you are mine—mine, Marian, and no power can save you now from hearing what I have to say."

His looks, even more than his manner, frightened her, and she said imploringly, "Give me the key, Mr. Raymond. Unlock the door and I will go away without hearing the reason."

"I frighten you, then," he answered, in a gentler tone, drawing her nearer to him, "and yet, Marian Grey, I would sell my life inch by inch rather than harm a hair of your dear head. Oh, Marian, Marian, I would to Heaven you had never crossed my path, for then I should not have known what it is to love as madly, as hopelessly, as wickedly as I now love you. What made you come to me in all your bright, girlish beauty, or why did Heaven suffer me to love you as I do? My punishment was before as great as I could bear, and now I must suffer this anguish, too. Oh, Marian Grey, Marian Grey!"

He wound his arms close around her, and she could feel his feverish breath as his lips almost touched her burning cheek. In the words "Marian Grey, Marian Grey," there was a deep pathos, as if all the loving tenderness of his nature were centered upon that name, and it brought the tears in torrents from her eyes. He saw them, and wiping them away, he said:

"The hardest part of all to me is the knowledge that you must suffer, too. Forgive me for saying it, but as I know that I love you, so by similar signs I know that you love me. Is it not so, darling?"

Involuntarily she laid her head upon his bosom, sobbing:

"I have loved you so long—so long."

But for her promise to Alice she would then have told him all, but she must keep her word, and when he rejoined, "It does, indeed seem long since that night you came to Riverside," she did not undeceive him, but listened while he continued, "Bless you for telling me of your love. When you are gone it will be a comfort for me to think that Marian Grey *once* loved me. I say *once* for you must overcome that love. You must tear it out and trample it beneath your feet. You can if you try. You are not as hard, as callous as I am. My heart is like adamant, and though I know that it is wicked to love you, and to tell you of my love, I cannot help it. I am a wretch, and when I tell you, as I must, just what a wretch I am, it will help you to forget me—to hate me, it may be. You have heard of my wife. You know she left me on my bridal night, and I have never known the joys of wedded bliss—never shall know, for even if she comes back to me now, *I cannot live with her!*"

"Oh, Frederic!" And again the hot tears trembled

through the hands which Marian clasped before her eyes.

"Don't call me thus," said Frederic, entreatingly, as he removed her hands, and held them both in his. "Don't say Frederic, for though it thrills me with strange joy to hear you, it is not right. Listen, Marian, while I tell you why I married her who bears your name, and then I'm sure you'll hate me—nor call me Frederic again. I have never told but one, and that one, William Gordon. I had thought never to tell it again, but it is right that you should know. Marian Lindsey was, or is, the Heiress of Redstone Hall. All my boasted wealth is hers—every cent of it is hers. But she didn't know it, for"—and Frederic's voice was very low and plaintive now as he told to Marian Grey how Marian Lindsey was an heiress—told her of his dead parent's fraud—of his desire to save that parent's name from disgrace, and his stronger desire to save him from poverty. "So I made her my wife," he said. "I promised to love and cherish her all the time my heart was longing for another."

Marian trembled now, as she lay helpless in his arms, and, observing it, he continued:

"I must confess the whole, and tell you that I loved, or thought I loved, Isabel Huntington, though how I could have fancied her is a mystery to me now. My poor Marian was plain, while Isabel was beautiful, and naught but Alice kept me from telling her my love. Alice stayed the act—Alice sent me to New York to look for Marian ——"

"And did you never hear from her? Did she never send you a letter?" Marian asked, and he replied:

"Never! If she had I should have known where to find her."

Then, as briefly as possible, for he knew time was hastening, he told of his fearful sickness, and of the little girl who took such care of him—told, too, of his weary search for her, and of the many dreary nights he had passed in thinking of her, and her probable fate.

"Then *you* came," he said, "and, struggle as I would, I could not mourn for Marian Lindsey as I had done before. I was satisfied to have you here until the conviction burst upon me, that far greater than any affection I had thought I could feel for that blue-eyed girl, and ten-fold greater than any love I had felt for Isabel Huntington, was my love for you. It has worn upon me terribly. Look!" And pushing back his thick brown locks, he showed her where the hair was turning white beneath. "These are for you," he said. "There are furrows upon my face—furrows upon my heart—and can you wonder that I bade you go, and so no longer tempt me to sin? And yet, could I keep you with me, Marian? Could I hold you to my bosom just as I hold you now, and know that I had a right so to do?—a right to call you mine—my Marian—my wife? Not Heaven itself, I'm sure, has greater happiness in store for those who merit its bliss than this would be to me! Oh, why is the boon denied to me? Why must I suffer on through wretched, dreary years, and know that somewhere in the world there is a Marian Grey, who might have been my wife?"

"Let me go for Alice," said Marian, struggling to release herself. "There is something she would tell you."

"Yes, in a moment," he replied; "but promise me first one thing. The news may come to me that I am free, and if it does, and you are still unmarried, will you then be my wife? Promise that you will, and the remembrance of that promise will help me to bear a little longer."

"I do!" said Marian, standing up before him, and holding one of his hands in hers. "I promise you, solemnly, that no other man shall ever call me wife save you."

There were tears in Frederic's eyes, and his whole

frame quivered with emotion, as, catching at her dress, for she was moving toward the door, he added:

"And you will wait for me, darling—wait for me *twenty* years, if it needs must be? You will never be old to me. I shall love you just the same when these sunny locks are grey," and he passed his hands caressingly over her bright hair. There was a world of love and tenderness in the answering look which Marian gave to him as he opened the door for her to pass out, and wringing his hands in anguish, he cried to himself, "Oh, how can I give her up—beautiful, beautiful Marian Grey!"

Swift as a bird Marian flew up the stairs in quest of Alice, who was to tell the wretched man that it was not a sin for him to love the beautiful Marian Grey.

"Alice, Alice! Go now—go quick!" she exclaimed, bursting into the room.

"Go whar—for the dear Lord's sake?" said Dinah, who had that moment come up, and consequently had made but little progress in dressing Alice. "Go whar? Not down stairs—'strue as yer born. She'll cotch her death o' cold!"

"Hurry—*do!*" cried Alice, standing first on one foot and then upon the other. "I must tell Frederic something before he goes away. There, he's going! Oh, Marian, help!" she fairly screamed, as she heard the carriage at the door, and Frederic in the hall below.

Marian was terribly excited, and in her attempts to assist, she only made matters worse by buttoning the wrong button, putting both stockings on the same foot, pulling the shoe-lacing into a hard knot, which baffled all her nervous efforts, while Dinah worked on leisurely, insisting that Alice "wasn't gwine down, and if there was anythin' killin' which marster 'or'to know, Miss Grey could tell him herself."

"Yes, Marian, go," said Alice, in despair, as she heard Dud bid Frederic good-by, and, scarcely conscious of what she was about, Marian ran down the stairs, just as Phil cracked his whip, and the spirited greys bounded off with a rapidity which left her faint call of "Stop, Frederic, stop!" far behind.

"I can write to him," she thought, as she slowly retraced her steps back to Alice, who was bitterly disappointed, and who, after Dinah was gone, threw herself upon the bed, refusing to be comforted.

"Three weeks was forever," she said, and she suggested sending Josh after the traveler, who, in a most unenviable frame of mind, was riding rapidly towards Frankfort.

"No, no," said Marian, "I will write immediately, so he can get the letter as soon almost as he reaches New Orleans. It won't be three weeks before he returns," and she strove to divert the child's mind by repeating to her as much as she thought proper of her exciting interview with Frederic.

But Alice could not be comforted, and all that day she lamented over the mischance which had taken Frederic away before she could tell him.

"There's Uncle Phil," she said, when towards night she heard the carriage drive into the yard; "and hark, hark!" she exclaimed, turning her quick ear in the direction of the sound, and rolling her bright eye around the room; "there's a step on the piazza that sounds like his—'tis him—'tis him! He's come back! I knew he would!" and in her weakness and excitement the little girl sunk exhausted at Marian's feet.

Raising her up, Marian listened breathlessly, but heard nothing save Phil, talking to his horses as he drove them to the stable.

"He has not come," she said, and Alice replied, "I tell you he has. There—there, don't you hear?" and Marian's heart gave one great bound as she, too, heard the well-known footstep upon the threshold and Frederick speaking to his favorite Dud, who had run to meet "his mars," asking for sugar-plums from New Orleans.

There had been a change in the time-table, and

Frederic did not reach Frankfort until after the train he intended to take had gone. His first thought was to remain in the city, and wait for the next train from Lexington. Accordingly he gave his parting directions to Phil, who being in no haste to return, loitered away the morning and a portion of the afternoon before he turned his horses homeward. As he was riding up the long hill which leads from Frankfort into the country beyond, he unexpectedly met his master, who had been to the cemetery, and was just returning to the Capitol Hotel.

All the day Frederic had thought of Marian Grey, and with each thought it had seemed to him more and more that he must see her again, if only to hear her say that she would wait all time for him, and when he came upon Phil, who he supposed was long ere this at Redstone Hall, his resolution was taken, and instead of the reproof he knew he merited, Phil was surprised at hearing his master say, as he made a motion for him to stop:

"Phil, I am going home."

And thus it was that he returned again to Redstone Hall, where his coming was hailed with eager joy by Marian and Alice, and created much surprise among the servants.

"My 'pinion he's a little out of his head," was all the satisfaction Phil could give, as he drove the carriage to the barn, while Frederic, half repenting of his rashness in returning, and wondering what good excuse he could render, went to his own room—the one formerly occupied by his father—where he sat before the glowing grate, when Alice appeared, covered with shawls, and her face all aglow with her excitement.

She would not be kept back another moment, lest he should go off again, so Marian had wrapped her up and sent her on her mission. Frederic sat with his face turned toward the fire, and though by the step he knew who it was that entered the door, he did not turn his head or evince the least knowledge of her presence until she stood before him, and said, inquiringly:

"Frederic, are you here?"

"Yes;" was the answer, rather curtly spoken, for he would rather be alone.

"Frederic!" and the bundle of shawls trembled violently. "I have come to tell you something about Marian."

"I don't wish to hear it," was his reply; and, nothing daunted, Alice continued:

"But you must hear me. Her name isn't Miss Grey. She is a married woman, and has a living husband; and you——"

She did not finish the sentence, for like a tiger Frederic started up, and seizing her by the shoulder, exclaimed: "You dare not tell me that again. Marian Grey is not married. She never had a husband," and as the maddening thought swept over him, that possibly the blind girl told him truly, he staggered against the mantel, where he stood panting for breath, and enduring, as it were, all the agonies of a lingering, painful death.

"Sit down," said Alice, and like a child he obeyed, while she proceeded, "Miss Grey has deceived us all, and it is strange, too, that none of us should know her —none but Bruno. Don't you remember how he wouldn't bite her, just because he knew her when we didn't? Don't you mind how I told you once maybe the Marian who went away would come back to us some day so beautiful we should not know her? You are listening, ain't you?"

"Yes, yes," came in a quick, short gasp from the arm-chair.

"Well, she has come back! She called herself Marian Grey so we would not guess right off who she was, but she ain't Marian Grey. She's the other one—she's MY MARIAN, Frederic, AND YOUR WIFE—"

As Alice was speaking Frederic had risen to his feet. Drop by drop every particle of blood receded from his face, leaving it colorless as ashes. There was a wild, unnatural light flashing from his eyes—his hands worked nervously together—his hair seemed starting from its roots, and with his head bent forward, he stood transfixed as it were by the dazzling light which had burst upon him. Then his lips parted slowly, and more like a wailing cry than a prayer of thanksgiving, the words "I thank thee, oh, my God," issued from them. The next moment the air near Alice was set in rapid motion—there was a heavy fall, and Frederic Raymond lay upon the carpet white and still as a block of marble.

Like lightning Alice flew across the floor, but swift as were her movements, another was there before her, and with his head upon her lap was pressing burning kisses upon his lips and dropping showers of tears upon his face. Marian had stood without the door, listening to that dialogue, and when by the fall she knew that it was ended, she came at once and knelt by the fainting man, who ere long began to show signs of consciousness. Alice was first to discover this, and when sure that he would come back to life, she glided silently from the room, for she knew that she would not be needed there.

She might have tarried yet a little longer, for the shock to Frederic had been so sudden and so great, that though his lips moved and his fingers clutched eagerly at the soft hand feeling for his pulse, he did not seem to heed aught else, until Marian whispered in his ear:

"My husband—may I call you so?"

Then, indeed, he started from his lethargy, and, struggling to his feet, clasped her in his arms, weeping over her passionately, and murmuring as he did so:

"My wife—my darling—my wife! Is it true that you have come to me again? Are you my Marian?"

Daylight was fading from the room, for the Winter sun had set behind the western hills, and leading her to the window, he turned her face to the light, gazing rapturously upon it, and saying to her:

"You are mine—all mine! God bless you, Marian!"

He kissed her hands, her neck, her lips, her forehead, her hair, and she could feel his hot tears falling amid the shining curls he parted so lovingly from her brow. They were not hateful to him now—and he passed his hand caressingly over them, whispering all the while:

"My own beautiful Marian—my bride—my wife!"

Surely, in this moment of bliss, Marian felt repaid for all that she had suffered, when at last as thoughts of the dreadful past came over Frederic, he led her to the sofa, and said, "Can you forgive me, darling?" she turned her bright eyes up to his, and by the expression of perfect happiness resting there, he knew she had forgotten the cold, heartless words he spoke to her, when once, at that very hour, and in that very place, he asked her to be his. That scene had faded away, leaving no cloud between them. All was sunshine and gladness, and with her fair head resting on his bosom — not timidly, as it had lain there in the morning, but trustingly, confidingly, as if that were its rightful resting-place—they sat together until the rose-red tinge faded from the western sky, and the night shadows had crept into the room.

More than once Alice stole on tiptoe to the door, to see if it were time for her to enter, but as often as she heard the low murmur of their voices, she went noiselessly back, saying to herself: "I won't disturb them yet."

At last as she came once she stumbled accidentally, and this woke Marian from the sweetest dream which ever had come to her.

"'Tis Alice," she said; and she called to the little girl who came gladly, and climbing into Frederic's lap, twined her arms around his neck and laid a cheek against his own, without word of comment.

"Blessed Alice, I owe you more than I can repay," he said, and Marian, far better than the child, appreciated the full meaning these words conveyed.

But for the helpless blind girl this hour might never have come to them, and the strong man felt it so, as he hugged the little creature closer to him, blessing her as his own and Marian's good angel. Observing that she shivered as if with the cold, he arose, and drawing the sofa directly before the fire, resumed his seat again, with Marian between himself and Alice, his arm around her neck and his lips almost constantly meeting hers. He could not remove his eyes from her, she seemed to him so beautiful, with the firelight falling on her sparkling face and shining on her hair. That hair—how it puzzled him, and winding one of the curls about his fingers he said, half laughingly, half reluctantly, "Your hair was not always this color."

Then the blue eyes flashed up into his, and Marian replied by telling whence came the change, and reminding him that she was the same young girl of whom the Yankee Ben had spoken when he visited Kentucky.

"And you had almost died, then, for me, my precious one," said Frederic, kissing the sunny locks.

Just at this point, old Dinah appeared in the door, which, like most Kentucky doors, was left ajar. She saw the position of the parties—saw Frederic kiss Marian Grey—saw Alice's look of satisfaction as he did so, and in an instant all the old lady's sense of propriety was roused to a boiling pitch.

Since Marian had revealed herself to Alice, the little girl had said to Dinah, by way of preparing her for the surprise when it should come, that "there was some doubt concerning the death of Marian—that Frederic believed she had been with him in New York, and had taken means to find her." This story was, of course, repeated among the servants, some of whom credited it, while others did not. Among the latter was Dinah. She wouldn't believe "she had done all her mournin' for nothin'," and in opposition to Hetty, she persisted in saying Marian was dead. When, however, she saw her master's familiarity with Miss Grey, she accepted of her young mistress's existence as a reality, and was terribly incensed against the offending Marian Grey.

"The trollop!" she muttered. "But I'll bring proof agin her," and hurrying back to the kitchen, she told to the astonished blacks, "how't marster done kissed Miss Grey spang on her har, and on her mouth, and hugged her into the bargain, when he didn't know for certain that t'other one was dead; and if they didn't b'lieve it, they could go and see for themselves, provided they went mighty still."

"Tole you he was crazy," said Uncle Phil, starting to see the wonderful sight, and followed by a troop of negroes, all of whom trod on tiptoe, a precaution wholly unnecessary, for Frederic and Marian were too much absorbed in each other to heed the dusky group assembled round the door, their white eyes growing larger as they all saw distinctly the arm thrown across Marian's neck.

"Listen to dat ar, will you?" whispered Hetty, as Frederic said, "Dear Marian," while old Dinah chimed in, "'Clar for't, it makes my blood bile, and he not a widower nuther!"

"Quit dat!" she exclaimed aloud, as her master showed signs of repeating the kissing offense; and, in an instant, Frederic sprang to his feet, an angry flush mounting to his face when he saw the crowd at the door.

Then, as he began to comprehend its meaning, the frown gave place to a good-humored laugh, and taking Marian's hand, he led her toward the assembled blacks, saying to them:

"Rejoice with me that the lost one has returned to us again, for this is *Marian Lindsey*—my wife and your mistress—changed, it is true, but the same Marian who went from us more than six years ago."

"Wonder if he 'spects us to swallow dat ar?" said the unbelieving Hetty.

Dinah, on the contrary, had not the shadow of a doubt, and she dropped on her knees at once, kissing the very hem of Marian's dress, and exclaiming through her tears:

"Lord bress you, Miss Marian. You've mightily altered, to be sure, but ain't none the wus for that. I'm nothin' but a poor old nigger, and can't say what's in my heart, but it's full and runnin' over, bless you, honey."

Dinah's example was contagious, and more than one prostrated themselves before their mistress, while their howling cries of surprise and delight were almost deafening. Particularly was Josh delighted, and while the noise went on, he took occasion to "balance to your partner," in the hall, with a young yellow girl, who thought his stammering was music, and his ungainly figure the most graceful that could be conceived. When the commotion had in a measure subsided, and Hetty had gone over to the popular side, saying, "she knew from the first Marian was somebody," Frederic made a few brief explanations as to where their mistress had been, and then dismissed them to their several duties, for he preferred being alone again with his wife and Alice.

Supper was soon announced, but little was eaten by any one. They were too much excited for that, and as soon as the meal was over, they returned to Frederic's room, where, sitting again between her husband and Alice, Marian told them, as far as possible, everything which had come to her since leaving Redstone Hall.

"Can't I ever know what made you go away?" Alice asked; and Frederic replied:

"Yes, birdie, you shall;" and, without sparing himself in the least, he told her all.

"Marian an heiress, too!" she exclaimed. "Will marvels never cease?" and she laid her head which was beginning to grow weary, upon Marian's lap, saying, "I never knew till now one half how good you are. No wonder Frederic thought that he had killed you. It was wicked in him, very," and the brown eyes looked sleepily into the fire, while Marian replied:

"But is all forgotten now."

It did seem to be, and in the long conversation which lasted till almost midnight, there was many a word of affection exchanged, many a confession made, many a forgiveness asked, and when, at last they parted, it was with the belief that each was all the world to the other.

Like lightning the news spread through the neighborhood that Frederid Raymond's governess was Frederic Raymond's wife; and, for many days the house was thronged with visitors, most of whom remembered little Marian Lindsey, and all of whom offered their sincere congratulations to the beautiful Marian Grey, for so she persisted in being called, until the night of the 20th of February, when they were to give a bridal party. Then she would answer to Mrs. Raymond, she said, but not before, and with this Frederic was fain to be satisfied. Great were the preparations for that party, to which all their friends were to be bidden, and as they were one evening making out the list, Marian suggested *Isabel*, more for the sake of seeing what Frederic would say, than from any desire to have her present.

"Isabel," he repeated, "never. I cannot so soon forget her treachery," and a frown darkened his handsome face, but Marian kissed it away as she said:

"You surely will not object to Ben, the best and truest friend I ever had."

"Certainly not," answered Frederic. "I owe Ben Burt more than I ever can repay, and I mean to keep him with us. He is just the man I want upon my farm—*your* farm, I mean," he added, smiling knowingly upon her, and catching in his the little hand raised to shut his mouth.

But Marian had her revenge by refusing to let him kiss her until he had promised never to allude to that again.

"I gave you Redstone Hall," she said, "that night I ran away, and I have never taken it back, but have brought you in instead an incumbrance which may prove a most expensive one." And amid such pleasantries as these Marian wrote the note to Ben, and then went back to her preparations for the party, which, together with the strange discovery, was the theme of the whole country.

CHAPTER XXIX.

BEN.

Ben sat among his boxes and barrels cracking hickory nuts and carrying on a one sided conversation with the well fed cat and six beautiful kittens, which were gamboling over the floor, the terror of rats and mice and the pride of their owner, who found his heart altogether too tender to destroy any one of them by the usual means of drowning or decapitation. So he was literally killing them with kindness, and with his seven cats and odd ways was the wonder and favorite of the entire village.

The night was dark and stormy, and fancying he had dismissed his last customer he had settled himself before the glowing stove with nearly half a peck of nuts at his side, when the door opened, and a little boy came in, his light hair covered with snow, which had also settled upon other portions of his person.

"Good evenin', Sandy," was Ben's salutation.

"What brung you here to-night?"

"Got you a letter," returned Sandy, who was the chore boy of the Post Master. "It's been a good while coming, too, for all it says 'in haste,'" and passing the note to Ben, he caught up five or six of the kittens, while Ben, tearing open the envelope and snuffing a tallow candle with his fingers read:

"Dear Ben,

"Frederic knows it all, and we are so happy. We are to have a great party on the 20th, and you must surely come. Don't fail us, that's a dear, good Ben, but come as soon as you get this. Then I will tell you what I can't write now, for Frederic keeps worrying me with teasing me to kiss him.

Yours truly,

"Marian.

"P. S.—Alice sends her love, so does Frederic, and so do I, dear Ben."

"I 'most wish she'd left off that last, and that about his kissin' her," said Ben, when, after the boy Sandy departed he was alone. "It makes me feel so streaked like. Guy, wouldn't I give all my groceries, and the six cats into the bargain, to be in Fred Raymond's boots;" and, taking up the kitten he called "Marian Grey," he fondled it tenderly, for the sake of her whose name it bore. "I shall go to this party," he continued, as his mind reverted again to the letter, "though I'll be as much out of place as a toad in a sugar bowl; but I can see Marian, and that little blind girl, and Josh. Wa'n't he a case, though?" And leaning back in his chair, Ben mentally made the necessary arrangements for leaving.

These arrangements were next day carried into effect, and as he must start at once if he would be there in time for the party, he took the night express for Albany, having left his feline family to the care of the boy Sandy. The second night found him on the train between Buffalo and Cleveland, and as the weather was very cold and the seat near the stove unoccupied, he appropriated it to himself, and was just falling away to sleep, when a lady, wrapped in velvet and furs, with a thickly dotted vail over her face, came up to him, and said, rather haughtily:

"Can I have this seat, sir? I prefer it to any other."

"So do I," returned Ben; "but bein' you're a woman, I'll give it up, I guess."

And he sought another, of which there were plenty, for it was the last car, and not one-third full.

"Considerable kind o' toppin'," was his mental comment, as he coiled himself in his shaggy overcoat for a second time, sleeping ere long so soundly that nothing disturbed him, until at last, as they turned a short curve, the car was detached from the others, and, leaving the track, was precipitated down an embankment, which, fortunately, was not very steep, so that none were killed, although several were wounded, and among them the lady who had so unceremoniously taken possession of Ben's comfortable seat.

"Wall, now," said Ben, crawling out of a window, and holding fast to his hat, which being new, was his special care, "if this ain't a little the imperlitest way of wakin' a feller out of a sound sleep, to pitch him head over heels in among these blackb'ry bushes and stuns; but who the plague is that a-screechin' so?—a woman's voice, too!"

And with all his gallantry aroused, Ben went to the rescue, feeling his way through briars and grass and broken pieces of the car, until he reached the human form struggling beneath the ruins, in close proximity to the hissing stove.

"Easy, now, my gal," he said, lifting her up. "Haul your foot out, can't you?"

"No, no, it's crushed;" and Ben's knees shook beneath him at the cry of pain.

Relief soon came from other sources, and as this lady seemed more seriously injured than either of the other passengers, she was carried carefully to a dwelling near by, and laid upon a bed, before Ben had a chance to see her features distinctly.

"Pretty well jammed," said he, examining the bonnet, which the women of the farm-house had removed.

Supposing he meant herself, the lady moaned,

"Oh, sir, is my face entirely crushed?"

"I meant your bonnet," returned Ben, "though if I was to pass judgment on you, I should say some of your feathers was crumpled a little; but law, beauty ain't but skin deep. It's good, honest actions that makes folks liked."

And taking the lamp, he bent to investigate, discovering to his utter amazement, that the lady was none other than Isabel Huntington!

Some weeks before, and ere Marian's identity with Frederic's wife had heen made known, Mrs. Rivers had invited her to visit Kentucky, and as there was now nothing in Yonkers to interest her she had accepted, with the forlorn hope that spite of Frederic's improbable story about a living wife, he might eventually be won back to his old allegiance. Accordingly she had taken the same train and car with Ben, and by rather rudely depriving him of his seat near the stove had been considerably injured, receiving several flesh wounds, besides breaking her ankle. For this last, however, she did not care; that would get well again; but her face—was it so disfigured as to spoil her boasted beauty? This was her constant thought as she lay moaning upon her pillows, and when for a few moments she was alone with Ben, whom she knew to be the Yankee peddler, and who considered it his duty to stay with her, she said to him:

"Please, Mr. Butterworth, tell me just how much I am bruised, and whether I shall probably be a fright the rest of my days."

"Wall, now," returned Ben, taking the lamp a second time and coming nearer to her, "there's no knowin' how you will look hereafter, but the fact is you ain't none too han'some now, with your face swelled as big as two, and all scratched up with them pesky briars."

"Yes, yes," interrupted Isabel, "but the swelling will go down and the scratches will get well. That isn't all."

"You're right," said Ben, peering curiously at her; "that ain't all. You know, I 'spose, that six of your front teeth are knocked out."

"Yes, but false ones will remedy that. I'll have

them made a little uneven so as to look natural; go on."

"Wall," continued Ben, "you've fixed your teeth, but what are you goin' to do with your *broke* nose?"

"Oh!" screamed Isabel, clasping her hand to that organ, which, from its classic shape had been her special pride. "Not broken—is it broken, true?"

"Looks mighty like it," answered Ben, "but law! doctors can do anything. They'll tinker it up so it will answer to sneeze out of and smell with as good as ever; and they'll sew up that ugly gash, too, that runs like a Virginny fence from your ear up onto your forehead and part of your cheek. Looks as though there'd been a scar of some kind there before," and looking closer, Ben saw the mark which the hot iron had made that night when the proud Isabel had given the cruel blow to the blind girl.

This she had heretofore managed to conceal by combing over it her hair, but nothing could hide the seam she knew would always be upon her forehead and cheek.

"Oh, I wish I could die," she groaned, "if I must be so mutilated."

"Pshaw! no you don't," returned Ben, now acting the part of a consoler. "Your eyes ain't damaged, nor your hair neither, only singed a little with the stove. There's some *white* ones, I see, but they must have been there before. Never used Wood's brimstony stuff, did you? That'll keep it from turnin.' I knew a chap once with a broke nose that looked like the notch in the White Mountains, and nobody thought of it, he was so good. Maybe your'n ain't so bad. Perhaps it's only out of jint. The doctor'll know—here he comes," and Ben stood back respectfully, while the physician examined the nature and extent of Isabel's injuries.

There was nothing serious, he said; nothing from which she would not recover. She was only stunned and bruised, besides having a broken ancle. The cut on the face would probably leave a scar, and the nose never be straight again, otherwise she would ere long be as well as ever, but she must of course remain where she was for two or three weeks, and he asked if she had friends with her.

"No," she said, while Ben said: "Yes, I'm her friend, and though I want to go on the wust way, I'll stay till her mother comes. We'd better telegraph, I guess."

This brought the tears from the heartless Isabel, for she appreciated Ben's kindness in not deserting her, and when again they were alone, she thanked him for so generously staying with her when she heard him say he wished to go on.

"Were you going to Kentucky?" she asked, and Ben replied: "Yes, goin' to see how Miss Raymond looks at the head of a family. You've heard, I s'pose, that Marian Grey was Fred's run-away wife, and that they are as happy now as two clams."

Unmindful of the fierce twinges of pain it gave her to move, Isabel started up exclaiming, "No, no, how can that be?"

"Just as easy," said Ben, proceeding to narrate a few particulars to his astonished listener, who, when he had finished, lay back again upon her pillow, weeping bitterly.

This, then, was the end of all her secret hopes. Frederic was surely lost to her; the beautiful Marian Grey was his wife, and what was worse than all, her treachery was undoubtedly suspected, and what must they think of her? Poor Isabel, she was in a measure suffering for her sins, and she continued to weep while Ben tried in vain to sooth her, talking to her upon the subject uppermost in his mind, namely, Marian's happiness and his own joy that it had all come right at last. Isabel would rather have heard of anything else, but when she saw how kind Ben was, she compelled herself to listen, even though every word he said of

Marian and Frederic pierced her with a keener pain than even her bruises produced.

"I shan't be in time for the doin's any way," thought Ben, when Mrs. Huntington did not come at the expected time, and as he fancied it his duty to let Marian know why he was not there, he telegraphed to her, "We've had a break down, and Isabel is knocked into a cocked hat."

This telegram, which created no little sensation at the office, was copied verbatim and sent to Frederic, who read it, while Marian, in her chamber, was dressing for the party. He could not forbear laughing heartily, it sounded so much like Ben, but he wisely determined to keep it from his wife and Alice, as it might cause them unnecessary anxiety. He accordingly thrust it in his pocket, and then, when it was time, went up for Marian, who, in her bridal dress of satin and lace, with pearls and diamonds woven among her shining hair, and flashing from her neck and arms, looked wondrously beautiful to him, and received many words of commendation from the guests, who soon began to appear, and who felt that the bride of Redstone Hall well became her high position. Many were the pleasant jokes passed at Frederic's expense, and the clergyman who had officiated at his wedding more than six years before, laughingly offered to repeat the ceremony. But Frederic shook his head, saying, he was satisfied if Marian was, while the look the beautiful, blushing bride gave to him, was quite as expressive of her answer as words would have been. And so, amid smiles and congratulations, the song and the dance moved on, and all went merry as a marriage bell, until at last, as the clock told the hour of midnight, the last guest had departed, and Frederic, with his arm round Marian, was calling her Mrs. Raymond, on purpose to see her blush, when there came up the avenue the sound of rapid wheels, followed by a bound on the piazza, and the next moment Ben burst into the room, holding up both hands, as he caught sight of Marian in her bridal robes.

"My goodness!" he exclaimed. "Ain't she pretty, though. It's curis how clothes will fix up a woman," and the tears came to Ben's eyes in his delight at seeing Marian so resplendent in jewels and costly lace.

The meeting between Frederic and Ben was like brother greeting brother, for the former felt that he almost owed his life to the great-hearted Yankee, and he grasped his hand warmly, bidding him welcome to Redstone Hall, and, by his kind, familiar manner, putting him at once at his ease. Alice, too, did her part well, and, pressing Ben's hand to her lips, she said:

"I love you, Ben Burt; love you a heap, for being so good to Marian."

"Don't now," said Ben, whiningly. "Don't set me to bellerin' the fust thing. I only did what anybody would have done, unless the milk of human kindness was all turned to bonny clabber!" Then, as he thought of Isabel, he continued, "I tried to get here sooner, but Miss Huntington didn't come till the last minute, and I couldn't leave Isabel. How she does take on about her sp'ilt beauty."

"What do you mean?" asked Marian. "Where is Isabel?" and as Frederic then passed her the telegram, she continued to ask questions, until she had learned the whole.

"Poor girl!" she sighed; "I pity her, and if she were here, I would so gladly take care of her."

Instantly there flashed upon Alice's mind an idea every way worthy of her, but she would not suggest it then, as it was growing late, and when she heard ere long a loud yawn from Ben, she thoughtfully rang the bell, bidding the servant who came "show Mr. Burt to his room;" then, kissing Frederic and Marian good-night, she, too, departed, leaving them alone.

Next morning, at the breakfast-table, she said to Frederic:

"Don't folks most always take a bridal tour?"

"Sometimes, when they can't be happy at home," returned Frederic. "Where does my blind birdie wish to go?"

"I don't really wish to go," answered Alice; "but wouldn't it be nice to surprise poor Isabel, lying so bruised and sick in that old farm-house in Ohio? Maybe she wants money? I heard them say at Yonkers that she had spent all Mr. Rivers left her, except the house, and that was mortgaged. I've got ten dollars that I'll give her."

"Blessed baby!" said Ben, bringing out his pocket-handkerchief, which he was pretty sure to need.

This suggestion was warmly seconded by Marian, and after a little further consultation, it was decided that they should start the next day for the place where Isabel lay sick.

"She may confess about the letters," said Marian, "and that will make me like her so much better."

This being settled, Alice's next inquiry was for her cat, and her brown eyes opened wide with wonder when told of the six young kittens which had a home in Ben Burt's grocery, and one of which was called for her.

"It ought to be blind," said the little girl, and, with a quivering chin, Ben answered:

"That's it, though I shouldn't have told you for fear of hurtin' your feelin's. The little cat *is* blind, and when Sandy—that's a boy who lives there—said how he would kill it for me, it struck to my stomick to once, for that little critter lies even nigher to my heart than the handsomest, sleekest one, which I call 'Marian Grey,' and 'tis grey, too, with mottled spots all over its back, while Alice is white as milk!"

The cat story being satisfactorily concluded, Ben went out to renew his acquaintance with the negroes, who vied with each other in paying him marked attention. Though they did not quite understand it, they knew that he was in some way connected with the return of their young mistress, and neither Dinah nor Hetty made the least objection when, before night, they saw the two black babies which had usurped the rights of *Dud* and *Victory*, seated upon his lap and "riding to Boston to buy penny cakes," at a rate which bade fair to throw them to the top of the ceiling at least, if not to land them somewhere in the vicinity of the bay state capital.

The next morning, Frederic, Marian and Alice started for Ohio, leaving Ben in charge at Redstone Hall.

"He'd tend to the niggers," he said, and he bade the "Square," as he persisted in calling Frederic, "not to worry at all about things to hum."

The family had scarcely been gone an hour when Dinah came in quest of Ben, whom she found in the parlor drumming Yankee Doodle upon the piano with one hand and whistling by way of accompaniment.

"Thar was the queerest actin' man in the dinin' room," she said, "and he done ax for marster, and when I tole him he had gone to the 'Hio with his wife, he laughed so hateful, and say how't she isn't his wife, that I come for you, 'case thar's a look in his eye I don't like."

"Catch him tellin' me Marian ain't a lawful wife," said Ben, starting from the stool and hurrying to the dining-room, where very much intoxicated, Rudolph McVicar was sitting.

He had landed not long before at New Orleans, and coming up the river as far as Louisville had stopped in that city, where he accidentally heard a young man speak of Frederic's wedding party, which had taken place the previous night.

"Who is the bride?" he asked eagerly. "Is it Miss Huntington?" and the young man who knew none of the particulars, and who had once heard that Frederic was to marry a lady of that name, replied: "Yes, I believe it is, or at all events she was his governess."

Rudolph waited for no more, but started at once for

Redstone Hall, chuckling with delight as he thought of the consternation his visit would create. He did not at first recognize Ben, neither did Ben know him, so bloated had he become with drink, and so rough and red with exposure upon the sea.

"Where is the woman they call Mrs. Raymond?" he asked with a sneer; and Ben replied: "Gone with her husband to Ohio."

"Her husband!" repeated Rudolph. "He isn't her husband. She has no right to be his wife, and I have come to tell her so."

"You say that again if you dare!" said Ben, bristling up in Marian's defense. "You say that Marian ain't Frederic's lawful wife, and I'll show you the door, plaguy quick. I'm boss here now."

As Ben was speaking, Rudolph remembered that they had met before, but he scarcely heeded that, so intent was he upon the name which Ben had uttered.

"Marian!" he repeated, a light breaking over him; "Is not Isabel Huntington the bride?"

"No, sir," answered Ben, snapping his fingers almost in the stranger's face. "She didn't come that game, though she tried it hard enough. But what do you know about it, any way?"

"I know I've been a fool," answered Rudolph, explaining, in a few words, what he once had done.

"So you wrote that letter, you scullion," returned Ben. "But it didn't do no good; and the smartest trick you ever done was to sign yourself *green*. Ugh! and Ben's voice was quite expressive of his contempt. "I don't blame you so much though," he continued, "for wantin' to pester that Isabel, but you'd better let the Lord 'tend to such critters in his own way. He can fix 'em better'n we can," and Ben proceeded to give an account of the accident in which Isabel's beauty had been seriously impaired.

"I am so glad," was Rudolph's exclamation, and he was proceeding further to express his malicious joy, when Ben cut him short by saying:

"It don't look well to rejoice over anybody's downfall, though I'm none too friendly to the gal, I shan't hear her berated, and you may as well quit."

On ordinary occasions, Rudolph would have resented any attempt at restraint, but he was too much intoxicated now fully to realize anything, and staring vacantly at Ben, he made no reply, but ere long fell asleep, dozing in his chair for several hours. Then, with faculties somewhat brightened, he announced his intention of leaving. With an immense degree of satisfaction Ben watched him as he went slowly down the avenue, saying to himself:

"Poor drunken critter, he's disappointed, I s'pose, in not gettin' revenge his own way; but I don't blame her much for givin' him the mitten. Wouldn't they have scratched each other's eyes out, if they'd come together! Better be as 'tis—she a nervous old maid, and he in a drunkard's grave, where he will be mighty soon—the bloat!" and having finished his soliloquy, Ben returned again to his music.

Meantime, in a most unenviable frame of mind, Isabel was chiding her mother for doing everything wrong, and bewailing her own sad fate:

"Oh, why didn't I stay at home," she said; "and so not have become the fright I know I am?"

It was in vain that her mother made her feel thankful that her life was spared. Isabel did not care for that. She thought only of her lost teeth, her disjointed nose, and ugly scar, and turning her face to the wall she was wishing she could die, when the woman of the house came in, telling her "some friends were there from Kentucky."

"Who are they?" she asked; but ere the woman could reply, a sweet voice said:

"It's me, and all of us;" and Alice's little hands were tenderly pressed to Isabel's feverish brow.

Then, indeed, the haughty girl wept aloud, for she knew she did not deserve this kindness either from Alice or Marian, the latter of whom soon came in, greeting her as pleasantly as if she had never received an injury from her hands. Frederic, too, was perfectly self-possessed, expressing his sympathy for her misfortune, and with these kind friends to cheer her sick room, Isabel recovered in a measure her former cheerfulness. But there was evidently something resting heavily upon her mind, and that night, when alone with Frederic and Marian, she confessed to them her wickedness in opening the letter, and sending it back with so cruel a message.

"We knew you must have done it," said Frederic, at the same time assuring her of his own and Marian's forgiveness. "It kept us apart for many years," he continued, "but I have found her at last, and love her all the more for what I suffered."

And Isabel, when she saw the look of deep affection he gave to his young wife, covered her face with her hands, and wept silently, until Marian asked "if she knew aught of the letter from Sarah Green?"

"No, no," she answered; "I am surely innocent of that," and they believed her, wondering all the more whence it could have come or why it had been sent.

Toward the close of the next day, they took their leave, cordially inviting Isabel to visit them at Redstone Hall, should she ever feel inclined so to do.

"We will let bygones be bygones," said Frederic, taking her hand at parting. "You and I have both learned that to deal fairly and openly is the best policy, and it is to be hoped we will profit by the experience."

Isabel did not answer, but she pressed his hand, and returned warmly the kiss which both Marian and Alice gave to her. As the latter was turning away she detained her a moment while she whispered in her ear, "Will you forgive me for that blow I gave you when I thought I was about to be exposed?"

"Yes, willingly," was the answer, and thrusting the golden eagle under the pillow, Alice hurried away. They found it after she was gone, and when at last

Isabel was able to go home, they found their bills paid, too, and were at no loss to know to whom they were indebted for the generous act. "I do not deserve this from him of all others," said Isabel, and drawing her thick, green veil close over her marred face she entered the carriage which had come to take them to the depot.

Not once during the journey home did she remove the veil, but in an obscure corner of the car she sat, a forlorn, wretched woman, brooding drearily over the past, and seeing in the future no star to cheer her pathway. Frederic lost, Redstone Hall lost, her little fortune wasted,—and worse than all, her boasted beauty gone forever. Poor, poor Isabel!

CHAPTER XXX.

SUMMING UP.

It is early June, and the balmy south wind is blowing soft and warm round Redstone Hall, which, with its countless roses in full bloom, and its profusion of flowering shrubs and vines, looked wondrously beautiful without, while within, the sunlight of domestic peace is shining with no cloud to dim its brightness. Frederic and Marian are perfectly happy, for the dark night which enshrouded them so long has passed away, and the day they fancy will never end has dawned upon them at last.

Ben, too, is there, ostensibly as an overseer, but really as a valued friend, free to do whatever he pleases, and greatly esteemed by those whom he worships with a devotion bordering upon idolatry. Everything pertaining to the place he calls his, and Frederic hardly knows whether himself or Ben is the master of Redstone Hall. The negroes acknowledge them both, though, as is quite natural, the aristocratic Higginses give the preference to Frederic, while the democratic Smitherses, with stammering Josh at their head, warmly advocate Marster Ben, "as sayin' the curisest things and singin' the drollest songs."

There is no spot in the world where Ben could be so supremely happy as he is at Redstone Hall, with Marian and Alice; and when Frederic, on his return from Ohio, suggested his remaining there, he evinced his delight in his usual way, lamenting the while that his extremely tender heart would always make him cry just when he did not wish to.

"I was never cut out for a nigger driver," he said; "but I guess I can coax as much out of 'em as that blusterin' Warren did;" and making his visit short, he hastened back to New England, where he found no difficulty of disposing of his grocery, and five of his numerous family.

These last he bestowed upon different people in the village, taking great care that none of them should go where there were children, and numerous were his injunctions that they should be well cared for, and suffered to die a natural death. Marian and Alice were destined for Kentucky, where they were welcomed joyfully by those whose names they bore. Particularly was the white one, with its bright, sightless eyes, the pet of the entire household, negroes and all; while even Bruno, who, on account of his recognition of Marian, was now allowed more liberty than before, and was consequently far less savage, took kindly to the little creature, tossing it up in his huge paws, licking its snowy face, and sometimes coaxing it into his kennel, where it was more than once found by the delighted Alice, sleeping half hidden under the mastiff's shaggy mane.

Frequently on bright days could Alice and her kitten be seen seated in a miniature waggon, which the Yankee ingenuity of Ben had devised, and in which he drew his blind pets from field to field, seeking out for them the shadiest spot and watching all their movements with a vigilance which told how dear to him was one of them at least. In all the wide world there is nothing Ben Burt loves half so well as the helpless blind girl, Alice—not as he loved Marian Grey, but with a tender, unselfish devotion, which would prompt him at any time to lay down his life for her, if it need must be. All the fairest flowers and choicest fruits are brought to her. And when he sees how she enjoys them, and how grateful she is to him, he murmurs softly:

"Blessed bird, I b'lieve I'd be blind myself, if she could only see."

But Alice does not care for sight, except at times, when she hears the people speak of Mrs. Raymond's beauty, and she wishes she could look upon the face whose praises so many ring. Still she is very happy in Frederic's and Marian's love, and happy, too, with her faithful friend, around whose neck she often twines her arms, blessing him for all he was to Marian and all he is to her.

Once she hoped to improve his peculiar dialect somewhat by imparting to him a greater knowledge of books than he already possessed, and Ben, willing to gratify her, waded industriously through the many volumes she recommended him to read, among which was "Watts on the Mind." But vain were all his efforts to grasp a single idea, and he returned it to Alice, saying that "he presumed it was a very excitin' story to some, but blamed if he could make out a word of sense from beginnin' to finis."

"'Taint much use tryin' to make a scholar of me," said he, winking slyly at Marian, who was present. "It's hard enough teachin' old dogs new tricks, and if I's to read all there is in the Squire's library, I shouldn't be no better off."

Marian thought so, too, and she dropped a few well-timed hints to Alice, who gradually relaxed her efforts to teach one who, had he been educated, would certainly not have been the simple-hearted, unselfish man we now know as Ben Burt.

Away to the northward among the New England hills there is a forsaken grave, where the inebriated Rudolph sleeps. His thirst for revenge is over and the forlorn girl who, in her mother's kitchen washes the dinner dishes for college students just as she used to when Frederic Raymond was a boarder there. has nothing to dread from him. Mrs. Huntington's house on the river has been sold to cancel the mortgage, and in the city of Elms she has returned to her old vocation, and Isabel, with her broken nose and ugly scar, has scarcely a hope, that among her mother's boarders there will ever one be found weak enough to offer her his hand. An humbled, and it is to be hoped, a better woman, she derives her greatest comfort from the letters which sometimes come to her from Marian, and which usually contain a more substantial token of regard than mere words convey.

One word now of William Gordon and our story is done. Ben had claimed the privilege of writing the news to him, and he did it in his charactistic way, first touching upon the note which, he said, was safe in his wallet and sure of being paid, then launching out into glowing descriptions of Marian's happines with Frederic.

This letter was a long time in finding Will, and the answer did not reach Redstone Hall until the family had returned from their summer residence at Riverside. Then it came to them one warm November day, just as the sun was setting, and its mellow rays fell upon the group assembled upon the piazza. Frederic, to whom it was directed, broke the seal and read the sincere congratulations which his early friend had sent to him from over the sea,—read, too, that 'mid the vine-clad hills of Bingen, in a cottage looking out upon the Rhine, there was a fair-haired German girl, with eyes like Marian Grey, and that when Will came next to America he would not be alone.

"For this fair-haired German girl," he wrote, "has promised to come with me. I have told her of my former love, and when last night I read to her Ben's letter, the tears glistened in her lustrous eyes as she whispered in her broken English tongue, 'God bless sweet Marian Grey,' and I, too, Fred, from a full heart respond the same, God bless sweet Marian Grey, the Heiress of Redstone Hall."

1863.

A NEW LIST OF

BOOKS

ISSUED BY

CARLETON, PUBLISHER,

(LATE RUDD & CARLETON,)

413 Broadway,

NEW YORK.

Artemus Ward, His Book.
The racy writings of this humorous author. Illustrated, $1.25.

The Old Merchants of New York.
Entertaining reminiscences of ancient mercantile New York City, by "Walter Barrett, clerk." First Series. $1.50 each.

Like and Unlike.
Novel by A. S. Roe, author of "I've been thinking," &c. $1 50.

Orpheus C. Kerr Papers.
Second series of letters by this comic military authority. $1.25.

Marian Grey.
New domestic novel, by the author of "Lena Rivers," etc. $1.50.

Lena Rivers.
A popular American novel, by Mrs. Mary J. Holmes, $1.50.

A Book about Doctors.
An entertaining volume about the medical profession. $1.50.

The Adventures of Verdant Green.
Humorous novel of English College life. Illustrated. $1.25.

The Culprit Fay.
Joseph Rodman Drake's faery poem, elegantly printed, 50 cts.

Doctor Antonio.
A charming love-tale of Italian life, by G. Ruffini, $1.50.

Lavinia.
A new love-story, by the author of "Doctor Antonio," $1.50.

Dear Experience.
An amusing Parisian novel, by author "Doctor Antonio," $1.00.

The Life of Alexander Von Humboldt.
A new and popular biography of this *savant*, including his travels and labors, with introduction by Bayard Taylor, $1.50.

Love (L'Amour.)
A remarkable volume, from the French of Michelet. $1.25.

Woman (La Femme.)
A continuation of "Love (L'Amour)," by same author, $1.25.

The Sea (La Mer.)
New work by Michelet, author "Love" and "Woman," $1.25.

The Moral History of Woman.
Companion to Michelet's "L'Amour," from the French, $1.25

Mother Goose for Grown Folks.
Humorous and satirical rhymes for grown people, 75 cts.

The Kelly's and the O'Kelly's.
Novel by Anthony Trollope, author of "Doctor Thorne," $1.50.

The Great Tribulation.
Or, Things coming on the earth, by Rev. John Cumming, D.D., author "Apocalyptic Sketches," etc., two series, each $1.00.

The Great Preparation.
Or, Redemption draweth nigh, by Rev. John Cumming, D.D., author "The Great Tribulation," etc., two series, each $1.00.

The Great Consummation.
Sequel "Great Tribulation," Dr. Cumming, two series, $1.00.

Teach us to Pray.
A new work on The Lord's Prayer, by Dr. Cumming, $1.00.

The Slave Power.
By Jas. E. Cairnes, of Dublin University, Lond. ed. $1.25.

Game Fish of the North.
A sporting work for Northern States and Canada. Illus., $1.50.

Drifting About.
By Stephen C. Massett ("Jeemes Pipes"), illustrated, $1.25

The Flying Dutchman.
A humorous Poem by John G. Saxe, with illustrations, 50 cts.

Notes on Shakspeare.
By Jas. H. Hackett, the American Comedian (portrait), $1.50.

The Spirit of Hebrew Poetry.
By Isaac Taylor, author "History of Enthusiasm," etc., $2.00.

A Life of Hugh Miller.
Author of "Testimony of the Rocks," &c., new edition, $1.50.

A Woman's Thoughts about Women.
By Miss Dinah Mulock, author of "John Halifax," etc., $1.00.

Curiosities of Natural History.
An entertaining vol., by F. T. Buckland; two series, each $1.25

The Partisan Leader.
Beverley Tucker's notorious Southern Disunion novel, $1.25

Cesar Birotteau.
First of a series of Honore de Balzac's best French novels, $1.00.

Petty Annoyances of Married Life.
The second of the series of Balzac's best French novels, $1.00.

The Alchemist.
The third of the series of the best of Balzac's novels, $1.00.

Eugenie Grandet.
The fourth of the series of Balzac's best French novels, $1.00

The National School for the Soldier.
Elementary work for the soldier; by Capt. Van Ness, 50 cts.

Tom Tiddler's Ground.
Charles Dickens's new Christmas Story, paper cover, 25 cts.

National Hymns.
An essay by Richard Grant White. 8vo. embellished, $1.00.

George Brimley.
Literary Essays reprinted from the British Quarterlies, $1.25

Thomas Bailey Aldrich.
First complete collection of Poems, blue and gold binding, $1.00.

Out of His Head.
A strange and eccentric romance by T. B. Aldrich, $1.00.

The Course of True Love
Never did run smooth. A Poem by Thomas B. Aldrich, 50 cts.

Poems of a Year.
By Thomas B. Aldrich, author of "Babie Bell," &c., 75 cts.

The King's Bell.
A Mediæval Legend in verse, by R. H. Stoddard, 75 cts.

The Morgesons.
A clever novel of American Life, by Mrs. R. H. Stoddard, $1.00.

Beatrice Cenci.
An historical novel by F. D. Guerrazzi, from the Italian, $1.50.

Isabella Orsini.
An historical novel by the author of "Beatrice Cenci," $1.25.

A Popular Treatise on Deafness.
For individuals and families, by E. B. Lighthill, M.D., $1:00.

Oriental Harems and Scenery.
A gossipy work, translated from the French of Belgiojoso, $1.25.

Lola Montez.
Her lectures and autobiography, with a steel portrait, $1.25.

John Doe and Richard Roe.
A novel of New York city life, by Edward S. Gould, $1.00.

Doesticks' Letters.
The original letters of this great humorist, illustrated, $1.50.

Plu-ri-bus-tah.
A comic history of America, by "Doesticks," illus., $1.50.

The Elephant Club.
A humorous description of club-life, by "Doesticks," $1.50.

Vernon Grove.
A novel by Mrs. Caroline H. Glover, Charleston, S. C., $1.00

The Book of Chess Literature.
A complete Encyclopædia of this subject, by D. W. Fiske, $1.50.

www.ingramcontent.com/pod-product-compliance
Lightning Source LLC
LaVergne TN
LVHW020109110826
845151LV00001B/104

* 9 7 8 1 4 2 5 5 4 4 0 5 8 *